Margaret Atwood's books have been published in over thirty-five countries. She is the author of more than thirty works, which include fiction, poetry and critical essays. *Oryx and Crake* is her eleventh novel, and was shortlisted for the Booker Prize 2003, as was *The Handmaid's Tale*, *Cat's Eye*, and *Alias Grace*. Her most recent novel, *The Blind Assassin*, won the 2000 Booker Prize. She lives in Toronto with writer Graeme Gibson.

BY MARGARET ATWOOD

FICTION

The Edible Woman (1969)
Surfacing (1972)
Lady Oracle (1976)
Dancing Girls (1977)
Life Before Man (1979)
Bodily Harm (1981)
Murder in the Dark (1983)
Bluebeard's Egg (1983)
The Handmaid's Tale (1985)
Cat's Eye (1988)
Wilderness Tips (1991)
Good Bones (1992)
The Robber Bride (1993)
Alias Grace (1996)
The Blind Assassin (2000)
Good Bones and *Simple Murders* (2001)
Oryx and Crake (2003)

FOR CHILDREN

Up in the Tree (1978)
Anna's Pet [with Joyce Barkhouse] (1980)
For the Birds (1990)
Princess Prunella and the Purple Peanut (1995)

NON-FICTION

Survival: A Thematic Guide to Canadian Literature (1972)
Days of the Rebels 1815–1840 (1977)
Second Words (1982)
Strange Things: The Malevolent North in Canadian Literature (1996)
Two Solicitudes: Conversations [with Victor-Lévy Beaulieu] (1998)
Negotiating with the Dead: A Writer on Writing (2002)

POETRY

Double Persephone (1961)
The Circle Game (1966)
The Animals in That Country (1968)
The Journals of Susanna Moodie (1970)
Procedures for Underground (1970)
Power Politics (1971)
You Are Happy (1974)
Selected Poems (1976)
Two-Headed Poems (1978)
True Stories (1981)
Interlunar (1984)
Selected Poems II: Poems Selected and New 1976–1986 (1986)
Morning in the Burned House (1995)

MARGARET ATWOOD

Oryx and Crake

Virago

A *Virago* Book
This edition published by Virago Press 2004
First published in Great Britain by Bloomsbury 2003

A CIP catalogue record for this book
is available from the British Library

ISBN 1 84408 056 0

Typeset in Bembo by M Rules
Printed and bound in Great Britain by
Clays Ltd, St Ives plc

Virago Press
An imprint of
Time Warner Books UK
Brettenham House
Lancaster Place
London WC2E 7EN

www.virago.co.uk

For my family

I could perhaps like others have astonished you with strange improbable tales; but I rather chose to relate plain matter of fact in the simplest manner and style; because my principal design was to inform you, and not to amuse you

Jonathan Swift, *Gulliver's Travels*

Was there no safety? No learning by heart of the ways of the world? No guide, no shelter, but all was miracle and leaping from the pinnacle of a tower into the air?

Virginia Woolf, *To the Lighthouse*.

Contents

Oryx and Crake

1

Mango

Snowman wakes before dawn. He lies unmoving, listening to the tide coming in, wave after wave sloshing over the various barricades, wish-wash, wish-wash, the rhythm of heartbeat. He would so like to believe he is still asleep.

On the eastern horizon there's a greyish haze, lit now with a rosy, deadly glow. Strange how that colour still seems tender. The offshore towers stand out in dark silhouette against it, rising improbably out of the pink and pale blue of the lagoon. The shrieks of the birds that nest out there and the distant ocean grinding against the ersatz reefs of rusted car parts and jumbled bricks and assorted rubble sound almost like holiday traffic.

Out of habit he looks at his watch – stainless-steel case, burnished aluminum band, still shiny although it no longer works. He wears it now as his only talisman. A blank face is what it shows him: zero hour. It causes a jolt of terror to run through him, this absence of official time. Nobody nowhere knows what time it is.

"Calm down," he tells himself. He takes a few deep breaths, then scratches his bug bites, around but not on the itchiest places, taking care not to knock off any scabs: blood poisoning is the last thing he needs. Then he scans the ground below for wildlife: all quiet, no scales and tails. Left hand, right foot, right hand, left foot, he makes his way down from the tree. After brushing off the twigs and bark, he winds his dirty bedsheet around himself like a toga. He's hung his authentic-replica Red Sox baseball cap on a branch overnight for safekeeping; he checks inside it, flicks out a spider, puts it on.

He walks a couple of yards to the left, pisses into the bushes. "Heads up," he says to the grasshoppers that whir away at the impact. Then he goes to the other side of the tree, well away from his customary urinal, and rummages around in the cache he's improvised from a few slabs of concrete, lining it with wire mesh to keep out the rats and mice. He's stashed some mangoes there, knotted in a plastic bag, and a can of Sveltana No-Meat Cocktail Sausages, and a precious half-bottle of Scotch – no, more like a third – and a chocolate-flavoured energy bar scrounged from a trailer park, limp and sticky inside its foil. He can't bring himself to eat it yet: it might be the last one he'll ever find. He keeps a can opener there too, and for no particular reason an ice pick; and six empty beer bottles, for sentimental reasons and for storing fresh water. Also his sunglasses; he puts them on. One lens is missing but they're better than nothing.

He undoes the plastic bag: there's only a single mango left. Funny, he remembered more. The ants have got in, even though he tied the bag as tightly as he could. Already they're running up his arms, the black kind and the vicious little yellow kind. Surprising what a sharp sting they can give, especially the yellow ones. He rubs them away.

"It is the strict adherence to daily routine that tends

towards the maintenance of good morale and the preservation of sanity," he says out loud. He has the feeling he's quoting from a book, some obsolete, ponderous directive written in aid of European colonials running plantations of one kind or another. He can't recall ever having read such a thing, but that means nothing. There are a lot of blank spaces in his stub of a brain, where memory used to be. Rubber plantations, coffee plantations, jute plantations. (What was jute?) They would have been told to wear solar topis, dress for dinner, refrain from raping the natives. It wouldn't have said *raping*. Refrain from fraternizing with the female inhabitants. Or, put some other way . . .

He bets they didn't refrain, though. Nine times out of ten.

"In view of the mitigating," he says. He finds himself standing with his mouth open, trying to remember the rest of the sentence. He sits down on the ground and begins to eat the mango.

Flotsam

On the white beach, ground-up coral and broken bones, a group of the children are walking. They must have been swimming, they're still wet and glistening. They should be more careful: who knows what may infest the lagoon? But they're unwary; unlike Snowman, who won't dip a toe in there even at night, when the sun can't get at him. Revision: especially at night.

He watches them with envy, or is it nostalgia? It can't be that: he never swam in the sea as a child, never ran around on a beach without any clothes on. The children scan the terrain, stoop, pick up flotsam; then they deliberate among themselves, keeping some items, discarding others; their treasures go into a torn sack. Sooner or later – he can count on it – they'll seek him out where he sits wrapped in his decaying sheet, hugging his shins and sucking on his mango, in under the shade of the trees because of the punishing sun. For the children – thick-skinned, resistant to ultraviolet – he's a creature of dimness, of the dusk.

Here they come now. "Snowman, oh Snowman," they chant in their singsong way. They never stand too close to him. Is that from respect, as he'd like to think, or because he stinks?

(He does stink, he knows that well enough. He's rank, he's gamy, he reeks like a walrus – oily, salty, fishy – not that he's ever smelled such a beast. But he's seen pictures.)

Opening up their sack, the children chorus, "Oh Snowman, what have we found?" They lift out the objects, hold them up as if offering them for sale: a hubcap, a piano key, a chunk of pale-green pop bottle smoothed by the ocean. A plastic BlyssPluss container, empty; a ChickieNobs Bucket O'Nubbins, ditto. A computer mouse, or the busted remains of one, with a long wiry tail.

Snowman feels like weeping. What can he tell them? There's no way of explaining to them what these curious items are, or were. But surely they've guessed what he'll say, because it's always the same.

"These are things from before." He keeps his voice kindly but remote. A cross between pedagogue, soothsayer, and benevolent uncle – that should be his tone.

"Will they hurt us?" Sometimes they find tins of motor oil, caustic solvents, plastic bottles of bleach. Booby traps from the past. He's considered to be an expert on potential accidents: scalding liquids, sickening fumes, poison dust. Pain of odd kinds.

"These, no," he says. "These are safe." At this they lose interest, let the sack dangle. But they don't go away: they stand, they stare. Their beachcombing is an excuse. Mostly they want to look at him, because he's so unlike them. Every so often they ask him to take off his sunglasses and put them on again: they want to see whether he has two eyes really, or three.

"Snowman, oh Snowman," they're singing, less to him than to one another. To them his name is just two syllables.

They don't know what a snowman is, they've never seen snow.

It was one of Crake's rules that no name could be chosen for which a physical equivalent – even stuffed, even skeletal – could not be demonstrated. No unicorns, no griffins, no manticores or basilisks. But those rules no longer apply, and it's given Snowman a bitter pleasure to adopt this dubious label. The Abominable Snowman – existing and not existing, flickering at the edges of blizzards, apelike man or manlike ape, stealthy, elusive, known only through rumours and through its backward-pointing footprints. Mountain tribes were said to have chased it down and killed it when they had the chance. They were said to have boiled it, roasted it, held special feasts; all the more exciting, he supposes, for bordering on cannibalism.

For present purposes he's shortened the name. He's only Snowman. He's kept the *abominable* to himself, his own secret hair shirt.

After a few moments of hesitation the children squat down in a half-circle, boys and girls together. A couple of the younger ones are still munching on their breakfasts, the green juice running down their chins. It's discouraging how grubby everyone gets without mirrors. Still, they're amazingly attractive, these children – each one naked, each one perfect, each one a different skin colour – chocolate, rose, tea, butter, cream, honey – but each with green eyes. Crake's aesthetic.

They're gazing at Snowman expectantly. They must be hoping he'll talk to them, but he isn't in the mood for it today. At the very most he might let them see his sunglasses, up close, or his shiny, dysfunctional watch, or his baseball cap. They like the cap, but don't understand his need for such a thing – removable hair that isn't hair – and he hasn't yet invented a fiction for it.

They're quiet for a bit, staring, ruminating, but then the oldest one starts up. "Oh Snowman, please tell us – what is that moss growing out of your face?" The others chime in. "Please tell us, please tell us!" No nudging, no giggling: the question is serious.

"Feathers," he says.

They ask this question at least once a week. He gives the same answer. Even over such a short time – two months, three? He's lost count – they've accumulated a stock of lore, of conjecture about him: *Snowman was once a bird but he's forgotten how to fly and the rest of his feathers fell out, and so he is cold and he needs a second skin, and he has to wrap himself up. No: he's cold because he eats fish, and fish are cold. No: he wraps himself up because he's missing his man thing, and he doesn't want us to see. That's why he won't go swimming. Snowman has wrinkles because he once lived underwater and it wrinkled up his skin. Snowman is sad because the others like him flew away over the sea, and now he is all alone.*

"I want feathers too," says the youngest. A vain hope: no beards on the men, among the Children of Crake. Crake himself had found beards irrational; also he'd been irritated by the task of shaving, so he'd abolished the need for it. Though not of course for Snowman: too late for him.

Now they all begin at once. "Oh Snowman, oh Snowman, can we have feathers too, please?"

"No," he says.

"Why not, why not?" sing the two smallest ones.

"Just a minute, I'll ask Crake." He holds his watch up to the sky, turns it around on his wrist, then puts it to his ear as if listening to it. They follow each motion, enthralled.

"No," he says. "Crake says you can't. No feathers for you. Now piss off."

"Piss off? Piss off?" They look at one another, then at him. He's made a mistake, he's said a new thing, one that's impossible to explain. Piss isn't something they'd find insulting. "What is *piss off*?"

"Go away!" He flaps his sheet at them and they scatter, running along the beach. They're still not sure whether to be afraid of him, or how afraid. He hasn't been known to harm a child, but his nature is not fully understood. There's no telling what he might do.

Voice

"Now I'm alone," he says out loud. "All, all alone. Alone on a wide, wide sea." One more scrap from the burning scrapbook in his head.

Revision: seashore.

He feels the need to hear a human voice – a fully human voice, like his own. Sometimes he laughs like a hyena or roars like a lion – his idea of a hyena, his idea of a lion. He used to watch old DVDs of such creatures when he was a child: those animal-behaviour programs featuring copulation and growling and innards, and mothers licking their young. Why had he found them so reassuring?

Or he grunts and squeals like a pigoon, or howls like a wolvog: *Aroo! Aroo!* Sometimes in the dusk he runs up and down on the sand, flinging stones at the ocean and screaming, *Shit, shit, shit, shit, shit!* He feels better afterwards.

He stands up and raises his arms to stretch, and his sheet falls off. He looks down at his body with dismay: the grimy, bug-bitten skin, the salt-and-pepper tufts of hair, the thickening yellow toenails. Naked as the day he was born, not that he can remember a thing about that. So many crucial events take place behind people's backs, when they aren't in a position to watch: birth and death, for instance. And the temporary oblivion of sex.

"Don't even think about it," he tells himself. Sex is like drink, it's bad to start brooding about it too early in the day.

He used to take good care of himself; he used to run, work out at the gym. Now he can see his own ribs: he's wasting away. Not enough animal protein. A woman's voice says caressingly in his ear, *Nice buns!* It isn't Oryx, it's some other woman. Oryx is no longer very talkative.

"Say anything," he implores her. She can hear him, he needs to believe that, but she's giving him the silent treatment. "What can I do?" he asks her. "You know I . . ."

Oh, nice abs! comes the whisper, interrupting him. *Honey, just lie back.* Who is it? Some tart he once bought. Revision, professional sex-skills expert. A trapeze artist, rubber spine, spangles glued onto her like the scales of a fish. He hates these echoes. Saints used to hear them, crazed lice-infested hermits in their caves and deserts. Pretty soon he'll be seeing beautiful demons, beckoning to him, licking their lips, with red-hot nipples and flickering pink tongues. Mermaids will rise from the waves, out there beyond the crumbling towers, and he'll hear their lovely singing and swim out to them and be eaten by sharks. Creatures with the heads and breasts of women and the talons of eagles will swoop down on him, and he'll open his arms to them, and that will be the end. Brainfrizz.

Or worse, some girl he knows, or knew, will come walking towards him through the trees, and she'll be happy to see him but she'll be made of air. He'd welcome even that, for the company.

He scans the horizon, using his one sunglassed eye:

nothing. The sea is hot metal, the sky a bleached blue, except for the hole burnt in it by the sun. Everything is so empty. Water, sand, sky, trees, fragments of past time. Nobody to hear him.

"Crake!" he yells. "Asshole! Shit-for-brains!"

He listens. The salt water is running down his face again. He never knows when that will happen and he can never stop it. His breath is coming in gasps, as if a giant hand is clenching around his chest – clench, release, clench. Senseless panic.

"You did this!" he screams at the ocean.

No answer, which isn't surprising. Only the waves, wish-wash, wish-wash. He wipes his fist across his face, across the grime and tears and snot and the derelict's whiskers and sticky mango juice. "Snowman, Snowman," he says. "Get a life."

2

Bonfire

Once upon a time, Snowman wasn't Snowman. Instead he was Jimmy. He'd been a good boy then.

Jimmy's earliest complete memory was of a huge bonfire. He must have been five, maybe six. He was wearing red rubber boots with a smiling duck's face on each toe; he remembers that, because after seeing the bonfire he had to walk through a pan of disinfectant in those boots. They'd said the disinfectant was poisonous and he shouldn't splash, and then he was worried that the poison would get into the eyes of the ducks and hurt them. He'd been told the ducks were only like pictures, they weren't real and had no feelings, but he didn't quite believe it.

So let's say five and a half, thinks Snowman. That's about right.

The month could have been October, or else November; the leaves still turned colour then, and they were orange and red. It was muddy underfoot – he must have been standing in a field – and it was drizzling. The bonfire was an enormous pile of cows and sheep and pigs. Their legs stuck out stiff and straight; gasoline had been poured onto them; the flames shot up and out, yellow and white and red and orange, and a smell of charred flesh filled the air. It was like the barbecue in the backyard when his father cooked things but a lot stronger, and mixed in with it was a gas-station smell, and the odour of burning hair.

Jimmy knew what burning hair smelled like because he'd cut off some of his own hair with the manicure scissors and set fire to it with his mother's cigarette lighter. The hair had frizzled up, squiggling like a clutch of tiny black worms, so he'd cut off some more and done it again. By the time he was caught, his hair was ragged all along the front. When accused he'd said it was an experiment.

His father had laughed then, but his mother hadn't. At least (his father said) Jimmy'd had the good sense to cut the hair off before torching it. His mother said it was lucky he hadn't burned the house down. Then they'd had an argument about the cigarette lighter, which wouldn't have been there (said his father) if his mother didn't smoke. His mother said that all children were arsonists at heart, and if not for the lighter he'd have used matches.

Once the fight got going Jimmy felt relieved, because he'd known then that he wouldn't be punished. All he had to do was say nothing and pretty soon they'd forget why they'd started arguing in the first place. But he also felt guilty, because look what he'd made them do. He knew it would end with a door being slammed. He scrunched down lower and lower in his chair with the words whizzing back and forth over his head, and finally there was the bang of the door – his mother this time – and the wind that came with it. There was always a wind when the door got slammed, a small puff – whuff! – right in his ears.

"Never mind, old buddy," said his father. "Women always get hot under the collar. She'll cool down. Let's have some ice cream." So that's what they did, they had Raspberry Ripple in the cereal bowls with the blue and red birds on them that were handmade in Mexico so you shouldn't put them in the dishwasher, and Jimmy ate his all up to show his father that everything was okay.

Women, and what went on under their collars. Hotness and coldness, coming and going in the strange musky flowery variable-weather country inside their clothes – mysterious, important, uncontrollable. That was his father's take on things. But men's body temperatures were never dealt with; they were never even mentioned, not when he was little, except when his dad said, "Chill out." Why weren't they? Why nothing about the hot collars of men? Those smooth, sharp-edged collars with their dark, sulphurous, bristling undersides. He could have used a few theories on that.

The next day his father took him to a haircut place where there was a picture of a pretty girl in the window with pouty lips and a black T-shirt pulled down off one shoulder, glaring out through smudgy charcoal eyes with a mean stare and her hair standing up stiff like quills. Inside, there was hair all over the tiled floor, in clumps and wisps; they were sweeping it up with a push broom. First Jimmy had a black cape put on him, only it was more like a bib, and Jimmy didn't want that, because it was babyish. The haircut man laughed and said it wasn't a bib, because who ever heard of a baby with a black bib on? So it was okay; and then Jimmy got a short all-over cut to even out the ragged places, which maybe was what he'd wanted in the first place – shorter hair. Then he had stuff out of a jar put on to make it spiky. It smelled like orange peels. He smiled at himself in the mirror, then scowled, thrusting down his eyebrows.

"Tough guy," said the haircut man, nodding at Jimmy's father. "What a tiger." He whisked Jimmy's cut-off hair onto the floor with all the other hair, then removed the black cape with a flourish and lifted Jimmy down.

At the bonfire Jimmy was anxious about the animals, because they were being burned and surely that would hurt them. No, his father told him. The animals were dead. They were like steaks and sausages, only they still had their skins on.

And their heads, thought Jimmy. Steaks didn't have heads. The heads made a difference: he thought he could see the animals looking at him reproachfully out of their burning eyes. In some way all of this – the bonfire, the charred smell, but most of all the lit-up, suffering animals – was his fault, because he'd done nothing to rescue them. At the same time he found the bonfire a beautiful sight – luminous, like a Christmas tree, but a Christmas tree on fire. He hoped there might be an explosion, as on television.

Jimmy's father was beside him, holding on to his hand. "Lift me up," said Jimmy. His father assumed he wanted to be comforted, which he did, and picked him up and hugged him. But also Jimmy wanted to see better.

"This is where it ends up," said Jimmy's father, not to Jimmy but to a man standing with them. "Once things get going." Jimmy's father sounded angry; so did the man when he answered.

"They say it was brought in on purpose."

"I wouldn't be surprised," said Jimmy's father.

"Can I have one of the cow horns?" said Jimmy. He didn't see why they should be wasted. He wanted to ask for two but that might be pushing it.

"No," said his father. "Not this time, old buddy." He patted Jimmy's leg.

"Drive up the prices," said the man. "Make a killing on their own stuff, that way."

"It's a killing all right," said Jimmy's father in a disgusted tone. "But it could've been just a nutbar. Some cult thing, you never know."

"Why not?" said Jimmy. Nobody else wanted the horns. But this time his father ignored him.

"The question is, how did they do it?" he said. "I thought our people had us sealed up tight as a drum."

"I thought they did too. We fork out enough. What were the guys doing? They're not paid to sleep."

"It could've been bribery," said Jimmy's father. "They'll check out the bank transfers, though you'd have to be pretty dumb to stick that kind of money into a bank. Anyway, heads will roll."

"Fine-tooth comb, and I wouldn't want to be them," said the man. "Who comes in from outside?"

"Guys who repair things. Delivery vans."

"They should bring all that in-house."

"I hear that's the plan," said his father. "This bug is something new though. We've got the bioprint."

"Two can play at that game," said the man.

"Any number can play," said Jimmy's father.

★

"Why were the cows and sheep on fire?" Jimmy asked his father the next day. They were having breakfast, all three of them together, so it must have been a Sunday. That was the day when his mother and his father were both there at breakfast.

Jimmy's father was on his second cup of coffee. While he drank it, he was making notes on a page covered with numbers. "They had to be burned," he said, "to keep it from spreading." He didn't look up; he was fooling with his pocket calculator, jotting with his pencil.

"What from spreading?"

"The disease."

"What's a disease?"

"A disease is like when you have a cough," said his mother.

"If I have a cough, will I be burned up?"

"Most likely," said his father, turning over the page.

Jimmy was frightened by this because he'd had a cough the week before. He might get another one at any moment: already there was something sticking in his throat. He could see his hair on fire, not just a strand or two on a saucer, but all of it, still attached to his head. He didn't want to be put in a heap with the cows and pigs. He began to cry.

"How many times do I have to tell you?" said his mother. "He's too young."

"Daddy's a monster once again," said Jimmy's father. "It was a joke, pal. You know – joke. Ha ha."

"He doesn't understand those kinds of jokes."

"Sure he does. Don't you, Jimmy?"

"Yes," said Jimmy, sniffling.

"Leave Daddy alone," said his mother. "Daddy is thinking. That's what they pay him for. He doesn't have time for you right now."

His father threw down the pencil. "Cripes, can't you give it a rest?"

His mother stuck her cigarette into her half-empty coffee cup. "Come on, Jimmy, let's go for a walk." She hauled Jimmy up by one wrist, closed the back door with exaggerated care behind them. She didn't even put their coats on. No coats, no hats. She was in her dressing gown and slippers.

The sky was grey, the wind chilly; she walked head down, her hair blowing. Around the house they went, over the soggy lawn at a double-quick pace, hand in hand. Jimmy felt he was being dragged through deep water by something with an iron claw. He felt buffeted, as if everything was about to be wrenched apart and whirled away. At the same time he felt exhilarated. He watched his mother's slippers: already they were stained with damp earth. He'd get in big trouble if he did that to his own slippers.

They slowed down, then stopped. Then his mother was talking to him in the quiet, nice-lady TV-teacher voice that meant she was furious. A disease, she said, was invisible, because it was so small. It could fly through the air or hide in the water, or on little boys' dirty fingers, which was why you shouldn't stick your fingers up your nose and then put them into your mouth, and why you should always wash your hands after you went to the bathroom, and why you shouldn't wipe . . .

"I know," said Jimmy. "Can I go inside? I'm cold."

His mother acted as if she hadn't heard him. A disease, she continued in that calm, stretched voice, a disease got into you and changed things inside you. It rearranged you, cell by cell, and that made the cells sick. And since you were all made up of tiny cells, working together to make sure you stayed alive, and if enough of the cells got sick, then you . . .

"I could get a cough," said Jimmy. "I could get a cough, right now!" He made a coughing sound.

"Oh, never mind," said his mother. She often tried to explain things to him; then she got discouraged. These were the worst moments, for both of them. He resisted her, he pretended he didn't understand even when he did, he acted stupid, but he didn't want her to give up on him. He wanted her to be brave, to try her best with him, to hammer away at the wall he'd put up against her, to keep on going.

"I want to hear about the tiny cells," he said, whining as much as he dared. "I want to!"

"Not today," she said. "Let's just go in."

OrganInc Farms

Jimmy's father worked for OrganInc Farms. He was a genographer, one of the best in the field. He'd done some of the key studies on mapping the proteonome when he was still a post-grad, and then he'd helped engineer the Methuselah Mouse as part of Operation Immortality. After that, at OrganInc Farms, he'd been one of the foremost architects of the pigoon project, along with a team of transplant experts and the microbiologists who were splicing against infections. *Pigoon* was only a nickname: the official name was *sus multiorganifer*. But pigoon was what everyone said. Sometimes they said Organ-Oink Farms, but not as often. It wasn't really a farm anyway, not like the farms in pictures.

The goal of the pigoon project was to grow an assortment of foolproof human-tissue organs in a transgenic knockout pig host – organs that would transplant smoothly and avoid rejection, but would also be able to fend off attacks by opportunistic microbes and viruses, of which there were more strains every year. A rapid-maturity gene was spliced in so the pigoon kidneys and livers and hearts would be ready sooner, and now they were perfecting a pigoon that could grow five or six kidneys at a time. Such a host animal could be reaped of its extra kidneys; then, rather than being destroyed, it could keep on living and grow more organs, much as a lobster could grow another claw to replace a missing one. That would be less wasteful, as it took a lot of food and care to grow a pigoon. A great deal of investment money had gone into OrganInc Farms.

All of this was explained to Jimmy when he was old enough.

Old enough, Snowman thinks as he scratches himself, around but not on top of the insect bites. Such a dumb concept. Old enough for what? To drink, to fuck, to know better? What fathead was in charge of making those decisions? For example, Snowman himself isn't old enough for this, this – what can it be called? This situation. He'll never be old enough, no sane human being could ever . . .

Each one of us must tread the path laid out before him, or her, says the voice in his head, a man's this time, the style bogus guru, *and each path is unique. It is not the nature of the path itself that should concern the seeker, but the grace and strength and patience with which each and every one of us follows the sometimes challenging . . .*

"Stuff it," says Snowman. Some cheap do-it-yourself enlightenment handbook, Nirvana for halfwits. Though he has the nagging feeling that he may well have written this gem himself.

In happier days, naturally. Oh, so much happier.

★

The pigoon organs could be customized, using cells from individual human donors, and the organs were frozen until needed. It was much cheaper than getting yourself cloned for spare parts – a few wrinkles left to be ironed out there, as Jimmy's dad used to say – or keeping a for-harvest child or two stashed away in some illegal baby orchard. In the OrganInc brochures and promotional materials, glossy and discreetly worded, stress was laid on the efficacy and comparative health benefits of the pigoon procedure. Also, to set the queasy at ease, it was claimed that none of the defunct pigoons ended up as bacon and sausages: no one would want to eat an animal whose cells might be identical with at least some of their own.

Still, as time went on and the coastal aquifers turned salty and the northern permafrost melted and the vast tundra bubbled with methane, and the drought in the midcontinental plains regions went on and on, and the Asian steppes turned to sand dunes, and meat became harder to come by, some people had their doubts. Within OrganInc Farms itself it was noticeable how often back bacon and ham sandwiches and pork pies turned up on the staff café menu. André's Bistro was the official name of the café, but the regulars called it Grunts. When Jimmy had lunch there with his father, as he did when his mother was feeling harried, the men and women at nearby tables would make jokes in bad taste.

"Pigoon pie again," they would say. "Pigoon pancakes, pigoon popcorn. Come on, Jimmy, eat up!" This would upset Jimmy; he was confused about who should be allowed to eat what. He didn't want to eat a pigoon, because he thought of the pigoons as creatures much like himself. Neither he nor they had a lot of say in what was going on.

"Don't pay any attention to them, sweetheart," said Ramona. "They're only teasing, you know?" Ramona was one of his dad's lab technicians. She often ate lunch with the two of them, him and his dad. She was young, younger than his father and even his mother; she looked something like the picture of the girl in the haircut man's window, she had the same sort of puffed-out mouth, and big eyes like that, big and smudgy. But she smiled a lot, and she didn't have her hair in quills. Her hair was soft and dark. Jimmy's mother's hair was what she herself called *dirty blonde*. ("Not dirty enough," said his father. "Hey! Joke. Joke. Don't kill me!")

Ramona would always have a salad. "How's Sharon doing?" she would say to Jimmy's father, looking at him with her eyes wide and solemn. Sharon was Jimmy's mother.

"Not so hot," Jimmy's father would say.

"Oh, that's too bad."

"It's a problem. I'm getting worried."

Jimmy watched Ramona eat. She took very small bites, and managed to chew up the lettuce without crunching. The raw carrots too. That was amazing, as if she could liquefy those hard, crisp foods and suck them into herself, like an alien mosquito creature on DVD.

"Maybe she should, I don't know, see someone?" Ramona's eyebrows lifted in concern. She had mauve powder on her eyelids, a little too much; it made them crinkly. "They can do all sorts of things, there's so many new pills . . ." Ramona was supposed to be a tech genius but she talked like a shower-gel babe in an ad. She wasn't stupid, said Jimmy's dad, she just didn't want to put her neuron power into long sentences. There were a lot of people like that at OrganInc, and not all of them were women. It was because they were numbers people, not word people, said Jimmy's father. Jimmy already knew that he himself was not a numbers person.

"Don't think I haven't suggested it. I asked around, found the top guy, made the appointment, but she wouldn't go," said Jimmy's father, looking down at the table. "She's got her own ideas."

"It's such a shame, a waste. I mean, she was so smart!"

"Oh, she's still smart enough," said Jimmy's father. "She's got *smart* coming out of her ears."

"But she used to be so, you know . . ."

Ramona's fork would slide out of her fingers, and the two of them would stare at each other as if searching for the perfect adjective to describe what Jimmy's mother used to be. Then they'd notice Jimmy listening, and beam their attention down on him like extraterrestrial rays. Way too bright.

"So, Jimmy sweetheart, how's it going at school?"

"Eat up, old buddy, eat the crusts, put some hair on your chest!"

"Can I go look at the pigoons?" Jimmy would say.

The pigoons were much bigger and fatter than ordinary pigs, to leave room for all of the extra organs. They were kept in special buildings, heavily secured: the kidnapping of a pigoon and its finely honed genetic material by a rival outfit would have been a disaster. When Jimmy went in to visit the pigoons he had to put on a biosuit that was too big for him, and wear a face mask, and wash his hands first with disinfectant soap. He especially liked the small pigoons, twelve to a sow and lined up in a row, guzzling milk. Pigoonlets. They were cute. But the adults were slightly frightening, with their runny noses and tiny, white-lashed pink eyes. They glanced up at him as if they saw him, really saw him, and might have plans for him later.

"Pigoon, balloon, pigoon, balloon," he would chant to pacify them, hanging over the edge of the pen. Right after the pens had been washed out they didn't smell too bad. He was glad he didn't live in a pen, where he'd have to lie around in poop and pee. The pigoons had no toilets and did it anywhere; this caused him a vague sensation of shame. But he hadn't wet his bed for a long time, or he didn't think he had.

"Don't fall in," said his father. "They'll eat you up in a minute."

"No they won't," said Jimmy. Because I'm their friend, he thought. Because I sing to them. He wished he had a long stick, so he could poke them – not to hurt them, just to make them run around. They spent far too much time doing nothing.

When Jimmy was really little they'd lived in a Cape Cod-style frame house in one of the Modules – there were pictures of him, in a carry-cot on the porch, with dates and everything, stuck into a photo album at some time when his mother was still bothering – but now they lived in a large Georgian centre-plan with an indoor swimming pool and a small gym. The furniture in it was called *reproduction*. Jimmy was quite old before he realized what this word meant – that for each reproduction item, there was supposed to be an original somewhere. Or there had been once. Or something.

The house, the pool, the furniture – all belonged to the OrganInc Compound, where the top people lived.

Increasingly, the middle-range execs and the junior scientists lived there too. Jimmy's father said it was better that way, because nobody had to commute to work from the Modules. Despite the sterile transport corridors and the high-speed bullet trains, there was always a risk when you went through the city.

Jimmy had never been to the city. He'd only seen it on TV – endless billboards and neon signs and stretches of buildings, tall and short; endless dingy-looking streets, countless vehicles of all kinds, some of them with clouds of smoke coming out the back; thousands of people, hurrying, cheering, rioting. There were other cities too, near and far; some had better neighbourhoods in them, said his father, almost like the Compounds, with high walls around the houses, but those didn't get on TV much.

Compound people didn't go to the cities unless they had to, and then never alone. They called the cities *the pleeblands*. Despite the fingerprint identity cards now carried by everyone, public security in the pleeblands was leaky: there were people cruising around in those places who could forge anything and who might be anybody, not to mention the loose change – the addicts, the muggers, the paupers, the crazies. So it was best for everyone at OrganInc Farms to live all in one place, with foolproof procedures.

Outside the OrganInc walls and gates and searchlights, things were unpredictable. Inside, they were the way it used to be when Jimmy's father was a kid, before things got so serious, or that's what Jimmy's father said. Jimmy's mother said it was all artificial, it was just a theme park and you could never bring the old ways back, but Jimmy's father said why knock it? You could walk around without fear, couldn't you? Go for a bike ride, sit at a sidewalk café, buy an ice-cream cone? Jimmy knew his father was right, because he himself had done all of these things.

Still, the CorpSeCorps men – the ones Jimmy's father called *our people* – these men had to be on constant alert. When there was so much at stake, there was no telling what the other side might resort to. The other side, or the other sides: it wasn't just one other side you had to watch out for. Other companies, other countries, various factions and plotters. There was too much hardware around, said Jimmy's father. Too much hardware, too much software, too many hostile bioforms, too many weapons of every kind. And too much envy and fanaticism and bad faith.

Long ago, in the days of knights and dragons, the kings and dukes had lived in castles, with high walls and drawbridges and slots on the ramparts so you could pour hot pitch on your enemies, said Jimmy's father, and the Compounds were the same idea. Castles were for keeping you and your buddies nice and safe inside, and for keeping everybody else outside.

"So are we the kings and dukes?" asked Jimmy.

"Oh, absolutely," said his father, laughing.

Lunch

At one time Jimmy's mother had worked for OrganInc Farms. That was how his mother had met his father: they'd both worked at the same Compound, on the same project. His mother was a microbiologist: it had been her job to study the proteins of the bioforms unhealthy to pigoons, and to modify their receptors in such a way that they could not bond with the receptors on pigoon cells, or else to develop drugs that would act as blockers.

"It's very simple," she said to Jimmy in one of her explaining moods. "The bad microbes and viruses want to get in through the cell doors and eat up the pigoons from the inside. Mummy's job was to make locks for the doors." On her computer screen she showed Jimmy pictures of the cells, pictures of the microbes, pictures of the microbes getting into the cells and infecting them and bursting them open, close-up pictures of the proteins, pictures of the drugs she had once tested. The pictures looked like the candy bins at the supermarket: a clear plastic bin of round candies, a clear plastic bin of jelly beans, a clear plastic bin of long licorice twizzles. The cells were like the clear plastic bins, with the lids you could lift up.

"Why aren't you making the locks for the doors any more?" said Jimmy.

"Because I wanted to stay home with you," she said, looking over the top of Jimmy's head and puffing on her cigarette.

"What about the pigoons?" said Jimmy, alarmed. "The microbes will get into them!" He didn't want his animal pals to burst open like the infected cells.

"Other people are in charge of that now," said his mother. She didn't seem to care at all. She let Jimmy play with the pictures on her computer, and once he learned how to run the programs, he could play war games with them – cells versus microbes. She said it was all right if he lost stuff off the computer, because all that material was out of date anyway. Though on some days – days when she appeared brisk and purposeful, and aimed, and steady – she would want to fool around on the computer herself. He liked it when she did that – when she seemed to be enjoying herself. She was friendly then, too. She was like a real mother and he was like a real child. But those moods of hers didn't last long.

When had she stopped working at the lab? When Jimmy started at the OrganInc School full-time, in the first grade. Which didn't make sense, because if she'd wanted to stay home with Jimmy, why had she started doing that when Jimmy stopped being at home? Jimmy could never figure out the reasons, and when he'd first heard this explanation he'd been too young to even think about them. All he'd known was that Dolores, the live-in from the Philippines, had been sent away, and he'd missed her a lot. She'd called him Jim-Jim and had smiled and laughed and cooked his egg just the way he liked it, and had sung songs and indulged him. But Dolores had to go, because now Jimmy's real mummy would be there all the time – this was held out to him like a treat – and nobody needed two mummies, did they?

Oh yes they did, thinks Snowman. Oh yes, they really did.

Snowman has a clear image of his mother – of Jimmy's mother – sitting at the kitchen table, still in her bathrobe when he came home from school for his lunch. She would have a cup of coffee in front of her, untouched; she would be looking out the window and smoking. The bathrobe was magenta, a colour that still makes him anxious whenever he sees it. As a rule there would be no lunch ready for him and he would have to make it himself, his mother's only participation being to issue directions in a flat voice. ("The milk's in the fridge. To the right. No, the *right*. Don't you know which is your right hand?") She sounded so tired; maybe she was tired of him. Or maybe she was sick.

"Are you infected?" he asked her one day.

"What do you mean, Jimmy?"

"Like the cells."

"Oh. I see. No, I'm not," she said. Then, after a moment, "Maybe I am." But when his face crumpled, she took it back.

More than anything, Jimmy had wanted to make her laugh – to make her happy, as he seemed to remember her being once. He would tell her funny things that had happened at school, or things he tried to make funny, or things he simply invented. ("Carrie Johnston went poo on the floor.") He would caper around the room, crossing his eyes and cheeping like a monkey, a trick that worked with several of the little girls in his class and almost all of the boys. He would put peanut butter on his nose and try to lick it off with his tongue. Most of the time these activities just irritated his mother: "That is not amusing, that is disgusting." "Stop it, Jimmy, you're giving me a headache." But then he might get a smile out of her, or more. He never knew what would work.

Once in a while there would be a real lunch waiting for him, a lunch that was so arranged and extravagant it frightened him, for what was the occasion? Place setting, paper napkin – *coloured* paper napkin, like parties – the sandwich peanut butter and jelly, his preferred combo; only it would be open-face and round, a peanut butter head with a jelly smile-face. His mother would be carefully dressed, her lipstick smile an echo of the jelly smile on the sandwich, and she would be all sparkling attention, for him and his silly stories, looking at him directly, her eyes bluer than blue. What she reminded him of at such times was a porcelain sink: clean, shining, hard.

He knew he was expected to appreciate all the effort she had put into this lunch, and so he too made an effort. "Oh boy, my favourite!" he would say, rolling his eyes, rubbing his stomach in a caricature of hunger, overdoing it. But he'd get what he wanted, because then she would laugh.

As he grew older and more devious, he found that on the days when he couldn't grab some approval, he could at least get a reaction. Anything was better than the flat voice, the blank eyes, the tired staring out of the window.

"Can I have a cat?" he would begin.

"No, Jimmy, you cannot have a cat. We've been over this before. Cats might carry diseases that would be bad for the pigoons."

"But you don't care." This in a sly voice.

A sigh, a puff of smoke. "Other people care."

"Can I have a dog then?"

"No. No dogs either. Can't you find something to do in your room?"

"Can I have a parrot?"

"No. Now stop it." She wouldn't really be listening.

"Can I have nothing?"

"No."

"Oh good," he would crow. "I can't have nothing! So I get to have something! What do I get to have?"

"Jimmy, sometimes you are a pain in the ass, do you know that?"

"Can I have a baby sister?"

"No!"

"A baby brother then? Please?"

"No means no! Didn't you hear me? I said no!"

"Why not?"

That was the key, that would do it. She might start crying and jump up and run out of the room, banging the door behind her, whuff. Or else she might start crying and hugging him. Or she might throw the coffee cup across the room and start yelling, "It's all shit, it's total shit, it's hopeless!" She might even slap him, and then cry and hug him. It could be any combination of those things.

Or it would just be the crying, with her head down on her arms. She would shake all over, gasp for breath, choking and sobbing. He wouldn't know what to do then. He loved her so much when he made her unhappy, or else when she made him unhappy: at these moments he scarcely knew which was which. He would pat her, standing well back as with strange dogs, stretching out his hand, saying, "I'm sorry, I'm sorry." And he was sorry, but there was more to it: he was also gloating, congratulating himself, because he'd managed to create such an effect.

He was frightened, as well. There was always that knife-edge: had he gone too far? And if he had, what came next?

3

Nooners

Noon is the worst, with its glare and humidity. At about eleven o'clock Snowman retreats back into the forest, out of sight of the sea altogether, because the evil rays bounce off the water and get at him even if he's protected from the sky, and then he reddens and blisters. What he could really use is a tube of heavy-duty sunblock, supposing he could ever find one.

In the first week, when he'd had more energy, he'd made himself a lean-to, using fallen branches and a roll of duct tape and a plastic tarp he'd found in the trunk of a smashed-up car. At that time he'd had a knife, but he lost it a week later, or was it two weeks? He must keep better track of such things as weeks. The knife was one of those pocket items with two blades, an awl, a tiny saw, a nail file, and a corkscrew. Also a little pair of scissors, which he'd used to cut his toenails and the duct tape as well. He regrets the loss of the scissors.

He was given a knife like that for his ninth birthday, by his father. His father was always giving him tools, trying to make him more practical. In his father's opinion Jimmy couldn't screw in a light bulb. *So who wants to screw in a light bulb?* says the voice in Snowman's head, a stand-up comic this time. *I'd rather do it in bed.*

"Shut up," says Snowman.

"Did you give him a dollar?" Oryx had asked him when he told her about the knife.

"No. Why?"

"You need to give money when someone gives you a knife. So the bad luck won't cut you. I wouldn't like it for you to be cut by the bad luck, Jimmy."

"Who told you that?"

"Oh, someone," said Oryx. *Someone* played a big part in her life.

"Someone who?" Jimmy hated him, this someone – faceless, eyeless, mocking, all hands and dick, now singular, now double, now a multitude – but Oryx had her mouth right next to his ear and was whispering, *Oh*, *oh*, *some*, *one*, and laughing at the same time, so how could he concentrate on his stupid old hate?

In the short period of the lean-to he'd slept on a fold-up cot he'd dragged from a bungalow half a mile away, a metal frame with a foam mattress on top of a grillwork of springs. The first night he'd been attacked by ants, and so he'd filled four tin cans with water and stuck the cot legs into them. That put a stop to the ants. But the build-up of hot, damp air under the tarp was too uncomfortable: at night, at ground level, with no breeze, the humidity felt like a hundred per cent: his breath fogged the plastic.

Also the rakunks were a nuisance, scuffling through the leaves and sniffing at his toes, nosing around him as if he were already garbage; and one morning he'd woken to find three pigoons gazing in at him through the plastic. One was a male; he thought he could see the gleaming point of a white tusk. Pigoons were supposed to be tusk-free, but maybe they were reverting to type now they'd gone feral, a fast-forward process considering their rapid-maturity genes. He'd shouted at them and waved his arms and they'd run off, but who could tell what they might do the next time they came around? Them, or the wolvogs: it wouldn't take them forever to figure out that he no longer had a spraygun. He'd thrown it away when he'd run out of virtual bullets for it. Dumb not to have swiped a recharger for it: a mistake, like setting up his sleeping quarters at ground level.

So he'd moved to the tree. No pigoons or wolvogs up there, and few rakunks: they preferred the undergrowth. He'd constructed a rough platform in the main branches out of scrap wood and duct tape. It's not a bad job: he's always been handier at putting things together than his father gave him credit for. At first he'd taken the foam mattress up there, but he had to toss it when it began to mildew, and to smell tantalizingly of tomato soup.

The plastic tarp on the lean-to was torn away during an unusually violent storm. The bed frame remains, however; he can still use it at noon. He's found that if he stretches out on it flat on his back, with his arms spread wide and his sheet off, like a saint arranged ready for frying, it's better than lying on the ground: at least he can get some air on all the surfaces of his body.

From nowhere, a word appears: *Mesozoic.* He can see the word, he can hear the word, but he can't reach the word. He can't attach anything to it. This is happening too much lately, this dissolution of meaning, the entries on his cherished wordlists drifting off into space.

"It's only the heat," he tells himself. "I'll be fine once it rains." He's sweating so hard he can almost hear it; trickles of sweat crawl down him, except that sometimes the trickles are insects. He appears to be attractive to beetles. Beetles, flies, bees, as if he's dead meat, or one of the nastier flowers.

The best thing about the noon hours is that at least he doesn't get hungry: even the thought of food makes him queasy, like chocolate cake in a steam bath. He wishes he could cool himself by hanging out his tongue.

Now the sun is at full glare; the zenith, it used to be called. Snowman lies splayed out on the grillwork of the bed, in the liquid shade, giving himself up to the heat. *Let's pretend this is a vacation!* A schoolteacher's voice this time, perky, condescending. Ms. Stratton Call-Me-Sally, with the big butt. *Let's pretend this, let's pretend that.* They spent the first three years of school getting you to pretend stuff and then the rest of it marking you down if you did the same thing. *Let's pretend I'm here with you, big butt and all, getting ready to suck your brains right out your dick.*

Is there a faint stirring? He looks down at himself: no action. Sally Stratton vanishes, and just as well. He has to find more and better ways of occupying his time. *His time,* what a bankrupt idea, as if he's been given a box of time belonging to him alone, stuffed to the brim with hours and minutes that he can spend like money. Trouble is, the box has holes in it and the time is running out, no matter what he does with it.

He might whittle, for instance. Make a chess set, play games with himself. He used to play chess with Crake but they'd played by computer, not with actual chessmen. Crake won mostly. There must be another knife somewhere; if he sets his mind to it, goes foraging, scrapes around in the leftovers, he'd be sure to find one. Now that he's thought of it he's surprised he hasn't thought of it before.

He lets himself drift back to those after-school times with Crake. It was harmless enough at first. They might play Extinctathon, or one of the others. Three-Dimensional Waco, Barbarian Stomp, Kwiktime Osama. They all used parallel strategies: you had to see where you were headed before you got there, but also where the other guy was headed. Crake was good at those games because he was a master of the sideways leap. Jimmy could sometimes win at Kwiktime Osama though, as long as Crake played the Infidel side.

No hope of whittling that kind of game, however. It would have to be chess.

Or he could keep a diary. Set down his impressions. There must be lots of paper lying around, in unburned interior spaces that are still leak-free, and pens and pencils; he's seen them on his scavenging forays but he's never bothered taking any. He could emulate the captains of ships, in olden times – the ship going down in a storm, the captain in his cabin, doomed but intrepid, filling in the logbook. There were movies like that. Or castaways on desert islands, keeping their journals day by tedious day. Lists of supplies, notations on the weather, small actions performed – the sewing on of a button, the devouring of a clam.

He too is a castaway of sorts. He could make lists. It could give his life some structure.

But even a castaway assumes a future reader, someone who'll come along later and find his bones and his ledger, and learn his fate. Snowman can make no such assumptions:

he'll have no future reader, because the Crakers can't read. Any reader he can possibly imagine is in the past.

A caterpillar is letting itself down on a thread, twirling slowly like a rope artist, spiralling towards his chest. It's a luscious, unreal green, like a gumdrop, and covered with tiny bright hairs. Watching it, he feels a sudden, inexplicable surge of tenderness and joy. Unique, he thinks. There will never be another caterpillar just like this one. There will never be another such moment of time, another such conjunction.

These things sneak up on him for no reason, these flashes of irrational happiness. It's probably a vitamin deficiency.

The caterpillar pauses, feeling around in the air with its blunt head. Its huge opaque eyes look like the front end of a riot-gear helmet. Maybe it's smelling him, picking up on his chemical aura. "We are not here to play, to dream, to drift," he says to it. "We have hard work to do, and loads to lift."

Now, what atrophying neural cistern in his brain did that come from? The Life Skills class, in junior high. The teacher had been a shambling neo-con reject from the heady days of the legendary dot.com bubble, back in prehistory. He'd had a stringy ponytail stuck to the back of his balding head, and a faux-leather jacket; he'd worn a gold stud in his bumpy, porous old nose, and had pushed self-reliance and individualism and risk-taking in a hopeless tone, as if even he no longer believed in them. Once in a while he'd come out with some hoary maxim, served up with a wry irony that did nothing to reduce the boredom quotient; or else he'd say, "I coulda been a contender," then glare meaningfully at the class as if there was some deeper-than-deep point they were all supposed to get.

Double-entry on-screen bookkeeping, banking by fingertip, using a microwave without nuking your egg, filling out housing applications for this or that Module and job applications for this or that Compound, family heredity research, negotiating your own marriage-and-divorce contracts, wise genetic match-mating, the proper use of condoms to avoid sexually transmitted bioforms: those had been the Life Skills. None of the kids had paid much attention. They either knew it already or didn't want to. They'd treated the class as a rest hour. *We are not here to play, to dream, to drift. We are here to practise Life Skills.*

"Whatever," says Snowman.

Or, instead of chess or a journal, he could focus on his living conditions. There's room for improvement in that department, a lot of room. More food sources, for one thing. Why didn't he ever bone up on roots and berries and pointed-stick traps for skewering small game, and how to eat snakes? Why had he wasted his time?

Oh honey, don't beat yourself up! breathes a female voice, regretfully, in his ear.

If only he could find a cave, a nice cave with a high ceiling and good ventilation and maybe some running water, he'd be better off. True, there's a stream with fresh water a quarter of a mile away; at one place it widens into a pool. Initially he'd gone there to cool off, but the Crakers might be splashing around in it or resting on the banks, and the kids would pester him to go swimming, and he didn't like being seen by them without his sheet. Compared to them he is just too weird; they make him feel deformed. If not people, there might well be animals: wolvogs, pigoons, bobkittens. Watering holes attract carnivores. They lie in wait. They slaver. They pounce. Not very cozy.

The clouds are building, the sky darkening. He can't see much through the trees but he senses the change in light. He slides off into half-sleep and dreams of Oryx, floating on her back in a swimming pool, wearing an outfit that appears to be made of delicate white tissue-paper petals. They spread out around her, expanding and contracting like the valves of a jellyfish. The pool is painted a vibrant pink. She smiles up at him and moves her arms gently to keep afloat, and he knows they are both in great danger. Then there's a hollow booming sound, like the door of a great vault shutting.

Downpour

He awakes to thunder and a sudden wind: the afternoon storm is upon him. He scrambles to his feet, grabs his sheet. Those howlers can come on very fast, and a metal bed frame in a thunderstorm is no place to be. He's built himself an island of car tires back in the woods; it's simply a matter of crouching on them, keeping their insulation between himself and the ground until the storm is over. Sometimes there are hailstones as big as golf balls, but the forest canopy slows their fall.

He reaches the pile of tires just as the storm breaks. Today it's only rain, the usual deluge, so heavy the impact turns the air to mist. Water sluices down onto him as the lightning sizzles. Branches thrash around overhead, rivulets amble along the ground. Already it's cooling down; the scent of freshly washed leaves and wet earth fills the air.

Once the rain has slowed to a drizzle and the rumbles of thunder have receded, he slogs back to his cement-slab cache to collect the empty beer bottles. Then he makes his way to a jagged concrete overhang that was once part of a bridge. Beneath it there's a triangular orange sign with the black silhouette of a man shovelling. Men at Work, that used to mean. Strange to think of the endless labour, the digging, the hammering, the carving, the lifting, the drilling, day by day, year by year, century by century; and now the endless crumbling that must be going on everywhere. Sandcastles in the wind.

Runoff is pouring through a hole in the side of the concrete. He stands under it with his mouth open, gulping water full of grit and twigs and other things he doesn't want to think about – the water must have found a channel through derelict houses and pungent cellars and clotted-up ditches and who knows what else. Then he rinses himself off, wrings out his sheet. He doesn't get himself very clean this way, but at least he can shed the surface layer of grime and scum. It would be useful to have a bar of soap: he keeps forgetting to pick one up during his pilfering excursions.

Lastly he fills up the beer bottles. He should get himself a better vessel, a Thermos or a pail – something that would hold more. Also the bottles are awkward: they're slippery and hard to position. He keeps imagining he can still smell beer inside them, though it's only wishful thinking. *Let's pretend this is beer.*

He shouldn't have brought that up. He shouldn't torture himself. He shouldn't dangle impossibilities in front of himself, as if he were some caged, wired-up lab animal, trapped into performing futile and perverse experiments on his own brain.

Get me out! he hears himself thinking. But he isn't locked up, he's not in prison. What could be more *out* than where he is?

"I didn't do it on purpose," he says, in the snivelling child's voice he reverts to in this mood. "Things happened, I had no idea, it was out of my control! What could I have done? Just someone, anyone, listen to me please!"

What a bad performance. Even he isn't convinced by it. But now he's weeping again.

It is important, says the book in his head, *to ignore minor irritants, to avoid pointless repinings, and to turn one's mental energies to immediate realities and to the tasks at hand*. He must have read that somewhere. Surely his own mind would never have come up with *pointless repinings*, not all by itself.

He wipes his face on a corner of the sheet. "Pointless repinings," he says out loud. As often, he feels he has a listener: someone unseen, hidden behind the screen of leaves, watching him slyly.

4

Rakunk

He does have a listener: it's a rakunk, a young one. He can see it now, its bright eyes peering out at him from under a bush.

"Here girl, here girl," he says to it coaxingly. It backs away into the underbrush. If he worked at it, if he really tried, he could probably tame one of those, and then he'd have someone to talk to. Someone to talk to was nice, Oryx used to tell him. "You should try it sometime, Jimmy," she'd say, kissing him on the ear.

"But I talk to you," he'd protest.

Another kiss. "Do you?"

When Jimmy was ten he'd been given a pet rakunk, by his father.

What did his father look like? Snowman can't get a fix on it. Jimmy's mother persists as a clear image, full colour, with a glossy white paper frame around her like a Polaroid, but he can recall his father only in details: the Adam's apple going up and down when he swallowed, the ears backlit against the kitchen window, the left hand lying on the table, cut off by the shirt cuff. His father is a sort of pastiche. Maybe Jimmy could never get far enough away from him to see all the parts at once.

The occasion for the gift of the rakunk must have been his birthday. He's repressed his birthdays: they weren't a matter for general celebration, not after Dolores the live-in Philippina left. When she was there, she'd always remember his birthday; she'd make a cake, or maybe she'd buy one, but anyway there it would be, a genuine cake, with icing and candles – isn't that true? He clutches on to the reality of those cakes; he closes his eyes, conjures them up, hovering all in a row, their candles alight, giving off their sweet, comforting scent of vanilla, like Dolores herself.

His mother on the other hand could never seem to recall how old Jimmy was or what day he was born. He'd have to remind her, at breakfast; then she'd snap out of her trance and buy him some mortifying present – pyjamas for little kids with kangaroos or bears on them, a disk nobody under forty would ever listen to, underwear ornamented with whales – and tape it up in tissue paper and dump it on him at the dinner table, smiling her increasingly weird smile, as if someone had yelled *Smile!* and goosed her with a fork.

Then his father would put them all through an awkward excuse about why this really, really special and important date had somehow just slid out of his head, and ask Jimmy if everything was okay, and send him an e-birthday card – the OrganInc standard design with five winged pigoons doing a conga line and *Happy Birthday, Jimmy, May All Your Dreams Come True* – and come up with a gift for him the day after, a gift that would not be a gift but some tool or intelligence-enhancing game or other hidden demand that he measure up. But measure up to what? There was never any standard; or there was one, but it was so cloudy and immense that nobody could see it, especially not Jimmy. Nothing he could achieve would ever be the right idea, or enough. By OrganInc's math-and-chem-and-applied-bio yardstick he must have seemed dull normal: maybe that was why his father stopped telling him he could do much better if he'd only try, and switched to doling out secretly disappointed praise, as if Jimmy had a brain injury.

So Snowman has forgotten everything else about Jimmy's tenth birthday except the rakunk, brought home by his father in a carry-cage. It was a tiny one, smallest of the litter born from the second generation of rakunks, the offspring of the first pair that had been spliced. The rest of the litter had been snapped up immediately. Jimmy's father made out that he'd had to spend a great deal of his time and throw his weight around and pull a lot of strings to get hold of this one, but all the effort had been worth it for this really, really special day, which had just happened as usual to fall on the day before.

The rakunks had begun as an after-hours hobby on the part of one of the OrganInc biolab hotshots. There'd been a lot of fooling around in those days: create-an-animal was so much fun, said the guys doing it; it made you feel like God. A number of the experiments were destroyed because they were too dangerous to have around – who needed a cane toad with a prehensile tail like a chameleon's that might climb in through the bathroom window and blind you while you were brushing your teeth? Then there was the snat, an unfortunate blend of snake and rat: they'd had to get rid of those. But the rakunks caught on as pets, inside OrganInc. They hadn't come in from the outside world – the world outside the Compound – so they had no foreign microbes and were safe for the pigoons. In addition to which they were cute.

The little rakunk let Jimmy pick it up. It was black and white – black mask, white stripe down its back, black and white rings around its fluffy tail. It licked Jimmy's fingers, and he fell in love with it.

"No smell to it, not like a skunk," said Jimmy's father. "It's a clean animal, with a nice disposition. Placid. Racoons never made good pets once they were grown up, they got crabby, they'd tear your house to pieces. This thing is supposed to be calmer. We'll see how the little guy does. Right, Jimmy?"

Jimmy's father had been apologetic towards him lately, as if he'd punished Jimmy for something Jimmy hadn't done and was sorry about it. He was saying *Right, Jimmy?* a bit too much. Jimmy didn't like that – he didn't like being the one handing out the good marks. There were a few other moves of his father's he could do without as well – the sucker punches, the ruffling of the hair, the way of pronouncing the word *son*, in a slightly deeper voice. This hearty way of talking was getting worse, as if his father were auditioning for the role of Dad, but without much hope. Jimmy had done enough faking himself so he could spot it in others, most of the time. He stroked the little rakunk and didn't answer.

"Who's going to feed it and empty the litter box?" said Jimmy's mother. "Because it won't be me." She didn't say this angrily, but in a detached, matter-of-fact voice, as if she was a bystander, someone on the sidelines; as if Jimmy and the chore of taking care of him, and his unsatisfactory father, and the scufflings between her and him, and the increasingly heavy baggage of all their lives, had nothing to do with her. She didn't seem to get angry any more, she didn't go charging out of the house in her slippers. She had become slowed-down and deliberate.

"Jimmy hasn't asked you to. He'll do it himself. Right, Jimmy?" said his father.

"What are you going to call it?" said his mother. She didn't really want to know, she was getting at Jimmy in some way. She didn't like it when he warmed up to anything his father gave him. "Bandit, I suppose."

That was exactly the name Jimmy had been thinking of, because of the black mask. "No," he said. "That's boring. I'm calling him Killer."

"Good choice, son," said his father.

"Well, if Killer wets on the floor, be sure you clean it up," said his mother.

Jimmy took Killer up to his room, where it made a nest in his pillow. It did have a faint smell, strange but not unpleasant, leathery and sharp, like a bar of designer soap for men. He slept with his arm crooked around it, his nose next to its own small nose.

It must have been a month or two after he got the rakunk that Jimmy's father changed jobs. He was headhunted by NooSkins and hired at the second-in-command level – the Vice level, Jimmy's mother called it. Ramona the lab tech from OrganInc made the move with him; she was part of the deal because she was an invaluable asset, said Jimmy's father; she was his right-hand man. ("Joke," he would say to Jimmy, to show that he knew Ramona wasn't really a man. But Jimmy knew that anyway.) Jimmy was more or less glad he might still be seeing Ramona at lunch – at least she was someone familiar – even though his lunches with his father had become few in number and far between.

NooSkins was a subsidiary of HelthWyzer, and so they moved into the HelthWyzer Compound. Their house this time was in the style of the Italian Renaissance, with an arched portico and a lot of glazed earth-tone tiles, and the indoor pool was bigger. Jimmy's mother called it "this barn." She complained about the tight security at the HelthWyzer gates – the guards were ruder, they were suspicious of everyone, they liked to strip search people, women especially. They got a kick out of it, she said.

Jimmy's father said she was making a big deal about nothing. Anyway, he said, there'd been an incident only a few weeks before they'd moved in – some fanatic, a woman, with a hostile bioform concealed in a hairspray bottle. Some vicious Ebola or Marburg splice, one of the fortified hemorrhagics. She'd nuked a guard who'd unwisely had his face mask off, contrary to orders but because of the heat. The woman had been spraygunned at once and neutralized in a vat of bleach, and the poor guard had been whisked into HotBioform and stuck into an isolation room, where he'd dissolved into a puddle of goo. No greater damage done, but naturally the guards were jumpy.

Jimmy's mother said that didn't change the fact that she felt like a prisoner. Jimmy's father said she didn't understand the reality of the situation. Didn't she want to be safe, didn't she want her son to be safe?

"So it's for my own good?" she said. She was cutting a piece of French toast into even-sided cubes, taking her time.

"For *our* own good. For us."

"Well, I happen to disagree."

"No news there," said Jimmy's father.

According to Jimmy's mother their phones and e-mail were bugged, and the sturdy, laconic HelthWyzer house-cleaners that came twice a week – always in pairs – were spies. Jimmy's father said she was getting paranoid, and anyway they had nothing to hide, so why worry about it?

The HelthWyzer Compound was not only newer than the OrganInc layout, it was bigger. It had two shopping malls instead of one, a better hospital, three dance clubs, even its own golf course. Jimmy went to the HelthWyzer Public School, where at first he didn't know anyone. Despite his initial loneliness, that wasn't too bad. Actually it was good, because he could recycle his old routines and jokes: the kids at OrganInc had become used to his antics. He'd moved on from the chimpanzee act and was into fake vomiting and choking to death – both popular – and a thing where he drew a bare-naked girl on his stomach with her crotch right where his navel was, and made her wiggle.

He no longer came home for lunch. He got picked up by the school's combo ethanol-solarvan in the morning and returned by it at night. There was a bright and cheerful school cafeteria with balanced meals, ethnic choices – perogies, felafels – and a kosher option, and soy products for the vegetarians. Jimmy was so pleased to be able to eat lunch with neither one of his parents present that he felt light-headed. He even put on some weight, and stopped being the skinniest kid in class. If there was any lunchtime left over and nothing else going on, he could go to the library and watch old instructional CD-ROMs. Alex the parrot was his favourite, from *Classics in Animal Behaviour Studies*. He liked the part where Alex invented a new word – *cork-nut*, for almond – and, best of all, the part where Alex got fed up with the blue-triangle and yellow-square exercise and said, *I'm going away now. No, Alex, you come back here! Which is the blue triangle – no, the* blue *triangle?* But Alex was out the door. Five stars for Alex.

One day Jimmy was allowed to bring Killer to school, where she – it was now officially a she – made a big hit. "Oh Jimmy, you are so lucky," said Wakulla Price, the first girl he'd ever had a crush on. She stroked Killer's fur, brown hand, pink nails, and Jimmy felt shivery, as if her fingers were running over his own body.

Jimmy's father spent more and more time at his work, but talked about it less and less. There were pigoons at NooSkins, just as at OrganInc Farms, but these were smaller and were being used to develop skin-related biotechnologies. The main idea was to find a method of replacing the older epidermis with a fresh one, not a laser-thinned or dermabraded short-term resurfacing but a genuine start-over skin that would be wrinkle- and blemish-free. For that, it would be useful to grow a young, plump skin cell that would eat up the worn cells in the skins of those on whom it was planted and replace them with replicas of itself, like algae growing on a pond.

The rewards in the case of success would be enormous, Jimmy's father explained, doing the straight-talking man-to-man act he had recently adopted with Jimmy. What well-to-do and once-young, once-beautiful woman or man, cranked up on hormonal supplements and shot full of vitamins but hampered by the unforgiving mirror, wouldn't sell their house, their gated retirement villa, their kids, and their soul to get a second kick at the sexual can? NooSkins for Olds, said the snappy logo. Not that a totally effective method had been found yet: the dozen or so ravaged hopefuls who had volunteered themselves as subjects, paying no fees but signing away their rights to sue, had come out looking like the Mould Creature from Outer Space – uneven in tone, greenish brown, and peeling in ragged strips.

But there were other projects at NooSkins as well. One evening Jimmy's father came home late and a little drunk, with a bottle of champagne. Jimmy took one look at this and got himself out of the way. He'd hidden a tiny mike behind the picture of the seashore in the living room and another one behind the kitchen wall clock – the one that gave a different irritating bird call for every hour – so he could listen in on stuff that was none of his business. He'd put the mikes together in the Neotechnology class at school; he'd used standard components out of the mini-mikes for wireless computer dictating, which, with a few adjustments, worked fine for eavesdropping.

"What's that for?" said the voice of Jimmy's mother. She meant the champagne.

"We've done it," said Jimmy's father's voice. "I think a little celebration is in order." A scuffle: maybe he'd tried to kiss her.

"Done what?"

Pop of the champagne cork. "Come on, it won't bite you." A pause: he must be pouring it out. Yes: the clink of glasses. "Here's to us."

"Done what? I need to know what I'm drinking to."

Another pause: Jimmy pictured his father swallowing, his Adam's apple going up and down, bobbity-bobble. "It's the neuro-regeneration project. We now have genuine human neocortex tissue growing in a pigoon. Finally, after all those duds! Think of the possibilities, for stroke victims, and . . ."

"That's all we need," said Jimmy's mother. "More people with the brains of pigs. Don't we have enough of those already?"

"Can't you be positive, just for once? All this negative stuff, *this is no good, that's no good*, nothing's ever good enough, according to you!"

"Positive about what? That you've thought up yet another way to rip off a bunch of desperate people?" said Jimmy's mother in that new slow, anger-free voice.

"God, you're cynical!"

"No, you are. You and your smart partners. Your colleagues. It's wrong, the whole organization is wrong, it's a moral cesspool and you know it."

"We can give people hope. Hope isn't ripping off!"

"At NooSkins' prices it is. You hype your wares and take all their money and then they run out of cash, and it's no more treatments for them. They can rot as far as you and your pals are concerned. Don't you remember the way we used to talk, everything we wanted to do? Making life better for people – not just people with money. You used to be so . . . you had ideals, then."

"Sure," said Jimmy's father in a tired voice. "I've still got them. I just can't afford them."

A pause. Jimmy's mother must've been mulling that over. "Be that as it may," she said – a sign that she wasn't going to give in. "Be that as it may, there's research and there's research. What you're doing – this pig brain thing. You're interfering with the building blocks of life. It's immoral. It's . . . sacrilegious."

Bang, on the table. Not his hand. The bottle? "I don't believe I'm hearing this! Who've you been listening to? You're an educated person, you did this stuff yourself! It's just proteins, you know that! There's nothing sacred about cells and tissue, it's just . . ."

"I'm familiar with the theory."

"Anyway it's been paying for your room and board, it's been putting the food on your table. You're hardly in a position to take the high ground."

"I know," said Jimmy's mother's voice. "Believe me, that is one thing I really do know. Why can't you get a job doing something honest? Something basic."

"Like what and like where? You want me to dig ditches?"

"At least your conscience would be clean."

"No, *yours* would. You're the one with the neurotic guilt. Why don't you dig a few ditches yourself, at least it would get you off your butt. Then maybe you'd quit smoking – you're a one-woman emphysema factory, plus you're single-handedly supporting the tobacco companies. Think about that if you're so ethical. They're the folks who get six-year-olds hooked for life by passing out free samples."

"I know all that." A pause. "I smoke because I'm depressed. The tobacco companies depress me, *you* depress me, Jimmy depresses me, he's turning into a . . ."

"Take some pills if you're so fucking depressed!"

"There's no need for swearing."

"I think maybe there is!" Jimmy's father yelling wasn't a complete novelty, but combined with the swearing it got Jimmy's full attention. Maybe there would be action, broken glass. He felt afraid – that cold lump in his stomach was back again – but he also felt compelled to listen. If there was going to be a catastrophe, some final collapse, he needed to witness it.

Nothing happened though, there was just the sound of footsteps going out of the room. Which one of them?

Whoever it was would now come upstairs and check to make sure Jimmy was asleep and hadn't heard. Then they could tick off that item on the Terrific Parenting checklist they both carted around inside their heads. It wasn't the bad stuff they did that made Jimmy so angry, it was the good stuff. The stuff that was supposed to be good, or good enough for him. The stuff they patted themselves on the backs for. They knew nothing about him, what he liked, what he hated, what he longed for. They thought he was only what they could see. A nice boy but a bit of a goof, a bit of a show-off. Not the brightest star in the universe, not a numbers person, but you couldn't have everything you wanted and at least he wasn't a total washout. At least he wasn't a drunk or an addict like a lot of boys his age, so touch wood. He'd actually heard his dad say that: *touch wood*, as if Jimmy was bound to fuck up, wander off the tracks, but he just hadn't got around to it yet. About the different, secret person living inside him they knew nothing at all.

He turned off his computer and unplugged the earphones and doused the lights and got into bed, quietly and also carefully, because Killer was in there already. She was down at the bottom, she liked it there; she'd taken to licking his feet to get the salt off. It was ticklish; head under the covers, he shook with silent laughter.

Hammer

Several years passed. They must have passed, thinks Snowman: he can't actually remember much about them except that his voice cracked and he began to sprout body hair. Not a big thrill at the time except that it would have been worse not to. He got some muscles too. He started having sexy dreams and suffering from lassitude. He thought about girls a lot in the abstract, as it were – girls without heads – and about Wakulla Price with her head on, though she wouldn't hang out with him. Did he have zits, was that it? He can't remember having any; though, as he recalls, the faces of his rivals were covered in them.

Cork-nut, he'd say to anyone who pissed him off. Anyone who wasn't a girl. No one but him and Alex the parrot knew exactly what cork-nut meant, so it was pretty demolishing. It became a fad, among the kids at the HelthWyzer Compound, so Jimmy was considered medium-cool. *Hey, cork-nut!*

His secret best friend was Killer. Pathetic, that the only person he could really talk to was a rakunk. He avoided his parents as much as possible. His dad was a cork-nut and his mother was a drone. He was no longer frightened by their negative electrical field, he simply found them tedious, or so he told himself.

At school, he enacted a major piece of treachery against them. He'd draw eyes on each of his index-finger knuckles and tuck his thumbs inside his fists. Then, by moving the thumbs up and down to show the mouths opening and closing, he could make these two hand-puppets argue together. His right hand was Evil Dad, his left hand was Righteous Mom. Evil Dad blustered and theorized and dished out pompous bullshit, Righteous Mom complained and accused. In Righteous Mom's cosmology, Evil Dad was the sole source of hemorrhoids, kleptomania, global conflict, bad breath, tectonic-plate fault lines, and clogged drains, as well as every migraine headache and menstrual cramp Righteous Mom had ever suffered. This lunchroom show of his was a hit; a crowd would collect, with requests. *Jimmy, Jimmy – do Evil Dad!* The other kids had lots of variations and routines to suggest, filched from the private lives of their own parental units. Some of them tried drawing eyes on their own knuckles, but they weren't as good at the dialogue.

Jimmy felt guilty sometimes, afterwards, when he'd gone too far. He shouldn't have had Righteous Mom weeping in the kitchen because her ovaries had burst; he shouldn't have done that sex scene with the Monday Special Fish Finger, 20% Real Fish – Evil Dad falling upon it and tearing it apart with lust because Righteous Mom was sulking inside an empty Twinkies package and wouldn't come out. Those skits were undignified, though that alone wouldn't have stopped him. They were also too close to an uncomfortable truth Jimmy didn't want to examine. But the other kids egged him on, and he couldn't resist the applause.

"Was that out of line, Killer?" he would ask. "Was that too vile?" *Vile* was a word he'd recently discovered: Righteous Mom was using it a lot these days.

Killer would lick his nose. She always forgave him.

One day Jimmy came home from school and there was a note on the kitchen table. It was from his mother. He knew as soon as he saw the writing on the outside – *For Jimmy*, underlined twice in black – what sort of note it would be.

Dear Jimmy, it said. *Blah blah blah, suffered with conscience long enough, blah blah, no longer participate in a lifestyle that is not only meaningless in itself but blah blah.* She knew that when Jimmy was old enough to consider the implications of *blah blah*, he would agree with her and understand. She would be in contact with him later, if there was any possibility. *Blah blah* search will be conducted, inevitably; thus necessary to go into hiding. A decision not taken without much soul-searching and thought and anguish, but *blah*. She would always love him very much.

Maybe she had loved Jimmy, thinks Snowman. In her own manner. Though he hadn't believed it at the time. Maybe, on the other hand, she hadn't loved him. She must have had some sort of positive emotion about him though. Wasn't there supposed to be a maternal bond?

P.S., she'd said. *I have taken Killer with me to liberate her, as I know she will be happier living a wild, free life in the forest.*

Jimmy hadn't believed that either. He was enraged by it. How dare she? Killer was his! And Killer was a tame animal, she'd be helpless on her own, she wouldn't know how to fend for herself, everything hungry would tear her into furry black and white pieces. But Jimmy's mother and her ilk must have been right, thinks Snowman, and Killer and the other liberated rakunks must have been able to cope just fine, or how else to account for the annoyingly large population of them now infesting this neck of the woods?

Jimmy had mourned for weeks. No, for months. Which one of them was he mourning the most? His mother, or an altered skunk?

His mother had left another note. Not a note – a wordless message. She'd trashed Jimmy's father's home computer, and not only the contents: she'd taken the hammer to it. Actually she'd employed just about every single tool in Jimmy's father's neatly arranged and seldom-used Mr. Home Handyman tool box, but the hammer seemed to have been her main weapon of choice. She'd done her own computer too, if anything more thoroughly. Thus neither Jimmy's father nor the CorpSeCorps men who were soon all over the place had any idea of what coded messages she might have been sending, what information she may or may not have downloaded and taken out with her.

As for how she'd got through the checkpoints and the gates, she'd said she was going for a root canal procedure, to a dentist in one of the Modules. She'd had the paperwork, all the necessary clearances, and the backstory was real: the root canal specialist at the HelthWyzer dental clinic had toppled over with a heart attack and his replacement hadn't arrived, so they were contracting out. She'd even made a genuine appointment with the Module dentist, who'd billed Jimmy's dad for the time when she hadn't shown up.

(Jimmy's dad refused to pay, because it wasn't his missed appointment; he and the dentist had a shouting match about it later, over the phone.) She hadn't packed any luggage, she'd been smarter than that. She'd booked a CorpSeCorps man as protection in the taxi ride from the sealed bullet-train station through the short stretch of pleebland that had to be crossed before reaching the perimeter wall of the Module, which was the usual thing to do. No one questioned her, she was a familiar sight and she had the requisition and the pass and everything. No one at the Compound gate had looked inside her mouth, though there wouldn't have been much to see: nerve pain wouldn't have shown.

The CorpSeCorps man must have been in cahoots with her, or else he'd been done away with; in any case he didn't come back and he was never found. Or so it was said. That really stirred things up. It meant there had been others involved. But what others, and what were their goals? It was urgent that these matters be clarified, said the Corps guys who grilled Jimmy. Had Jimmy's mother ever said anything to him, the Corpsmen asked?

Like, what did they mean by *anything*? said Jimmy. There were the conversations he'd overheard on his mini-mikes, but he didn't want to talk about those. There were the things his mother rambled on about sometimes, about how everything was being ruined and would never be the same again, like the beach house her family had owned when she was little, the one that got washed away with the rest of the beaches and quite a few of the eastern coastal cities when the sea-level rose so quickly, and then there was that huge tidal wave, from the Canary Islands volcano. (They'd taken it in school, in the Geolonomics unit. Jimmy had found the video simulation pretty exciting.) And she used to snivel about her grandfather's Florida grapefruit orchard that had dried up like a giant raisin when the rains had stopped coming, the same year Lake Okeechobee had shrunk to a reeking mud puddle and the Everglades had burned for three weeks straight.

But everyone's parents moaned on about stuff like that. *Remember when you could drive anywhere? Remember when everyone lived in the pleeblands? Remember when you could fly anywhere in the world, without fear? Remember hamburger chains, always real beef, remember hot-dog stands? Remember before New York was* New *New York? Remember when voting mattered?* It was all standard lunchtime hand-puppet stuff. *Oh it was all so great once. Boohoo. Now I'm going into the Twinkies package. No sex tonight!*

His mother was just a mother, Jimmy told the CorpSeCorps man. She did what mothers did. She smoked a lot.

"She belong to any, like, organizations? Any strange folk come to the house? She spend a lot of time on the cellphone?"

"Anything you could help us out with, we'd appreciate it, son," said the other Corpsman. It was the *son* that clinched it. Jimmy said he didn't think so.

Jimmy's mother had left some new clothes for him, in the sizes she said he would soon grow into. They were sucky, like the clothes she always bought. Also they were too small. He put them away in a drawer.

His father was rattled, you could tell; he was scared. His wife had broken every rule in the book, she must've had a whole other life and he'd had no idea. That sort of thing reflected badly on a man. He said he hadn't kept any crucial information on the home computer she'd wrecked, but of course he would have said that, and there was no way of proving otherwise. Then he'd been debriefed, elsewhere, for quite a long time. Maybe he was being tortured, as in old movies or on some of the nastier Web sites, with electrodes and truncheons and red-hot nails, and Jimmy worried about that and felt bad. Why hadn't he seen it all coming and headed it off, instead of playing at mean ventriloquism?

Two cast-iron CorpSeCorps women had stayed in the house while Jimmy's father was away, looking after Jimmy, or so it was called. A smiling one and a flat-faced one. They made a lot of phone calls on their ether cells; they went through the photo albums and Jimmy's mother's closets, and tried to get Jimmy to talk. *She looks really pretty. You think she had a boyfriend? Did she go to the pleeblands much?* Why would she go there, said Jimmy, and they said some people liked to. Why, said Jimmy again, and the flat-faced one said some people were twisted, and the smiling one laughed and blushed, and said you could get things out there you couldn't get in here. What sorts of things, Jimmy wanted to ask, but he didn't because the answer might entangle him in more questions, about what his mother liked or might want to get. He'd done all of his betrayal of her in the HelthWyzer High lunchroom, he wasn't going to do any more.

The two of them cooked terrible leathery omelettes in an attempt to throw Jimmy off guard by feeding him. After that didn't work, they microwaved frozen dinners and ordered in pizza. *So, your mother go to the mall a lot? Did she go dancing? I bet she did.* Jimmy wanted to slug them. If he'd been a girl he could have burst into tears and got them to feel sorry for him, and shut them up that way.

After Jimmy's dad came back from wherever he'd been taken, he'd had counselling. He looked like he needed it, his face was green and his eyes were red and puffy. Jimmy had counselling too, but it was a waste of time.

You must be unhappy that your mother's gone.

Yeah, right.

You mustn't blame yourself, son. It's not your fault she left.

How do you mean?

It's okay, you can express your emotions.

Which ones would you like me to express?

No need to be hostile, Jimmy, I know how you feel.

So, if you already know how I feel, why are you asking me, and so on.

Jimmy's dad told Jimmy that they two fellows would just have to forge ahead the best way they could. So they did forge ahead. They forged and they forged, they poured out their own orange juice in the morning and put the dishes in the dishwasher when they remembered, and after a few weeks of forging Jimmy's dad lost his greenish tint and started playing golf again.

Underneath you could tell he wasn't feeling too shabby, now that the worst was over. He began whistling while he shaved. He shaved more. After a decent interval Ramona moved in. Life took on a different pattern, which involved bouts of giggly, growly sex going on behind doors that were closed but not soundproof, while Jimmy turned his music up high and tried not to listen. He could have put a bug in their room, taken in the whole show, but he had a strong aversion to that. Truth to tell, he found it embarrassing. Once there was a difficult encounter in the upstairs hall, Jimmy's father in a bath towel, ears standing out from the sides of his head, jowls flushed with the energy of his latest erotic tussle,

Jimmy red with shame and pretending not to notice. The two hormone-sodden love bunnies might have had the decency to do it in the garage, instead of rubbing Jimmy's nose in it all the time. They made him feel invisible. Not that he wanted to feel anything else.

How long had they been going at it? Snowman wonders now. Had the two of them been having it off behind the pigoon pens in their biosuits and germ-filtering face masks? He doesn't think so: his father was a nerd, not a shit. Of course you could be both: a nerdy shit, a shitty nerd. But his father (or so he believes) was too awkward and bad at lying to have become involved in full-fledged treachery and betrayal without Jimmy's mother noticing.

Though maybe she had noticed. Maybe that was why she'd fled, or part of the reason. You don't take a hammer – not to mention an electric screwdriver and a pipe wrench – to a guy's computer without being quite angry.

Not that she hadn't been angry in general: her anger had gone way beyond any one motive.

The more Snowman thinks about it, the more he's convinced that Ramona and his father had refrained. They'd waited till Jimmy's mother had buggered off in a splatter of pixels before toppling into each other's arms. Otherwise they wouldn't have done so much earnest, blameless gazing at each other in André's Bistro at OrganInc. If they'd been having a thing already they'd have been brusque and businesslike in public, they'd have avoided each other if anything; they'd have had quick and dirty trysts in grungy corners, weltering around in their own popped buttons and stuck zippers on the office carpet, chewing each other's ears in car parks. They wouldn't have bothered with those antiseptic lunches, with his father staring at the tabletop while Ramona liquefied the raw carrots. They wouldn't have salivated on each other over the greenery and pork pies while using young Jimmy as a human shield.

Not that Snowman passes judgment. He knows how these things go, or used to go. He's a grown-up now, with much worse things on his conscience. So who is he to blame them?

(He blames them.)

Ramona sat Jimmy down and gazed at him with her big black-fringed smudgy sincere eyes, and told him that she knew this was very hard on him and it was a trauma for them all, it was hard on her too, though maybe he, you know, might not think so, and she was aware that she couldn't replace his real mother but she hoped, maybe, they could be buddies? Jimmy said, *Sure, why not*, because apart from her connection with his father he liked her well enough and wanted to please her.

She did try. She laughed at his jokes, a little late sometimes – she was not a word person, he reminded himself – and sometimes when Jimmy's father was away she microwaved dinner for just herself and Jimmy; lasagna and Caesar salad were her staples. Sometimes she would watch DVD movies with him, sitting beside him on the couch, making them a bowl of popcorn first, pouring melted butter substitute onto it, dipping into it with greasy fingers she'd lick during the scary parts while Jimmy tried not to look at her breasts. She asked him if there was anything he wanted to ask her about, like, you know. Her and his dad, and what had happened to the marriage. He said there wasn't.

In secret, in the night, he yearned for Killer. Also – in some corner of himself he could not quite acknowledge – for his real, strange, insufficient, miserable mother. Where had she gone, what danger was she in? That she was in danger of some sort was a given. They'd be looking for her, he knew that, and if he were her he wouldn't want to be found.

But she'd said she would contact him, so why wasn't she doing it? After a while he did get a couple of postcards, with stamps from England, then Argentina. They were signed *Aunt Monica*, but he knew they were from her. *Hope you're well*, was all they said. She must have known they'd be read by about a hundred snoops before ever getting to Jimmy, and that was right, because along came the Corpsmen after each one, asking who Aunt Monica was. Jimmy said he didn't know. He didn't think his mother was in any of the countries the stamps were from, because she was way smarter than that. She must have got other people to mail them for her.

Didn't she trust him? Evidently not. He felt he'd disappointed her, he'd failed her in some crucial way. He'd never understood what was required of him. If only he could have one more chance to make her happy.

"I am not my childhood," Snowman says out loud. He hates these replays. He can't turn them off, he can't change the subject, he can't leave the room. What he needs is more inner discipline, or a mystic syllable he could repeat over and over to tune himself out. What were those things called? Mantras. They'd had that in grade school. Religion of the Week. *All right, class, now quiet as mice, that means you, Jimmy. Today we're going to pretend we live in India, and we're going to do a mantra. Won't that be fun? Now let's all choose a word, a different word, so we can each have our own special mantra.*

"Hang on to the words," he tells himself. The odd words, the old words, the rare ones. *Valance. Norn. Serendipity. Pibroch. Lubricious.* When they're gone out of his head, these words, they'll be gone, everywhere, forever. As if they had never been.

Crake

A few months before Jimmy's mother vanished, Crake appeared. The two things happened in the same year. What was the connection? There wasn't one, except that the two of them seemed to get on well together. Crake was among the scant handful of Jimmy's friends that his mother liked. Mostly she'd found his male pals juvenile, his female ones airheaded or sluttish. She'd never used those words but you could tell.

Crake though, Crake was different. More like an adult, she'd said; in fact, more adult than a lot of adults. You could have an objective conversation with him, a conversation in which events and hypotheses were followed through to their logical conclusions. Not that Jimmy ever witnessed the two of them having such a conversation, but they must have done or else she wouldn't have said that. When and how did these logical, adult conversations take place? He's often wondered.

"Your friend is intellectually honourable," Jimmy's mother would say. "He doesn't lie to himself." Then she'd gaze at Jimmy with that blue-eyed, wounded-by-him look he knew so well. If only *he* could be like that – intellectually honourable. Another baffling item on the cryptic report card his mother toted around in some mental pocket, the report card on which he was always just barely passing. *Jimmy would do better at intellectual honourableness if only he would try harder.* Plus, if he had any fucking clues about what the fuck it meant.

"I don't need supper," he'd tell her yet again. "I'll just grab a snack." If she wanted to do that wounded thing she could do it for the kitchen clock. He'd fixed it so the robin said *hoot* and the owl said *caw caw*. Let her be disappointed with them for a change.

He had his doubts about Crake's honourableness, intellectual or otherwise. He knew a bit more about Crake than his mother did.

When Jimmy's mother took off like that, after the rampage with the hammer, Crake didn't say much. He didn't seem surprised or shocked. All he said was that some people needed to change, and to change they needed to be elsewhere. He said a person could be in your life and then not in it any more. He said Jimmy should read up on the Stoics. That last part was mildly aggravating: Crake could be a little too instructive sometimes, and a little too free with the *should*s. But Jimmy appreciated his calmness and lack of nosiness.

Of course Crake wasn't Crake yet, at that time: his name was Glenn. Why did it have two n's instead of the usual spelling? "My dad liked music," was Crake's explanation, once Jimmy got around to asking him about it, which had taken a while. "He named me after a dead pianist, some boy genius with two n's."

"So did he make you take music lessons?"

"No," said Crake. "He never made me do much of anything."

"Then what was the point?

"Of what?"

"Of your name. The two n's."

"Jimmy, Jimmy," said Crake. "Not everything has a point."

Snowman has trouble thinking of Crake as Glenn, so thoroughly has Crake's later persona blotted out his earlier one. The Crake side of him must have been there from the beginning, thinks Snowman: there was never any real Glenn, *Glenn* was only a disguise. So in Snowman's reruns of the story, Crake is never Glenn, and never *Glenn-alias-Crake* or *Crake/Glenn*, or *Glenn, later Crake*. He is always just Crake, pure and simple.

Anyway *Crake* saves time, thinks Snowman. Why hyphenate, why parenthesize, unless absolutely necessary?

Crake turned up at HelthWyzer High in September or October, one of those months that used to be called *autumn*. It was a bright warm sunny day, otherwise undistinguished. He was a transfer, the result of some headhunt involving a parental unit: these were frequent among the Compounds. Kids came and went, desks filled and emptied, friendship was always contingent.

Jimmy wasn't paying much attention when Crake was introduced to the class by Melons Riley, their Hoodroom and Ultratexts teacher. Her name wasn't Melons – that was a nickname used among the boys in the class – but Snowman can't remember her real name. She shouldn't have bent down so closely over his Read-A-Screen, her large round breasts almost touching his shoulder. She shouldn't have worn her NooSkins T-shirt tucked so tightly into her zipleg shorts: it was too distracting. So that when Melons announced that Jimmy would be showing their new classmate Glenn around the school, there was a pause while Jimmy scrambled to decipher what it was she'd just said.

"Jimmy, I made a request," said Melons.

"Sure, anything," said Jimmy, rolling his eyes and leering, but not taking it too far. There was some class laughter; even Ms. Riley gave him a remote, unwilling smile. He could usually get round her with his boyish-charm act. He liked to imagine that if he hadn't been a minor, and she his teacher and subject to abuse charges, she'd have been gnawing her way through his bedroom walls to sink her avid fingers into his youthful flesh.

Jimmy had been full of himself back then, thinks Snowman with indulgence and a little envy. He'd been unhappy too, of course. It went without saying, his unhappiness. He'd put a lot of energy into it.

When Jimmy got around to focusing on Crake, he wasn't too cheered. Crake was taller than Jimmy, about two inches; thinner too. Straight brown-black hair, tanned skin, green eyes, a half-smile, a cool gaze. His clothes were dark in tone, devoid of logos and visuals and written commentary – a no-name look. He was possibly older than the rest of them, or trying to act it. Jimmy wondered what kinds of sports he played. Not football, nothing too brawny. Not tall enough for basketball. He didn't strike Jimmy as a team player, or one who would stupidly court injury. Tennis, maybe. (Jimmy himself played tennis.)

At lunch hour Jimmy collected Crake and the two of them grabbed some food – Crake put down two giant soy-sausage dogs and a big slab of coconut-style layer cake, so maybe he was trying to bulk up – and then they trudged up and down the halls and in and out of the classrooms and labs, with Jimmy giving the running commentary. *Here's the gym, here's the library, those are the readers, you have to sign up for them before noon, in there's the girls' shower room, there's supposed to be a hole drilled through the wall but I've never found it. If you want to smoke dope don't use the can, they've got it bugged; there's a microlens for Security in that air vent, don't stare at it or they'll know you know.*

Crake looked at everything, said nothing. He volunteered no information about himself. The only comment he made was that the Chemlab was a dump.

Well stuff it, Jimmy thought. If he wants to be an asshole it's a free country. Millions before him have made the same life choice. He was annoyed with himself for jabbering and capering, while Crake gave him brief, indifferent glances, and that one-sided demi-smile. Nevertheless there was something about Crake. That kind of cool slouchiness always impressed Jimmy, coming from another guy: it was the sense of energies being held back, held in reserve for something more important than present company.

Jimmy found himself wishing to make a dent in Crake, get a reaction; it was one of his weaknesses, to care what other people thought of him. So after school he asked Crake if he'd like to go to one of the malls, hang out, see the sights, maybe there would be some girls there, and Crake said why not. There wasn't much else to do after school in the HelthWyzer Compound, or in any of the Compounds, not for kids their age, not in any sort of group way. It wasn't like the pleeblands. There, it was rumoured, the kids ran in packs, in hordes. They'd wait until some parent was away, then get right down to business – they'd swarm the place, waste themselves with loud music and toking and boozing, fuck everything including the family cat, trash the furniture, shoot up, overdose. Glamorous, thought Jimmy. But in the Compounds the lid was screwed down tight. Night patrols, curfews for growing minds, sniffer dogs after hard drugs. Once, they'd loosened up, let in a real band – The Pleebland Dirtballs, it had been – but there'd been a quasi-riot, so no repeats. No need to apologize to Crake, though. He was a Compound brat himself, he'd know the score.

Jimmy was hoping he might catch a glimpse of Wakulla Price, at the mall; he was still sort of in love with her, but after the I-value-you-as-my-friend speech she'd ruined him with, he'd tried one girl and then another, ending up – currently – with blonde LyndaLee. LyndaLee was on the rowing team and had muscular thighs and impressive pecs, and had smuggled him up to her bedroom on more than one occasion. She had a foul mouth and more experience than Jimmy, and every time he went with her he felt as if he'd been sucked into a Pachinko machine, all flashing lights and random tumbling and cascades of ball bearings. He didn't like her much, but he needed to keep up with her, make sure he was still on her list. Maybe he could get Crake into the queue – do him a favour, build up some gratitude equity. He wondered what kind of girls Crake preferred. So far there'd been zero signals.

At the mall there was no Wakulla to be seen, and no Lynda-Lee. Jimmy tried calling LyndaLee, but her cellphone was off. So Jimmy and Crake played a few games of Three-Dimensional Waco in the arcade and had a couple of

SoyOBoyburgers – no beef that month, said the chalkboard menu – and an iced Happicuppuchino, and half a Joltbar each to top up their energy and mainline a few steroids. Then they ambled down the enclosed hallway with its fountains and plastic ferns, through the warm-bathwater music they always played in there. Crake was not exactly voluble, and Jimmy was about to say he had to go do his homework, when up ahead there was a noteworthy sight: it was Melons Riley with a man, heading towards one of the adults-only dance clubs. She'd changed out of her school clothes and had on a loose red jacket over a tight black dress, and the man had his arm around her waist, inside the jacket.

Jimmy nudged Crake. "You think he's got his hand on her ass?" he said.

"That's a geometrical problem," said Crake. "You'd have to work it out."

"What?" said Jimmy. Then, "How?"

"Use your neurons," said Crake. "Step one: calculate length of man's arm, using single visible arm as arm standard. Assumption: that both arms are approximately the same length. Step two: calculate angle of bend at elbow. Step three: calculate curvature of ass. Approximation of this may be necessary, in absence of verifiable numbers. Step four: calculate size of hand, using visible hand, as above."

"I'm not a numbers person," said Jimmy, laughing, but Crake kept on: "All potential hand positions must now be considered. Waist, ruled out. Upper right cheek, ruled out. Lower right cheek or upper thigh would seem by deduction to be the most likely. Hand between both upper thighs a possibility, but this position would impede walking on the part of the subject, and no limping or stumbling is detectable." He was doing a pretty good imitation of their

Chemlab teacher – the use-your-neurons line, and that clipped, stiff delivery, sort of like a bark. More than pretty good, good.

Already Jimmy liked Crake better. They might have something in common after all, at least the guy had a sense of humour. But he was also a little threatened. He himself was a good imitator, he could do just about all the teachers. What if Crake turned out to be better at it? He could feel it within himself to hate Crake, as well as liking him.

But in the days that followed, Crake gave no public performances.

Crake had had a thing about him even then, thinks Snowman. Not that he was popular, exactly, but people felt flattered by his regard. Not just the kids, the teachers too. He'd look at them as if he was listening, as if what they were talking about was worthy of his full attention, though he would never say so exactly. He generated awe – not an overwhelming amount of it, but enough. He exuded potential, but potential for what? Nobody knew, and so people were wary of him. All of this in his dark laconic clothing.

Brainfrizz

Wakulla Price had been Jimmy's lab partner in Nanotech Biochem, but her father was headhunted by a Compound on the other side of the continent, and she'd taken the high-speed sealed bullet train and was never seen again. After she'd gone Jimmy moped for a week, and not even LyndaLee's dirty-mouthed convulsions could console him.

Wakulla's vacant place at the lab table was filled by Crake, who was moved up from his solitary latecomer's position at the back of the room. Crake was very smart – even in the world of HelthWyzer High, with its overstock of borderline geniuses and polymaths, he had no trouble floating at the top of the list. He turned out to be excellent at Nanotech Biochem, and together he and Jimmy worked on their single-molecular-layer splicing project, managing to produce the required purple nematode – using the colour-coder from a primitive seaweed – before schedule, and with no alarming variations.

Jimmy and Crake took to hanging out together at lunch hour, and then – not every day, they weren't gay or anything, but at least twice a week – after school. At first they'd play tennis, on the clay court behind Crake's place, but Crake combined method with lateral thinking and hated to lose, and Jimmy was impetuous and lacked finesse, so that wasn't too productive and they dropped it. Or, under pretence of doing their homework, which sometimes they really would do, they would shut themselves up in Crake's room, where they would play computer chess or Three-Dimensionals, or Kwiktime Osama, tossing to see who got Infidels. Crake had two computers, so they could sit with their backs to each other, one at each.

"Why don't we use a real set?" Jimmy asked one day when they were doing some chess. "The old kind. With plastic men." It did seem weird to have the two of them in the same room, back to back, playing on computers.

"Why?" said Crake. "Anyway, this *is* a real set."

"No it's not."

"Okay, granted, but neither is plastic men."

"What?"

"The real set is in your head."

"Bogus!" Jimmy yelled. It was a good word, he'd got it off an old DVD; they'd taken to using it to tear each other down for being pompous. "Way too bogus!"

Crake laughed.

Crake would get fixated on a game, and would want to play it and play it and perfect his attack until he was sure he could win, nine times out of ten anyway. For a whole month they'd had to play Barbarian Stomp (See If You Can Change History!). One side had the cities and the riches and the other side had the hordes, and – usually but not always – the most viciousness. Either the barbarians stomped the cities or else they got stomped, but you had to start out with the historical disposition of energies and go on from there. Rome versus the Visigoths, Ancient Egypt versus the Hyksos, Aztecs versus the Spaniards. That was a cute one, because it was the Aztecs who represented civilization, while the Spaniards were the barbarian hordes. You could customize the game as long as you used real societies and tribes, and for a while Crake and Jimmy vied with each other to see who could come up with the most obscure pairing.

"Petchenegs versus Byzantium," said Jimmy, one memorable day.

"Who the fuck are the Petchenegs? You made that up," said Crake.

But Jimmy had found it in the *Encyclopedia Britannica*, 1957 edition, which was stored on CD-ROM – for some forgotten reason – in the school library. He had chapter and verse. "'Matthew of Edessa referred to them as wicked blood-drinking beasts,'" he was able to say with authority. "'They were totally ruthless and had no redeeming features.'" So they tossed for sides, and Jimmy got Petchenegs, and won. The Byzantines were slaughtered, because that was what Petchenegs did, Jimmy explained. They always slaughtered everyone immediately. Or they slaughtered the men, at least. Then they slaughtered the women after a while.

Crake took the loss of all of his players badly, and sulked a little. After that he'd switched his loyalty to Blood and Roses. It was more cosmic, said Crake: the field of battle was larger, both in time and space.

Blood and Roses was a trading game, along the lines of Monopoly. The Blood side played with human atrocities for the counters, atrocities on a large scale: individual rapes and murders didn't count, there had to have been a large number of people wiped out. Massacres, genocides, that sort of thing. The Roses side played with human achievements. Artworks, scientific breakthroughs, stellar works of architecture, helpful inventions. *Monuments to the soul's magnificence*, they were called in the game. There were sidebar buttons, so that if you didn't know what *Crime and Punishment* was, or the Theory of Relativity, or the Trail of Tears, or *Madame Bovary*, or the Hundred Years' War, or *The Flight into Egypt*, you could double-click and get an illustrated rundown, in two choices: R for children, PON for Profanity, Obscenity, and Nudity. That was the thing about history, said Crake: it had lots of all three.

You rolled the virtual dice and either a Rose or a Blood item would pop up. If it was a Blood item, the Rose player had a chance to stop the atrocity from happening, but he had to put up a Rose item in exchange. The atrocity would then vanish from history, or at least the history recorded on the screen. The Blood player could acquire a Rose item, but only by handing over an atrocity, thus leaving himself with less ammunition and the Rose player with more. If he was a skilful player he could attack the Rose side by means of the atrocities in his possession, loot the human achievement, and transfer it to his side of the board. The player who managed to retain the most human achievements by Time's Up was the winner. With points off, naturally, for achievements destroyed through his own error and folly and cretinous play.

The exchange rates – one *Mona Lisa* equalled Bergen-Belsen, one Armenian genocide equalled the *Ninth Symphony* plus three Great Pyramids – were suggested, but there was room for haggling. To do this you needed to know the numbers – the total number of corpses for the atrocities, the latest open-market price for the artworks; or, if the artworks had been stolen, the amount paid out by the insurance policy. It was a wicked game.

"Homer," says Snowman, making his way through the dripping-wet vegetation. "*The Divine Comedy*. Greek statuary. Aqueducts. *Paradise Lost*. Mozart's music. Shakespeare, complete works. The Brontës. Tolstoy. The Pearl Mosque. Chartres Cathedral. Bach. Rembrandt. Verdi. Joyce. Penicillin. Keats. Turner. Heart transplants. Polio vaccine. Berlioz. Baudelaire. Bartok. Yeats. Woolf."

There must have been more. There were more.

The sack of Troy, says a voice in his ear. *The destruction of Carthage. The Vikings. The Crusades. Ghenghis Khan. Attila the Hun. The massacre of the Cathars. The witch burnings. The destruction of the Aztec. Ditto the Maya. Ditto the Inca. The Inquisition. Vlad the Impaler. The massacre of the Huguenots. Cromwell in Ireland. The French Revolution. The Napoleonic Wars. The Irish Famine. Slavery in the American South. King Leopold in the Congo. The Russian Revolution. Stalin. Hitler. Hiroshima. Mao. Pol Pot. Idi Amin. Sri Lanka. East Timor. Saddam Hussein.*

"Stop it," says Snowman.

Sorry, honey. Only trying to help.

That was the trouble with Blood and Roses: it was easier to remember the Blood stuff. The other trouble was that the Blood player usually won, but winning meant you inherited a wasteland. This was the point of the game, said Crake, when Jimmy complained. Jimmy said if that was the point, it was pretty pointless. He didn't want to tell Crake that he was having some severe nightmares: the one where the Parthenon was decorated with cut-off heads was, for some reason, the worst.

By unspoken consent they'd given up on Blood and Roses, which was fine with Crake because he was into something new – Extinctathon, an interactive biofreak masterlore game he'd found on the Web. *EXTINCTATHON, Monitored by MaddAddam. Adam named the living animals, MaddAddam names the dead ones. Do you want to play?* That was what came up when you logged on. You then had to click Yes, enter your codename, and pick one of the two chat rooms – Kingdom Animal, Kingdom Vegetable. Then some challenger would come on-line, using his own codename – Komodo, Rhino, Manatee, Hippocampus Ramulosus – and propose a contest. *Begins with, number of legs, what is it?* The *it* would be some bioform that had kakked out within the past fifty years – no T-Rex, no roc, no dodo, and points off for getting the time frame wrong. Then you'd narrow it down, Phylum Class Order Family Genus Species, then the habitat and when last seen, and what had snuffed it. (Pollution, habitat destruction, credulous morons who thought that eating its horn would give them a boner.) The longer the challenger held out, the more points he got, but you could win big bonuses for speed. It helped to have the MaddAddam printout of every extinct species, but that gave you only the Latin names, and anyway it was a couple of hundred pages of fine print and filled with obscure bugs, weeds, and frogs nobody had ever heard of. Nobody except, it seemed, the Extinctathon Grandmasters, who had brains like search engines.

You always knew when you were playing one of those because a little Coelacanth symbol would come up on the screen. *Coelacanth. Prehistoric deep-sea fish, long supposed extinct until specimens found in mid-twentieth. Present status unknown.* Extinctathon was nothing if not informative. It was like some tedious pedant you got trapped beside on the school van, in Jimmy's view. It wouldn't shut up.

"Why do you like this so much?" said Jimmy one day, to Crake's hunched-over back.

"Because I'm good at it," said Crake. Jimmy suspected him of wanting to make Grandmaster, not because it meant anything but just because it was there.

Crake had picked their codenames. Jimmy's was Thickney, after a defunct Australian double-jointed bird that used to hang around in cemeteries, and – Jimmy suspected – because Crake liked the sound of it as applied to Jimmy. Crake's codename was Crake, after the Red-necked Crake, another Australian bird – never, said Crake, very numerous. For a while they called each other Crake and Thickney, as an in-joke. After Crake had realized Jimmy was not wholeheartedly participating and they'd stopped playing Extinctathon, Thickney as a name had faded away. But Crake had stuck.

When they weren't playing games they'd surf the Net – drop in on old favourites, see what was new. They'd watch open-heart surgery in live time, or else the Noodie News, which was good for a few minutes because the people on it tried to pretend there was nothing unusual going on and studiously avoided looking at one another's jujubes.

Or they'd watch animal snuff sites, Felicia's Frog Squash and the like, though these quickly grew repetitious: one stomped frog, one cat being torn apart by hand, was much like another. Or they'd watch dirtysockpuppets.com, a current-affairs show about world political leaders. Crake said that with digital genalteration you couldn't tell whether any of these generals and whatnot existed any more, and if they did, whether they'd actually said what you'd heard. Anyway they were toppled and replaced with such rapidity that it hardly mattered.

Or they might watch hedsoff.com, which played live coverage of executions in Asia. There they could see enemies of the people being topped with swords in someplace that looked like China, while thousands of spectators cheered. Or they could watch alibooboo.com, with various supposed thieves having their hands cut off and adulterers and lipstick-wearers being stoned to death by howling crowds, in dusty enclaves that purported to be in fundamentalist countries in the Middle East. The coverage was usually poor on that site: filming was said to be prohibited, so it was just some desperate pauper with a hidden minivideocam, risking his life for filthy Western currency. You saw mostly the backs and heads of the spectators, so it was like being trapped inside a huge clothes rack unless the guy with the camera got caught, and then there would be a flurry of hands and cloth before the picture went black. Crake said these bloodfests were probably taking place on a back lot somewhere in California, with a bunch of extras rounded up off the streets.

Better than these were the American sites, with their sports-event commentary – "Here he comes now! Yes! It's Joe 'The Ratchet Set' Ricardo, voted tops by you viewers!" Then a rundown of the crimes, with grisly pictures of the victims. These sites would have spot commercials, for things like car batteries and tranquilizers, and logos painted in bright yellow on the background walls. At least the Americans put some style into it, said Crake.

Shortcircuit.com, brainfrizz.com, and deathrowlive.com were the best; they showed electrocutions and lethal injections. Once they'd made real-time coverage legal, the guys being executed had started hamming it up for the cameras. They were mostly guys, with the occasional woman, but Jimmy didn't like to watch those: a woman being croaked was a solemn, weepy affair, and people tended to stand around with lighted candles and pictures of the kids, or show up with poems they'd written themselves. But the guys could be a riot. You could watch them making faces, giving the guards the finger, cracking jokes, and occasionally breaking free and being chased around the room, trailing restraint straps and shouting foul abuse.

Crake said these incidents were bogus. He said the men were paid to do it, or their families were. The sponsors required them to put on a good show because otherwise people would get bored and turn off. The viewers wanted to see the executions, yes, but after a while these could get monotonous, so one last fighting chance had to be added in, or else an element of surprise. Two to one it was all rehearsed.

Jimmy said this was an awesome theory. *Awesome* was another old word, like *bogus*, that he'd dredged out of the DVD archives. "Do you think they're really being executed?" he said. "A lot of them look like simulations."

"You never know," said Crake.

"You never know what?"

"What is *reality*?"

"Bogus!"

There was an assisted-suicide site too – nitee-nite.com, it was called – which had a this-was-your-life component:

family albums, interviews with relatives, brave parties of friends standing by while the deed was taking place to background organ music. After the sad-eyed doctor had declared that life was extinct, there were taped testimonials from the participants themselves, stating why they'd chosen to depart. The assisted-suicide statistics shot way up after this show got going. There was said to be a long lineup of people willing to pay big bucks for a chance to appear on it and snuff themselves in glory, and lotteries were held to choose the participants.

Crake grinned a lot while watching this site. For some reason he found it hilarious, whereas Jimmy did not. He couldn't imagine doing such a thing himself, unlike Crake, who said it showed flair to know when you'd had enough. But did Jimmy's reluctance mean he was a coward, or was it just that the organ music sucked?

These planned departures made him uneasy: they reminded him of Alex the parrot saying *I'm going away now*. There was too fine a line between Alex the parrot and the assisted suicides and his mother and the note she'd left for him. All three gave notice of their intentions; then all vanished.

Or they would watch At Home With Anna K. Anna K. was a self-styled installation artist with big boobs who'd wired up her apartment so that every moment of her life was sent out live to millions of voyeurs. "This is Anna K., thinking always about my happiness and my unhappiness," was what you'd get as you joined her. Then you might watch her tweezing her eyebrows, waxing her bikini line, washing her underwear. Sometimes she'd read scenes from old plays out loud, taking all the parts, while sitting on the can with her retro-look bell-bottom jeans around her ankles. This was how Jimmy first encountered Shakespeare – through Anna K.'s rendition of *Macbeth*.

> Tomorrow, and tomorrow, and tomorrow.
> Creeps in this petty pace from day to day,
> To the last syllable of recorded time;
> And all our yesterdays have lighted fools
> The way to dusty death,

read Anna K. She was a terrible ham, but Snowman has always been grateful to her because she'd been a doorway of sorts. Think what he might not have known if it hadn't been for her. Think of the words. *Sere*, for instance. *Incarnadine*.

"What is this shit?" said Crake. "Channel change!"

"No, wait, wait," said Jimmy, who had been seized by – what? Something he wanted to hear. And Crake waited, because he did humour Jimmy sometimes.

Or they would watch the Queek Geek Show, which had contests featuring the eating of live animals and birds, timed by stopwatches, with prizes of hard-to-come-by foods. It was amazing what people would do for a couple of lamb chops or a chunk of genuine Brie.

Or they would watch porn shows. There were a lot of those.

When did the body first set out on its own adventures? Snowman thinks; after having ditched its old travelling companions, the mind and the soul, for whom it had once been considered a mere corrupt vessel or else a puppet acting out their dramas for them, or else bad company, leading the other two astray. It must have got tired of the soul's constant nagging and whining and the anxiety-driven intellectual web-spinning of the mind, distracting it whenever it was getting its teeth into something juicy or its fingers into something good. It had dumped the other two back there somewhere, leaving them stranded in some damp sanctuary or stuffy lecture hall while it made a beeline for the topless bars, and it had dumped culture along with them: music and painting and poetry and plays. Sublimation, all of it; nothing but sublimation, according to the body. Why not cut to the chase?

But the body had its own cultural forms. It had its own art. Executions were its tragedies, pornography was its romance.

To access the more disgusting and forbidden sites – those for which you had to be over eighteen, and for which you needed a special password – Crake used his Uncle Pete's private code, via a complicated method he called a lily-pad labyrinth. He'd construct a winding pathway through the Web, hacking in at random through some easy-access commercial enterprise, then skipping from lily pad to lily pad, erasing his footprints as he went. That way when Uncle Pete got the bill he couldn't find out who'd run it up.

Crake had also located Uncle Pete's stash of high-grade Vancouver skunkweed, kept in orange-juice cans in the freezer; he'd take out about a quarter of the can, then mix in some of the low-octane carpet sweepings you could buy at the school tuck shop for fifty bucks a baggie. He said Uncle

Pete would never know because he never smoked except when he wanted to have sex with Crake's mother, which – judging from the number of orange-juice cans and the rate at which they were getting used up – wasn't often. Crake said Uncle Pete got his real kicks at the office, bossing people around, whipping the wage slaves. He used to be a scientist, but now he was a large managerial ultra-cheese at Helth-Wyzer, on the financial end of things.

So they'd roll a few joints and smoke them while watching the executions and the porn – the body parts moving around on the screen in slow motion, an underwater ballet of flesh and blood under stress, hard and soft joining and separating, groans and screams, close-ups of clenched eyes and clenched teeth, spurts of this or that. If you switched back and forth fast, it all came to look like the same event. Sometimes they'd have both things on at once, each on a different screen.

These sessions would take place for the most part in silence, except for the sound effects coming from the machines. It would be Crake who'd decide what to watch and when to stop watching it. Fair enough, they were his computers. He might say, "Finished with that?" before changing. He didn't seem to be affected by anything he saw, one way or the other, except when he thought it was funny. He never seemed to get high, either. Jimmy suspected he didn't really inhale.

Jimmy on the other hand would wobble homewards, still fuzzy from the dope and feeling as if he'd been to an orgy, one at which he'd had no control at all over what had happened to him. What had been done to him. He also felt very light, as if he were made of air; thin, dizzying air, at the top of some garbage-strewn Mount Everest. Back at home base, his parental units – supposing they were there, and downstairs – never seemed to notice a thing.

"Getting enough to eat?" Ramona might say to him. She'd interpret his mumble as a yes.

HottTotts

Late afternoons were the best time for doing these things at Crake's place. Nobody interrupted them. Crake's mother was out a lot, or in a hurry; she worked as a diagnostician at the hospital complex. She was an intense, square-jawed, dark-haired woman with not much of a chest. On the rare occasions when Jimmy had been there at the same time as Crake's mother, she hadn't said much. She'd dug around in the kitchen cupboards for something that would pass as a snack for "you boys," as she called the two of them. Sometimes she would stop in the middle of her preparations – the dumping of stale crackers onto a plate, the sawing up of chewy orange-and-white-marbled hunks of cheesefood – and stand stock-still, as if she could see someone else in the room. Jimmy had the impression she couldn't remember his name; not only that, she couldn't remember Crake's name either. Sometimes she would ask Crake if his room was tidy, though she never went in there herself.

"She believes in respecting a child's privacy," said Crake, straight-faced.

"I bet it's your mouldy socks," said Jimmy. "All the perfumes of Arabia will not sweeten these little socks." He'd recently discovered the joys of quotation.

"For that we've got room spray," said Crake.

As for Uncle Pete, he was rarely home before seven. HelthWyzer was expanding like helium, and therefore he had a lot of new responsibilities. He wasn't Crake's real uncle, he was just Crake's mother's second husband. He'd taken on that status when Crake had been twelve, a couple of years too old for the "uncle" tag to have been viewed by him as anything but totally rancid. Yet Crake had accepted the status quo, or so it appeared. He'd smile, he'd say *Sure, Uncle Pete* and *That's right, Uncle Pete* when the man was around, even though Jimmy knew Crake disliked him.

One afternoon in – what? March, it must have been, because it was already hot as hell outside – the two of them were watching porn in Crake's room. Already it felt like old time's sake, already it felt like nostalgia – something they were too grown-up for, like middle-aged guys cruising the pleebland teeny clubs. Still, they dutifully lit up a joint, hacked into Uncle Pete's digital charge card via a new labyrinth, and started surfing. They checked into Tart of the Day, which featured elaborate confectionery in the usual orifices, then went to Superswallowers; then to a Russian site that employed ex-acrobats, ballerinas, and contortionists.

"Whoever said a guy can't suck his own?" was Crake's comment. The high-wire act with the six flaming torches was pretty good, but they'd seen things like that before.

Then they went to HottTotts, a global sex-trotting site. "The next best thing to being there," was how it was advertised. It claimed to show real sex tourists, filmed while doing things they'd be put in jail for back in their home countries. Their faces weren't visible, their names weren't used, but the possibilities for blackmail, Snowman realizes now, must have been extensive. The locations were supposed to be countries where life was cheap and kids were plentiful, and where you could buy anything you wanted.

This was how the two of them first saw Oryx. She was only about eight, or she looked eight. They could never find out for certain how old she'd been then. Her name wasn't Oryx, she didn't have a name. She was just another little girl on a porno site.

None of those little girls had ever seemed real to Jimmy – they'd always struck him as digital clones – but for some reason Oryx was three-dimensional from the start. She was small-boned and exquisite, and naked like the rest of them, with nothing on her but a garland of flowers and a pink hair ribbon, frequent props on the sex-kiddie sites. She was on her knees, with another little girl on either side of her, positioned in front of the standard gargantuan Gulliver-in-Lilliput male torso – a life-sized man shipwrecked on an island of delicious midgets, or stolen away and entranced, forced to experience agonizing pleasures by a trio of soulless pixies. The guy's distinguishing features were concealed – bag with eyeholes over the head, surgical tape over the tattoos and scars: few of these types wanted to be spotted by the folks back home, though the possibility of detection must have been part of the thrill.

The act involved whipped cream and a lot of licking. The effect was both innocent and obscene: the three of them were going over the guy with their kittenish tongues and their tiny fingers, giving him a thorough workout to the sound of moans and giggles. The giggles must have been recorded, because they weren't coming from the three girls: they all looked frightened, and one of them was crying.

Jimmy knew the drill. They were supposed to look like that, he thought; if they stopped the action, a walking stick would come in from offside and prod them. This was a feature of the site. There were at least three layers of contradictory make-believe, one on top of the other. *I want to, I want to not, I want to.*

Oryx paused in her activities. She smiled a hard little smile that made her appear much older, and wiped the whipped cream from her mouth. Then she looked over her shoulder and right into the eyes of the viewer – right into Jimmy's eyes, into the secret person inside him. *I see you*, that look said. *I see you watching. I know you. I know what you want.*

Crake pushed the reverse, then the freeze, then the download. Every so often he froze frames; by now he had a small archive of them. Sometimes he'd print them out and give a copy to Jimmy. It could be dangerous – it could leave a footprint for anyone who might manage to trace a way through the labyrinth – but Crake did it anyway. So now he saved that one moment, the moment when Oryx looked.

Jimmy felt burned by this look – eaten into, as if by acid. She'd been so contemptuous of him. The joint he'd been smoking must have had nothing in it but lawn mowings: if it had been stronger he might have been able to bypass guilt. But for the first time he'd felt that what they'd been doing was wrong. Before, it had always been entertainment, or else far beyond his control, but now he felt culpable. At the same time he felt hooked through the gills: if he'd been offered instant teleportation to wherever Oryx was he'd have taken it, no question. He'd have begged to go there. It was all too complicated.

"This a keeper?" Crake said. "You want it?"

"Yeah," said Jimmy. He could barely get the word out. He hoped he sounded normal.

So Crake had printed it, the picture of Oryx looking, and Snowman had saved it and saved it. He'd shown it to Oryx many years later.

"I don't think this is me," was what she'd said at first.

"It has to be!" said Jimmy. "Look! It's your eyes!"

"A lot of girls have eyes," she said. "A lot of girls did these things. Very many." Then, seeing his disappointment, she said, "It might be me. Maybe it is. Would that make you happy, Jimmy?"

"No," said Jimmy. Was that a lie?

"Why did you keep it?"

"What were you thinking?" Snowman said instead of answering.

Another woman in her place would have crumpled up the picture, cried, denounced him as a criminal, told him he understood nothing about her life, made a general scene. Instead she smoothed out the paper, running her fingers gently over the soft, scornful child's face that had – surely – once been hers.

"You think I was thinking?" she said. "Oh Jimmy! You always think everyone is thinking. Maybe I wasn't thinking anything."

"I know you were," he said.

"You want me to pretend? You want me to make something up?"

"No. Just tell me."

"Why?"

Jimmy had to think about that. He remembered himself watching. How could he have done that to her? And yet it hadn't hurt her, had it? "Because I need you to." Not much of a reason, but it was all he could come up with.

She sighed. "I was thinking," she said, tracing a little circle on his skin with her fingernail, "that if I ever got the chance, it would not be me down on my knees."

"It would be someone else?" said Jimmy. "Who? What someone?"

"You want to know everything," said Oryx.

5

Toast

Snowman in his tattered sheet sits hunched at the edge of the trees, where grass and vetch and sea grapes merge into sand. Now that it's cooler he feels less dejected. Also he's hungry. There's something to be said for hunger: at least it lets you know you're still alive.

A breeze riffles the leaves overhead; insects rasp and trill; red light from the setting sun hits the tower blocks in the water, illuminating an unbroken pane here and there, as if a scattering of lamps has been turned on. Several of the buildings once held roof gardens, and now they're top-heavy with overgrown shrubbery. Hundreds of birds are streaming across the sky towards them, roostward bound. Ibis? Herons? The black ones are cormorants, he knows that for sure. They settle down into the darkening foliage, croaking and squabbling. If he ever needs guano he'll know where to find it.

Across the clearing to the south comes a rabbit, hopping, listening, pausing to nibble at the grass with its gigantic teeth. It glows in the dusk, a greenish glow filched from the iridicytes of a deep-sea jellyfish in some long-ago experiment. In the half-light the rabbit looks soft and almost translucent, like a piece of Turkish delight; as if you could suck off its fur like sugar. Even in Snowman's boyhood there were luminous green rabbits, though they weren't this big and they hadn't yet slipped their cages and bred with the wild population, and become a nuisance.

This one has no fear of him, though it fills him with carnivorous desires: he longs to whack it with a rock, tear it apart with his bare hands, then cram it into his mouth, fur and all. But rabbits belong to the Children of Oryx and are sacred to Oryx herself, and it would be a bad idea to offend the women.

It's his own fault. He must have been stupefied with drink when he was laying down the laws. He should have made rabbits edible, by himself at any rate, but he can't change that now. He can almost hear Oryx, laughing at him with indulgent, faintly malicious delight.

The Children of Oryx, the Children of Crake. He'd had to think of something. Get your story straight, keep it simple, don't falter: this used to be the expert advice given by lawyers to criminals in the dock. *Crake made the bones of the Children of Crake out of the coral on the beach, and then he made their flesh out of a mango. But the Children of Oryx hatched out of an egg, a giant egg laid by Oryx herself. Actually she laid two eggs: one full of animals and birds and fish, and the other one full of words. But the egg full of words hatched first, and the Children of Crake had already been created by then, and they'd eaten up all the words because they were hungry, and so there were no words left over when the second egg hatched out. And that is why the animals can't talk.*

Internal consistency is best. Snowman learned this earlier in his life, when lying had posed more of a challenge for him. Now even when he's caught in a minor contradiction he can make it stick, because these people trust him. He's the only one left who'd known Crake face to face, so he can lay claim to the inside track. Above his head flies the invisible banner of Crakedom, of Crakiness, of Crakehood, hallowing all he does.

The first star appears. "Star light, star bright," he says. Some grade-school teacher. Big-bum Sally. *Now close your eyes right up tight. Tighter! Really tight! There! See the wishing star? Now we will all wish for the thing we want the very, very most of all in the whole wide world. But shhh – don't tell anyone, or the wish won't come true!*

Snowman screws his eyes shut, pushes his fists into them, clenches his entire face. There's the wishing star all right: it's blue. "I wish I may, I wish I might," he says. "Have the wish I wish tonight."

Fat chance.

"Oh Snowman, why are you talking to no one?" says a voice. Snowman opens his eyes: three of the older children are standing just out of reach, regarding him with interest. They must have crept up on him in the dusk.

"I'm talking to Crake," he says.

"But you talk to Crake through your shiny thing! Is it broken?"

Snowman lifts his left arm, holds out his watch. "This is for *listening* to Crake. *Talking* to him is different."

"Why are you talking to him about stars? What are you telling to Crake, oh Snowman?"

What, indeed? thinks Snowman. *When dealing with indigenous peoples,* says the book in his head – a more modern book this time, late twentieth century, the voice a confident female's – *you must attempt to respect their traditions and confine your explanations to simple concepts that can be understood within the contexts of their belief systems.* Some earnest aid worker in a khaki jungle outfit, with netting under the arms and a hundred pockets. Condescending self-righteous cow, thinks she's got all the answers. He'd known girls like that at college. If she were here she'd need a whole new take on *indigenous.*

"I was telling him," says Snowman, "that you ask too many questions." He holds his watch to his ear. "And he's telling me that if you don't stop doing that, you'll be toast."

"Please, oh Snowman, what is toast?"

Another error, Snowman thinks. He should avoid arcane metaphors. "Toast," he says, "is something very, very bad. It's so bad I can't even describe it. Now it's your bedtime. Go away."

"What is toast?" says Snowman to himself, once they've run off. *Toast is when you take a piece of bread – What is bread? Bread is when you take some flour – What is flour? We'll skip that part, it's too complicated. Bread is something you can eat, made from a ground-up plant and shaped like a stone. You cook it . . . Please, why do you cook it? Why don't you just eat the plant? Never mind that part – Pay attention. You cook it, and then you cut it into slices, and you put a slice into a toaster, which is a metal box that heats up with electricity – What is electricity? Don't worry about that. While the slice is in the toaster, you get out the butter – butter is a yellow grease, made from the mammary glands of – skip the butter. So, the toaster turns the slice of bread black on both sides with smoke coming out, and then this "toaster" shoots the slice up into the air, and it falls onto the floor . . .*

"Forget it," says Snowman. "Let's try again." *Toast was a pointless invention from the Dark Ages. Toast was an implement of torture that caused all those subjected to it to regurgitate in verbal form the sins and crimes of their past lives. Toast was a ritual item devoured by fetishists in the belief that it would enhance their kinetic and sexual powers. Toast cannot be explained by any rational means.*

Toast is me.

I am toast.

Fish

The sky darkens from ultramarine to indigo. God bless the namers of oil paints and high-class women's underwear, Snowman thinks. Rose-Petal Pink, Crimson Lake, Sheer Mist, Burnt Umber, Ripe Plum, Indigo, Ultramarine – they're fantasies in themselves, such words and phrases. It's comforting to remember that *Homo sapiens sapiens* was once so ingenious with language, and not only with language. Ingenious in every direction at once.

Monkey brains, had been Crake's opinion. Monkey paws, monkey curiosity, the desire to take apart, turn inside out, smell, fondle, measure, improve, trash, discard – all hooked up to monkey brains, an advanced model of monkey brains but monkey brains all the same. Crake had no very high opinion of human ingenuity, despite the large amount of it he himself possessed.

There's a murmuring of voices from the direction of the village, or from what would be a village if it had any houses.

Right on schedule, here come the men, carrying their torches, and behind them the women.

Every time the women appear, Snowman is astonished all over again. They're every known colour from deepest black to whitest white, they're various heights, but each one of them is admirably proportioned. Each is sound of tooth, smooth of skin. No ripples of fat around their waists, no bulges, no dimpled orange-skin cellulite on their thighs. No body hair, no bushiness. They look like retouched fashion photos, or ads for a high-priced workout program.

Maybe this is the reason that these women arouse in Snowman not even the faintest stirrings of lust. It was the thumbprints of human imperfection that used to move him, the flaws in the design: the lopsided smile, the wart next to the navel, the mole, the bruise. These were the places he'd single out, putting his mouth on them. Was it consolation he'd had in mind, kissing the wound to make it better? There was always an element of melancholy involved in sex. After his indiscriminate adolescence he'd preferred sad women, delicate and breakable, women who'd been messed up and who needed him. He'd liked to comfort them, stroke them gently at first, reassure them. Make them happier, if only for a moment. Himself too, of course; that was the payoff. A grateful woman would go the extra mile.

But these new women are neither lopsided nor sad: they're placid, like animated statues. They leave him chilled.

The women are carrying his weekly fish, grilled the way he's taught them and wrapped in leaves. He can smell it, he's starting to drool. They bring the fish forward, put it on the ground in front of him. It will be a shore fish, a species too paltry and tasteless to have been coveted and sold and exterminated, or else a bottom-feeder pimply with toxins, but Snowman couldn't care less, he'll eat anything.

"Here is your fish, oh Snowman," says one of the men, the one called Abraham. Abraham as in Lincoln: it had amused Crake to name his Crakers after eminent historical figures. It had all seemed innocent enough, at the time.

"This is the one fish chosen for you tonight," says the woman holding it; the Empress Josephine, or else Madame Curie or Sojourner Truth, she's in the shade so he can't tell which. "This is the fish Oryx gives you."

Oh good, thinks Snowman. Catch of the Day.

Every week, according to the phases of the moon – dark, first quarter, full, second quarter – the women stand in the tidal pools and call the unlucky fish by name – only *fish*, nothing more specific. Then they point it out, and the men kill it with rocks and sticks. That way the unpleasantness is shared among them and no single person is guilty of shedding the fish's blood.

If things had gone as Crake wanted, there would be no more such killing – no more human predation – but he'd reckoned without Snowman and his beastly appetites. Snowman can't live on clover. The people would never eat a fish themselves, but they have to bring him one a week because he's told them Crake has decreed it. They've accepted Snowman's monstrousness, they've known from the beginning he was a separate order of being, so they weren't surprised by this.

Idiot, he thinks. I should have made it three a day. He unwraps the warm fish from its leaves, trying to keep his hands from trembling. He shouldn't get too carried away. But he always does.

The people keep their distance and avert their eyes while he crams handfuls of fishiness into his mouth and sucks out the eyes and cheeks, groaning with pleasure. Perhaps it's like hearing a lion gorge itself, at the zoo, back when there were zoos, back when there were lions – a rending and crunching, a horrible gobbling and gulping – and, like those long-gone zoo visitors, the Crakers can't help peeking. The spectacle of depravity is of interest even to them, it seems, purified by chlorophyll though they are.

When Snowman has finished he licks his fingers and wipes them on his sheet, and places the bones back in their leaf wrappings, ready to be returned to the sea. He's told them Oryx wants that – she needs the bones of her children so she can make other children out of them. They've accepted this without question, like everything he says about Oryx. In reality it's one of his smarter ploys: no sense leaving the scraps around on land, to attract rakunks and wolvogs and pigoons and other scavengers.

The people move closer, men and women both, gathering around, their green eyes luminescent in the semi-darkness, just like the rabbit; same jellyfish gene. Sitting all together like this, they smell like a crateful of citrus fruit – an added feature on the part of Crake, who'd thought those chemicals would ward off mosquitoes. Maybe he was right, because all the mosquitoes for miles around appear to be biting Snowman. He resists the urge to swat: his fresh blood only excites them. He shifts to the left so he's more in the smoke of the torches.

"Snowman, tell us please about the deeds of Crake."

A story is what they want, in exchange for every slaughtered fish. Well, I owe them, Snowman thinks. God of Bullshit, fail me not.

"What part would you like to hear tonight?" he says.

"In the beginning," prompts a voice. They're fond of repetition, they learn things by heart.

"In the beginning, there was chaos," he says.

"Show us chaos, please, oh Snowman!"

"Show us a picture of chaos!"

They'd struggled with pictures, at first – flowers on beach-trash lotion bottles, fruits on juice cans. *Is it real? No, it is not real. What is this not real? Not real can tell us about real.* And so forth. But now they appear to have grasped the concept.

"Yes! Yes! A picture of chaos!" they urge.

Snowman has known this request would be made – all the stories begin with chaos – and so he's ready for it. From behind his concrete-slab cache he brings out one of his finds – an orange plastic pail, faded to pink but otherwise undamaged. He tries not to imagine what has happened to the child who must once have owned it. "Bring some water," he says, holding out the pail. There's a scramble around the ring of torches: hands reach out, feet scamper off into the darkness.

"In the chaos, everything was mixed together," he says. "There were too many people, and so the people were all mixed up with the dirt." The pail comes back, sloshing, and is set down in the circle of light. He adds a handful of earth, stirs it with a stick. "There," he says. "Chaos. You can't drink it . . ."

"No!" A chorus.

"You can't eat it . . ."

"No, you can't eat it!" Laughter.

"You can't swim in it, you can't stand on it . . ."

"No! No!" They love this bit.

"The people in the chaos were full of chaos themselves, and the chaos made them do bad things. They were killing other people all the time. And they were eating up all the Children of Oryx, against the wishes of Oryx and Crake. Every day they were eating them up. They were killing them and killing them, and eating them and eating them. They ate them even when they weren't hungry."

Gasping here, widened eyes: it's always a dramatic moment. Such wickedness! He continues: "And Oryx had only one desire – she wanted the people to be happy, and to be at peace, and to stop eating up her children. But the people couldn't be happy, because of the chaos. And then Oryx said to Crake, *Let us get rid of the chaos*. And so Crake took the chaos, and he poured it away." Snowman demonstrates, sloshing the water off to the side, then turns the pail upside down. "There. Empty. And this is how Crake did the Great Rearrangement and made the Great Emptiness. He cleared away the dirt, he cleared room . . ."

"For his children! For the Children of Crake!"

"Right. And for . . ."

"And for the Children of Oryx, as well!"

"Right," says Snowman. Is there no end to his shameless inventions? He feels like crying.

"Crake made the Great Emptiness . . . " say the men.

"For us! For us!" say the women. It's becoming a liturgy. "Oh, good, kind Crake!"

Their adulation of Crake enrages Snowman, though this adulation has been his own doing. The Crake they're praising is his fabrication, a fabrication not unmixed with spite: Crake was against the notion of God, or of gods of any kind, and would surely be disgusted by the spectacle of his own gradual deification.

If he were here. But he's not here, and it's galling for Snowman to listen to all this misplaced sucking up. Why don't they glorify Snowman instead? Good, kind Snowman, who deserves glorification more – much more – because who got them out, who got them here, who's been watching over them all this time? Well, sort of watching. It sure as hell wasn't Crake. Why can't Snowman revise the mythology? *Thank me, not him! Lick my ego instead!*

But for now his bitterness must be swallowed. "Yes," he says. "Good, kind Crake." He twists his mouth into what he hopes is a gracious and benevolent smile.

At first he'd improvised, but now they're demanding dogma: he would deviate from orthodoxy at his peril. He might not lose his life – these people aren't violent or given to bloodthirsty acts of retribution, or not so far – but he'd lose his audience. They'd turn their backs on him, they'd wander away. He is Crake's prophet now, whether he likes it or not; and the prophet of Oryx as well. That, or nothing. And he couldn't stand to be nothing, to know himself to be nothing. He needs to be listened to, he needs to be heard. He needs at least the illusion of being understood.

"Oh Snowman, tell us about when Crake was born," says one of the women. This is a new request. He isn't ready for it, though he should have expected it: children are of great interest to these women. Careful, he tells himself. Once he provides a mother and a birth scene and an infant Crake for them, they'll want the details. They'll want to know when Crake cut his first tooth and spoke his first word and ate his first root, and other such banalities.

"Crake was never born," says Snowman. "He came down

out of the sky, like thunder. Now go away please, I'm tired."
He'll add to this fable later. Maybe he'll endow Crake with horns, and wings of fire, and allow him a tail for good measure.

Bottle

After the Children of Crake have filed away, taking their torches with them, Snowman clambers up his tree and tries to sleep. All around him are noises: the slurping of the waves, insect chirpings and whirrings, bird whistles, amphibious croaks, the rustling of leaves. His ears deceive him: he thinks he can hear a jazz horn, and under that a rhythmic drumming, as if from a muffled nightclub. From somewhere farther along the shore comes a booming, bellowing sound: now what? He can't think of any animal that makes such a noise. Perhaps it's a crocodile, escaped from a defunct Cuban handbag farm and working its way north along the shore. That would be bad news for the kids in swimming. He listens again, but the sound doesn't recur.

There's a distant, peaceful murmur from the village: human voices. If you can call them human. As long as they don't start singing. Their singing is unlike anything he ever heard in his vanished life: it's beyond the human level, or below it. As if crystals are singing; but not that, either. More like ferns unscrolling – something old, carboniferous, but at the same time newborn, fragrant, verdant. It reduces him, forces too many unwanted emotions upon him. He feels excluded, as if from a party to which he will never be invited. All he'd have to do is step forward into the firelight and there'd be a ring of suddenly blank faces turned towards him. Silence would fall, as in tragic plays of long ago when the doomed protagonist made an entrance, enveloped in his cloak of contagious bad news. On some non-conscious level Snowman must serve as a reminder to these people, and not a pleasant one: he's what they may have been once. *I'm your past*, he might intone. *I'm your ancestor, come from the land of the dead. Now I'm lost, I can't get back, I'm stranded here, I'm all alone. Let me in!*

Oh Snowman, how may we be of help to you? The mild smiles, the polite surprise, the puzzled goodwill.

Forget it, he would say. There's no way they can help him, not really.

There's a chilly breeze blowing; the sheet is damp; he shivers. If only this place had a thermostat. Maybe he could figure out some way of building a little fire, up here in his tree.

"Go to sleep," he orders himself. With no result. After a long session of tossing, turning, and scratching, he climbs back down to seek out the Scotch bottle in his cache. There's enough starlight so he can get his bearings, more or less. He's made this trip many times in the past: for the first month and a half, after he was fairly sure it was safe to relax his vigilance, he got pissed out of his mind every night. This was not a wise or mature thing for him to have done, granted, but of what use are wisdom and maturity to him now?

So every night had been party night, party of one. Or every night he'd had the makings, whenever he'd been able to locate another stash of alcohol in the abandoned pleebland buildings within reach. He'd scoured the nearby bars first, then the restaurants, then the houses and trailers. He'd done cough medicine, shaving lotion, rubbing alcohol; out behind the tree he'd accumulated an impressive dump of empty bottles. Once in a while he'd come across a stash of weed and he'd done that too, though often enough it was mouldy; still, he might manage to get a buzz out of it. Or he might find some pills. No coke or crack or heroin – that would have been used up early, stuffed into veins and noses in one last burst of *carpe diem*; anything for a vacation from reality, under the circumstances. There'd been empty BlyssPluss containers everywhere, all you'd need for a non-stop orgy. The revellers hadn't managed to get through all the booze, though often enough on his hunting and gathering trips he's discovered that others had been there before him and there was nothing left but broken glass. There must have been riotous behaviour of all sorts imaginable, until finally there had been no one left to keep it up.

At ground level it's dark as an armpit. A flashlight would come in handy, one of the windup kind. He should keep an eye out. He gropes and stumbles in the right direction, scanning the ground for a glimmer of the vicious white land crabs that come out of their burrows and scuttle around after dark – those things can give you quite a nip – and after a short detour into a clump of bushes, he locates his cement hidey-hole by stubbing his toe on it. He refrains from swearing: no way of telling what else might be prowling around in the night. He slides open the cache, fumbles blindly within it, retrieves the third of Scotch.

He's been saving it up, resisting the urge to binge, keeping it as a sort of charm – as long as he's known it was still there it's been easier to get through time. This might be the last of it. He's certain he has explored every likely site within a day's out-and-back radius of his tree. But he's feeling reckless. Why hoard the stuff? Why wait? What's his life worth anyway, and who cares? Out, out, brief candle. He's served his evolutionary purpose, as fucking Crake knew he would. He's saved the children.

"*Fucking* Crake!" he can't help yelling.

Clutching the bottle with one hand, feeling his way with the other, he reaches his tree again. He needs both hands for climbing, so he knots the bottle securely into his sheet. Once up, he sits on his platform, gulping down the Scotch and howling at the stars – *Aroo! Aroo!* – until he's startled by a chorus of replies from right near the tree.

Is that the gleam of eyes? He can hear panting.

"Hello, my furry pals," he calls down. "Who wants to be man's best friend?" In answer there's a supplicating whine. That's the worst thing about wolvogs: they still look like dogs, still behave like dogs, pricking up their ears, making playful puppy leaps and bounces, wagging their tails. They'll sucker you in, then go for you. It hasn't taken much to reverse fifty thousand years of man-canid interaction. As for the real dogs, they never stood a chance: the wolvogs have simply killed and eaten all those who'd shown signs of vestigial domesticated status. He's seen a wolvog advance to a yapping Pekinese in a friendly manner, sniff its bum, then lunge for its throat, shake it like a mop, and canter off with the limp body.

For a while there were still a few woebegone house pets scrounging around, skinny and limping, their fur matted and dull, begging with bewildered eyes to be taken in by some human, any human. The Children of Crake hadn't fit their bill – they must have smelled weird to a dog, sort of like walking fruits, especially at dusk when the citrus-oil insect repellant kicked in – and in any case they'd shown no interest in puppy-dogs as a concept, so the strays had concentrated on Snowman. He'd almost given in a couple of times, he'd found it hard to resist their ingratiating wriggles, their pitiful whining, but he couldn't afford to feed them; anyway they were useless to him. "It's sink or swim," he'd told them. "Sorry, old buddy." He'd driven them away with stones, feeling like a complete shit, and there haven't been any more lately.

What a fool he'd been. He'd let them go to waste. He should have eaten them. Or taken one in, trained it to catch rabbits. Or to defend him. Or something.

Wolvogs can't climb trees, which is one good thing. If they get numerous enough and too persistent, he'll have to start swinging from vine to vine, like Tarzan. That's a funny idea, so he laughs. "All you want is my body!" he yells at them. Then he drains the bottle and throws it down. There's a yelp, a scuttling: they still respect missiles. But how long can that last? They're smart; very soon they'll sense his vulnerability, start hunting him. Once they begin he'll never be able to go anywhere, or anywhere without trees. All they'll have to do is get him out in the open, encircle him, close in for the kill. There's only so much you can do with stones and pointed sticks. He really needs to find another spraygun.

After the wolvogs have gone he lies on his back on the platform, gazing up at the stars through the gently moving leaves. They seem close, the stars, but they're far away. Their light is millions, billions of years out of date. Messages with no sender.

Time passes. He wants to sing a song but can't think of one. Old music rises up in him, fades; all he can hear is the percussion. Maybe he could whittle a flute, out of some branch or stem or something, if only he could find a knife.

"Star light, star bright," he says. What comes next? It's gone right out of his head.

No moon, tonight is the dark of the moon, although the moon is there nevertheless and must be rising now, a huge invisible ball of stone, a giant lump of gravity, dead but powerful, drawing the sea towards itself. Drawing all fluids. *The human body is ninety-eight per cent water*, says the book in his head. This time it's a man's voice, an encyclopedia voice; no one he knows, or knew. *The other two per cent is made up of minerals, most importantly the iron in the blood and the calcium of which the skeletal frame and the teeth are comprised.*

"Who gives a rat's ass?" says Snowman. He doesn't care about the iron in his blood or the calcium in his skeletal frame; he's tired of being himself, he wants to be someone else. Turn over all his cells, get a chromosome transplant, trade in his head for some other head, one with better things in it. Fingers moving over him, for instance, little fingers with oval nails, painted Ripe Plum or Crimson Lake or Rose-Petal Pink. *I wish I may, I wish I might, Have the wish I wish tonight.* Fingers, a mouth. A dull heavy ache begins, at the base of his spine.

"Oryx," he says. "I know you're there." He repeats the name. It's not even her real name, which he'd never known anyway; it's only a word. It's a mantra.

Sometimes he can conjure her up. At first she's pale and

shadowy, but if he can say her name over and over, then maybe she'll glide into his body and be present with him in his flesh, and his hand on himself will become her hand. But she's always been evasive, you can never pin her down. Tonight she fails to materialize and he is left alone, whimpering ridiculously, jerking off all by himself in the dark.

6

Oryx

Snowman wakes up suddenly. Has someone touched him? But there's nobody there, nothing.

It's totally dark, no stars. Clouds must have come in.

He turns over, pulls his sheet around him. He's shivering: it's the night breeze. Most likely he's still drunk; sometimes it's hard to tell. He stares up into the darkness, wondering how soon it will be morning, hoping he'll be able to go back to sleep.

There's an owl hooting somewhere. That fierce vibration, up close and far away at once, like the lowest note on a Peruvian flute. Maybe it's hunting. Hunting what?

Now he can feel Oryx floating towards him through the air, as if on soft feathery wings. She's landing now, settling; she's very close to him, stretched out on her side just a skin's distance away. Miraculously she can fit onto the platform beside him, although it isn't a large platform. If he had a candle or a flashlight he'd be able to see her, the slender outline of her, a pale glow against the darkness. If he put out his hand he could touch her; but that would make her vanish.

"It wasn't the sex," he says to her. She doesn't answer, but he can feel her disbelief. He's making her sad because he's taking away some of her knowledge, her power. "It wasn't just the sex." A dark smile from her: that's better. "You know I love you. You're the only one." She isn't the first woman he's ever said that to. He shouldn't have used it up so much earlier in his life, he shouldn't have treated it like a tool, a wedge, a key to open women. By the time he got around to meaning it, the words had sounded fraudulent to him and he'd been ashamed to pronounce them. "No, really," he says to Oryx.

No answer, no response. She was never very forthcoming at the best of times.

"Tell me just one thing," he'd say, back when he was still Jimmy.

"Ask me a question," she'd reply.

So he would ask, and then she might say, "I don't know. I've forgotten." Or, "I don't want to tell you that." Or, "Jimmy, you are so bad, it's not your business." Once she'd said, "You have a lot of pictures in your head, Jimmy. Where did you get them? Why do you think they are pictures of me?"

He thought he understood her vagueness, her evasiveness. "It's all right," he'd told her, stroking her hair. "None of it was your fault."

"None of what, Jimmy?"

How long had it taken him to piece her together from the slivers of her he'd gathered and hoarded so carefully? There was Crake's story about her, and Jimmy's story about her as well, a more romantic version; and then there was her own story about herself, which was different from both, and not very romantic at all. Snowman riffles through these three stories in his head. There must once have been other versions of her: her mother's story, the story of the man who'd bought her, the story of the man who'd bought her after that, and the third man's story – the worst man of them all, the one in San Francisco, a pious bullshit artist; but Jimmy had never heard those.

Oryx was so delicate. Filigree, he would think, picturing her bones inside her small body. She had a triangular face – big eyes, a small jaw – a Hymenoptera face, a mantid face, the face of a Siamese cat. Skin of the palest yellow, smooth and translucent, like old, expensive porcelain. Looking at her, you knew that a woman of such beauty, slightness, and one-time poverty must have led a difficult life, but that this life would not have consisted in scrubbing floors.

"Did you ever scrub floors?" Jimmy asked her once.

"Floors?" She thought a minute. "We didn't have floors. When I got as far as the floors, it wasn't me scrubbing them." One thing about that early time, she said, the time without floors: the pounded-earth surfaces were swept clean every day. They were used for sitting on while eating, and for sleeping on, so that was important. Nobody wanted to get old food on themselves. Nobody wanted fleas.

When Jimmy was seven or eight or nine, Oryx was born. Where, exactly? Hard to tell. Some distant, foreign place.

It was a village though, said Oryx. A village with trees all around and fields nearby, or possibly rice paddies. The huts had thatch of some kind on the roofs – palm fronds? – although the best huts had roofs of tin. A village in Indonesia, or else Myanmar? Not those, said Oryx, though she couldn't be sure. It wasn't India though. Vietnam? Jimmy guessed. Cambodia? Oryx looked down at her hands, examining her nails. It didn't matter.

She couldn't remember the language she'd spoken as a child. She'd been too young to retain it, that earliest language: the words had all been scoured out of her head. But it wasn't the same as the language of the city to which she'd first been taken, or not the same dialect, because she'd had to learn a different way of speaking. She did remember that: the clumsiness of the words in her mouth, the feeling of being struck dumb.

This village was a place where everyone was poor and there were many children, said Oryx. She herself was quite little when she was sold. Her mother had a number of children, among them two older sons who would soon be able to work in the fields, which was a good thing because the father was sick. He coughed and coughed; this coughing punctuated her earliest memories.

Something wrong with the lungs, Jimmy had guessed. Of course they all probably smoked like maniacs when they could get the cigarettes: smoking dulled the edge. (He'd congratulated himself on this insight.) The villagers set the father's illness down to bad water, bad fate, bad spirits. Illness had an element of shame to it; no one wanted to be contaminated by the illness of another. So the father of Oryx was pitied, but also blamed and shunned. His wife tended him with silent resentment.

Bells were rung, however. Prayers were said. Small images were burned in the fire. But all of this was useless, because the father died. Everyone in the village knew what would happen next, because if there was no man to work in the fields or in the rice paddies, then the raw materials of life had to come from somewhere else.

Oryx had been a younger child, often pushed to the side, but suddenly she was made much of and given better food than usual, and a special blue jacket, because the other village women were helping out and they wanted her to look pretty and healthy. Children who were ugly or deformed, or who were not bright or couldn't talk very well – such children went for less, or might not be sold at all. The village women might need to sell their own children one day, and if they helped out they would be able to count on such help in return.

In the village it was not called "selling," this transaction. The talk about it implied apprenticeship. The children were being trained to earn their living in the wide world: this was the gloss put on it. Besides, if they stayed where they were, what was there for them to do? Especially the girls, said Oryx. They would only get married and make more children, who would then have to be sold in their turn. Sold, or thrown into the river, to float away to the sea; because there was only so much food to go around.

One day a man came to the village. It was the same man who always came. Usually he arrived in a car, bumping over the dirt track, but this time there had been a lot of rain and the road was too muddy. Each village had its own such man, who would make the dangerous journey from the city at irregular intervals, although it was always known ahead of time that he was on his way.

"What city?" asked Jimmy.

But Oryx only smiled. Talking about this made her hungry, she said. Why didn't sweet Jimmy phone out for some pizza? Mushrooms, artichoke hearts, anchovies, no pepperoni. "You want some too?" she said.

"No," said Jimmy. "Why won't you tell me?"

"Why do you care?" said Oryx. "I don't care. I never think about it. It's long ago now."

This man – said Oryx, contemplating the pizza as if it were a jigsaw puzzle, then picking off the mushrooms, which she liked to eat first – would have two other men with him, who were his servants and who carried rifles to fend off the bandits. He wore expensive clothes, and except for the mud and dust – everyone got muddy and dusty on the way to the village – he was clean and well-kempt. He had a watch, a shiny gold-coloured watch he consulted often, pulling up his sleeve to display it; this watch was reassuring, a badge of quality. Maybe the watch was real gold. There were some who said it was.

This man wasn't regarded as a criminal of any sort, but as an honourable businessman who didn't cheat, or not much, and who paid in cash. Therefore he was treated with respect and shown hospitality, because no one in the village wanted to get on his bad side. What if he ceased to visit? What if a family needed to sell a child and he would not buy it because he'd been offended on a previous visit? He was the villagers' bank, their insurance policy, their kind rich uncle, their only charm against bad luck. And he had been needed more and more often, because the weather had become so strange and could no longer be predicted – too much rain or not enough, too much wind, too much heat – and the crops were suffering.

The man smiled a lot, greeted many of the village men by name. He always gave a little speech, the same one every time. He wanted everyone to be happy, he would say. He wanted satisfaction on both sides. He didn't want any hard feelings. Hadn't he bent over backwards for them, taking children that were plain and stupid and a burden on his hands, just to oblige them? If they had any criticism of the way he conducted affairs, they should tell him. But there was never any criticism, though there was grumbling behind his back: he never paid any more than he had to, it was said. He was admired for this, however: it showed he was good at his trade, and the children would be in competent hands.

Each time the gold-wristwatch man came to the village he would take several children away with him, to sell flowers to tourists on the city streets. The work was easy and the children would be well treated, he assured the mothers: he wasn't a low-down thug or a liar, he wasn't a pimp. They would be well fed and given a safe place to sleep, they would be carefully guarded, and they would be paid a sum of money, which they could send home to their families, or not, whatever they chose. This sum would be a percentage of their earnings minus the expense of their room and board. (No money was ever sent to the village. Everyone knew it would not be.) In exchange for the child apprentice, he would give the fathers, or else the widowed mothers, a good price, or what he said was a good price; and it was a decent-enough price, considering what people were used to. With this money, the mothers who sold their children would be able to give the remaining children a better chance in life. So they told one another.

*

Jimmy was outraged by this the first time he heard about it. That was in the days of his outrage. Also in the days of his making a fool of himself over anything concerning Oryx.

"You don't understand," said Oryx. She was still eating the pizza in bed; with that she was having a Coke, and a side of fries. She'd finished with the mushrooms and now she was eating the artichoke hearts. She never ate the crust. She said it made her feel very rich to throw away food. "Many people did it. It was the custom."

"An asshole custom," said Jimmy. He was sitting on a chair beside the bed, watching her pink cat's tongue as she licked her fingers.

"Jimmy, you are bad, don't swear. You want a pepperoni? You didn't order them but they put them on anyway. I guess they heard you wrong."

"*Asshole* isn't swearing, it's only graphic description."

"Well, I don't think you should say it." She was eating the anchovies now: she always saved them till last.

"I'd like to kill this guy."

"What guy? You want this Coke? I can't finish it."

"The guy you just told me about."

"Oh Jimmy, you would like it better maybe if we all starved to death?" said Oryx, with her small rippling laugh. This was the laugh he feared most from her, because it disguised amused contempt. It chilled him: a cold breeze on a moonlit lake.

Of course he'd marched his outrage off to Crake. He'd whammed the furniture: those were his furniture-whamming days. What Crake had to say was this: "Jimmy, look at it realistically. You can't couple a minimum access to food with an expanding population indefinitely. *Homo sapiens* doesn't seem able to cut himself off at the supply end. He's one of the few species that doesn't limit reproduction in the face of dwindling resources. In other words – and up to a point, of course – the less we eat, the more we fuck."

"How do you account for that?" said Jimmy.

"Imagination," said Crake. "Men can imagine their own deaths, they can see them coming, and the mere thought of impending death acts like an aphrodisiac. A dog or a rabbit doesn't behave like that. Take birds – in a lean season they cut down on the eggs, or they won't mate at all. They put their energy into staying alive themselves until times get better. But human beings hope they can stick their souls into someone else, some new version of themselves, and live on forever."

"As a species we're doomed by hope, then?"

"You could call it hope. That, or desperation."

"But we're doomed without hope, as well," said Jimmy.

"Only as individuals," said Crake cheerfully.

"Well, it sucks."

"Jimmy, grow up."

Crake wasn't the first person who'd ever said that to Jimmy.

The wristwatch man would stay overnight in the village with his two servants and their guns, and would eat and then drink with the men. He would hand out cigarettes, entire packs of them, in gold and silver paper boxes with the cellophane still on. In the morning he would look over the children on offer and ask some questions about them – had they been sick, were they obedient? And he'd check their teeth. They had to have good teeth, he said, because they would need to smile a lot. Then he would make his selections, and the money would change hands, and he'd say his farewells, and there would be polite nods and bows all round. He would take three or four children with him, never more; that was the number he could manage. This meant he could pick the best of the crop. He did the same in the other villages in his territory. He was known for his taste and judgment.

Oryx said it must have been too bad for a child not to be chosen. Things would be worse for it in the village then, it would lose value, it would be given less to eat. She herself had been chosen first of all.

Sometimes the mothers would cry, and also the children, but the mothers would tell the children that what they were doing was good, they were helping their families, and they should go with the man and do everything he told them. The mothers said that after the children had worked in the city for a while and things were better, then they could come back to the village. (No children ever came back.)

All of this was understood, and if not condoned, at least pardoned. Still, after the man had left, the mothers who had sold their children felt empty and sad. They felt as if this act, done freely by themselves (no one had forced them, no one had threatened them), had not been performed willingly. They felt cheated as well, as if the price had been too low. Why hadn't they demanded more? And yet, the mothers told themselves, they'd had no choice.

The mother of Oryx sold two of her children at the same time, not only because she was hard up. She thought the two might keep each other company, look out for each other. The other child was a boy, a year older than Oryx. Fewer boys were sold than girls, but they were not therefore more valued.

(Oryx took this double sale as evidence that her mother had loved her. She had no images of this love. She could offer no anecdotes. It was a belief rather than a memory.)

The man said he was doing Oryx's mother a special favour, as boys were more trouble and did not obey, and ran away more often, and who would pay him for his trouble then? Also this boy did not have a right attitude, that much was clear at a glance, and he had a blackened front tooth that gave him a criminal expression. But as he knew she needed the money he would be generous, and would take the boy off her hands.

Birdcall

Oryx said she couldn't remember the trip from the village to the city, but she could remember some of the things that had happened. It was like pictures hanging on a wall, with around them the blank plaster. It was like looking through other people's windows. It was like dreams.

The man with the watch said his name was Uncle En, and they must call him that or there would be very big trouble.

"Was that En as in a name, or N as in an initial?" Jimmy asked.

"I don't know," said Oryx.

"Did you ever see it written?"

"Nobody in our village could read," said Oryx. "Here, Jimmy. Open your mouth. I give you the last piece."

Remembering this, Snowman can almost taste it. The pizza, then Oryx's fingers in his mouth.

Then the Coke can rolling onto the floor. Then joy, crushing his whole body in its boa-constrictor grip.

Oh stolen secret picnics. Oh sweet delight. Oh clear memory, oh pure pain. Oh endless night.

*

This man – Oryx continued, later that night, or on some other night – this man said he was their uncle from now on. Now that they were out of sight of the village he wasn't smiling so much. They must walk very quickly, he said, because the forest around them was full of wild animals with red eyes and long sharp teeth, and if they ran in among the trees or walked too slowly, these animals would come and tear them to pieces. Oryx was frightened and wanted to hold hands with her brother, but that wasn't possible.

"Were there tigers?" Jimmy asked.

Oryx shook her head for no. No tigers.

"What were these animals then?" Jimmy wanted to know. He thought he might get some clues that way, as to the location. He could look at the list of habitats, that might help.

"They didn't have names," said Oryx, "but I knew what they were."

At first they went single file along the muddy road, walking on the side where it was higher, watching out for snakes. A gun-carrying man was at the front, then Uncle En, then the brother, then the two other children who had also been sold – both girls, both older – and then Oryx. At the end came the other gun man. They stopped for a noon meal – cold rice, it was, packed for them by the villagers – and then they walked some more. When they came to a river one of the men with the guns carried Oryx across. He said she was so heavy he would have to drop her into the water and then the fish would eat her, but that was a joke. He smelled of sweaty cloth and smoke, and some sort of perfume or grease that was in his hair. The water came up to his knees.

After that the sun was on a slant and got into her eyes – they must have been going west then, thought Jimmy – and she was very tired.

As the sun got lower and lower the birds began singing and calling, unseen, hidden in the branches and vines of the forest: raucous croaks and whistles, and four clear sounds in a row, like a bell. These were the same birds that always called like this as dusk approached, and at dawn just before the sun came up, and Oryx was consoled by their sounds. The birdcalls were familiar, they were part of what she knew. She imagined that one of them – the one like a bell – was her mother's spirit, sent out in the shape of a bird to keep watch over her, and that it was saying *You will come back*.

In that village, she told him, some of the people could send their spirits out like that even before they were dead. It was well known. You could learn how to do it, the old women could teach you, and that way you could fly everywhere, you could see what was coming in the future, and send messages, and appear in other people's dreams.

The bird called and called and then fell silent. Then the sun went down abruptly and it was dark. That night they slept in a shed. Possibly it was a shed for livestock; it had that smell. They had to pee in the bushes, all together in a row, with one of the gun men standing guard. The men made a fire outside and laughed and talked, and smoke came in, but Oryx didn't care because she went to sleep. Did they sleep on the ground, or in hammocks, or on cots, asked Jimmy, but she said it wasn't important. Her brother was there beside her. He'd never paid very much attention to her before, but now he wanted to be close to her.

The next morning they walked some more and came to the place where Uncle En's car had been left, under the protection of several men in a small village: smaller than their own village, and dirtier. Women and children peered at them from the doorways but did not smile. One woman made a sign against evil.

Uncle En checked to make sure nothing was missing from the car and then he paid the men, and the children were told to get in. Oryx had never been inside a car before and she didn't like the smell. It wasn't a solarcar, it was the gasoline kind, and not new. One of the men drove, Uncle En beside him; the other man sat in the back with all four children jammed in beside him. Uncle En was in a bad temper and told the children not to ask any questions. The road was bumpy and it was hot inside the car. Oryx felt sick and thought she would vomit, but then she dozed off.

They must have driven for a long time; they stopped when it was night again. Uncle En and the man in front went into a low building, some sort of inn perhaps; the other man stretched out on the front seat and soon began to snore. The children slept in the back of the car, as best they could. The back doors were locked: they couldn't get out of the car without climbing over the man, and they were afraid to do that because he would think they were trying to run away. Somebody wet their pants during the night, Oryx could smell it, but it wasn't her. In the morning they were all herded around to the back of the building where there was an open latrine. A pig on the other side of it watched them while they squatted.

After more hours of bumpy driving they stopped where there was a gate across the road, with two soldiers. Uncle En told the soldiers that the children were his nieces and his nephew: their mother had died and he was taking them to live in his own house, with his own family. He was smiling again.

"You have a lot of nieces and nephews," said one of the soldiers, grinning.

"That is my misfortune," said Uncle En.

"And all their mothers die."

"This is the sad truth."

"We aren't sure we should believe you," said the other soldier, also grinning.

"Here," said Uncle En. He pulled Oryx out of the car. "What's my name?" he said to her, putting his smiling face down close.

"Uncle En," she said. The two soldiers laughed and Uncle En laughed also. He patted Oryx on the shoulder and told her to get back into the car, and shook hands with the soldiers, putting his hand into his pocket first, and then the soldiers swung the gate open. Once the car was going along the road again Uncle En gave Oryx a hard candy, in the shape of a tiny lemon. She sucked it for a while and then took it out to keep. She had no pocket so she held it in her sticky fingers. That night she comforted herself by licking her own hand.

The children cried at night, not loudly. They cried to themselves. They were frightened: they didn't know where they were going, and they had been taken away from what they knew. Also, said Oryx, they had no more love, supposing they'd had some in the first place. But they had a money value: they represented a cash profit to others. They must have sensed that – sensed they were worth something.

Of course (said Oryx), having a money value was no substitute for love. Every child should have love, every person should have it. She herself would rather have had her mother's love – the love she still continued to believe in, the love that had followed her through the jungle in the form of a bird so she would not be too frightened or lonely – but love was undependable, it came and then it went, so it was good to have a money value, because then at least those who wanted to make a profit from you would make sure you were fed enough and not damaged too much. Also there were many who had neither love nor a money value, and having one of these things was better than having nothing.

Roses

The city was a chaos, filled with people and cars and noise and bad smells and a language that was hard to understand. The four new children were shocked by it at first, as if they'd been plunged into a cauldron of hot water – as if the city was physically hurtful to them. Uncle En had experience, however: he treated the new children as if they were cats, he gave them time to get used to things. He put them into a small room in a three-storey building, on the third floor, with a barred window they could look out but not climb out, and then he led them outside gradually, a short distance at first and an hour at a time. There were already five children staying in the room, so it was crowded; but there was enough space for a thin mattress for each child, laid down at night so the entire floor was covered with mattresses and children, then rolled up during the day. These mattresses were worn and stained, and smelled of urine; but rolling them up neatly was the first thing the new children had to learn.

From the other, more seasoned children they learned more things. The first was that Uncle En would always be watching them, even when it appeared they had been left in the city on their own. He would always know where they were: all he had to do was hold his shiny watch up to his ear and it would tell him, because there was a little voice inside it that knew everything. This was reassuring, as nobody else would be allowed to harm them. On the other hand, Uncle En would see if you didn't work hard enough or tried to run away, or if you kept for yourself any of the money you got from the tourists. Then you would be punished. Uncle En's men would beat you and then you would have bruises. They might burn you as well. Some of the children claimed to have endured these punishments, and were proud of it: they had scars. If you tried these forbidden things often enough – laziness, theft, running away – you would be sold, to someone much worse – it was said – than Uncle En. Or else you would be killed and tossed on a rubbish heap, and nobody would care because nobody would know who you were.

Oryx said that Uncle En really knew his business, because children would believe other children about punishments more readily than they would believe adults. Adults threatened to do things they never did, but children told what would happen. Or what they were afraid would happen. Or what had happened already, to them or to other children they'd known.

The week after Oryx and her brother arrived in the mattress room, three of the older children were taken away. They were going to another country, said Uncle En. This country was called San Francisco. Was it because they'd been bad? No, said Uncle En, it was a reward for being good. All who were obedient and diligent might go there some day. There was nowhere Oryx wanted to go except home, but "home" was becoming hazy in her mind. She could still hear her mother's spirit calling *You will come back*, but that voice was becoming fainter and more indistinct. It was no longer like a bell, it was like a whisper. It was a question now, rather than a statement; a question with no answer.

Oryx and her brother and the other two newcomers were taken to watch the more experienced children selling flowers. The flowers were roses, red and white and pink; they were collected at the flower market early in the morning. The thorns had been removed from the stems so the roses could be passed from hand to hand without pricking anyone. You had to loiter around the entranceways to the best hotels – the banks where foreign money could be changed and the expensive shops were good locations too – and you had to keep an eye out for policemen. If a policeman came near or stared hard at you, you should walk the other way quickly. Selling flowers to the tourists was not allowed unless you had an official permit, and such permits were too expensive. But there was nothing to worry about, said Uncle En: the police knew all about it, only they had to appear as if they didn't know.

When you saw a foreigner, especially one with a foreign woman beside him, you should approach and hold up the roses, and you should smile. You should not stare or laugh at their strange foreign hair and water-coloured eyes. If they took a flower and asked how much, you should smile even more and hold out your hand. If they spoke to you, asking questions, you should look as if you didn't understand. That part was easy enough. They would always give you more – sometimes much more – than the flower was worth.

The money had to be put into a little bag hanging inside your clothes; that was to protect against pickpockets and random snatching from street urchins, those unlucky ones without an Uncle En to look after them. If anyone – especially any man – tried to take you by the hand and lead you off somewhere, you should pull your hand away. If they held on too tight you should sit down. That would be a signal, and one of Uncle En's men would come, or Uncle En himself. You should never get into a car or go into a hotel. If a man asked you to do that, you should tell Uncle En as soon as possible.

Oryx had been given a new name by Uncle En. All the children got new names from him. They were told to forget their old names, and soon they did. Oryx was now SuSu. She was good at selling roses. She was so small and fragile, her features so clear and pure. She was given a dress that was too big for her, and in it she looked like an angelic doll. The other children petted her, because she was the littlest one. They took turns sleeping beside her at night; she was passed from one set of arms to another.

Who could resist her? Not many of the foreigners. Her smile was perfect – not cocky or aggressive, but hesitant, shy, taking nothing for granted. It was a smile with no ill will in it: it contained no resentment, no envy, only the promise of heartfelt gratitude. "Adorable," the foreign ladies would murmur, and the men with them would buy a rose and hand it to the lady, and that way the men would become adorable too; and Oryx would slip the coins into the bag down the front of her dress and feel safe for one more day, because she had sold her quota.

Not so her brother. He had no luck. He didn't want to sell flowers like a girl, and he hated smiling; and when he did smile, the effect was not good because of his blackened tooth. So Oryx would take some of his leftover roses and try to sell them for him. Uncle En didn't mind at first – money was money – but then he said Oryx shouldn't be seen too much in the same locations because it wouldn't do for people to become tired of her.

Something else would have to be found for the brother – some other occupation. He would have to be sold elsewhere. The older children in the room shook their heads: the brother would be sold to a pimp, they said; a pimp for hairy white foreign men or bearded brown men or fat yellow men, any kind of men who liked little boys. They described in detail what these men would do; they laughed about it. He would be a melon-bum boy, they said: that's what boys like him were called. Firm and round on the outside, soft and sweet on the inside; a nice melon bum, for anyone who paid. Either that or he would be put to work as a messenger, sent from street to street, doing errands for gamblers, and that was hard work and very dangerous, because the rival gamblers would kill you. Or he could be a messenger and a melon boy, both. That was the most likely thing.

Oryx saw her brother's face darken and grow hard, and she wasn't surprised when he ran away; and whether he was ever caught and punished Oryx never knew. Nor did she ask, because asking – she had now found out – would do no good.

One day a man did take Oryx by the hand and say she should come into the hotel with him. She gave him her shy smile, and looked up sideways and said nothing, and pulled her hand away and told Uncle En afterwards. Then Uncle En said a surprising thing. If the man asked again, he said, she was to go into the hotel with him. He would want to take her up to his room, and she must go with him. She should do whatever the man asked, but she shouldn't worry, because Uncle En would be watching and would come to get her. Nothing bad would happen to her.

"Will I be a melon?" she asked. "A melon-bum girl?" and Uncle En laughed and said where did she pick up that word. But no, he said. That was not what would happen.

Next day the man appeared and asked Oryx if she would like some money, a lot more money than she could make by selling roses. He was a long white hairy man with a thick accent, but she could make out the words. This time Oryx went with him. He held her hand and they went up in an elevator – this was the frightening part, a tiny room with doors that shut, and when the doors opened you were in a different place, and Uncle En hadn't explained about that. She could feel her heart thumping. "Don't be afraid," said the man, thinking she was afraid of him. But it was the other way around, he was afraid of her, because his hand had a tremor. He unlocked a door with a key and they went in, and he locked the door behind them, and they were in a mauve-and-gold-coloured room with a giant bed in it, a bed for giants, and the man asked Oryx to take off her dress.

Oryx was obedient and did as she was told. She had a general idea of what else the man might want – the other children already knew about such things and discussed them freely, and laughed about them. People paid a lot of money for the kinds of things this man wanted, and there were special places in the city for men like him to go; but some wouldn't go there because it was too public and they were ashamed, and they foolishly wanted to arrange things for themselves, and this man was one of that kind. So Oryx knew the man would now take off his own clothes, or some of them, and he did, and seemed pleased when she stared at his penis, which was long and hairy like himself, with a bend in it like a little elbow. Then he kneeled down so he was on her level, with his face right next to hers.

What did this face look like? Oryx couldn't remember. She could remember the singularity of his penis but not the singularity of his face. "It was like no face," she said. "It was all soft, like a dumpling. There was a big nose on it, a carrot nose. A long white penis nose." She laughed, holding her two hands over her mouth. "Not like your nose, Jimmy," she added in case he felt self-conscious. "Your nose is beautiful. It is a sweet nose, believe me."

"I won't hurt you," said the man. His accent was so ridiculous that Oryx wanted to giggle, but she knew that would be wrong. She smiled her shy smile, and the man took hold of one of her hands and placed it on himself. He did this gently enough, but at the same time he seemed angry. Angry, and in a hurry.

That was when Uncle En plunged suddenly into the room – how? He must have had a key, he must have been given a key by someone at the hotel. He picked Oryx up and hugged her and called her his little treasure, and yelled at the man, who seemed very frightened and tried to scramble into his clothes. He got caught in his trousers and hopped around on one foot while trying to explain something with his bad accent, and Oryx felt bad for him. Then the man gave money to Uncle En, a lot of money, all the money in his wallet, and Uncle En went out of the room carrying Oryx like a precious vase and still muttering and scowling. But out on the street he laughed, and made jokes about the man hopping around in his snarled-up trousers, and told Oryx she was a good girl and wouldn't she like to play this game again?

So that became her game. She felt a little sorry for the men: although Uncle En said they deserved what happened to them and they were lucky he never called the police, she somewhat regretted her part. But at the same time she enjoyed it. It made her feel strong to know that the men thought she was helpless but she was not. It was they who were helpless, they who would soon have to stammer apologies in their silly accents and hop around on one foot in their luxurious hotel rooms, trapped in their own pant legs with their bums sticking out, smooth bums and hairy bums, bums of different sizes and colours, while Uncle En berated them. From time to time they would cry. As for the money, they emptied their pockets, they threw all the money they had at Uncle En, they thanked him for taking it. They didn't want to spend any time in jail, not in that city, where the jails were not hotels and it took a very long time for charges to be laid and for trials to be held. They wanted to get into taxis, as soon as they could, and climb onto big airplanes, and fly away through the sky.

"Little SuSu," Uncle En would say, as he set Oryx down on the street outside the hotel. "You are a smart girl! I wish I could marry you. Would you like that?"

This was as close to love as Oryx could get right then, so she felt happy. But what was the right answer, yes or no? She knew it was not a serious question but a joke: she was only five, or six, or seven, so she couldn't get married. Anyway the other children said that Uncle En had a grown-up wife who lived in a house elsewhere, and he had other children as well. His real children. They went to school.

"Can I listen to your watch?" said Oryx with her shy smile. *Instead of,* was what she meant. *Instead of marrying you, instead of answering your question, instead of being your real child.* And he laughed some more, and he did let her listen to his watch, but she didn't hear any little voice inside.

Pixieland Jazz

One day a different man came, one they'd never seen before – a tall thin man, taller than Uncle En, with ill-fitting clothes and a pock-marked face – and said that all of them would have to come with him. Uncle En had sold his flower business, this man said; the flowers, and the flower-sellers, and everything else. He'd gone away, he'd moved to a different city. So this tall man was the boss now.

A year or so later, Oryx was told – by a girl who'd been with her the first weeks in the room with the mattresses, and had turned up again in her new life, her life of movie-making – that this wasn't the real story. The real story was that Uncle En had been found floating in one of the city's canals with his throat cut.

This girl had seen him. No, that was wrong – she hadn't seen him, but she knew somebody who had. There was no doubt about who it was. His stomach was puffed up like a pillow, his face was bloated, but it was Uncle En all right. He had no clothes on – someone must have taken them. Maybe someone else, not the one who'd cut his throat, or maybe the same one, because what use did a corpse have for good clothes like his? No watch on him either. "No money," the girl had said, and she'd laughed. "No pockets, so no money!"

"There were canals in this city?" Jimmy asked. He thought maybe that would give him a clue as to which city it had been. In those days he'd wanted to know whatever it was possible to know, about Oryx, about anywhere she'd been. He'd wanted to track down and personally injure anyone who had ever done harm to her or made her unhappy. He'd tortured himself with painful knowledge: every white-hot factoid he could collect he'd shove up under his fingernails. The more it hurt, the more – he was convinced – he loved her.

"Oh yes, there were canals," Oryx said. "The farmers used them, and the flower-growers, to get to the markets. They tied up their boats and sold what they had right there, right at the quays. That was a pretty sight, from a distance. So many flowers." She looked at him: she could often tell what he was thinking. "But a lot of cities have canals," she said. "And rivers. The rivers are so useful, for the garbage and the dead people and the babies that get thrown away, and the shit." Although she didn't like it when he swore, she sometimes liked to say what she called *bad words* herself, because it shocked him. She had a large supply of bad words once she got going. "Don't worry so much, Jimmy," she added more gently. "It was a long time ago." More often than not she acted as if she wanted to protect him, from the image of herself – herself in the past. She liked to keep only the bright side of herself turned towards him. She liked to shine.

*

So Uncle En had ended up in the canal. He'd been unlucky. He hadn't paid off the right people, or he hadn't paid them off enough. Or maybe they'd tried to buy his business and the price was too low and he wouldn't do it. Or his own men had sold him out. There were many things that could have happened to him. Or maybe it was nothing planned – just an accident, a random killing, just a thief. Uncle En had been careless, he'd gone out walking by himself. Though he wasn't a careless man.

"I cried when I heard about it," said Oryx. "Poor Uncle En."

"Why are you defending him?" Jimmy asked. "He was vermin, he was a cockroach!"

"He liked me."

"He liked the money!"

"Of course, Jimmy," said Oryx. "Everyone likes that. But he could have done much worse things to me, and he didn't do them. I cried when I heard he was dead. I cried and cried."

"What worse things? What much worse?"

"Jimmy, you worry too much."

The children were herded out of the room with the grey mattresses, and Oryx never saw it again. She never saw most of the other children again. They were divided up, and one went this way and one that. Oryx was sold to a man who made movies. She was the only one of them that went with the movie man. He told her she was a pretty little girl and asked how old she was, but she didn't know the answer to that. He asked her wouldn't she like to be in a movie. She'd never seen a movie so she didn't know whether she would like it or not; but it sounded like an offer of a treat, so she said yes. By this time she was good at knowing when *yes* was the expected answer.

The man drove her in a car with some other girls, three or four, girls she didn't know. They stayed overnight at a house, a big house. It was a house for rich people; it had a high wall around it with broken glass and barbed wire on the top, and they went in through a gate. Inside, it had a rich smell.

"What do you mean, a rich smell?" Jimmy asked, but Oryx couldn't say. *Rich* was just a thing you learned to tell. The house smelled like the better hotels she'd been in: many different foods cooking, wooden furniture, polishes and soap, all those smells mixed in. There must have been flowers, flowering trees or bushes nearby, because that was some of the smell. There were carpets on the floor but the children didn't walk on them; the carpets were in a big room, and they went past the open door and looked in and saw them. They were blue and pink and red, such beauty.

The room they were put in was next to the kitchen. Perhaps it was a storeroom, or it had been one: there was the smell of rice and of the bags it was packed in, though no rice was in that room then. They were fed – better food than usual, said Oryx, there was chicken in it – and told not to make any noise. Then they were locked in. There were dogs at that house; you could hear them outside in the yard, barking.

The next day some of them went in a truck, in the back of a truck. There were two other children, both girls, both of them small like Oryx. One of them had just come from a village and missed her people there, and cried a lot, silently, hiding her face. They were lifted up into the back of the truck and locked in, and it was dark and hot and they got thirsty, and when they had to pee they had to do it in the truck because there was no stopping. There was a little window though, up high, so some air got in.

It was only a couple of hours, but it seemed like more because of the heat and the darkness. When they got to where they were going they were handed over to another man, a different one, and the truck drove off.

"Was there any writing on it? The truck?" asked Jimmy, sleuthing.

"Yes. It was red writing."

"What did it say?"

"How would I know?" said Oryx reproachfully.

Jimmy felt foolish. "Was there a picture, then?"

"Yes. There was a picture," said Oryx after a moment.

"A picture of what?"

Oryx thought. "It was a parrot. A red parrot."

"Flying, or standing?"

"Jimmy, you are too strange!"

Jimmy held on to it, this red parrot. He kept it in mind. Sometimes it would appear to him in reveries, charged with mystery and hidden significance, a symbol free of all contexts. It must have been a brand name, a logo. He searched the Internet for Parrot, Parrot Brand, Parrot Inc., Redparrot. He found Alex the cork-nut parrot who'd said *I'm going away now*, but that was no help to him because Alex was the wrong colour. He wanted the red parrot to be a link between the story Oryx had told him and the so-called real world. He wanted to be walking along a street or trolling through the Web, and eureka, there it would be, the red parrot, the code, the password, and then many things would become clear.

The building where the movies were made was in a different city, or it might have been in a different part of the same city, because the city was very big, said Oryx. The room she stayed in with the other girls was in that building too. They almost never went outside, except up onto the flat roof sometimes when the movie was to be made up there. Some of the men who came to the building wanted to be outside while the movie was being filmed. They wanted to be seen, and at the same time they wanted to be hidden: the roof had a wall around it. "Maybe they wanted God to see them," said Oryx. "What do you think, Jimmy? They were showing off to God? I think so."

These men all had ideas about what should be in their movie. They wanted things in the background, chairs or trees, or they wanted ropes or screaming, or shoes. Sometimes they would say, *Just do it, I'm paying for it*, or things like that, because everything in these movies had a price. Every hair bow, every flower, every object, every gesture. If the men thought up something new, there would have to be a discussion about how much that new thing ought to cost.

"So I learned about life," said Oryx.

"Learned what?" said Jimmy. He shouldn't have had the pizza, and the weed they'd smoked on top of that. He was feeling a little sick.

"That everything has a price."

"Not everything. That can't be true. You can't buy time. You can't buy . . ." He wanted to say *love*, but hesitated. It was too soppy.

"You can't buy it, but it has a price," said Oryx. "Everything has a price."

"Not me," said Jimmy, trying to joke. "I don't have a price."

Wrong, as usual.

Being in a movie, said Oryx, was doing what you were told. If they wanted you to smile then you had to smile, if they wanted you to cry you had to do that too. Whatever it was, you had to do it, and you did it because you were afraid not to. You did what they told you to do to the men who came, and then sometimes those men did things to you. That was movies.

"What sort of things?" said Snowman.

"You know," said Oryx. "You saw. You have the picture of it."

"I only saw that one," said Snowman. "Only the one, with you in."

"I bet you saw more with me in. You don't remember. I could look different, I could wear different clothes and wigs, I could be someone else, do other things."

"Like what else? What else did they make you do?"

"They were all the same, those movies," said Oryx. She'd washed her hands, she was painting her nails now, her delicate oval nails, so perfectly shaped. Peach-coloured, to match the flowered wrapper she was wearing. Not a smudge on her. Later on she would do her toes.

It was less boring for the children to make the movies than to do what they did the rest of the time, which was nothing much. They watched cartoons on the old DVD in one of the rooms, mice and birds being chased around by other animals that could never catch them; or they brushed and braided one another's hair, or they ate and slept. Sometimes other people came to use the space, to make different kinds of movies. Grown-up women came, women with breasts, and grown-up men – actors. The children could watch them making those movies if they didn't get in the way. Though sometimes the actors objected because the little girls would giggle at their penises – so big, and then sometimes, all of a sudden, so small – and then the children had to go back into their room.

They washed a lot – that was important. They took showers with a bucket. They were supposed to be pure-looking. On a bad day when there was no business they would get tired and restless, and then they would argue and fight. Sometimes they'd be given a toke or a drink to calm them down – beer, maybe – but no hard drugs, those would shrivel them up; and they weren't allowed to smoke. The man in charge – the big man, not the man with the camera – said they shouldn't smoke because it would make their teeth brown. They did smoke sometimes anyway, because the man with the camera might give them a cigarette to share.

The man with the camera was white, and his name was Jack. He was the one they mostly saw. He had hair like frayed rope and he smelled too strong, because he was a meat-eater. He ate so much meat! He didn't like fish. He didn't like rice either, but he liked noodles. Noodles with lots of meat.

Jack said that where he came from the movies were bigger and better, the best in the world. He kept saying he wanted to go home. He said it was only pure dumb chance he wasn't dead – that this fucking country hadn't killed him with its lousy food. He said he'd almost died from some disease he'd got from the water and the only thing that had saved him was getting really, really pissed, because alcohol killed germs. Then he had to explain to them about germs. The little girls laughed about the germs, because they didn't believe in them; but they believed about the disease, because they'd seen that happen. Spirits caused it, everyone knew that. Spirits and bad luck. Jack had not said the right prayers.

Jack said he would get sick more often from the rotten food and water, only he had a really strong stomach. He said you needed a strong stomach in this business. He said the videocam was antique-roadshow junk and the lights were poor so no wonder everything looked like cheap shit. He said he wished he had a million dollars but he'd pissed all his money away. He said he couldn't hold on to money, it slid off him like water off a greased whore. "Don't be like me when you grow up," he would say. And the girls would laugh, because whatever else happened to them they would never be like him, a rope-haired clownish giant with a cock like a wrinkly old carrot.

Oryx said she had many chances to see that old carrot up close, because Jack wanted to do movie things with her when there were no movies. Then he would be sad and tell her he was sorry. That was puzzling.

"You did it for nothing?" said Jimmy. "I thought you said everything has a price." He didn't feel he'd won the argument about money, he wanted another turn.

Oryx paused, lifting the nail-polish brush. She looked at her hand. "I traded him," she said.

"Traded him for what?" said Jimmy. "What did that pathetic prick of a loser have to offer?"

"Why do you think he is bad?" said Oryx. "He never did anything with me that you don't do. Not nearly so many things!"

"I don't do them against your will," said Jimmy. "Anyway you're grown up now."

Oryx laughed. "What is my will?" she said. Then she must have seen his pained look, so she stopped laughing. "He taught me to read," she said quietly. "To speak English, and to read English words. Talking first, then reading, not so good at first, and I still don't talk so good but you always have to start somewhere, don't you think so, Jimmy?"

"You talk perfectly," said Jimmy.

"You don't need to tell lies to me. So that is how. It took a long time, but he was very patient. He had one book, I don't know where he got it but it was a book for children. It had a girl in it with long braids, and stockings – that was a hard word, *stockings* – who jumped around and did whatever she liked. So this is what we read. It was a good trade, because, Jimmy, if I hadn't done it I couldn't be talking to you, no?"

"Done what?" said Jimmy. He couldn't stand it. If he had this Jack, this piece of garbage, in the room right now he'd wring his neck like a wormy old sock. "What did you do for him? You sucked him off?"

"Crake is right," said Oryx coldly. "You do not have an elegant mind."

Elegant mind was just mathtalk, that patronizing jargon the math nerds used, but it hurt Jimmy anyway. No. What hurt was the thought of Oryx and Crake discussing him that way, behind his back.

"I'm sorry," he said. He ought to know better than to speak so bluntly to her.

"Now maybe I wouldn't do it, but I was a child then," said Oryx more softly. "Why are you so angry?"

"I don't buy it," said Jimmy. Where was her rage, how far down was it buried, what did he have to do to dig it up?

"You don't buy what?"

"Your whole fucking story. All this sweetness and acceptance and crap."

"If you don't want to buy that, Jimmy," said Oryx, looking at him tenderly, "what is it that you would like to buy instead?"

Jack had a name for the building where the movies went on. He called it Pixieland. None of the children knew what that meant – *Pixieland* – because it was an English word and an English idea, and Jack couldn't explain it. "All right, pixies, rise and shine," he'd say. "Candy time!" He brought candies for them as a treat, sometimes. "Want a candy, candy?" he'd say. That also was a joke, but they didn't know what it meant either.

He let them see the movies of themselves if he felt like it, or if he'd just been doing drugs. They could tell when he'd been shooting or snorting, because he was happier then. He liked to play pop music while they were working, something with a bounce. Upbeat, he called it. Elvis Presley, things like that. He said he liked the golden oldies, from back when songs had words. "Call me sentimental," he said, causing puzzlement. He liked Frank Sinatra too, and Doris Day: Oryx knew all the words to "Love Me or Leave Me" before she had any idea what they meant. "Sing us some pixieland jazz," Jack would say, and so that was what Oryx would sing. He was always pleased.

"What was this guy's name?" said Jimmy. What a jerk, this Jack. Jack the jerk, the jerkoff. Name-calling helped, thought Jimmy. He'd like to twist the guy's head off.

"His name was Jack. I told you. He told us a poem about it, in English. *Jack be nimble, Jack be quick, Jack has got a big candlestick.*"

"I mean his other name."

"He didn't have another name."

Working was what Jack called what they did. *Working girls*, he called them. He used to say, *Whistle while you work*. He used to say, *Work harder*. He used to say, *Put some jazz into it*. He used to say, *Act like you mean it, or you want to get hurt?* He used to say, *Come on, sex midgets, you can do better*. He used to say, *You're only young once*.

"That's all," said Oryx.

"What do you mean, that's all?"

"That's all there was," she said. "That's all there was to it."

"What about, did they ever . . ."

"Did they ever what?"

"They didn't. Not when you were that young. They couldn't have."

"Please, Jimmy, tell me what you are asking." Oh, very cool. He wanted to shake her.

"Did they rape you?" He could barely squeeze it out. What answer was he expecting, what did he want?

"Why do you want to talk about ugly things?" she said. Her voice was silvery, like a music box. She waved one hand in the air to dry the nails. "We should think only beautiful things, as much as we can. There is so much beautiful in the world if you look around. You are looking only at the dirt under your feet, Jimmy. It's not good for you."

She would never tell him. Why did this drive him so crazy? "It wasn't real sex, was it?" he asked. "In the movies. It was only acting. Wasn't it?"

"But Jimmy, you should know. All sex is real."

7

Sveltana

Snowman opens his eyes, shuts them, opens them, keeps them open. He's had a terrible night. He doesn't know which is worse, a past he can't regain or a present that will destroy him if he looks at it too clearly. Then there's the future. Sheer vertigo.

The sun is above the horizon, lifting steadily as if on a pulley; flattish clouds, pink and purple on top and golden underneath, stand still in the sky around it. The waves are waving, up down up down. The thought of them makes him queasy. He's violently thirsty, and he has a headache and a hollow cottony space between his ears. It takes him some moments to register the fact that he has a hangover.

"It's your own fault," he tells himself. He behaved foolishly the night before: he guzzled, he yelled, he gibbered, he indulged in pointless repinings. Once he wouldn't have had a hangover after so little booze, but he's out of practice now, and out of shape.

At least he didn't fall out of the tree. "Tomorrow is another day," he declaims to the pink and purple clouds. But if tomorrow is another day, what's today? The same day as it always is, except that he feels as if he has tongue fur all over his body.

A long scrawl of birds unwinds from the empty towers – gulls, egrets, herons, heading off to fish along the shore. A mile or so to the south, a salt marsh is forming on a one-time landfill dotted with semi-flooded townhouses. That's where all the birds are going: minnow city. He watches them with resentment: everything is fine with them, not a care in the world. Eat, fuck, poop, screech, that's all they do. In a former life he might have snuck up on them, studied them through binoculars, wondering at their grace. No, he never would have done that, it hadn't been his style. Some grade-school teacher, a nature snoop – Sally Whatshername? – herding them along on what she called field trips. The Compound golf course and lily ponds had been their hunting grounds. *Look! See the nice ducks? Those are called mallards!* Snowman had found birds tedious even then, but he wouldn't have wished to harm them. Whereas right now he yearns for a big slingshot.

He climbs down from the tree, more carefully than usual: he's still a bit dizzy. He checks his baseball cap, dumps out a butterfly – attracted by the salt, no doubt – and pisses on the grasshoppers, as usual. I have a daily routine, he thinks. Routines are good. His entire head is becoming one big stash of obsolete fridge magnets.

Then he opens up his cement-block cache, puts on his one-eyed sunglasses, drinks water from a stored beer bottle. If only he had a real beer, or an aspirin, or more Scotch.

"Hair of the dog," he says to the beer bottle. He mustn't drink too much water at a time, he'll throw up. He pours the rest of the water over his head, gets himself a second bottle, and sits down with his back against the tree, waiting for his stomach to settle. He wishes he had something to read. To read, to view, to hear, to study, to compile. Rag ends of language are floating in his head: *mephitic, metronome, mastitis, metatarsal, maudlin.*

"I used to be erudite," he says out loud. *Erudite.* A hopeless word. What are all those things he once thought he knew, and where have they gone?

After a while he finds he's hungry. What's in the cache, foodwise? Shouldn't there be a mango? No, that was yesterday. All that's left of it is a sticky ant-covered plastic bag. There's the chocolate energy Joltbar, but he doesn't feel up to that, so he opens the can of Sveltana No-Meat Cocktail Sausages with his rusty can opener. He could use a better one of those. The sausages are a diet brand, beige and unpleasantly soft – babies' turds, he thinks – but he manages to get them down. Sveltanas are always better if you don't look.

They're protein, but they're not enough for him. Not enough calories. He drinks the warm, bland sausage juice, which – he tells himself – must surely be full of vitamins. Or minerals, at least. Or something. He used to know. What's happening to his mind? He has a vision of the top of his neck, opening up into his head like a bathroom drain. Fragments of words are swirling down it, in a grey liquid he realizes is his dissolving brain.

Time to face reality. Crudely put, he's slowly starving to death. A fish a week is all he can depend on, and the people take that literally: it can be a decent-sized fish or a very small one, all spikes and bones. He knows that if he doesn't balance out the protein with starches and that other stuff – carbohydrates, or are those the same as starches? – he'll start dissolving his own fat, what's left of it, and after that his own muscles. The heart is a muscle. He pictures his heart, shrivelling up until it's no bigger than a walnut.

At first he'd been able to get fruit, not only from the cans of it he'd been able to scrounge, but also from the deserted arboretum an hour's walk to the north. He'd known how to find it, he'd had a map then, but it's long gone, blown away in a thunderstorm. Fruits of the World was the section he'd headed for. There'd been some bananas ripening in the Tropicals area, and several other things, round, green, and knobbly, that he hadn't wanted to eat because they might have been poisonous. There'd been some grapes too, on a trellis, in the Temperate zone. The solar air conditioning was still functioning, inside the greenhouse, though one of the panes was broken. There'd been some apricots as well, espaliered against a wall; though only a few, browning where the wasps had eaten into them and beginning to rot. He'd devoured them anyway; also some lemons. They'd been very sour, but he'd forced himself to drink the juice: he was familiar with scurvy from old seafaring movies. Bleeding gums, teeth coming out in handfuls. That hasn't happened to him yet.

Fruits of the World is cleaned out now. How long till more fruits of the world appear and ripen? He has no clue. There ought to be some wild berries. He'll ask the kids about that, the next time they come poking around: they'll know about berries. But though he can hear them farther down the beach, laughing and calling to one another, they don't seem to be coming his way this morning. Maybe they're getting bored with him, tired of pestering him for answers he won't give or that make no sense to them. Maybe he's old hat, an outworn novelty, a mangy toy. Maybe he's lost his charisma, like some shoddy, balding pop star of yesteryear. He ought to welcome the possibility of being left alone, but he finds the thought dispiriting.

If he had a boat he might row out to the tower blocks, climb up, rob nests, steal some eggs, if he had a ladder. No, bad idea: the towers are too unstable, even in the months he's been here several of them have come crashing down. He could walk to the area of the bungalows and trailers, hunt for rats, barbecue them over the glowing coals. It's something to consider. Or he could try going as far as the closest Module, better pickings than the trailers because the goodies there had been thicker on the ground. Or one of the retirement colonies, the gated communities, something like that. But he has no maps any more and he can't risk getting lost, wandering around at dusk with no cover and no suitable tree. The wolvogs would be after him for sure.

He could trap a pigoon, bludgeon it to death, butcher it in secret. He'd have to hide the mess: he has a notion that the sight of full frontal blood and guts might take him over the threshold as far as the Children of Crake are concerned. But a pigoon feast would do him a world of good. Pigoons are fat, and fat is a carbohydrate. Or is it? He searches his mind for some lesson or long-lost chart that would tell him: he knew that stuff once, but it's no use, the file folders are empty.

"Bring home the bacon," he says. He can almost smell it, that bacon, frying in a pan, with an egg, to be served up with toast and a cup of coffee . . . *Cream with that?* whispers a woman's voice. Some naughty, nameless waitress, out of a white-aprons-and-feather-dusters porno farce. He finds himself salivating.

Fat isn't a carbohydrate. Fat is a fat. He whacks his own forehead, lifts his shoulders, spreads his hands. "So, wise guy," he says. "Next question?"

Do not overlook a plentiful source of nutrition that may be no farther away than your feet, says another voice, in an annoying, instructive tone he recognizes from a survival manual he once leafed through in someone else's bathroom. When jumping off a bridge, clench your bum so the water won't rush up your anus. When drowning in quicksand, take a ski pole. Great advice! This is the same guy who said you could catch an alligator with a pointed stick. Worms and grubs were what he recommended for a snack food. You could toast them if you wanted.

Snowman can see himself turning over logs, but not just yet. There's something else he'll try first: he'll retrace his steps, go back to the RejoovenEsense Compound. It's a long hike, longer than any he's taken yet, but worth it if he can get there. He's sure there will still be a lot left, back there: not only canned goods, booze as well. Once they'd figured out what was going on, the Compound inhabitants had dropped everything and fled. They wouldn't have stayed long enough to clean out the supermarkets.

What he really needs is a spraygun, though – with one of those, he could shoot pigoons, hold off the wolvogs – and, Idea! Light bulb over head! – he knows exactly where to find one. Crake's bubble-dome contains a whole arsenal, which ought to be right where he left it. *Paradice*, was what they'd named the place. He'd been one of the angels guarding the gate, in a manner of speaking, so he knows where everything is, he'll be able to lay his hands on the necessary items. A quick in and out, a snatch and grab. Then he'll be equipped for anything.

But you don't want to go back there, do you? a soft voice whispers.

"Not particularly."

Because?

"Because nothing."

Go on, say it.

"I forget."

No, you don't. You've forgotten nothing.

"I'm a sick man," he pleads. "I'm dying of scurvy! Go away!"

What he needs to do is concentrate. Prioritize. Whittle things down to essentials. The essentials are: *Unless you eat, you die.* You can't get any more essential than that.

The Rejoov Compound is too far away for a casual day trip: it's more like an expedition. He'll have to stay out overnight. He doesn't welcome that thought – where will he sleep? – but if he's careful he should be okay.

With the can of Sveltana sausages inside him and a goal in sight, Snowman's beginning to feel almost normal. He has a mission: he's even looking forward to it. He might unearth all sorts of things. Cherries preserved in brandy; dry-roasted peanuts; a precious can of imitation Spam, if serendipity strikes. A truckload of booze. The Compounds hadn't stinted themselves, you could find the full range of goods and services there when there were shortages everywhere else.

He gets to his feet, stretches, scratches around the old scabs on his back – they feel like misplaced toenails – then walks back along the path behind his tree, picking up the empty Scotch bottle he threw down at the wolvogs the night before. He gives it a wistful sniff, then tosses it and the Sveltana can onto his midden-heap of empty containers, where a whole crowd of debauched flies is making merry. Sometimes at night he can hear the rakunks pawing through this private dump of his, searching for a free meal among the leavings of catastrophe, as he himself has often done, and is about to do again.

Then he sets about making his preparations. He reties his sheet, arranging it over his shoulders and pulling the extra up through his legs and tucking it in through the belt effect at the front, and knotting his last chocolate energy bar into a corner. He finds himself a stick, long and fairly straight. He decides to take only one bottle of water: most likely there'll be water along the way. If not, he can always catch the runoff from the afternoon storm.

He'll have to tell the Children of Crake he's going. He doesn't want them to discover he's missing and set out looking for him. They could run into dangers, or get lost. Despite their irritating qualities – among which he counts their naive optimism, their open friendliness, their calmness, and their limited vocabularies – he feels protective towards them. Intentionally or not, they've been left in his care, and they simply have no idea. No idea, for instance, of how inadequate his care really is.

Stick in hand, rehearsing the story he'll tell them, he goes along the path to their encampment. They call this path the Snowman Fish Path, because they carry his fish along it every week. It skirts the edge of the beach while keeping to the shade; nevertheless he finds it too bright, and tilts his baseball cap down to keep out the rays. He whistles as he approaches them, as he always does to let them know he's coming. He doesn't want to startle them, strain their politeness, cross their boundaries without being invited – loom up on them suddenly out of the shrubbery, like some grotesque flasher exposing himself to schoolkids.

His whistle is like a leper's bell: all those bothered by cripples can get out of his way. Not that he's infectious: what he's got they'll never catch. They're immune from him.

Purring

The men are performing their morning ritual, standing six feet apart in a long line curving off into the trees at either side. They're facing outward as in pictures of muskoxen, pissing along the invisible line that marks their territory. Their expressions are grave, as befits the seriousness of their task. They remind Snowman of his father heading out the door in the morning, briefcase in hand, an earnest aiming-for-the-target frown between his eyes.

The men do this twice a day, as they've been taught: it's necessary to keep the volume constant, the odour renewed. Crake's model had been the canids and the mustelids, and a couple of other families and species as well. Scent-marking was a wide-ranging mammalian leitmotif, he'd said, nor was it confined to the mammals. Certain reptiles, various lizards . . .

"Never mind about the lizards," said Jimmy.

According to Crake – and Snowman has seen nothing since to disprove it – the chemicals programmed into the men's urine are effective against wolvogs and rakunks, and to a lesser extent against bobkittens and pigoons. The wolvogs and bobkittens are reacting to the scent of their own kind and must imagine a huge wolvog or bobkitten, from which they would be wise to keep their distance. The rakunks and pigoons imagine large predators. Or this was the theory.

Crake allotted the special piss to men only; he said they'd need something important to do, something that didn't involve childbearing, so they wouldn't feel left out. Woodworking, hunting, high finance, war, and golf would no longer be options, he'd joked.

There are some disadvantages to this plan, in action – the ring-of-pee boundary line smells like a rarely cleaned zoo – but the circle is large enough so that there's ample smell-free room inside it. Anyway Snowman is used to it by now.

He waits politely for the men to finish. They don't ask him to join them: they already know his piss is useless. Also it's their habit to say nothing while performing their task: they need to concentrate, to make sure their urine lands in exactly the right place. Each has his own three feet of borderland, his own area of responsibility. It's quite a sight: like the women, these men – smooth-skinned, well-muscled – look like statues, and grouped like this they resemble an entire Baroque fountain. A few mermaids and dolphins and cherubs and the scene would be complete. Into Snowman's head comes the image of a circle of naked car mechanics, each holding a wrench. A whole squad of Mr. Fix-its. A gay magazine centrefold. Witnessing their synchronized routine, he almost expects them to break into some campy chorus line from one of the seedier nightclubs.

The men shake off, break their circle, look over at

Snowman with their uniformly green eyes, smile. They're always so goddamn affable.

"Welcome, oh Snowman," says the one called Abraham Lincoln. "Will you join us inside our home?" He's getting to be a bit of a leader, that one. *Watch out for the leaders*, Crake used to say. *First the leaders and the led, then the tyrants and the slaves, then the massacres. That's how it's always gone.*

Snowman steps over the wet line on the ground, ambles along with the men. He'd just had a brilliant idea: what if he were to take some of the saturated earth with him on his journey, as a protective device? It might ward off the wolvogs. But on second thought, the men would find the gap dug in their defences and would know he'd done it. Such an act could be misinterpreted: he wouldn't want to be suspected of weakening their fortress, exposing their young to danger.

He'll have to cook up a new directive from Crake, present it to them later. *Crake has told me you must collect an offering of your scent*. Get them all to piss in a tin can. Sprinkle it around his tree. Make a fairy ring. Draw his own line in the sand.

They reach the open space at the centre of the territorial circle. Off to one side, three of the women and one man are tending to a little boy, who appears to be hurt in some way. These people are not immune from wounds – the children fall down or bash their heads on trees, the women burn their fingers tending the fires, there are cuts and scrapes – but so far the injuries have been minor, and easily cured by purring.

Crake had worked for years on the purring. Once he'd discovered that the cat family purred at the same frequency as the ultrasound used on bone fractures and skin lesions and were thus equipped with their own self-healing mechanism, he'd turned himself inside out in the attempt to install that feature. The trick was to get the hyoid apparatus modified and the voluntary nerve pathways connected and the neocortex control systems adapted without hampering the speech abilities. There'd been quite a few botched experiments, as Snowman recalled. One of the trial batch of kids had manifested a tendency to sprout long whiskers and scramble up the curtains; a couple of the others had vocal-expression impediments; one of them had been limited to nouns, verbs, and roaring.

Crake did it though, thinks Snowman. He pulled it off. Just look at the four of them now, heads down close to the child, purring away like car engines.

"What happened to him?" he asks.

"He was bitten," says Abraham. "One of the Children of Oryx bit him."

This is something new. "What kind?"

"A bobkitten. For no reason."

"It was outside our circle, it was in the forest," says one of the women – Eleanor Roosevelt? Empress Josephine? – Snowman can't always remember their names.

"We were forced to hit it with rocks, to make it go away," says Leonardo da Vinci, the man in the purring quartet.

So the bobkittens are hunting kiddies now, thinks Snowman. Maybe they're getting hungry – as hungry as he is himself. But they have lots of rabbits to choose from, so it can't be simple hunger. Maybe they see the Children of Crake, the little ones anyway, as just another kind of rabbit, though easier to catch.

"Tonight we will apologize to Oryx," says one of the women – Sacajawea? – "for the rocks. And we will request her to tell her children not to bite us."

He's never seen the women do this – this communion with Oryx – although they refer to it frequently. What form does it take? They must perform some kind of prayer or invocation, since they can hardly believe that Oryx appears to them in person. Maybe they go into trances. Crake thought he'd done away with all that, eliminated what he called the G-spot in the brain. *God is a cluster of neurons*, he'd maintained. It had been a difficult problem, though: take out too much in that area and you got a zombie or a psychopath. But these people are neither.

They're up to something though, something Crake didn't anticipate: they're conversing with the invisible, they've developed reverence. Good for them, thinks Snowman. He likes it when Crake is proved wrong. He hasn't caught them making any graven images yet, however.

"Will the child be all right?" he asks.

"Yes," says the woman calmly. "Already the tooth holes are closing. See?"

The rest of the women are doing the things they usually do in the morning. Some are tending the central fire; others squat around it, warming themselves. Their body thermostats are set for tropical conditions, so they sometimes find it cold before the sun is high. The fire is fed with dead twigs and branches, but primarily with dung, made into patties the size and shape of hamburgers and dried in the noonday sun. Since the Children of Crake are vegetarians and eat mostly grass and leaves and roots, this material burns well enough. As far as Snowman can tell, fire-tending is about the only thing the women do that might be classified as work. Apart from helping to catch his weekly fish, that is. And cooking it for him. On their own behalf they do no cooking.

"Greetings, oh Snowman," says the next woman he comes to. Her mouth is green from the breakfast she's been chewing. She's breastfeeding a year-old boy, who looks up at Snowman, lets the nipple pop out of his mouth, and begins to cry. "It's only Snowman!" she says. "He won't hurt you."

Snowman still hasn't got used to it, the growth rate of these kids. The yearling looks like a five-year-old. By the age of four he'll be an adolescent. Far too much time was wasted in childrearing, Crake used to say. Childrearing, and being a child. No other species used up sixteen years that way.

Some of the older children have spotted him; they come closer, chanting, "Snowman, Snowman!" So he hasn't yet lost his allure. Now all the people are gazing at him curiously, wondering what he's doing here. He never arrives without a reason. On his first visits they'd thought – judging from his appearance – that he must be hungry, and they'd offered him food – a couple of handfuls of choice leaves and roots and grass, and several caecotrophs they'd kept especially for him – and he'd had to explain carefully that their food was not his food.

He finds the caecotrophs revolting, consisting as they do of semi-digested herbage, discharged through the anus and reswallowed two or three times a week. This had been another boy-genius concept on the part of Crake. He'd used the vermiform appendix as the base on which to construct the necessary organ, reasoning that at an earlier evolutionary stage, when the ancestral diet had been higher in roughage, the appendix must have fulfilled some such function. But he'd stolen the specific idea from the *Leporidae*, the hares and rabbits, which depend on caecotrophs rather than on several stomachs like the ruminants. Maybe this is why bobkittens have started hunting the young Crakers, Snowman thinks:

beneath the citrus overlay, they can smell the rabbity aroma of the caecotrophs.

Jimmy had argued with Crake over this feature. However you look at it, he'd said, what it boiled down to was eating your own shit. But Crake had merely smiled. For animals with a diet consisting largely of unrefined plant materials, he'd pointed out, such a mechanism was necessary to break down the cellulose, and without it the people would die. Also, as in the *Leporidae*, the caecotrophs were enriched with Vitamin B1, and with other vitamins and minerals as well, at four or five times the level of ordinary waste material. Caecotrophs were simply a part of alimentation and digestion, a way of making maximum use of the nutrients at hand. Any objections to the process were purely aesthetic.

That was the point, Jimmy had said.

Crake had said that if so it was a bad one.

Snowman is now surrounded by an attentive circle. "Greetings, Children of Crake," he says. "I have come to tell you that I'm going on a journey." The adults must have deduced this already, from his long stick and the way he's tied his sheet: he's gone on journeys before, or that's what he's called his looting forays into the trailer parks and adjacent pleeblands.

"Are you going to see Crake?" asks one of the children.

"Yes," says Snowman. "I'll try to see him. I'll see him if he's there."

"Why?" says one of the older children.

"There are some things I need to ask him," says Snowman cautiously.

"You must tell him about the bobkitten," says Empress Josephine. "The one that bit."

"That is a matter for Oryx," says Madame Curie. "Not for Crake." The other women nod.

"We want to see Crake too," the children begin. "We too, we too! We want to see Crake too!" It's one of their favourite ideas, going to see Crake. Snowman blames himself: he shouldn't have told them such exciting lies at the beginning. He'd made Crake sound like Santa Claus.

"Don't bother Snowman," says Eleanor Roosevelt gently. "Surely he is making this journey to help us. We must thank him."

"Crake is not for children," says Snowman, looking as stern as he can manage.

"Let us come too! We want to see Crake!"

"Only Snowman can ever see Crake," Abraham Lincoln says mildly. That seems to settle it.

"This will be a longer journey," Snowman says. "Longer than the other journeys. Maybe I won't come back for two days." He holds up two fingers. "Or three," he adds. "So you shouldn't worry. But while I'm away, be sure to stay here in your home, and do everything the way Crake and Oryx have taught you."

A chorus of yeses, much nodding of heads. Snowman doesn't mention the possibility of danger to himself. Perhaps it isn't a thing they ever consider, nor is it a subject he brings up – the more invulnerable they think he is, the better.

"We will come with you," says Abraham Lincoln. Several of the other men look at him, then nod.

"No!" says Snowman, taken aback. "I mean, you can't see Crake, it isn't allowed." He doesn't want them tagging along, absolutely not! He doesn't want them witnessing any weaknesses or failures on his part. Also, some of the sights along the way might be bad for their state of mind. Inevitably they would shower him with questions. In addition to all of which, a day in their company would bore the pants off him.

But you don't have any pants, says a voice in his head – a small voice this time, a sad little child's voice. *Joke! Joke! Don't kill me!*

Please, not now, thinks Snowman. Not in company. In company, he can't answer back.

"We would come with you to protect you," says Benjamin Franklin, looking at Snowman's long stick. "From the bobkittens that bite, from the wolvogs."

"Your smell is not very strong," adds Napoleon.

Snowman finds this offensively smug. Also it's too euphemistic by half: as they all know, his smell is strong enough, it just isn't the right kind. "I'll be fine," he says. "You stay here."

The men look dubious, but he thinks they'll do as he says. To reinforce his authority he holds his watch up to his ear. "Crake says he'll be watching over you," he says. "To keep you safe." *Watch, watching over*, says the small child's voice. *It's a pun, you cork-nut.*

"Crake watches over us in the daytime, and Oryx watches over us at night," Abraham Lincoln says dutifully. He doesn't sound too convinced.

"Crake always watches over us," says Simone de Beauvoir serenely. She's a yellow-brown woman who reminds Snowman of Dolores, his long-lost Philippina nanny; he sometimes has to resist the urge to drop to his knees and throw his arms around her waist.

"He takes good care of us," says Madame Curie. "You must tell him that we are grateful."

Snowman goes back along the Snowman Fish Path. He feels mushy: nothing breaks him up like the generosity of these people, their willingness to be of help. Also their gratitude towards Crake. It's so touching, and so misplaced.

"Crake, you dickhead," he says. He feels like weeping. Then he hears a voice – his own! – saying *boohoo*; he sees it, as if it's a printed word in a comic-strip balloon. Water leaks down his face.

"Not this again," he says. What's the sensation? It isn't anger exactly; it's vexation. An old word but serviceable. *Vexation* takes in more than Crake, and indeed why blame Crake alone?

Maybe he's merely envious. Envious yet again. He too would like to be invisible and adored. He too would like to be elsewhere. No hope for that: he's up to his neck in the here and now.

He slows to a shamble, then to a halt. *Oh, boohoo!* Why can't he control himself? On the other hand, why bother, since nobody's watching? Still, the noise he's making seems to him like the exaggerated howling of a clown – like misery performed for applause.

Stop snivelling, son, says his father's voice. *Pull yourself together. You're the man around here.*

"Right!" Snowman yells. "What exactly would you suggest? You were such a great example!"

But irony is lost on the trees. He wipes his nose with his stick-free hand and keeps walking.

Blue

It's nine in the morning, sun clock, by the time Snowman leaves the Fish Path to turn inland. As soon as he's out of the sea breeze the humidity shoots up, and he attracts a coterie of small green biting flies. He's barefoot – his shoes disintegrated some time ago, and in any case they were too hot and damp – but he doesn't need them now because the soles of his feet are hard as old rubber. Nevertheless he walks cautiously: there might be broken glass, torn metal. Or there might be snakes, or other things that could give him a nasty bite, and he has no weapon apart from the stick.

At first he's walking under trees, formerly parkland. Some distance away he hears the barking cough of a bobkitten. That's the sound they make as a warning: perhaps it's a male, and it's met another male bobkitten. There'll be a fight, with the winner taking all – all the females in the territory – and dispatching their kittens, if he can get away with it, to make room for his own genetic package.

Those things were introduced as a control, once the big green rabbits had become such a prolific and resistant pest. Smaller than bobcats, less aggressive – that was the official story about the bobkittens. They were supposed to eliminate feral cats, thus improving the almost non-existent songbird population. The bobkittens wouldn't bother much about birds, as they would lack the lightness and agility necessary to catch them. Thus went the theory.

All of which came true, except that the bobkittens soon got out of control in their turn. Small dogs went missing from backyards, babies from prams; short joggers were mauled. Not in the Compounds, of course, and rarely in the Modules, but there'd been a lot of grousing from the pleeblanders. He should keep a lookout for tracks, and be careful of overhanging branches: he doesn't like the thought of one of those things landing on his head.

There are always the wolvogs to worry about. But wolvogs are nocturnal hunters: in the heat of the day they tend to sleep, like most things with fur.

Every so often there's a more open space – the remains of a drive-in campsite, with a picnic table and one of those outdoor-barbecue fireplaces, though nobody used them very much once it got so warm and began to rain every afternoon. He comes upon one now, fungi sprouting from the decaying table, the barbecue covered in bindweed.

Off to the side, from what is probably a glade where the tents and trailers used to be set up, he can hear laughter and singing, and shouts of admiration and encouragement. There must be a mating going on, a rare-enough occasion among the people: Crake had worked out the numbers, and had decreed that once every three years per female was more than enough.

There'll be the standard quintuplet, four men and the woman in heat. Her condition will be obvious to all from the bright-blue colour of her buttocks and abdomen – a trick of variable pigmentation filched from the baboons, with a contribution from the expandable chromosphores of the octopus. As Crake used to say, *Think of an adaptation, any adaptation, and some animal somewhere will have thought of it first.*

Since it's only the blue tissue and the pheromones released by it that stimulate the males, there's no more unrequited love these days, no more thwarted lust; no more shadow between the desire and the act. Courtship begins at the first whiff, the first faint blush of azure, with the males presenting flowers to the females – just as male penguins present round stones, said Crake, or as the male silverfish presents a sperm packet. At the same time they indulge in musical outbursts, like songbirds. Their penises turn bright blue to match the blue abdomens of the females, and they do a sort of blue-dick dance number, erect members waving to and fro in unison, in time to the foot movements and the singing: a feature suggested to Crake by the sexual semaphoring of crabs. From amongst the floral tributes the female chooses four flowers, and the sexual ardour of the unsuccessful candidates dissipates immediately, with no hard feelings left. Then, when the blue of her abdomen has reached its deepest shade, the female and her quartet find a secluded spot and go at it until the woman becomes pregnant and her blue colouring fades. And that is that.

No more *No means yes*, anyway, thinks Snowman. No more prostitution, no sexual abuse of children, no haggling over the price, no pimps, no sex slaves. No more rape. The five of them will roister for hours, three of the men standing guard and doing the singing and shouting while the fourth one copulates, turn and turn about. Crake has equipped these women with ultra-strong vulvas – extra skin layers, extra muscles – so they can sustain these marathons. It no longer matters who the father of the inevitable child may be, since there's no more property to inherit, no father–son loyalty required for war. Sex is no longer a mysterious rite, viewed with ambivalence or downright loathing, conducted in the dark and inspiring suicides and murders. Now it's more like an athletic demonstration, a free-spirited romp.

Maybe Crake was right, thinks Snowman. Under the old dispensation, sexual competition had been relentless and cruel: for every pair of happy lovers there was a dejected onlooker, the one excluded. Love was its own transparent bubble-dome: you could see the two inside it, but you couldn't get in there yourself.

That had been the milder form: the single man at the window, drinking himself into oblivion to the mournful strains of the tango. But such things could escalate into violence. Extreme emotions could be lethal. *If I can't have you nobody will*, and so forth. Death could set in.

"How much misery," Crake said one lunchtime – this must have been when they were in their early twenties and Crake was already at the Watson-Crick Institute – "how much needless despair has been caused by a series of biological mismatches, a misalignment of the hormones and pheromones? Resulting in the fact that the one you love so passionately won't or can't love you. As a species we're pathetic in that way: imperfectly monogamous. If we could only pair-bond for life, like gibbons, or else opt for total guilt-free promiscuity, there'd be no more sexual torment. Better plan – make it cyclical and also inevitable, as in the other mammals. You'd never want someone you couldn't have."

"True enough," Jimmy replied. Or Jim, as he was now insisting, without results: everyone still called him Jimmy. "But think what we'd be giving up."

"Such as?"

"Courtship behaviour. In your plan we'd just be a bunch of hormone robots." Jimmy thought he should put things in Crake's terms, which was why he said *courtship behaviour*. What he meant was the challenge, the excitement, the chase. "There'd be no free choice."

"There's courtship behaviour in my plan," said Crake, "except that it would always succeed. And we're hormone robots anyway, only we're faulty ones."

"Well, what about art?" said Jimmy, a little desperately. He was, after all, a student at the Martha Graham Academy, so he felt some need to defend the art-and-creativity turf.

"What about it?" said Crake, smiling his calm smile.

"All that mismatching you talk about. It's been an inspiration, or that's what they say. Think of all the poetry – think Petrarch, think John Donne, think the *Vita Nuova*, think . . ."

"Art," said Crake. "I guess they still do a lot of jabbering about that, over where you are. What is it Byron said? Who'd write if they could do otherwise? Something like that."

"That's what I mean," said Jimmy. He was alarmed by the reference to Byron. What right had Crake to poach on his own shoddy, threadbare territory? Crake should stick to science and leave poor Byron to Jimmy.

"What *do* you mean?" said Crake, as if coaching a stutterer.

"I mean, when you can't get the *otherwise*, then . . ."

"Wouldn't you rather be fucking?" said Crake. He wasn't

including himself in this question: his tone was one of detached but not very strong interest, as if he were conducting a survey of people's less attractive personal habits, such as nose-picking.

Jimmy found that his face got redder and his voice got squeakier the more outrageous Crake became. He hated that. "When any civilization is dust and ashes," he said, "art is all that's left over. Images, words, music. Imaginative structures. Meaning – human meaning, that is – is defined by them. You have to admit that."

"That's not quite all that's left over," said Crake. "The archeologists are just as interested in gnawed bones and old bricks and ossified shit these days. Sometimes more interested. They think human meaning is defined by those things too."

Jimmy would like to have said *Why are you always putting me down?* but he was afraid of the possible answers, *because it's so easy* being one of them. So instead he said, "What have you got against it?"

"Against what? Ossified shit?"

"Art."

"Nothing," said Crake lazily. "People can amuse themselves any way they like. If they want to play with themselves in public, whack off over doodling, scribbling, and fiddling, it's fine with me. Anyway it serves a biological purpose."

"Such as?" Jimmy knew that everything depended on keeping his cool. These arguments had to be played through like a game: if he lost his temper, Crake won.

"The male frog, in mating season," said Crake, "makes as much noise as it can. The females are attracted to the male frog with the biggest, deepest voice because it suggests a more powerful frog, one with superior genes. Small male frogs – it's been documented – discover that if they position themselves in empty drainpipes, the pipe acts as a voice amplifier, and the small frog appears much larger than it really is."

"So?"

"So that's what art is, for the artist," said Crake. "An empty drainpipe. An amplifier. A stab at getting laid."

"Your analogy falls down when it comes to female artists," said Jimmy. "They're not in it to get laid. They'd gain no biological advantage from amplifying themselves, since potential mates would be deterred rather than attracted by that sort of amplification. Men aren't frogs, they don't want women who are ten times bigger than them."

"Female artists are biologically confused," said Crake. "You must have discovered that by now." This was a snide dig at Jimmy's current snarled romance, with a brunette poet who'd renamed herself Morgana and refused to tell him what her given name had been, and who was currently on a twenty-eight-day sex fast in honour of the Great Moon-Goddess Oestre, patroness of soybeans and bunnies. Martha Graham attracted those kinds of girls. An error, though, to have confided this affair to Crake.

Poor Morgana, thinks Snowman. I wonder what happened to her. She'll never know how useful she's been to me, her and her claptrap. He feels a little paltry for having pawned Morgana's drivel off on the Crakers as cosmogony. But it seems to make them happy enough.

Snowman leans against a tree, listening to the noises off. My love is like a blue, blue rose. Moon on, harvest shine. So now Crake's had his way, he thinks. Hooray for him. There's no more jealousy, no more wife-butcherers, no more husband-poisoners. It's all admirably good-natured: no pushing and shoving, more like the gods cavorting with willing nymphs on some golden-age Grecian frieze.

Why then does he feel so dejected, so bereft? Because he doesn't understand this kind of behaviour? Because it's beyond him? Because he can't jump in?

And what would happen if he tried? If he burst out of the bushes in his filthy tattered sheet, reeking, hairy, tumescent, leering like a goat-balled, cloven-hoofed satyr or a patch-eyed buccaneer from some ancient pirate film – *Aarr, me hearties!* – and attempted to join the amorous, blue-bottomed tussle? He can imagine the dismay – as if an orang-utang had crashed a formal waltzfest and started groping some sparkly pastel princess. He can imagine his own dismay too. What right does he have to foist his pustulant, cankered self and soul upon these innocent creatures?

"Crake!" he whimpers. "Why am I on this earth? How come I'm alone? Where's my Bride of Frankenstein?"

He needs to ditch this morbid tape-loop, flee the discouraging scene. *Oh honey*, a woman's voice whispers, *Cheer up! Look on the bright side! You've got to think positive!*

He hikes doggedly onward, muttering to himself. The forest blots up his voice, the words coming out of him in a string of colourless and soundless bubbles, like air from the mouths of the drowning. The laughter and singing dwindle behind him. Soon he can't hear them at all.

8

SoYummie

Jimmy and Crake graduated from HelthWyzer High on a warm humid day in early February. The ceremony used to take place in June; the weather then used to be sunny and moderate. But June was now the wet season all the way up the east coast, and you couldn't have held an outdoor event then, what with the thunderstorms. Even early February was pushing it: they'd ducked a twister by only one day.

HelthWyzer High liked to do things in the old style, with marquees and awnings and the mothers in flowered hats and the fathers in panamas, and fruit-flavoured punch, with or without alcohol, and Happicuppa coffee, and little plastic tubs of SoYummie Ice Cream, a HelthWyzer Own Brand, in chocolate soy, mango soy, and roasted-dandelion green-tea soy. It was a festive scene.

Crake was top of the class. The bidding for him by the rival EduCompounds at the Student Auction was brisk, and he was snatched up at a high price by the Watson-Crick Institute. Once a student there and your future was assured. It was like going to Harvard had been, back before it got drowned.

Jimmy on the other hand was a mid-range student, high on his word scores but a poor average in the numbers columns. Even those underwhelming math marks had been achieved with the help of Crake, who'd coached Jimmy weekends, taking time away from his own preparations. Not that he himself needed any extra cramming, he was some sort of mutant, he could crank out the differential equations in his sleep.

"Why are you doing this?" Jimmy asked in the middle of one exasperating session. (*You need to look at it differently. You have to get the beauty of it. It's like chess. Here – try this. See? See the pattern? Now it all comes clear.* But Jimmy did not see, and it did not all come clear.) "Why help me out?"

"Because I'm a sadist," Crake said. "I like to watch you suffer."

"Anyway, I appreciate it," said Jimmy. He did appreciate it, for several reasons, the best being that because Crake was known to be tutoring him Jimmy's dad had no grounds for nagging.

If Jimmy had been from a Module school, or – better – from one of those dump bins they still called "the public system," he'd have shone like a diamond in a drain. But the Compound schools were awash in brilliant genes, none of which he'd inherited from his geeky, kak-hearted parents, so his talents shrank by comparison. Nor had he been given any extra points for being funny. He was less funny now, anyway: he'd lost interest in the general audience.

After a humiliating wait while the brainiacs were tussled over by the best EduCompounds and the transcripts of the mediocre were fingered and skimmed and had coffee spilled on them and got dropped on the floor by mistake, Jimmy was knocked down at last to the Martha Graham Academy; and even that only after a long spell of lacklustre bidding. Not to mention some arm-twisting – Jimmy suspected – on the part of his dad, who'd known the Martha Graham president from their long-defunct mutual summer camp and probably had the dirt on him. Shagging smaller boys, dabbling in black-market pharmaceuticals. Or this was Jimmy's suspicion, in view of the ill grace and excessive force with which his hand was shaken.

"Welcome to Martha Graham, son," said the president with a smile fake as a vitamin-supplement salesman's.

When can I stop being a son? thought Jimmy.

Not yet. Oh, not yet. "Attaboy, Jimmy," said his father at the garden party afterwards, giving him the arm punch. He had chocolate soy goo on his dweeby tie, which had a pattern of pigs with wings. Just don't hug me, Jimmy prayed.

"Honey, we're so proud of you," said Ramona, who'd come decked out like a whore's lampshade in an outfit with a low neckline and pink frills. Jimmy'd seen something like that on HottTotts once, only it was worn by an eight-year-old. Ramona's push-up-bra breast tops were freckled from too much sun, not that Jimmy was much interested in those any more. He was familiar with the tectonics of cantilevered mammary-gland support devices by now, and anyway he found Ramona's new matronly air repellent. She was getting little creases on either side of her mouth, despite the collagen injections; her biological clock was ticking, as she was fond of pointing out. Pretty soon it would be the NooSkins BeauToxique Treatment for her – Wrinkles Paralyzed Forever, Employees Half-Price – plus, in say five years, the Fountain of Yooth Total Plunge, which rasped off your entire epidermis. She kissed him beside the nose, leaving a smooch of cerise lipstick; he could feel it resting on his cheek like bicycle grease.

She was allowed to say *we* and to kiss him, because she was now officially his stepmother. His real mother had been divorced from his father *in absentia*, for "desertion," and the bogus wedding of his father had been celebrated, if that was the word for it, soon after. Not that his real mother would have given a wombat's anus, thought Jimmy. She wouldn't have cared. She was off having cutting-edge adventures on her own, far from the dolorous festivities. He hadn't had a postcard from her in months; the last one had shown a Komodo dragon and had borne a Malaysian stamp, and had prompted another visit from the CorpSeCorps.

At the wedding Jimmy got as drunk as it took. He propped himself against a wall, grinning stupidly as the happy couple cut the sugary cake, All Real Ingredients, as Ramona had made known. Lots of cackling over the fresh eggs. Any minute now Ramona would be planning a baby, a more satisfactory baby than Jimmy had ever been to anybody.

"Who cares, who cares," he'd whispered to himself. He didn't want to have a father anyway, or be a father, or have a son or be one. He wanted to be himself, alone, unique, self-created and self-sufficient. From now on he was going to be fancy-free, doing whatever he liked, picking globes of ripe life off the life trees, taking a bite or two, sucking out the juice, throwing away the rinds.

It was Crake who'd got him back to his room. By that time Jimmy had been morose, and barely ambulatory. "Sleep it off," said Crake in his genial fashion. "I'll call you in the morning."

★

Now here was Crake at the graduation garden party, looming up out of the crowd, shining with achievement. No, he wasn't, Snowman amends. Give him credit for that at least. He was never a triumphalist.

"Congratulations," Jimmy made himself say. It was easier because he was the only one at this gathering who'd known Crake well for any length of time. Uncle Pete was in attendance, but he didn't count. Also, he was staying as far away from Crake as possible. Maybe he'd finally figured out who'd been running up his Internet bill. As for Crake's mother, she'd died the month before.

It was an accident, or so went the story. (Nobody liked to say the word *sabotage*, which was notoriously bad for business.) She must have cut herself at the hospital – although, said Crake, her job didn't involve scalpels – or scratched herself, or maybe she'd been careless and had taken her latex gloves off and had been touched on a raw spot by some patient who was a carrier. It was possible: she was a nail-biter, she might have had what they called an integumental entry point. In any case she'd picked up a hot bioform that had chewed through her like a solar mower. It was a transgenetic staph, said some labcoat, mixed with a clever gene from the slime mould family; but by the time they'd pinned it down and started what they hoped would be effective treatment, she was in Isolation and losing shape rapidly. Crake couldn't go in to see her, of course – nobody could, everything in there was done with robotic arms, as in nuclear-materials procedures – but he could watch her through the observation window.

"It was impressive," Crake told Jimmy. "Froth was coming out."

"Froth?"

"Ever put salt on a slug?"

Jimmy said he hadn't.

"Okay. So, like when you brush your teeth."

His mother was supposed to be able to speak her last words to him via the mike system, said Crake, but there was a digital failure; so though he could see her lips moving, he couldn't hear what she was saying. "Otherwise put, just like daily life," said Crake. He said anyway he hadn't missed much, because by that stage she'd been incoherent.

Jimmy didn't understand how he could be so nil about it – it was horrible, the thought of Crake watching his own mother dissolve like that. He himself wouldn't have been able to do it. But probably it was just an act. It was Crake preserving his dignity, because the alternative would have been losing it.

Happicuppa

For the vacation following graduation, Jimmy was invited to the Moosonee HelthWyzer Gated Vacation Community on the western shore of Hudson's Bay, where the top brass of HelthWyzer went to beat the heat. Uncle Pete had a nice place there, "nice place" being his term. Actually it was like a combination mausoleum and dirty-weekend hideaway – a lot of stonework, king-sized magic-finger beds, bidets in every bathroom – though it was hard to imagine Uncle Pete getting up to anything of much interest in there. Jimmy had been invited, he was pretty sure, so that Uncle Pete wouldn't have to be alone with Crake. Uncle Pete spent most of his time on the golf course and the rest of it in the hot tub, and Jimmy and Crake were free to do whatever they liked.

They probably would have gone back to interactives and state-sponsored snuff, and porn, as relaxation after their final exams, but that was the summer the gen-mod coffee wars got underway, so they watched those instead. The wars were over the new Happicuppa bean, developed by a HelthWyzer subsidiary. Until then the individual coffee beans on each bush had ripened at different times and had needed to be handpicked and processed and shipped in small quantities, but the Happicuppa coffee bush was designed so that all of its beans would ripen simultaneously, and coffee could be grown on huge plantations and harvested with machines. This threw the small growers out of business and reduced both them and their labourers to starvation-level poverty.

The resistance movement was global. Riots broke out, crops were burned, Happicuppa cafés were looted, Happicuppa personnel were car-bombed or kidnapped or shot by snipers or beaten to death by mobs; and, on the other side, peasants were massacred by the army. Or by the armies, various armies; a number of countries were involved. But the soldiers and dead peasants all looked much the same wherever they were. They looked dusty. It was amazing how much dust got stirred up in the course of such events.

"Those guys should be whacked," said Crake.

"Which ones? The peasants? Or the guys killing them?"

"The latter. Not because of the dead peasants, there's always been dead peasants. But they're nuking the cloud forests to plant this stuff."

"The peasants would do that too if they had half a chance," said Jimmy.

"Sure, but they don't have half a chance."

"You're taking sides?"

"There aren't any sides, as such."

Nothing much to be said to that. Jimmy thought about shouting *bogus*, decided it might not apply. Anyway they'd used up that word. "Let's change channels," he said.

But there was Happicuppa coverage, it seemed, wherever you turned. There were protests and demonstrations, with tear gas and shooting and bludgeoning; then more protests, more demonstrations, more tear gas, more shooting, more bludgeoning. This went on day after day. There hadn't been anything like it since the first decade of the century. Crake said it was history in the making.

Don't Drink Death! said the posters. Union dockworkers in Australia, where they still had unions, refused to unload Happicuppa cargoes; in the United States, a Boston Coffee Party sprang up. There was a staged media event, boring because there was no violence – only balding guys with retro tattoos or white patches where they'd been taken off, and severe-looking baggy-boobed women, and quite a few overweight or spindly members of marginal, earnest religious groups, in T-shirts with smiley-faced angels flying with birds or Jesus holding hands with a peasant or God Is Green on the front. They were filmed dumping Happicuppa products into the harbour, but none of the boxes sank. So there was the Happicuppa logo, lots of copies of it, bobbing around on the screen. It could have been a commercial.

"Makes me thirsty," said Jimmy.

"Shit for brains," said Crake. "They forgot to add rocks."

As a rule they watched the unfolding of events on the Noodie News, via the Net, but for a change they sometimes watched fully clothed newscasters on the wall-sized plasma screen in Uncle Pete's leatherette-upholstered TV room. The suits and shirts and ties seemed bizarre to Jimmy, especially if he was mildly stoned. It was weird to imagine what all those serious-faced talking heads would look like minus their fashion items, full frontal on the Noodie News.

Uncle Pete sometimes watched too, in the evenings, when he was back from the golf course. He'd pour himself a drink, then provide a running commentary. "The usual uproar," he said. "They'll get tired of it, they'll settle down. Everybody wants a cheaper cup of coffee – you can't fight that."

"No, you can't," Crake would say agreeably. Uncle Pete had a chunk of Happicuppa stock in his portfolio, and not just a little chunk. "What a mort," Crake would say as he scanned Uncle Pete's holdings on his computer.

"You could trade his stuff," said Jimmy. "Sell the Happicuppa, buy something he really hates. Buy windpower. No, better – buy a croaker. Get him some South American cattle futures."

"Nah," said Crake. "I can't risk that with a labyrinth. He'd notice. He'd find out I've been getting in."

Things escalated after a cell of crazed anti-Happicuppa fanatics bombed the Lincoln Memorial, killing five visiting Japanese schoolkids that were part of a Tour of Democracy. *Stop the Hipocrissy*, read the note left at a safe distance.

"That's pathetic," said Jimmy. "They can't even spell."

"They made their point though," said Crake.

"I hope they fry," said Uncle Pete.

Jimmy didn't answer, because now they were looking at the blockade of the Happicuppa head-office compound in Maryland. There in the shouting crowd, clutching a sign that read A Happicup Is a Crappi Cup, with a green bandanna over her nose and mouth, was – wasn't it? – his vanished mother. For a moment the bandanna slipped down and Jimmy saw her clearly – her frowning eyebrows, her candid blue eyes, her determined mouth. Love jolted through him, abrupt and painful, followed by anger. It was like being kicked: he must have let out a gasp. Then there was a CorpSeCorps charge and a cloud of tear gas and a smattering of what sounded like gunfire, and when Jimmy looked again his mother had disappeared.

"Freeze the frame!" he said. "Turn back!" He wanted to be sure. How could she be taking such a risk? If they got hold of her she'd really disappear, this time forever. But after a brief glance at him Crake had already switched to another channel.

I shouldn't have said anything, thought Jimmy. I shouldn't have called attention. He was cold with fear now. What if Uncle Pete made the connection and phoned the Corpsmen? They'd be right on her trail, she'd be roadkill.

But Uncle Pete didn't seem to have noticed. He was pouring himself another Scotch. "They should spraygun the whole bunch of them," he said. "Once they've smashed those cameras. Who took that footage anyway? Sometimes you wonder who's running this show."

"So what was that about?" said Crake when they were alone.

"Nothing," said Jimmy.

"I did freeze it," said Crake. "I got the whole sequence."

"I think you better erase it," said Jimmy. He was past being frightened, he'd entered full-blown dejection. Surely at this very moment Uncle Pete was turning on his cell-phone and punching in the numbers; hours from now it would be the CorpSeCorps interrogation all over again. His mother this, his mother that. He would just have to go through it.

"It's okay," said Crake, which Jimmy took to mean: *You can trust me*. Then he said, "Let me guess. Phylum Chordata, Class Vertebrata, Order Mammalia, Family Primates, Genus *Homo*, Species *sapiens sapiens*, subspecies your mother."

"Big points," said Jimmy listlessly.

"Not a stretch," said Crake. "I spotted her right away, those blue eyes. It was either her or a clone."

If Crake had recognized her, who else might have done so? Everyone in the HelthWyzer Compound had doubtless been shown pictures: *You seen this woman?* The story of his deviant mother had followed Jimmy around like an unwanted dog, and was probably half responsible for his poor showing at the Student Auction. He wasn't dependable, he was a security risk, he had a taint.

"My dad was the same," said Crake. "He buggered off too."

"I thought he died," said Jimmy. That's all he'd ever got out of Crake before: dad died, full stop, change the subject. It wasn't anything Crake would talk about.

"That's what I mean. He went off a pleebland overpass. It was rush hour, so by the time they got to him he was cat food."

"Did he jump, or what?" said Jimmy. Crake didn't seem too worked up about it, so he felt it was okay to ask that.

"It was the general opinion," said Crake. "He was a top researcher over at HelthWyzer West, so he got a really nice funeral. The tact was amazing. Nobody used the word *suicide*. They said 'your father's accident.'"

"Sorry about that," said Jimmy.

"Uncle Pete was over at our place all the time. My mother said he was really *supportive*." Crake said *supportive* like a quote. "She said, besides being my dad's boss and best friend, he was turning out to be a really good friend of the family, not that I'd ever seen him around much before. He wanted things to be *resolved* for us, he said he was anxious about that. He kept trying to have these heart-to-heart talks with me – tell me all about how my father had *problems*."

"Meaning your dad was a nutbar," said Jimmy.

Crake looked at Jimmy out of his slanty green eyes. "Yeah. But he wasn't. He was acting worried lately, but he didn't have *problems*. He had nothing like that on his mind. Nothing like jumping. I'd have known."

"You think he maybe fell off?"

"Fell off?"

"Off the overpass." Jimmy wanted to ask what he'd been doing on a pleebland overpass in the first place, but it didn't seem like the right time. "Was there a railing?"

"He was kind of uncoordinated," said Crake, smiling in an odd way. "He didn't always watch where he was going. He was head in the clouds. He believed in contributing to the improvement of the human lot."

"You get along with him?"

Crake paused. "He taught me to play chess. Before it happened."

"Well, I guess not *after*," said Jimmy, trying to lighten things up, because by this time he was feeling sorry for Crake, and he didn't like that at all.

How could I have missed it? Snowman thinks. What he was telling me. How could I have been so stupid?

No, not stupid. He can't describe himself, the way he'd been. Not unmarked – events had marked him, he'd had his own scars, his dark emotions. Ignorant, perhaps. Unformed, inchoate.

There had been something willed about it though, his ignorance. Or not willed, exactly: structured. He'd grown up in walled spaces, and then he had become one. He had shut things out.

Applied Rhetoric

At the end of that vacation, Crake went off to Watson-Crick and Jimmy to Martha Graham. They shook hands at the bullet-train station.

"See you around," said Jimmy.

"We'll e-mail," said Crake. Then, noticing Jimmy's dejection, he said, "Come on, you did okay, the place is famous."

"Was famous," said Jimmy.

"It won't be that bad."

Crake was wrong, for once. Martha Graham was falling apart. It was surrounded – Jimmy observed as the train pulled in – by the tackiest kind of pleeblands: vacant warehouses, burnt-out tenements, empty parking lots. Here and there were sheds and huts put together from scavenged materials – sheets of tin, slabs of plywood – and inhabited no doubt by squatters. How did such people exist? Jimmy had no idea. Yet there they were, on the other side of the razor wire. A couple of them raised their middle fingers at the train, shouted something that the bulletproof glass shut out.

The security at the Martha Graham gateway was a joke. The guards were half asleep, the walls – scrawled all over with faded graffiti – could have been scaled by a one-legged dwarf. Inside them, the Bilbao-ripoff cast-concrete buildings leaked, the lawns were mud, either baked or liquid depending on the season, and there were no recreational facilities apart from a swimming pool that looked and smelled like a giant sardine can. Half the time the air conditioning in the dorms didn't work; there was a brownout problem with the electrical supply; the food in the cafeteria was mostly beige and looked like rakunk shit. There were arthropods in the bedrooms, families and genera various, but half of them were cockroaches. Jimmy found the place depressing, as did – it seemed – everyone there with any more neural capacity than a tulip. But this was the hand life had dealt him, as his dad had said during their awkward goodbye, and now Jimmy would just have to play it as well as he could.

Right, Dad, Jimmy had thought. I've always known I could count on you for really, really sage advice.

The Martha Graham Academy was named after some gory old dance goddess of the twentieth century who'd apparently mowed quite a swath in her day. There was a gruesome statue of her in front of the administration building, in her role – said the bronze plaque – as Judith, cutting off the head of a guy in a historical robe outfit called Holofernes. Retro feminist shit, was the general student opinion. Every once in a while the statue got its tits decorated or steel wool glued onto its pubic region – Jimmy himself had done some of this glueing – and so comatose was the management that the ornaments often stayed up there for months before they were noticed. Parents were always objecting to this statue – poor role model, they'd say, too aggressive, too bloodthirsty, blah blah – whereupon the students would rally to its defence. Old Martha was their mascot, they'd say, the scowl, the dripping head and all. She represented life, or art, or something. Hands off Martha. Leave her alone.

The Academy had been set up by a clutch of now-dead rich liberal bleeding hearts from Old New York as an Arts-and-Humanities college at some time in the last third of the twentieth century, with special emphasis on the Performing Arts – acting, singing, dancing, and so forth. To that had been added Film-making in the 1980s, and Video Arts after that. These things were still taught at Martha Graham – they still put on plays, and it was there Jimmy saw *Macbeth* in the flesh and reflected that Anna K. and her Web site for peeping Toms had done a more convincing job of Lady Macbeth while sitting on her toilet.

The students of song and dance continued to sing and dance, though the energy had gone out of these activities and the classes were small. Live performance had suffered in the sabotage panics of the early twenty-first century – no one during those decades had wanted to form part of a large group at a public event in a dark, easily destructible walled space, or no one with any cool or status. Theatrical events had dwindled into versions of the singalong or the tomato bombardment or the wet T-shirt contest. And though various older forms had dragged on – the TV sitcom, the rock video – their audience was ancient and their appeal mostly nostalgic.

So a lot of what went on at Martha Graham was like studying Latin, or book-binding: pleasant to contemplate in its way, but no longer central to anything, though every once in a while the college president would subject them to some yawner about the vital arts and their irresistible reserved seat in the big red-velvet amphitheatre of the beating human heart.

As for Film-making and Video Arts, who needed them? Anyone with a computer could splice together whatever they wanted, or digitally alter old material, or create new animation. You could download one of the standard core plots and add whatever faces you chose, and whatever bodies too. Jimmy himself had put together a naked *Pride and Prejudice* and a naked *To the Lighthouse*, just for laughs, and in sophomore VizArts at HelthWyzer he'd done *The Maltese Falcon*, with costumes by Kate Greenaway and depth-and-shadow styling by Rembrandt. That one had been good. A dark tonality, great chiaroscuro.

With this kind of attrition going on – this erosion of its former intellectual territory – Martha Graham had found itself without a very convincing package to offer. As the initial funders had died off and the enthusiasm of the dedicated artsy money had waned and endowment had been sought in more down-to-earth quarters, the curricular emphasis had switched to other arenas. *Contemporary* arenas, they were called. Webgame Dynamics, for instance; money could still be made from that. Or Image Presentation, listed in the calendar as a sub-branch of Pictorial and Plastic Arts. With a degree in PicPlarts, as the students called it, you could go into advertising, no sweat.

Or Problematics. Problematics was for word people, so that was what Jimmy took. Spin and Grin was its nickname among the students. Like everything at Martha Graham it had utilitarian aims. Our Students Graduate With Employable Skills, ran the motto underneath the original Latin motto, which was *Ars Longa Vita Brevis*.

★

Jimmy had few illusions. He knew what sort of thing would be open to him when he came out the other end of Problematics with his risible degree. Window dressing was what he'd be doing, at best – decorating the cold, hard, numerical real world in flossy 2-D verbiage. Depending on how well he did in his Problematics courses – Applied Logic, Applied Rhetoric, Medical Ethics and Terminology, Applied Semantics, Relativistics and Advanced Mischaracterization, Comparative Cultural Psychology, and the rest – he'd have a choice between well-paid window-dressing for a big Corp or flimsy cut-rate stuff for a borderline one. The prospect of his future life stretched before him like a sentence; not a prison sentence, but a long-winded sentence with a lot of unnecessary subordinate clauses, as he was soon in the habit of quipping during Happy Hour pickup time at the local campus bars and pubs. He couldn't say he was looking forward to it, this rest-of-his-life.

Nevertheless, he dug himself in at Martha Graham as if into a trench, and hunkered down for the duration. He shared a dorm suite – one cramped room either side, silverfish-ridden bathroom in the middle – with a fundamentalist vegan called Bernice, who had stringy hair held back with a wooden clip in the shape of a toucan and wore a succession of God's Gardeners T-shirts, which – due to her aversion to chemical compounds such as underarm deodorants – stank even when freshly laundered.

Bernice let him know how much she disapproved of his carnivorous ways by kidnapping his leather sandals and incinerating them on the lawn. When he protested that they hadn't been real leather, she said they'd been posing as it, and as such deserved their fate. After he'd had a few girls up to his room – none of Bernice's business, and they'd been quiet enough, apart from some pharmaceutically induced giggling and a lot of understandable moans – she'd manifested her views on consensual sex by making a bonfire of all Jimmy's jockey shorts.

He'd complained about that to Student Services, and after a few tries – Student Services at Martha Graham was notoriously grumpy, staffed as it was by burnt-out TV-series actors who could not forgive the world for their plunge from marginal fame – he got himself moved to a single room. (*First my sandals, then my underwear. Next it'll be me. The woman is a pyromaniac, let me rephrase that, she is reality-challenged in a major way. You wish to see the concrete evidence of her crotchwear auto-da-fé? Look into this tiny envelope. If you see me next in an urn, gritty ashes, couple of teeth, you want the responsibility? Hey, I'm the Student here and you're the Service. Here it is, right on the letterhead, see? I've e-mailed this to the president.*)

(This is not what he actually said, of course. He knew better than that. He smiled, he presented himself as a reasonable human being, he enlisted their sympathy.)

After that, after he got his new room, things were a little better. At least he was free to pursue his social life unhampered. He'd discovered that he projected a form of melancholy attractive to a certain kind of woman, the semi-artistic, wise-wound kind in large supply at Martha Graham. Generous, caring, idealistic women, Snowman thinks of them now. They had a few scars of their own, they were working on healing. At first Jimmy would rush to their aid: he was tender-hearted, he'd been told, and nothing if not chivalrous. He'd draw out of them their stories of hurt, he'd apply himself to them like a poultice. But soon the process would reverse, and Jimmy would switch from bandager to bandagee. These women would begin to see how fractured he was, they'd want to help him gain perspective on life and access the positive aspects of his own spirituality. They saw him as a creative project: the raw material, Jimmy in his present gloomy form; the end product, a happy Jimmy.

Jimmy let them labour away on him. It cheered them up, it made them feel useful. It was touching, the lengths to which they would go. Would this make him happy? Would this? Well then, how about *this*? But he took care never to get any less melancholy on a permanent basis. If he were to do that they'd expect a reward of some sort, or a result at least; they'd demand a next step, and then a pledge. But why would he be stupid enough to give up his grey rainy-day allure – the crepuscular essence, the foggy aureole, that had attracted them to him in the first place?

"I'm a lost cause," he would tell them. "I'm emotionally dyslexic." He would also tell them they were beautiful and they turned him on. True enough, no falsehood there, he always meant it. He would also say that any major investment on their part would be wasted on him, he was an emotional landfill site, and they should just enjoy the here and now.

Sooner or later they'd complain that he refused to take things seriously. This, after having begun by saying he needed to lighten up. When their energy flagged at last and the weeping began, he'd tell them he loved them. He took care to do this in a hopeless voice: being loved by him was a poison pill, it was spiritually toxic, it would drag them down to the murky depths where he himself was imprisoned, and it was because he loved them so much that he wanted them out of harm's way, i.e., out of his ruinous life. Some of them saw through it – *Grow up, Jimmy!* – but on the whole, how potent that was.

He was always sad when they decamped. He disliked the part where they'd get mad at him, he was upset by any woman's anger, but once they'd lost their tempers with him he'd know it was over. He hated being dumped, even though he himself had manoeuvred the event into place. But another woman with intriguing vulnerabilities would happen along shortly. It was a time of simple abundance.

He wasn't lying though, not all the time. He really did love these women, sort of. He really did want to make them feel better. It was just that he had a short attention span.

"You scoundrel," says Snowman out loud. It's a fine word, *scoundrel*; one of the golden oldies.

They knew about his scandalous mother, of course, these women. Ill winds blow far and find a ready welcome. Snowman is ashamed to remember how he'd used that story – a hint here, a hesitation there. Soon the women would be consoling him, and he'd roll around in their sympathy, soak in it, massage himself with it. It was a whole spa experience in itself.

By then his mother had attained the status of a mythical being, something that transcended the human, with dark wings and eyes that burned like Justice, and a sword. When he got to the part where she'd stolen Killer the rakunk away from him he could usually wring out a tear or two, not from himself but from his auditors.

What did you do? (Eyes wide, single pat of hand on arm, sympathetic gaze.)

Oh, you know. (Shrug, look away, change subject.)

It wasn't all acting.

Only Oryx had not been impressed by this dire, feathered

mother of his. *So Jimmy, your mother went somewhere else? Too bad. Maybe she had some good reasons. You thought of that?* Oryx had neither pity for him nor self-pity. She was not unfeeling: on the contrary. But she refused to feel what he wanted her to feel. Was that the hook – that he could never get from her what the others had given him so freely? Was that her secret?

Asperger's U.

Crake and Jimmy kept in touch by e-mail. Jimmy whined about Martha Graham in what he hoped was an entertaining way, applying unusual and disparaging adjectives to his professors and fellow students. He described the diet of recycled botulism and salmonella, sent lists of the different multi-legged creatures he'd found in his room, moaned about the inferior quality of the mood-altering substances for sale in the dismal student mall. Out of self-protection, he concealed the intricacies of his sex life except for what he considered the minimum of hints. (*These babes may not be able to count to ten, but hey, who needs numeracy in the sack? Just so long as they think it's ten, haha, joke,* ☺.)

He couldn't help boasting a little, because this seemed to be – from any indications he'd had so far – the one field of endeavour in which he had the edge over Crake. At HelthWyzer, Crake hadn't been what you'd call sexually active. Girls had found him intimidating. True, he'd attracted a couple of obsessives who'd thought he could walk on water, and who'd followed him around and sent him slushy, fervent e-mails and threatened to slit their wrists on his behalf. Perhaps he'd even slept with them on occasion; but he'd never gone out of his way. Falling in love, although it resulted in altered body chemistry and was therefore real, was a hormonally induced delusional state, according to him. In addition it was humiliating, because it put you at a disadvantage, it gave the love object too much power. As for sex per se, it lacked both challenge and novelty, and was on the whole a deeply imperfect solution to the problem of intergenerational genetic transfer.

The girls Jimmy accumulated had found Crake more than a little creepy, and it had made Jimmy feel superior to come to his defence. "He's okay, he's just on another planet," was what he used to say.

But how to know about Crake's present circumstances? Crake divulged few factoids about himself. Did he have a roommate, a girlfriend? He never mentioned either, but that meant nothing. His e-mail descriptions were of the campus facilities, which were awesome – an Aladdin's treasure-trove of bio-research gizmos – and of, well, what else? What *did* Crake have to say in his terse initial communications from the Watson-Crick Institute? Snowman can't remember.

They'd played long-drawn-out games of chess though, two moves a day. Jimmy was better at chess by now; it was easier without Crake's distracting presence, and the way he had of drumming his fingers and humming to himself, as if he already saw thirty moves ahead and was patiently waiting for Jimmy's tortoiselike mind to trundle up to the next rook sacrifice. Also, Jimmy could look up grandmasters and famous games of the past on various Net programs, in between moves. Not that Crake wasn't doing the same thing.

★

After five or six months Crake loosened up a bit. He was having to work harder than at HelthWyzer High, he wrote, because there was a lot more competition. Watson-Crick was known to the students there as Asperger's U. because of the high percentage of brilliant weirdos that strolled and hopped and lurched through its corridors. Demi-autistic, genetically speaking; single-track tunnel-vision minds, a marked degree of social ineptitude – these were not your sharp dressers – and luckily for everyone there, a high tolerance for mildly deviant public behaviour.

More than at HelthWyzer? asked Jimmy.

Compared to this place, HelthWyzer was a pleebland, Crake replied. *It was wall-to-wall NTs.*

NTs?

Neurotypicals.

Meaning?

Minus the genius gene.

So, are you a neurotypical? Jimmy asked the next week, having had some time to think this over. Also to worry about whether he himself was a neurotypical, and if so, was that now bad, in the gestalt of Crake? He suspected he was, and that it was.

But Crake never answered that one. This was his way: when there was a question he didn't want to address, he acted as if it hadn't been asked.

You should come and see this joint, he told Jimmy in late October of their sophomore year. *Give yourself a lifetime experience. I'll pretend you're my dull-normal cousin. Come for Thanksgiving Week.*

The alternative for Jimmy was turkey with the parental-unit turkeys, *joke, haha,* ☺, said Jimmy, and he wasn't up for that; so it would be his pleasure to accept. He told himself he was being a pal and doing Crake a favour, for who did lone Crake have to visit with on his holidays, aside from his boring old australopithecine not-really-an-uncle Uncle Pete? But also he found he was missing Crake. He hadn't seen him now for more than a year. He wondered if Crake had changed.

Jimmy had a couple of term papers to finish before the holidays. He could have bought them off the Net, of course – Martha Graham was notoriously lax about scorekeeping, and plagiarism was a cottage industry there – but he'd taken a position on that. He'd write his own papers, eccentric though it seemed; a line that played well with the Martha Graham type of woman. They liked a dash of originality and risk-taking and intellectual rigour.

For the same reason he'd taken to spending hours in the more obscure regions of the library stacks, ferreting out arcane lore. Better libraries, at institutions with more money, had long ago burned their actual books and kept everything on CD-ROM, but Martha Graham was behind the times in that, as in everything. Wearing a nose-cone filter to protect against the mildew, Jimmy grazed among the shelves of mouldering paper, dipping in at random.

Part of what impelled him was stubbornness; resentment, even. The system had filed him among the rejects, and what he was studying was considered – at the decision-making levels, the levels of real power – an archaic waste of time. Well then, he would pursue the superfluous as an end in itself. He would be its champion, its defender and preserver. Who was it who'd said that all art was completely useless?

Jimmy couldn't recall, but hooray for him, whoever he was. The more obsolete a book was, the more eagerly Jimmy would add it to his inner collection.

He compiled lists of old words too – words of a precision and suggestiveness that no longer had a meaningful application in today's world, or *toady's world*, as Jimmy sometimes deliberately misspelled it on his term papers. (*Typo*, the profs would note, which showed how alert they were.) He memorized these hoary locutions, tossed them left-handed into conversation: *wheelwright, lodestone, saturnine, adamant.* He'd developed a strangely tender feeling towards such words, as if they were children abandoned in the woods and it was his duty to rescue them.

One of his term papers – for his Applied Rhetoric course – was titled "Self-Help Books of the Twentieth Century: Exploiting Hope and Fear," and it supplied him with a great stand-up routine for use in the student pubs. He'd quote snatches of this and that – *Improve Your Self-Image*; *The Twelve-Step Plan for Assisted Suicide*; *How to Make Friends and Influence People*; *Flat Abs in Five Weeks*; *You Can Have It All*; *Entertaining Without a Maid*; *Grief Management for Dummies* – and the circle around him would crack up.

He now had a circle around him again: he'd rediscovered that pleasure. *Oh Jimmy, do* Cosmetic Surgery for Everyone*! Do* Access Your Inner Child*! Do* Total Womanhood*! Do* Raising Nutria for Fun and Profit*! Do* The Survival Handbook of Dating and Sex*!* And Jimmy, the ever-ready song-and-dance man, would oblige. Sometimes he'd make up books that didn't exist – *Healing Diverticulitis Through Chanting and Prayer* was one of his best creations – and nobody would spot the imposture.

He'd turned that paper topic into his senior dissertation, later. He'd got an A.

There was a bullet-train connection between Martha Graham and Watson-Crick, with only one change. Jimmy spent a lot of the three-hour trip looking out the window at the pleeblands they were passing through. Rows of dingy houses; apartment buildings with tiny balconies, laundry strung on the railings; factories with smoke coming out of the chimneys; gravel pits. A huge pile of garbage, next to what he supposed was a high-heat incinerator. A shopping mall like the ones at HelthWyzer, only there were cars in the parking lots instead of electric golf carts. A neon strip, with bars and girlie joints and what looked like an archeological-grade movie theatre. He glimpsed a couple of trailer parks, and wondered what it was like to live in one of them: just thinking about it made him slightly dizzy, as he imagined a desert might, or the sea. Everything in the pleeblands seemed so boundless, so porous, so penetrable, so wide-open. So subject to chance.

Accepted wisdom in the Compounds said that nothing of interest went on in the pleeblands, apart from buying and selling: there was no life of the mind. Buying and selling, plus a lot of criminal activity; but to Jimmy it looked mysterious and exciting, over there on the other side of the safety barriers. Also dangerous. He wouldn't know the ways to do things there, he wouldn't know how to behave. He wouldn't even know how to pick up girls. They'd turn him upside down in no time, they'd shake his head loose. They'd laugh at him. He'd be fodder.

*

The security going into Watson-Crick was very thorough, unlike the sloppy charade that took place at Martha Graham: the fear must have been that some fanatic would sneak in and blow up the best minds of the generation, thus dealing a crippling blow to something or other. There were dozens of CorpSeCorps men, complete with sprayguns and rubber clubs; they had Watson-Crick insignia, but you could tell who they really were. They took Jimmy's iris imprint and ran it through the system, and then two surly weightlifters pulled him aside for questioning. As soon as it happened he guessed why.

"You seen your runaway mother lately?"

"No," he said truthfully.

"Heard from her? Had a phone call, another postcard?" So they were still tracking his snail mail. All of the postcards must be stored on their computers; plus his present whereabouts, which was why they hadn't asked where he'd come from.

No again, he said. They had him hooked up to the neural-impulse monitor so they knew he wasn't lying; they must also have known that the question distressed him. He was on the verge of saying *And if I had I wouldn't tell you, apeface*, but he was old enough by then to realize that nothing would be served by that, and it was likely to land him on the next bullet train back to Martha Graham, or worse.

"Know what she's been doing? Who she's hanging out with?"

Jimmy didn't, but he had a feeling they themselves might have some idea. They didn't mention the Happicuppa demonstration in Maryland though, so maybe they were less informed than he feared.

"Why are you here, son?" Now they were bored. The important part was over.

"I'm visiting an old friend for Thanksgiving Week," said Jimmy. "A friend from HelthWyzer High. He's a student here. I've been invited." He gave the name, and the visitor authorization number supplied to him by Crake.

"What sort of a student? What's he taking?"

Transgenics, Jimmy told them.

They pulled up the file to check, frowned at it, looked moderately impressed. Then they made a cellcall, as if they hadn't quite believed him. What was a serf like him doing visiting the nobility? their manner implied. But finally they let him through, and there was Crake in his no-name dark clothing, looking older and thinner and also smarter than ever, leaning on the exit barrier and grinning.

"Hi there, cork-nut," said Crake, and nostalgia swept through Jimmy like sudden hunger. He was so pleased to see Crake he almost wept.

Wolvogs

Compared with Martha Graham, Watson-Crick was a palace. At the entranceway was a bronzed statue of the Institute's mascot, the spoat/gider – one of the first successful splices, done in Montreal at the turn of the century, goat crossed with spider to produce high-tensile spider silk filaments in the milk. The main application nowadays was bulletproof vests. The CorpSeCorps swore by the stuff.

The extensive grounds inside the security wall were beautifully laid out: the work, said Crake, of the JigScape Faculty. The students in Botanical Transgenics (Ornamental Division) had created a whole array of drought-and-flood-resistant tropical blends, with flowers or leaves in lurid shades of chrome yellow and brilliant flame red and phosphorescent blue and neon purple. The pathways, unlike the crumbling cement walks at Martha Graham, were smooth and wide. Students and faculty were beetling along them in their electric golf carts.

Huge fake rocks, made from a combo-matrix of recycled plastic bottles and plant material from giant tree cacti and various lithops – the living-stone members of the Mesembryanthemaceae – were dotted here and there. It was a patented process, said Crake, originally developed at Watson-Crick and now a nice little money spinner. The fake rocks looked like real rocks but weighed less; not only that, they absorbed water during periods of humidity and released it in times of drought, so they acted like natural lawn regulators. Rockulators, was the brand name. You had to avoid them during heavy rainfalls, though, as they'd been known to explode.

But most of the bugs had now been ironed out, said Crake, and new varieties were appearing every month. The student team was thinking of developing something called the Moses Model, for dependable supplies of fresh drinking water in times of crisis. Just Hit It With a Rod, was the proposed slogan.

"How do those things work?' asked Jimmy, trying not to sound impressed.

"Search me," said Crake. "I'm not in NeoGeologicals."

"So, are the butterflies – are they recent?" Jimmy asked after a while. The ones he was looking at had wings the size of pancakes and were shocking pink, and were clustering all over one of the purple shrubs.

"You mean, did they occur in nature or were they created by the hand of man? In other words, are they real or fake?"

"Mm," said Jimmy. He didn't want to get into the *what is real* thing with Crake.

"You know when people get their hair dyed or their teeth done? Or women get their tits enlarged?"

"Yeah?"

"After it happens, that's what they look like in real time. The process is no longer important."

"No way fake tits feel like real tits," said Jimmy, who thought he knew a thing or two about that.

"If you could tell they were fake," said Crake, "it was a bad job. These butterflies fly, they mate, they lay eggs, caterpillars come out."

"Mm," said Jimmy again.

Crake didn't have a roommate. Instead he had a suite, accented in wood tones, with push-button venetians and air conditioning that really worked. It consisted of a large bedroom, an enclosed bath and shower unit with steam function, a main living-dining room with a pullout couch – that was where Jimmy would camp out, said Crake – and a study with a built-in sound system and a full array of compu-gizmos. It had maid service too, and they picked up and delivered your laundry. (Jimmy was depressed by this news, as he had to do his own laundry at Martha Graham, using the clanking, wheezy washers and the dryers that fried your clothes. You had to slot plastic tokens into them because the machines had been jimmied regularly when they'd taken coins.)

Crake also had a cheery kitchenette. "Not that I microwave much," said Crake. "Except for snack food. Most of us eat at our dining halls. There's one for each faculty."

"How's the food?" Jimmy asked. He was feeling more and more like a troglodyte. Living in a cave, fighting off the body parasites, gnawing the odd bone.

"It's food," said Crake indifferently.

On day one they toured some of the wonders of Watson-Crick. Crake was interested in everything – all the projects that were going on. He kept saying "Wave of the future," which got irritating after the third time.

First they went to Décor Botanicals, where a team of five seniors was developing Smart Wallpaper that would change colour on the walls of your room to complement your mood. This wallpaper – they told Jimmy – had a modified form of Kirilian-energy-sensing algae embedded in it, along with a sublayer of algae nutrients, but there were still some glitches to be fixed. The wallpaper was short-lived in humid weather because it ate up all the nutrients and then went grey; also it could not tell the difference between drooling lust and murderous rage, and was likely to turn your wallpaper an erotic pink when what you really needed was a murky, capillary-bursting greenish red.

That team was also working on a line of bathroom towels that would behave in much the same way, but they hadn't yet solved the marine-life fundamentals: when algae got wet it swelled up and began to grow, and the test subjects so far had not liked the sight of their towels from the night before puffing up like rectangular marshmallows and inching across the bathroom floor.

"Wave of the future," said Crake.

Next they went to NeoAgriculturals. AgriCouture was its nickname among the students. They had to put on biosuits before they entered the facility, and scrub their hands and wear nose-cone filters, because what they were about to see hadn't been bioform-proofed, or not completely. A woman with a laugh like Woody Woodpecker led them through the corridors.

"This is the latest," said Crake.

What they were looking at was a large bulblike object that seemed to be covered with stippled whitish-yellow skin. Out of it came twenty thick fleshy tubes, and at the end of each tube another bulb was growing.

"What the hell is it?" said Jimmy.

"Those are chickens," said Crake. "Chicken parts. Just the breasts, on this one. They've got ones that specialize in drumsticks too, twelve to a growth unit."

"But there aren't any heads," said Jimmy. He grasped the concept – he'd grown up with *sus multiorganifer*, after all – but this thing was going too far. At least the pigoons of his childhood hadn't lacked heads.

"That's the head in the middle," said the woman. "There's a mouth opening at the top, they dump the nutrients in there. No eyes or beak or anything, they don't need those."

"This is horrible," said Jimmy. The thing was a nightmare. It was like an animal-protein tuber.

"Picture the sea-anemone body plan," said Crake. "That helps."

"But what's it thinking?" said Jimmy.

The woman gave her jocular woodpecker yodel, and explained that they'd removed all the brain functions that had nothing to do with digestion, assimilation, and growth.

"It's sort of like a chicken hookworm," said Crake.

"No need for added growth hormones," said the woman, "the high growth rate's built in. You get chicken breasts in two weeks – that's a three-week improvement on the most efficient low-light, high-density chicken farming operation so far devised. And the animal-welfare freaks won't be able to say a word, because this thing feels no pain."

"Those kids are going to clean up," said Crake after they'd left. The students at Watson-Crick got half the royalties from anything they invented there. Crake said it was a fierce incentive. "ChickieNobs, they're thinking of calling the stuff."

"Are they on the market yet?" asked Jimmy weakly. He

couldn't see eating a ChickieNob. It would be like eating a large wart. But as with the tit implants – the good ones – maybe he wouldn't be able to tell the difference.

"They've already got the takeout franchise operation in place," said Crake. "Investors are lining up around the block. They can undercut the price of everyone else."

Jimmy was becoming annoyed by Crake's way of introducing him – "This is Jimmy, the neurotypical" – but he knew better than to show it. Still, it seemed to be like calling him a Cro-Magnon or something. Next step they'd be putting him in a cage, feeding him bananas, and poking him with electroprods.

Nor did he think much of the Watson-Crick women on offer. Maybe they weren't even on offer: they seemed to have other things on their minds. Jimmy's few attempts at flirtation got him some surprised stares – surprised and not at all pleased, as if he'd widdled on these women's carpets.

Considering their slovenliness, their casual approach to personal hygiene and adornment, they ought to have fainted at the attention. Plaid shirts were their formal wear, hairstyles not their strong suit: a lot of them looked as if they'd had a close encounter with the kitchen shears. As a group, they reminded him of Bernice, the God's Gardeners pyromaniac vegan. The Bernice model was an exception at Martha Graham, where the girls tried to give the impression they were, or had been once, or could well be, dancers or actresses or singers or performance artists or conceptual photographers or something else artistic. Willowy was their aim, style was their game, whether they played it well or not. But here the Bernice look was the rule, except that there were few religious T-shirts. More usual were ones with complex mathematical equations on them that caused snickers among those who could decode them.

"What's the T-shirt say?" asked Jimmy, when he'd had one too many of these experiences – high-fives among the others, himself standing with the foolish look of someone who's just had his pocket picked.

"That girl's a physicist," said Crake, as if this explained everything.

"So?"

"So, her T-shirt's about the eleventh dimension."

"What's the joke?"

"It's complicated," said Crake.

"Try me."

"You have to know about the dimensions and how they're supposed to be all curled up inside the dimensions we know about."

"And?"

"It's sort of like, I can take you out of this world, but the route to it is just a few nanoseconds long, and the way of measuring those nanoseconds doesn't exist in our space-frame."

"All that in symbols and numbers?"

"Not in so many words."

"Oh."

"I didn't say it was *funny*," said Crake. "These are physicists. It's only funny to them. But you asked."

"So it's sort of like she's saying they could make it together if he only had the right kind of dick, which he doesn't?" said Jimmy, who'd been thinking hard.

"Jimmy, you're a genius," said Crake.

*

"This is BioDefences," said Crake. "Last stop, I promise." He could tell Jimmy was flagging. The truth was that all this was too reminiscent. The labs, the peculiar bioforms, the socially spastic scientists – they were too much like his former life, his life as a child. Which was the last place he wanted to go back to. Even Martha Graham was preferable.

They were standing in front of a series of cages. Each contained a dog. There were many different breeds and sizes, but all were gazing at Jimmy with eyes of love, all were wagging their tails.

"It's a dog pound," said Jimmy.

"Not quite," said Crake. "Don't go beyond the guardrail, don't stick your hand in."

"They look friendly enough," said Jimmy. His old longing for a pet came over him. "Are they for sale?"

"They aren't dogs, they just look like dogs. They're wolvogs – they're bred to deceive. Reach out to pat them, they'll take your hand off. There's a large pit-bull component."

"Why make a dog like that?" said Jimmy, taking a step back. "Who'd want one?"

"It's a CorpSeCorps thing," said Jimmy. "Commission work. A lot of funding. They want to put them in moats, or something."

"Moats?"

"Yeah. Better than an alarm system – no way of disarming these guys. And no way of making pals with them, not like real dogs."

"What if they get out? Go on the rampage? Start breeding, then the population spirals out of control – like those big green rabbits?"

"That would be a problem," said Crake. "But they won't

get out. Nature is to zoos as God is to churches."

"Meaning what?" said Jimmy. He wasn't paying close attention, he was worrying about the ChickieNobs and the wolvogs. Why is it he feels some line has been crossed, some boundary transgressed? How much is too much, how far is too far?

"Those walls and bars are there for a reason," said Crake. "Not to keep us out, but to keep them in. Mankind needs barriers in both cases."

"Them?"

"Nature and God."

"I thought you didn't believe in God," said Jimmy.

"I don't believe in Nature either," said Crake. "Or not with a capital N."

Hypothetical

"So, you got a girlfriend?" said Jimmy on the fourth day. He'd been saving this question for the right time. "I mean, there's quite an array of babes to choose from." He meant this to be ironic. He couldn't picture himself with the Woody Woodpecker-laugh girl or the ones with numbers all over their chests, but he couldn't picture Crake with one of them either. Crake was too suave for that.

"Not as such," said Crake shortly.

"What do you mean, *not as such*? You've got a girl, but she's not a human being?"

"Pair-bonding at this stage is not encouraged," said Crake, sounding like a guidebook. "We're supposed to be focusing on our work."

"Bad for your health," said Jimmy. "You should get yourself fixed up."

"Easy for you to say," said Crake. "You're the grasshopper, I'm the ant. I can't waste time in unproductive random scanning."

For the first time in their lives, Jimmy wondered – could it be? – whether Crake might be jealous of him. Though maybe Crake was just being a pompous tightass; maybe Watson-Crick was having a bad effect on him. *So what's the super-cerebellum-triathlon ultralife mission?* Jimmy felt like saying. *Deign to divulge?* "I wouldn't call it a waste," he said instead, trying to lighten Crake up, "unless you fail to score."

"If you really need to, you can arrange that kind of thing through Student Services," Crake said, rather stiffly. "They deduct the price from your scholarship, same as room and board. The workers come in from the pleeblands, they're trained professionals. Naturally they're inspected for disease."

"Student Services? In your dreams! They do *what*?"

"It makes sense," said Crake. "As a system, it avoids the diversion of energies into unproductive channels, and short-circuits malaise. The female students have equal access, of course. You can get any colour, any age – well, almost. Any body type. They provide everything. If you're gay or some kind of a fetishist, they'll fix that too."

At first Jimmy thought Crake might be joking, but he wasn't. Jimmy longed to ask him what he'd tried – had he done a double amputee, for instance? But all of a sudden such a question seemed intrusive. Also it might be mistaken for mockery.

The food in Crake's faculty dining hall was fantastic – real shrimps instead of the CrustaeSoy they got at Martha Graham, and real chicken, Jimmy suspected, though he avoided that because he couldn't forget the ChickieNobs he'd seen; and something a lot like real cheese, though Crake said it came from a vegetable, a new species of zucchini they were trying out.

The desserts were heavy on the chocolate, real chocolate. The coffee was heavy on the coffee. No burnt grain products, no molasses mixed in. It was Happicuppa, but who cared? And real beer. For sure the beer was real.

So all of that was a welcome change from Martha Graham, though Crake's fellow students tended to forget about cutlery and eat with their hands, and wipe their mouths on their sleeves. Jimmy wasn't picky, but this verged on gross. Also they talked all the time, whether anyone was listening or not, always about the ideas they were developing. Once they found Jimmy wasn't working on a *space* – was attending, in fact, an institution they clearly regarded as a mud puddle – they lost any interest in him. They referred to other students in their own faculties as their conspecifics, and to all other human beings as nonspecifics. It was a running joke.

So Jimmy had no yen to mingle after hours. He was happy enough to hang out at Crake's, letting Crake beat him at chess or Three-Dimensional Waco, or trying to decode Crake's fridge magnets, the ones that didn't have numbers and symbols. Watson-Crick was a fridge-magnet culture: people bought them, traded them, made their own.

No Brain, No Pain (with a green hologram of a brain).
Siliconsciousness.
I wander from Space to Space.
Wanna Meet a Meat Machine?
Take Your Time, Leave Mine Alone.
Little spoat/gider, who made thee?
Life experiments like a rakunk at play.
I think, therefore I spam.
The proper study of Mankind is Everything.

Sometimes they'd watch TV or Web stuff, as in the old days. The Noodie News, brainfrizz, alibooboo, comfort eyefood like that. They'd microwave popcorn, smoke some of the enhanced weed the Botanical Transgenic students were raising in one of the greenhouses; then Jimmy could pass out on the couch. After he got used to his status in this brainpound, which was equivalent to that of a house plant, it wasn't too bad. You just had to relax and breathe into the stretch, as in workouts. He'd be out of here in a few days. Meanwhile it was always interesting to listen to Crake, when Crake was alone, and when he was in the mood to say anything.

On the second to last evening, Crake said, "Let me walk you through a hypothetical scenario."

"I'm game," said Jimmy. Actually he was sleepy – he'd had too much popcorn and beer – but he sat up and put on his paying-attention look, the one he'd perfected in high school. Hypothetical scenarios were a favourite thing of Crake's.

"Axiom: that illness isn't productive. In itself, it generates no commodities and therefore no money. Although it's an excuse for a lot of activity, all it really does moneywise is cause wealth to flow from the sick to the well. From patients to doctors, from clients to cure-peddlers. Money osmosis, you might call it."

"Granted," said Jimmy.

"Now, suppose you're an outfit called HelthWyzer. Suppose you make your money out of drugs and procedures that cure sick people, or else – better – that make it impossible for them to get sick in the first place."

"Yeah?" said Jimmy. Nothing hypothetical here: that was what HelthWyzer actually did.

"So, what are you going to need, sooner or later?"

"More cures?"

"After that."

"What do you mean, after that?"

"After you've cured everything going."

Jimmy made a pretence of thinking. No point doing any actual thought: it was a foregone conclusion that Crake would have some lateral-jump solution to his own question.

"Remember the plight of the dentists, after that new mouthwash came in? The one that replaced plaque bacteria with friendly ones that filled the same ecological niche, namely your mouth? No one ever needed a filling again, and a lot of dentists went bust."

"So?"

"So, you'd need more sick people. Or else – and it might be the same thing – more diseases. New and different ones. Right?"

"Stands to reason," said Jimmy after a moment. It did, too. "But don't they keep discovering new diseases?"

"Not discovering," said Crake. "They're *creating* them."

"Who is?" said Jimmy. Saboteurs, terrorists, is that what Crake meant? It was well known they went in for that kind of thing, or tried to. So far they hadn't had a lot of successes: their puny little diseases had been simple-minded, in Compound terms, and fairly easy to contain.

"HelthWyzer," said Crake. "They've been doing it for years. There's a whole secret unit working on nothing else. Then there's the distribution end. Listen, this is brilliant. They put the hostile bioforms into their vitamin pills – their HelthWyzer over-the-counter premium brand, you know?

They have a really elegant delivery system – they embed a virus inside a carrier bacterium, E. coli splice, doesn't get digested, bursts in the pylorus, and bingo! Random insertion, of course, and they don't have to keep on doing it – if they did they'd get caught, because even in the pleeblands they've got guys who could figure it out. But once you've got a hostile bioform started in the pleeb population, the way people slosh around out there it more or less runs itself. Naturally they develop the antidotes at the same time as they're customizing the bugs, but they hold those in reserve, they practise the economics of scarcity, so they're guaranteed high profits."

"Are you making this up?" said Jimmy.

"The best diseases, from a business point of view," said Crake, "would be those that cause lingering illnesses. Ideally – that is, for maximum profit – the patient should either get well or die just before all of his or her money runs out. It's a fine calculation."

"This would be really evil," said Jimmy.

"That's what my father thought," said Crake.

"He *knew*?" Jimmy really was paying attention now.

"He found out. That's how come they pushed him off a bridge."

"Who did?" said Jimmy.

"Into oncoming traffic."

"Are you going paranoid, or what?"

"Not in the least," said Crake. "This is the bare-naked truth. I hacked into my dad's e-mails before they deep-cleansed his computer. The evidence he'd been collecting was all there. The tests he'd been running on the vitamin pills. Everything."

Jimmy felt a chill up his spine. "Who knows that you know?"

"Guess who else he told?" said Crake. "My mother and Uncle Pete. He was going to do some whistle-blowing through a rogue Web site – those things have a wide viewership, it would have wrecked the pleebland sales of every single HelthWyzer vitamin supplement, plus it would have torched the entire scheme. It would have caused financial havoc. Think of the job losses. He wanted to warn them first." Crake paused. "He thought Uncle Pete didn't know."

"Wow," said Jimmy. "So one or the other of them . . ."

"Could have been both," said Crake. "Uncle Pete wouldn't have wanted the bottom line threatened. My mother may just have been scared, felt that if my dad went down, she could go too. Or it could have been the CorpSeCorps. Maybe he'd been acting funny at work. Maybe they were checking up. He encrypted everything, but if I could hack in, so could they."

"That is so weird," said Jimmy. "So they murdered your father?"

"Executed," said Crake. "That's what they'd have called it. They'd have said he was about to destroy an elegant concept. They'd have said they were acting for the general good."

The two of them sat there. Crake was looking up at the ceiling, almost as if he admired it. Jimmy didn't know what else to say. Words of comfort would be superfluous.

Finally Crake said, "How come your mother took off the way she did?"

"I don't know," said Jimmy. "A lot of reasons. I don't want to talk about it."

"I bet your dad was in on something like that. Some scam like the HelthWyzer one. I bet she found out."

"Oh, I don't think so," said Jimmy. "I think she got

involved with some God's Gardeners–type outfit. Some bunch of wackos. Anyway, my dad wouldn't have . . ."

"I bet she knew they were starting to know she knew."

"I'm really tired," said Jimmy. He yawned, and suddenly it was true. "I think I'll turn in."

Extinctathon

On the last evening, Crake said, "Want to play Extinctathon?"

"Extinctathon?" said Jimmy. It took him a moment, but then he remembered it: the boring Web interactive with all those defunct animals and plants. "When was it we used to play that? It can't still be going."

"It's never stopped," said Crake. Jimmy took in the implications: Crake had never stopped. He must've been playing it by himself, all these years. Well, he was a compulsive, no news there.

"So, how's your cumulative score?" he asked, to be polite.

"Once you rack up three thousand," said Crake, "you get to be a Grandmaster." Which meant Crake was one, because he wouldn't have mentioned it otherwise.

"Oh good," said Jimmy. "So do you get a prize? The tail and both ears?"

"Let me show you something," said Crake. He went onto the Web, found the site, pulled it up. There was the familiar gateway: *EXTINCTATHON, Monitored by MaddAddam. Adam named the living animals, MaddAddam names the dead ones. Do you want to play?*

Crake clicked Yes, and entered his codename: *Rednecked Crake*. The little coelacanth symbol appeared over his name, meaning Grandmaster. Then something new came up, a message Jimmy had never seen before: *Welcome Grandmaster Rednecked Crake. Do you want to play a general game or do you want to play another Grandmaster?*

Crake clicked the second. *Good. Find your playroom. MaddAddam will meet you there.*

"MaddAddam is a person?" asked Jimmy.

"It's a group," said Crake. "Or groups."

"So what do they do, this MaddAddam?" Jimmy was feeling silly. It was like watching some corny old spy DVD, James Bond or something. "Besides counting the skulls and pelts, I mean."

"Watch this." Crake left Extinctathon, then hacked into a local pleeb bank, and from there skipped to what looked to be a manufacturer of solarcar parts. He went into the image of a hubcap, which opened into a folder – HottTotts Pinups, it was titled. The files were dated, not named; he chose one of them, transferred it into one of his lily pads, used that to skip to another, erased his footprints, opened the file there, loaded an image.

It was the picture of Oryx, seven or eight years old, naked except for her ribbons, her flowers. It was the picture of the look she'd given him, the direct, contemptuous, knowing look that had dealt him such a blow when he was – what? Fourteen? He still had the paper printout, folded up, hidden deep. It was a private thing, this picture. His own private thing: his own guilt, his own shame, his own desire. Why had Crake kept it? *Stolen* it.

Jimmy felt ambushed. *What's she doing here?* he wanted to yell. *That's mine! Give it back!* He was in a lineup; fingers pointed at him, faces scowled, while some rabid Bernice clone set fire to his undershorts. Retribution was at hand, but for what? What had he done? Nothing. He'd only looked.

Crake moved to the girl's left eye, clicked on the iris. It was a gateway: the playroom opened up.

Hello, Grandmaster Crake. Enter pass number now.

Crake did so. A new sentence popped up: *Adam named the animals. MaddAddam customizes them.*

Then there was a string of e-bulletins, with places and dates – CorpSeCorps issue, by the look of them, marked For Secure Addresses Only.

A tiny parasitic wasp had invaded several ChickieNobs installations, carrying a modified form of chickenpox, specific to the ChickieNob and fatal to it. The installations had had to be incinerated before the epidemic could be brought under control.

A new form of the common house mouse addicted to the insulation on electric wiring had overrun Cleveland, causing an unprecedented number of house fires. Control measures were still being tested.

Happicuppa coffee bean crops were menaced by a new bean weevil found to be resistant to all known pesticides.

A miniature rodent containing elements of both porcupine and beaver had appeared in the northwest, creeping under the hoods of parked vehicles and devastating their fan belts and transmission systems.

A microbe that ate the tar in asphalt had turned several interstate highways to sand. All interstates were on alert, and a quarantine belt was now in place.

"What's going on?" said Jimmy. "Who's putting this stuff out there?"

The bulletins vanished, and a fresh entry appeared. *MaddAddam needs fresh initiatives. Got a bright idea? Share with us.*

Crake typed, *Sorry, interruption. Must go.*

Right, Grandmaster Rednecked Crake. We'll talk later. Crake closed down.

Jimmy had a cold feeling, a feeling that reminded him of the time his mother had left home: the same sense of the forbidden, of a door swinging open that ought to be kept locked, of a stream of secret lives, running underground, in the darkness just beneath his feet. "What was all that about?" he said. It might not be about anything, he told himself. It might be about Crake showing off. It might be an elaborate setup, an invention of Crake's, a practical joke to frighten him.

"I'm not sure," said Crake. "I thought at first they were just another crazy Animal Liberation org. But there's more to it than that. I think they're after the machinery. They're after the whole system, they want to shut it down. So far they haven't done any people numbers, but it's obvious they could."

"You shouldn't be messing around!" said Jimmy. "You don't want to be connected! Someone could think you're part of it. What if you get caught? You'll end up on brainfrizz!" He was frightened now.

"I won't get caught," said Crake. "I'm just cruising. But do me a favour and don't mention this when you e-mail."

"Sure," said Jimmy. "But why even take the chance?"

"I'm curious, that's all," said Crake. "They've let me into the waiting room, but not any further. They've got to be Compound, or Compound-trained. These are sophisticated bioforms they're putting together; I don't think a pleeblander would be able to make anything like that." He gave

Jimmy his green-eyed sideways look – a look (Snowman thinks now) that meant trust. Crake trusted him. Otherwise he wouldn't have shown him the hidden playroom.

"It could be a CorpSeCorps flytrap," said Jimmy. The Corpsmen were in the habit of setting up schemes of that sort, to capture subversives in the making. Weeding the pea patch, he'd heard it called. The Compounds were said to be mined with such potentially lethal tunnels. "You need to watch your step."

"Sure," said Crake.

What Jimmy really wanted to know was: *Out of all the possibilities you had, out of all the gateways, why did you choose her?*

He couldn't ask, though. He couldn't give himself away.

Something else happened during that visit; something important, though Jimmy hadn't realized it at the time.

The first night, as he was sleeping on Crake's pullout sofa bed, he'd heard shouting. He'd thought it was coming from outside – at Martha Graham it would have been student pranksters – but in fact it was coming from Crake's room. It was coming from Crake.

More than shouting: screaming. There were no words. It happened every night he was there.

"That was some dream you were having," said Jimmy the next morning, after the first time it happened.

"I never dream," said Crake. His mouth was full and he was looking out the window. For such a thin man he ate a lot. It was the speed, the high metabolic rate: Crake burned things up.

"Everyone dreams," Jimmy said. "Remember the REM-sleep study at HelthWyzer High?"

"The one where we tortured cats?"

"Virtual cats, yeah. And the cats that couldn't dream went crazy."

"I never remember my dreams," said Crake. "Have some more toast."

"But you must have them anyway."

"Okay, point taken, wrong words. I didn't mean *I never dream*. I'm not crazy, therefore I must dream. Hypothesis, demonstration, conclusion, if A then not B. Good enough?" Crake smiled, poured himself some coffee.

So Crake never remembered his dreams. It's Snowman that remembers them instead. Worse than remembers: he's immersed in them, he'd wading through them, he's stuck in them. Every moment he's lived in the past few months was dreamed first by Crake. No wonder Crake screamed so much.

9

Hike

After an hour of walking, Snowman comes out from the former park. He picks his way farther inland, heading along the trashed pleebland boulevards and avenues and roads and streets. Wrecked solarcars are plentiful, some piled up in multi-vehicle crashes, some burnt out, some standing intact as if temporarily parked. There are trucks and vans, fuel-cell models and also the old gas or diesel kind, and ATVs. A few bicycles, a few motorcycles – not a bad choice considering the traffic mayhem that must have lasted for days. On a two-wheeled item you'd have been able to weave in and out among the larger vehicles until someone shot you or ran into you, or you fell off.

This was once a semi-residential sector – shops on the ground floor, gutted now; small dim apartments above. Most of the signs are still in place despite the bullet holes in them. People had hoarded the lead bullets from the time before sprayguns, despite the ban on the pleebs having any kind of gun at all. Snowman's been unable to find any bullets; not that he had a rusty old firearm that would have taken them.

The buildings that didn't burn or explode are still standing, though the botany is thrusting itself through every crack. Given time it will fissure the asphalt, topple the walls, push aside the roofs. Some kind of vine is growing everywhere, draping the windowsills, climbing in through the broken windows and up the bars and grillwork. Soon this district will be a thick tangle of vegetation. If he'd postponed the trip much longer the way back would have become impassable. It won't be long before all visible traces of human habitation will be gone.

But suppose – just suppose, thinks Snowman – that he's not the last of his kind. Suppose there are others. He wills them into being, these possible remnants who might have survived in isolated pockets, cut off by the shutdown of the communications networks, keeping themselves alive somehow. Monks in desert hideaways, far from contagion; mountain goatherders who'd never mixed with the valley people; lost tribes in the jungles. Survivalists who'd tuned in early, shot all comers, sealed themselves into their underground bunkers. Hillbillies, recluses; wandering lunatics, swathed in protective hallucinations. Bands of nomads, following their ancient ways.

How did this happen? their descendants will ask, stumbling upon the evidence, the ruins. The ruinous evidence. *Who made these things? Who lived in them? Who destroyed them?* The Taj Mahal, the Louvre, the Pyramids, the Empire State Building – stuff he's seen on TV, in old books, on postcards, on Blood and Roses. Imagine coming upon them, 3-D, life-sized, with no preparation – you'd be freaked, you'd run away, and after that you'd need an explanation. At first they'll say giants or gods, but sooner or later they'll want to know the truth. Like him, they'll have the curious monkey brain.

Perhaps they'll say, *These things are not real. They are phantasmagoria. They were made by dreams, and now that no one is dreaming them any longer they are crumbling away.*

"Let's suppose for the sake of argument," said Crake one evening, "that civilization as we know it gets destroyed. Want some popcorn?"

"Is that real butter?" said Jimmy.

"Nothing but the best at Watson-Crick," said Crake. "Once it's flattened, it could never be rebuilt."

"Because why? Got any salt?"

"Because all the available surface metals have already been mined," said Crake. "Without which, no iron age, no bronze age, no age of steel, and all the rest of it. There's metals farther down, but the advanced technology we need for extracting those would have been obliterated."

"It could be put back together," said Jimmy, chewing. It was so long since he'd tasted popcorn this good. "They'd still have the instructions."

"Actually not," said Crake. "It's not like the wheel, it's too complex now. Suppose the instructions survived, suppose there were any people left with the knowledge to read them. Those people would be few and far between, and they wouldn't have the tools. Remember, no electricity. Then once those people died, that would be it. They'd have no apprentices, they'd have no successors. Want a beer?"

"Is it cold?"

"All it takes," said Crake, "is the elimination of one generation. One generation of anything. Beetles, trees, microbes, scientists, speakers of French, whatever. Break the link in time between one generation and the next, and it's game over forever."

"Speaking of games," said Jimmy, "it's your move."

The walking has become an obstacle course for Snowman: in several places he's needed to make detours. Now he's in a narrow sidestreet, choked with vines; they've festooned themselves across the street, from roof to roof. Through the clefts in the overhead greenery he can see a handful of vultures, circling idly in the sky. They can see him too, they have eyesight like ten magnifying glasses, those things can count the change in your pocket. He knows a thing or two about vultures. "Not yet," he calls up at them.

But why disappoint them? If he were to stumble and fall, cut himself open, knock himself out, then be set upon by wolvogs or pigoons, what difference would it make to anyone but himself? The Crakers are doing fine, they don't need him any more. For a while they'll wonder where he's gone, but he's already provided an answer to that: he's gone to be with Crake. He'll become a secondary player in their mythology, such as it is – a sort of backup demiurge. He'll be falsely remembered. He won't be mourned.

The sun is climbing higher, intensifying its rays. He feels light-headed. A thick tendril slithers away, flickering its tongue, as his foot comes down beside it. He needs to pay more attention. Are any of the snakes venomous? Did that long tail he almost stepped on have a small furry body at the front? He didn't see it clearly. He certainly hopes not. The claim was that all the snats had been destroyed, but it would take only one pair of them. One pair, the Adam and Eve of snats, and some weirdo with a grudge, bidding them go forth and multiply, relishing the idea of those things twirling up the drainpipes. Rats with long green scaly tails and rattlesnake fangs. He decides not to think about that.

Instead he begins to hum, to cheer himself up. What's the song? "Winter Wonderland." They used to recycle that in the malls every Christmas, long after the last time it snowed. Some tune about playing pranks on a snowman, before it got mushed.

Maybe he's not the Abominable Snowman after all. Maybe he's the other kind of snowman, the grinning dope set up as a joke and pushed down as an entertainment, his pebble smile and carrot nose an invitation to mockery and abuse. Maybe that's the real him, the last *Homo sapiens* – a white illusion of a man, here today, gone tomorrow, so easily shoved over, left to melt in the sun, getting thinner and thinner until he liquefies and trickles away altogether. As Snowman is doing now. He pauses, wipes the sweat off his face, drinks half of his bottle of water. He hopes there will be more somewhere, soon.

Up ahead, the houses thin out and vanish. There's an interval of parking lots and warehouses, then barbed wire strung between cement posts, an elaborate gate off its hinges. End of urban sprawl and pleeb city limits, beginning of Compound turfdom. Here's the last station of the sealed-tunnel bullet train, with its plastic jungle-gym colours. *No risks here*, the colours are saying. *Just kiddie fun*.

But this is the dangerous part. Up to here he's always had

something he could climb or scramble up or dodge around in case of a flank attack, but now comes an open space with no shelter and few verticals. He pulls the sheet up over his baseball cap to protect himself from the sun's glare, shrouding himself like an Arab, and plods on, picking up the pace as much as he can. He knows he'll burn some even through the sheet if he stays out here long enough: his best hope is speed. He'll need to get to shelter before noon, when the asphalt will be too hot to walk on.

Now he's reached the Compounds. He passes the turnoff to CryoJeenyus, one of the smaller outfits: he'd like to have been a fly on the wall when the lights went out and two thousand frozen millionaires' heads awaiting resurrection began to melt in the dark. Next comes Genie-Gnomes, with the elfin mascot popping its pointy-eared head in and out of a test tube. The neon was on, he noted: the solar hookup must still be functioning, though not perfectly. Those signs were supposed to go on only at night.

And, finally, RejoovenEsense. Where he'd made so many mistakes, misunderstood so much, gone on his last joyride. Bigger than OrganInc Farms, bigger than HelthWyzer. The biggest of them all.

He passes the first barricade with its crapped-out scopers and busted searchlights, then the checkpoint booth. A guard is lying half in, half out. Snowman isn't too surprised by the absence of a head: in times of crisis emotions run high. He checks to see if the guy still has his spraygun, but no dice.

Next comes a tract kept free of buildings. No Man's Land, Crake used to call it. No trees here: they'd mowed down anything you could hide behind, divided the territory into squares with lines of heat-and-motion sensors. The eerie chessboard effect is already gone; weeds are poking up like whiskers all over the flat surface. Snowman takes a few minutes to scan the field, but apart from a cluster of dark birds squabbling over some object on the ground, nothing's moving. Then he goes forward.

Now he's on the approach proper. Along the road is a trail of objects people must have dropped in flight, like a treasure hunt in reverse. A suitcase, a knapsack spilling out clothes and trinkets; an overnight bag, broken open, beside it a forlorn pink toothbrush. A bracelet; a woman's hair ornament in the shape of a butterfly; a notebook, its pages soaked, the handwriting illegible.

The fugitives must have had hope, to begin with. They must have thought they'd have a use for these things later. Then they'd changed their minds and let go.

RejoovenEsense

He's out of breath and sweating too much by the time he reaches the RejoovenEsense Compound curtain wall, still twelve feet high but no longer electrified, its iron spikes rusting. He goes through the outer gate, which looks as if someone blew it apart, pausing in its shadow to eat the chocolate energy bar and drink the rest of his water. Then he continues on, across the moat, past the sentry boxes where the CorpSeCorps armed guards once stood and the glassed-in cubicles where they'd monitored the surveillance equipment, then past the rampart watchtower with the steel door – standing forever open, now – where he'd once have been ordered to present his thumbprint and the iris of his eye.

Beyond is the vista he remembers so well: the residences laid out like a garden suburb with large houses in fake Georgian and fake Tudor and fake French provincial, the meandering streets leading to the employees' golf course and their restaurants and nightclubs and medical clinics and shopping malls and indoor tennis courts, and their hospitals. To the right are the off-bounds hot-bioform isolation facilities, bright orange, and the black cube-shaped shatterproofglass fortresses that were the business end of things. In the distance is his destination – the central park, with the top of Crake's charmed dome visible above the trees, round and white and glaring, like a bubble of ice. Looking at it, he shivers.

But no time for pointless repining. He hikes rapidly along the main street, stepping around the huddles of cloth and gnawed human carcasses. Not much left except the bones: the scavengers have done their work. At the time he walked out of here this place looked like a riot scene and stank like an abattoir, but now all is quiet and the stench is mostly gone. The pigoons have rooted up the lawns; their hoof-marks are everywhere, though luckily not too fresh.

His first object is food. It would make sense to go all the way along the road to where the malls are – more chance of a square meal there – but he's too hungry for that. Also he needs to get out of the sun, right now.

So he takes the second left, into one of the residential sections. Already the weeds are thick along the curbs. The street is circular; in the island in the middle, a clutch of shrubs, unpruned and scraggly, flares with red and purple flowers. Some exotic splice: in a few years they'll be overwhelmed. Or else they'll spread, make inroads, choke out the native plants. Who can tell which? The whole world is now one vast uncontrolled experiment – the way it always was, Crake would have said – and the doctrine of unintended consequences is in full spate.

The house he chooses is medium-sized, a Queen Anne. The front door's locked, but a diamond-paned window has been smashed: some doomed looter must have been there before him. Snowman wonders what the poor guy was looking for: food, useless money, or just a place to sleep?

Whatever it was, it wouldn't have done him much good.

He drinks a few handfuls of water from a stone birdbath, ornamented with witless-looking frogs and still mostly full from yesterday's downpour, and not too muddied with bird droppings. What disease do birds carry, and is it in their shit? He'll have to chance it. After splashing his face and neck he refills his bottle. Then he studies the house for signs, for movements. He can't rid himself of the notion that someone – someone like him – is lying in wait, around some corner, behind some half-opened door.

He takes off his sunglasses, knots them into his sheet. Then he climbs in through the broken window, one leg and then the other, throwing his stick in first. Now he's in the dimness. The hair on his arms prickles: claustrophobia and bad energy are already pressing him down. The air is thick, as if panic has condensed in here and hasn't yet had time to dissipate. It smells like a thousand bad drains.

"Hello!" he calls. "Anybody home?" He can't help it: any house speaks to him of potential inhabitants. He feels like turning back; nausea simmers in his throat. But he holds a corner of his rancid sheet over his nose – at least it's his own smell – and makes his away across the mouldering broadloom, past the dim shapes of the plump reproduction furniture. There's a squeaking, a scurrying: the rats have taken over. He picks his steps with care. He knows what he looks like to rats: carrion on the hoof. They sound like real rats though, not snats. Snats don't squeak, they hiss.

Did squeak, *did* hiss, he corrects himself. They were liquidated, they're extinct, he must insist on that.

First things first. He locates the liquor cabinet in the

dining room and goes through it quickly. A half-bottle of bourbon; nothing else, only a bunch of empties. No cigarettes. It must have been a non-smoking household, or else the looter before him pinched them. "Fuck you," he says to the fumed oak sideboard.

Then he tiptoes up the carpeted stairs to the second floor. Why so quietly, as if he's a real burglar? He can't help it. Surely there are people here, asleep. Surely they will hear him and wake up. But he knows that's foolish.

There's a man in the bathroom, sprawled on the earth-tone tiles, wearing – what's left of him – a pair of blue-and-maroon-striped pyjamas. Strange, thinks Snowman, how in an emergency a lot of people would head for the bathroom. Bathrooms were the closest things to sanctuaries in these houses, places where you could be alone to meditate. Also to puke, to bleed from the eyes, to shit your guts out, to grope desperately in the medicine cabinet for some pill that would save you.

It's a nice bathroom. A Jacuzzi, ceramic Mexican mermaids on the walls, their heads crowned with flowers, their blonde hair waving down, their painted nipples bright pink on breasts that are small but rounded. He wouldn't mind a shower – this place probably has a gravity-flow rainwater backup tank – but there's some form of hardened guck in the tub. He takes a bar of soap, for later, and checks the cabinet for sunblock, without success. A BlyssPluss container, half full; a bottle of aspirin, which he snags. He thinks about adding a toothbrush, but he has an aversion to sticking a dead person's toothbrush into his mouth, so he takes only the toothpaste. For a Whiter Smile, he reads. Fine with him, he needs a whiter smile, though he can't at the moment think what for.

The mirror on the front of the cabinet has been smashed: some last act of ineffectual rage, of cosmic protest – *Why this? Why me?* He can understand that, he'd have done the same. Broken something; turned his last glimpse of himself into fragments. Most of the glass is in the sink, but he's careful where he places his feet: like a horse, his life now depends on them. If he can't walk, he's rat food.

He continues along the hall. The lady of the house is in the bedroom, tucked under the king-sized pink and gold duvet, one arm and shoulder blade outside the covers, bones and tendons in a leopard-skin-print nightie. Her face is turned away from him, which is just as well, but her hair is intact, all of a piece, as if it's a wig: dark roots, frosted wisps, a sort of pixie look. On the right woman that could be attractive.

At one time in his life he used to go through other people's bureau drawers given half the chance, but in this room he doesn't want to. Anyway it would be the same sort of thing. Underwear, sex aids, costume jewellery, mixed in with pencil stubs, spare change, and safety pins, and a diary if he got lucky. When he was still in high school he'd liked reading girls' diaries, with their capital letters and multiple exclamation marks and extreme phrasing – *love love love, hate hate hate* – and their coloured underlining, like the crank letters he used to get, later, at work. He'd wait till the girl was in the shower, do a lightning-swift rummage. Of course it was his own name he'd be searching for, though he hadn't always liked what he'd found.

Once he'd read, *Jimmy you nosy brat I know your reading this, I* hate *it just because I fucked you doesn't mean I like you so* STAY OUT!!! Two red lines under *hate*, three under *stay out*. Her name had been Brenda. Cute, a gum-chewer, sat in front of him in Life Skills class. She'd had a solar-battery robodog on her dresser that barked, fetched a plastic bone, and lifted its leg to pee yellow water. It's always struck him how the toughest and most bitchy girls had the schmaltziest, squishiest doodads in their bedrooms.

The vanity table holds the standard collection of firming creams, hormone treatments, ampoules and injections, cosmetics, colognes. In the half-light that comes through the slatted blinds these things gleam darkly, like a still life muted with varnish. He sprays himself with the stuff in one of the bottles, a musky scent he hopes might cut the other smells in here. Crack Cocaine, its label says in raised gold lettering. He thinks briefly about drinking it, but remembers he has the bourbon.

Then he bends down to take stock of himself in the oval mirror. He can't resist the mirrors in the places he breaks into, he sneaks a peek at himself every chance he has. Increasingly it's a shock. A stranger stares back at him, bleary-eyed, hollow-cheeked, pocked with bug-bite scabs. He looks twenty years older than he is. He winks, grins at himself, sticks out his tongue: the effect is truly sinister. Behind him in the glass the husk of the woman in the bed seems almost like a real woman; as if at any moment she might turn towards him, open her arms, whisper to him to come and get her. Her and her pixie hair.

Oryx had a wig like that. She liked to dress up, change her appearance, pretend to be different women. She'd strut around the room, do a little strip, wiggle and pose. She said men liked variety.

"Who told you that?" Jimmy asked her.

"Oh, someone." Then she laughed. That was right before he scooped her up and her wig fell off . . . *Jimmee!* But he can't afford to think about Oryx right now.

He finds himself standing in the middle of the room, hands dangling, mouth open. "I have been unintelligent," he says out loud.

Next door there's a child's room, with a computer in gay red plastic, a shelf of teddy bears, a wallpaper frieze of giraffes, and a stash of CDs containing – judging from the pictures on them – some extremely violent computer games. But there's no child, no child's body. Maybe it died and was cremated in those first few days when cremations were still taking place; or maybe it was frightened when its parents keeled over and began gurgling blood, and it ran away somewhere else. Maybe it was one of the cloth and bone bundles he passed on the streets outside. Some of them were quite small.

He locates the linen closet in the hall and exchanges his filthy sheet for a fresh one, this time not plain but patterned with scrolls and flowers. That will make an impression among the Craker kids. "Look," they'll say. "Snowman is growing leaves!" They wouldn't put it past him. There's a whole stack of clean sheets in the closet, neatly folded, but he takes only the one. He doesn't want to weigh himself down with stuff he doesn't really need. If he has to he can always come back for more.

He hears his mother's voice telling him to put the discarded sheet into the laundry hamper – old neurological pathways die hard – but he drops it onto the floor instead and goes back downstairs, into the kitchen. He hopes he'll find some canned food there, soy stew or beans and fake wieners, anything with protein in it – even some vegetables would be nice, ersatz or not, he'll take anything – but whoever smashed the window also cleaned out the cupboard. There's a handful of dry cereal in a plastic snap-top container, so he eats that; it's unadulterated junk-gene cardboard and he has to chew it a lot and drink some water to get it down. He finds three packets of cashew nuts, snac-pacs from the bullet train, and gobbles one of them immediately; it isn't too stale. There's also a tin of SoyOBoy sardines. Otherwise there's only a half-empty bottle of ketchup, dark brown and fermenting.

He knows better than to open the refrigerator. Some of the smell in the kitchen is coming from there.

In one of the drawers under the counter there's a flashlight that works. He takes that, and a couple of candle ends, and some matches. He finds a plastic garbage bag, right where it should be, and puts everything into it, including the sardines and the other two packs of cashews, and the bourbon and the soap and aspirin. There are some knives, not very sharp; he chooses two, and a small cooking pot. That will come in handy if he can find something to cook.

Down the hallway, tucked in between the kitchen and the utility room, there's a small home office. A desk with a dead computer, a fax, a printer; also a container with plastic pens, a shelf with reference books – a dictionary, a thesaurus, a Bartlett's, the *Norton Anthology of Modern Poetry*. The striped-pyjamas guy upstairs must have been a word person, then: a RejoovenEsense speechwriter, an ideological plumber, a spin doctor, a hairsplitter for hire. Poor bugger, thinks Snowman.

Beside a vase of withered flowers and a framed father-and-son snapshot – the child was a boy then, seven or eight

– there's a telephone scratch pad. Scrawled across the top page are the words GET LAWN MOWED. Then, in smaller, fainter letters, *Call clinic . . .* The ballpoint pen is still on the paper, as if dropped from a slackening hand: it must have come suddenly, right then, the sickness and the realization of it both. Snowman can picture the guy figuring it out as he looked down at his own moving hand. He must have been an early case, or he wouldn't still have been worrying about his lawn.

The back of his neck prickles again. Why does he have the feeling that it's his own house he's broken into? His own house from twenty-five years ago, himself the missing child.

Twister

Snowman makes his way through the curtained demi-light of the living room to the front of the house, plotting his future course. He'll have to try for a house richer in canned goods, or even a mall. He could camp out there overnight, up on one of the top shelving racks; that way he could take his time, bag only the best. Who knows? There may still be some chocolate bars. Then, when he knows he's covered the nutrition angle, he can head for the bubble-dome, pilfer the arsenal. Once he's got a functional spraygun in his hands again he'll feel a lot safer.

He throws his stick out through the broken window, then climbs out himself, taking care not to rip his new flowered sheet or cut himself or tear his plastic bag on the jagged glass. Directly across from him on the overgrown lawn, cutting off access to the street, there's a quintuplet of pigoons, rooting around in a small heap of trash he hopes is only clothing. A boar, two sows, two young. When they hear him they stop feeding and lift their heads: they see him, all right. He raises his stick, shakes it at them. Usually they bolt if he does that – pigoons have long memories, and sticks look like electroprods

– but this time they stand their ground. They're sniffing in his direction, as if puzzled; maybe they smell the perfume he sprayed on himself. The stuff could have analogue mammalian sex pheromones in it, which would be just his luck. Trampled to death by lustful pigoons. What a moronic finish.

What can he do if they charge? Only one option: scramble back through the window. Does he have time for that? Despite the stubby legs carrying their enormous bulk, the damn things can run very fast. The kitchen knives are in his garbage bag; in any case they're too short and flimsy to do much damage to a full-sized pigoon. It would be like trying to stick a paring knife into a truck tire.

The boar lowers its head, hunching its massive neck and shoulders and swaying uneasily back and forth, making up its mind. But the others have already begun moving away, so the boar thinks better of it and follows them, marking its contempt and defiance by dropping a pile of dung as it goes. Snowman stands still until they're all out of sight, then proceeds with caution, looking frequently behind him. There are too many pigoon tracks around here. Those beasts are clever enough to fake a retreat, then lurk around the next corner. They'd bowl him over, trample him, then rip him open, munch up the organs first. He knows their tastes. A brainy and omnivorous animal, the pigoon. Some of them may even have human neocortex tissue growing in their crafty, wicked heads.

Yes: there they are, up ahead. They're coming out from behind a bush, all five of them; no, all seven. They're staring in his direction. It would be a mistake to turn his back, or to run. He raises the stick, and walks sideways, back in the direction from which he's come. If necessary he can take refuge inside the checkpoint gatehouse and stay there till they go away. Then he'll have to find a roundabout route to the bubble-dome, keeping to the sidestreets, where evasion is possible.

But in the time it takes him to cover the distance, slip-stepping as if in some grotesque dance with the pigoons still staring, dark clouds have come boiling up from the south, blotting out the sun. This isn't the usual afternoon storm: it's too early, and the sky has an ominous greenish-yellow tinge. It's a twister, a big one. The pigoons have vanished now, gone to seek shelter.

He stands outside the checkpoint cubicle watching the storm roll forward. It's a grand spectacle. He once saw an amateur documentary-maker with a camcorder sucked right up into one of those. He wonders how Crake's Children are getting along, back at the shore. Too bad for Crake if the living results of all his theories are whirled away into the sky or swept out to sea on a big wave. But that won't happen: in case of high seas, the breakwaters formed by fallen rubble will protect them. As for the twister, they've weathered one of those before. They'll retreat into the central cavern in the jumble of concrete blocks they call their thunder home and wait it out.

The advance winds hit, stirring up debris on the open field. Lightning zips between the clouds. He can see the thin dark cone, zigzagging downwards; then darkness descends. Luckily the checkpoint is built into the security building beside it, and those things are like bunkers, thick and solid. He ducks inside as the first rain strikes.

There's a shrieking of wind, a crashing of thunder, a vibrating sound as everything still nailed down hums like a gear in a giant engine. A large object hits the outer wall. He moves inward, through one doorway and then another, scrabbling in his garbage bag for the flashlight. He's got it out and is fumbling with it when there's another gigantic crash, and the overhead lights blink on. Some previously fried solar circuit must have been refried.

He almost wishes the lights hadn't gone on: there's a couple of biosuits off in the corner, with whatever's left inside them in a bad state of repair. Filing cabinets pulled open, paper scattered everywhere. Looks as if the guards were overwhelmed. Maybe they were trying to stop people from getting out through the gates; there was an attempt to enforce a quarantine, as he recalls. But the antisocial elements, which would have included just about everyone by then, must have broken in and trashed the secret files. How optimistic of them to have believed that any of the paperwork and storage disks might still have been of use to anyone.

He forces himself to go over to the suits; he prods them with his stick, turns them over. Not as bad as he thought, not too smelly, only a few beetles; anything soft is mostly gone. But he can't find any weapons. The antisocials must have made off with those, as he would have done. As he did do.

He leaves the inmost room, goes back to the receptionist's area, the part with the counter and the desk. All at once he's very tired. He sits down in the ergonomic chair. It's been a long time since he sat in a chair, and it feels strange. He decides to set out his matches and candle ends, in case the lights go out again; while he's at it he has a drink of birdbath water and the second package of cashews. From outside comes the howling of the wind, an unearthly noise like a huge animal unchained and raging. Gusts are coming in, past the doors he's closed, stirring up the dust; everything rattles. His hands are shaking. This is getting to him, more than he's allowed himself to admit.

What if there are rats in here? There must be rats. What if it starts to flood? They'll run up his legs! He pulls his legs up onto the chair, folds them over one of the ergonomic arms, tucks the floral sheet around them. No hope of hearing any telltale squeaking, the racket of the storm is too loud.

A great man must rise to meet the challenges in his life, says a voice. Who is it this time? A motivational lecturer from RejoovTV, some fatuous drone in a suit. A gabbler for hire. *This is surely the lesson taught to us by history. The higher the hurdle the greater the jump. Having to face a crisis causes you to grow as a person.*

"I haven't grown as a person, you cretin," Snowman shouts. "Look at me! I've shrunk! My brain is the size of a grape!"

But he doesn't know which it is, bigger or smaller, because there's nobody to measure himself by. He's lost in the fog. No benchmarks.

The lights go out. Now he's alone in the dark.

"So what?" he tells himself. "You were alone in the light. No big difference." But there is.

He's ready though. He gets a grip. He stands the flashlight on end, strikes a match in its feeble beam, manages to light a candle. It wavers in the drafty air but it burns, casting a small glowing circle of soft yellow on the desk, turning the room around him into an ancient cave, dark but protective.

He rummages in his plastic bag, finds the third pack of

cashews, rips it open, eats the contents. He takes out the bottle of bourbon, thinks about it, then unscrews the top and drinks. *Gluk gluk gluk*, goes the cartoon writing in his head. *Firewater.*

Oh sweetie, a woman's voice says from the corner of the room. *You're doing really well.*

"No I'm not," he says.

A puff of air – whuff! – hits his ears, blows out the candle. He can't be bothered relighting it, because the bourbon is taking over. He'd rather stay in the dark. He can sense Oryx drifting towards him on her soft feathery wings. Any moment now she'll be with him. He sits crouched in the chair with his head down on the desk and his eyes closed, in a state of misery and peace.

10

Vulturizing

After four deranged years Jimmy graduated from Martha Graham with his dingy little degree in Problematics. He didn't expect to get a job right away, and in this he was not deceived. For weeks he'd parcel up his meagre credentials, send them out, then get them back too quickly, sometimes with grease spots and fingerprints from whatever sub-basement-level cog had been flipping through them while eating lunch. Then he'd replace the dirty pages and send the package out again.

He'd snared a summer job at the Martha Graham library, going through old books and earmarking them for destruction while deciding which should remain on earth in digital form, but he lost this post halfway through its term because he couldn't bear to throw anything out. After that he shacked up with his girlfriend of the moment, a conceptual artist and long-haired brunette named Amanda Payne. This name was an invention, like much about her: her real name was Barb Jones. She'd had to reinvent herself, she told Jimmy, the original Barb having been so bulldozed by her abusive, white-trash, sugar-overdosed family that she'd been nothing but a yard-sale reject, like a wind chime made of bent forks or a three-legged chair.

This had been her appeal for Jimmy, for whom "yard sale" was in itself an exotic concept: he'd wanted to mend her, do the repairs, freshen up the paint. Make her like new. "You have a good heart," she'd told him, the first time she'd let him inside her defences. Revision: overalls.

Amanda had a rundown condo in one of the Modules, shared with two other artists, both men. The three of them were all from the pleeblands, they'd gone to Martha Graham on scholarship, and they considered themselves superior to the privileged, weak-spined, degenerate offspring of the Compounds, such as Jimmy. They'd had to be tough, take it on the chin, battle their way. They claimed a clarity of vision that could only have come from being honed on the grindstone of reality. One of the men had tried suicide, which conferred on him – he implied – a special vantage. The other one had shot a lot of heroin and dealt it too, before taking up art instead, or possibly in addition. After the first few weeks, during which he'd found them charismatic, Jimmy had decided these two were bullshit technicians, in addition to which they were puffed-up snots.

The two who were not Amanda tolerated Jimmy, but just marginally. In order to ingratiate himself with them he took a turn in the kitchen now and then – all three of the artists sneered at microwaves and were into boiling their own spaghetti – but he wasn't a very good cook. He made the mistake of bringing home a ChickieNobs Bucket O'Nubbins one night – a franchise had opened around the corner, and the stuff wasn't that bad if you could forget everything you knew about the provenance – and after that the two of them who were not Amanda barely spoke to him.

That didn't stop them from speaking to each other. They had lots to say about all kinds of junk they claimed to know something about, and would drone on in an instigated way, delivering themselves of harangues and oblique sermons that were in fact – Jimmy felt – aimed at himself. According to them it had been game over once agriculture was invented, six or seven thousand years ago. After that, the human experiment was doomed, first to gigantism due to a maxed-out food supply, and then to extinction, once all the available nutrients had been hoovered up.

"You've got the answers?" said Jimmy. He'd come to enjoy needling them, because who were they to judge? The artists, who were not sensitized to irony, said that correct analysis was one thing but correct solutions were another, and the lack of the latter did not invalidate the former.

Anyway, maybe there weren't any solutions. Human society, they claimed, was a sort of monster, its main by-products being corpses and rubble. It never learned, it made the same cretinous mistakes over and over, trading short-term gain for long-term pain. It was like a giant slug eating its way relentlessly through all the other bioforms on the planet, grinding up life on earth and shitting it out the backside in the form of pieces of manufactured and soon-to-be-obsolete plastic junk.

"Like your computers?" murmured Jimmy. "The ones you do your art on?"

Soon, said the artists, ignoring him, there would be nothing left but a series of long subterranean tubes covering the surface of the planet. The air and light inside them would be artificial, the ozone and oxygen layers of Planet Earth having been totally destroyed. People would creep along through this tubing, single file, stark naked, their only view the asshole of the one before them in the line, their urine and excrement flowing down through vents in the floor, until they were randomly selected by a digitalized mechanism, at which point they would be sucked into a side tunnel, ground up, and fed to the others through a series of nipple-shaped appendages on the inside of the tube. The system would be self-sustaining and perpetual, and would serve everybody right.

"So, I guess that would do away with war," said Jimmy, "and we'd all have very thick kneecaps. But what about sex? Not so easy, packed into a tube like that." Amanda shot him a dirty look. Dirty, but complicit: you could tell the same question had occurred to her.

Amanda herself wasn't very talkative. She was an image person, not a word person, she said: she claimed to think in pictures. That was fine with Jimmy, because a bit of synesthesia never went amiss.

"So what do you see when I do this?" he'd ask her, in their earliest, most ardent days.

"Flowers," she'd say. "Two or three. Pink."

"How about this? What do you see?"

"Red flowers. Red and purple. Five or six."

"How about this? Oh baby I love you!"

"Neon!" Afterwards she would sigh, and tell him, "That was the whole bouquet."

He was susceptible to those invisible flowers of hers: they were after all a tribute to his talents. She had a very fine ass too, and the tits were real, but – and he'd noticed this early – she was a little flinty around the eyes.

Amanda was from Texas, originally; she claimed to be able

to remember the place before it dried up and blew away, in which case, thought Jimmy, she was about ten years older than she made out. She'd been working for some time on a project called Vulture Sculptures. The idea was to take a truckload of large dead-animal parts to vacant fields or the parking lots of abandoned factories and arrange them in the shapes of words, wait until the vultures had descended and were tearing them apart, then photograph the whole scene from a helicopter. She'd attracted a lot of publicity at first, as well as a few sacks of hate mail and death threats from the God's Gardeners, and from isolated crazies. One of the letters was from Jimmy's old dorm roommate, Bernice, who'd cranked her rhetorical volume up considerably.

Then some wrinkly, corrupt old patron who'd made a couple of fortunes out of a string of heart-parts farms had given her a hefty grant, under the illusion that what she was doing was razor-sharp cutting-edge. This was good, said Amanda, because without that chunk of change she would have had to abandon her artwork: helicopters cost a lot of money, and then of course there was the security clearance. The Corpsmen were really anal about airspace, she said; they suspected everyone of wanting to nuke stuff from above, and you practically had to let them climb into your underpants before they'd let you fly anywhere in a hired copter, unless you were some graft-ridden prince from a Compound, that is.

The words she vulturized – her term – had to have four letters. She gave a great deal of thought to them: each letter of the alphabet had a vibe, a plus or minus charge, so the words had to be selected with care. Vulturizing brought them to life, was her concept, and then it killed them. It was a powerful process – "Like watching God thinking," she'd said on a Net Q&A. So far she'd done PAIN – a pun on her last name, as she'd pointed out in chat-room interviews – and WHOM, and then GUTS. She was having a hard time during the summer of Jimmy because she was blocked on the next word.

Finally, when Jimmy didn't think he could stand any more boiled spaghetti, and the sight of Amanda staring into space while chewing on a strand of her hair no longer brought on an attack of lust and rapture, he landed a job. It was with an outfit called AnooYoo, a minor Compound situated so close to one of the more dilapidated pleeblands that it might as well have been in it. Not too many people would work there if they'd had other choices, was what he felt on the day he went for the interview; which might have accounted for the slightly abject manner of the interviewers. He could bet they'd been rejected by a dozen or two job-hunters before him. Well, he beamed at them telepathically, I may not be what you had in mind, but at least I'm cheap.

What had impressed them, said the interviewers – there were two of them, a woman and a man – was his senior dissertation on self-help books of the twentieth century. One of their core products, they told him, was the improvement items – not books any more, of course, but the DVDs, the CD-ROMs, the Web sites, and so forth. It wasn't these instructionals as such that generated the cash surplus, they explained: it was the equipment and the alternative medicines you needed in order to get the optimum effect. Mind and body went hand in hand, and Jimmy's job would be to work on the mind end of things. In other words, the promotionals.

"What people want is perfection," said the man. "In themselves."

"But they need the steps to it to be pointed out," said the woman.

"In a simple order," said the man.

"With encouragement," said the woman. "And a positive attitude."

"They like to hear about the before and the after," said the man. "It's the art of the possible. But with no guarantees, of course."

"You showed great insight into the process," the woman said. "In your dissertation. We found it very mature."

"If you know one century, you know them all," said the man.

"But the adjectives change," said Jimmy. "Nothing's worse than last year's adjectives."

"Exactly!" said the man, as if Jimmy had just solved the riddle of the universe in one blinding flashbulb of light. He got a finger-cracking handshake from the man; from the woman he got a warm but vulnerable smile, which left him wondering whether or not she was married. The pay at AnooYoo wasn't that great, but there might be other advantages.

That evening he told Amanda Payne about his good fortune. She'd been carping about money lately – or not carping, but she'd inserted a few pointed remarks about pulling your own weight into the prolonged and intent silences that were her specialty – so he thought she'd be pleased. Things hadn't been that good in the sack lately, ever since his ChickieNobs blunder, in fact. Maybe they'd pick up now, in time for a heartfelt, plangent, and action-filled finale. Already he was rehearsing his exit lines: *I'm not what you need, you deserve better, I'll ruin your life*, and so forth. But it was best to work up to these things, so he elaborated on his new job.

"Now I'll be able to bring home the bacon," he concluded in what he hoped was a winsome but responsible tone.

Amanda wasn't impressed. "You're going to work where?" was her comment; point being, as it unfolded, that AnooYoo was a collection of cesspool denizens who existed for no other reason than to prey on the phobias and void the bank accounts of the anxious and the gullible. It seemed that Amanda, until recently, had had a friend who'd signed up for an AnooYoo five-month plan, touted as being able to cure depression, wrinkles, and insomnia all at the same time, and who'd pushed herself over the edge – actually, over the windowsill of her ten-storey-up apartment – on some kind of South American tree bark.

"I could always turn them down," said Jimmy, when this tale had been told. "I could join the ranks of the permanently unemployed. Or, hey, I could go on being a kept man, like now. Joke! Joke! Don't kill me!"

Amanda was more silent than ever for the next few days. Then she told him she'd unblocked herself artistically: the next key word for the Vulture Sculpture had come to her.

"And what's that?" said Jimmy, trying to sound interested.

She looked at him speculatively. "Love," she said.

AnooYoo

Jimmy moved into the junior apartment provided for him in the AnooYoo Compound: bedroom in an alcove, cramped kitchenette, reproduction 1950s furniture. As a dwelling place it was only a small step up from his dorm room at Martha Graham, but at least there was less insect life. He discovered quite soon that, corporately speaking, he was a drudge and a helot. He was to cudgel his brains and spend ten-hour days wandering the labyrinths of the thesaurus and cranking out the verbiage. Then those above would grade his offerings, hand them back for revision, hand them back again. *What we want is more . . . is less . . . that's not quite it.* But with time he improved, whatever that meant.

Cosmetic creams, workout equipment, Joltbars to build your muscle-scape into a breathtaking marvel of sculpted granite. Pills to make you fatter, thinner, hairier, balder, whiter, browner, blacker, yellower, sexier, and happier. It was his task to describe and extol, to present the vision of what – oh, so easily! – could come to be. Hope and fear, desire and revulsion, these were his stocks-in-trade, on these he rang his changes. Once in a while he'd make up a word

– *tensicity, fibracionous, pheromonimal* – but he never once got caught out. His proprietors liked those kinds of words in the small print on packages because they sounded scientific and had a convincing effect.

He should have been pleased by his success with these verbal fabrications, but instead he was depressed by it. The memos that came from above telling him he'd done a good job meant nothing to him because they'd been dictated by semi-literates; all they proved was that no one at AnooYoo was capable of appreciating how clever he had been. He came to understand why serial killers sent helpful clues to the police.

His social life was – for the first time in many years – a zero: he hadn't been stranded in such a sexual desert since he was eight. Amanda Payne shimmered in the past like a lost lagoon, its crocodiles for the moment forgotten. Why had he abandoned her so casually? Because he'd been looking forward to the next in the series. But the woman interviewer from AnooYoo about whom he'd had such hopes was never seen again, and the other women he encountered, at the office or in the AnooYoo bars, were either mean-minded eye-the-target sharks or so emotionally starved even Jimmy avoided them as if they were quagmires. He was reduced to flirting with waitpersons, and even they turned a cold shoulder. They'd seen fast-talking youngsters like him before, they knew he had no status.

In the company café he was a new boy, alone once more, starting over. He took to eating SoyOBoy burgers in the Compound mall, or taking out a greasy box of ChickieNobs Nubbins to munch on while working overtime at his computer terminal. Every week there was a Compound social barbecue, a comprehensive ratfuck that all employees were expected to attend. These were dire occasions for Jimmy. He lacked the energy to work the crowd, he was fresh out of innocuous drivel; he loitered on the edges gnawing on a burned soydog and silently ripping apart everyone within eyesight. *Saggy boobs*, ran the thought balloon in his head. *Bunfaced tofubrain. Thumbsucking posterboy. Fridgewoman. Sell his granny. Wobble-bummed bovine. Bladderheaded jerk.*

He got the occasional e-mail from his father; an e-birthday card perhaps, a few days later than his real birthday, something with dancing pigoons on it, as if he were still eleven. *Happy Birthday, Jimmy, May All Your Dreams Come True*. Ramona would write him chatty, dutiful messages: no baby brother for him yet, she'd say, but they were still "working on it." He did not wish to visualize the hormone-sodden, potion-ridden, gel-slathered details of such work. If nothing "natural" happened soon, she said, they'd try "something else" from one of the agencies – Infantade, Foetility, Perfectababe, one of those. Things had changed a lot in the field since Jimmy came along! (*Came along*, as if he hadn't actually been born, but had just sort of dropped by for a visit.) She was doing her "research," because of course they wanted the best for their money.

Terrific, thought Jimmy. They'd have a few trial runs, and if the kids from those didn't measure up they'd recycle them for the parts, until at last they got something that fit all their specs – perfect in every way, not only a math whiz but beautiful as the dawn. Then they'd load this hypothetical wonderkid up with their bloated expectations until the poor tyke burst under the strain. Jimmy didn't envy him.

(He envied him.)

Ramona invited Jimmy for the holidays, but he had no wish to go, so he pleaded overwork. Which was the truth, in a way, as he'd come to see his job as a challenge: how outrageous could he get, in the realm of fatuous neologism, and still achieve praise?

After a while he was granted a promotion. Then he could buy new toys. He got himself a better DVD player, a gym suit that cleaned itself overnight due to sweat-eating bacteria, a shirt that displayed e-mail on its sleeve while giving him a little nudge every time he had a message, shoes that changed colour to match his outfits, a talking toaster. Well, it was company. *Jimmy, your toast is done.* He upgraded to a better apartment.

Now that he was climbing up the ladder he found a woman, and then another one, and another one after that. He no longer thought of these women as girlfriends: now they were lovers. They were all married or the equivalent, looking for a chance to sneak around on their husbands or partners, to prove they were still young or else to get even. Or else they were wounded and wanted consolation. Or they simply felt ignored.

There was no reason he couldn't have several of them at once, as long as he was conscientious about his scheduling. At first he enjoyed the rushed impromptu visits, the secrecy, the sound of Velcro ripped open in haste, the slow tumbling onto the floor; though he figured out pretty soon that he was an extra for these lovers – not to be taken seriously, but instead to be treasured like some child's free gift dug out of a box of cereal, colourful and delightful but useless: the joker among the twos and threes they'd been dealt in their real lives. He was merely a pastime for them, as they were for him, though for them there was more at stake: a divorce, or a spate of non-routine violence; at the least, a dollop of verbal uproar if they got caught.

One good thing, they never told him to grow up. He suspected they kind of liked it that he hadn't.

None of them wanted to leave their husbands and settle down with him, or to run away to the pleeblands with him, not that this was very possible any more. The pleeblands were said to have become ultra-hazardous for those who didn't know their way around out there, and the CorpSeCorps security at the Compound gates was tighter than ever.

Garage

So this was the rest of his life. It felt like a party to which he'd been invited, but at an address he couldn't actually locate. Someone must be having fun at it, this life of his; only, right at the moment, it wasn't him.

His body had always been easy to maintain, but now he had to work at it. If he skipped the gym he'd develop flab overnight, where none was before. His energy level was sinking, and he had to watch his Joltbar intake: too many steroids could shrink your dick, and though it said on the package that this problem had been fixed due to the addition of some unpronounceable patented compound, he'd written enough package copy not to believe this. His hair was getting sparser around the temples, despite the six-week AnooYoo follicle-regrowth course he'd done. He ought to have known it was a scam – he'd put together the ads for it – but they were such good ads he'd convinced even himself. He found himself wondering what shape Crake's hairline was in.

Crake had graduated early, done post-grad work, then written his own ticket. He was at RejoovenEsense now – one of the most powerful Compounds of them all – and climbing fast. At first the two of them had continued to keep in touch by e-mail. Crake spoke vaguely of a special project he was doing, something white-hot. He'd been given carte blanche, he said; the sun shone out of his bum as far as the top brass were concerned. Jimmy should come and visit some time and he'd show him around. What was it that Jimmy was doing, again?

Jimmy countered with a suggestion that they play chess.

Crake's next news was that Uncle Pete had died suddenly. Some virus. Whatever it was had gone through him like shit through a goose. It was like watching pink sorbet on a barbecue – instant meltdown. Sabotage was suspected, but nothing had been proved.

Were you there? asked Jimmy.

In a manner of speaking, said Crake.

Jimmy pondered this; then he asked if anyone else had caught the virus. Crake said no.

As time went by, the intervals between their messages became longer and longer, the thread connecting them stretched thinner. What did they have to say to each other? Jimmy's wordserf job was surely one that Crake would despise, though affably, and Crake's pursuits might not be something Jimmy could understand any more. He realized he was thinking of Crake as someone he used to know.

Increasingly he was restless. Even sex was no longer what it had once been, though he was still as addicted to it as ever. He felt jerked around by his own dick, as if the rest of him was merely an inconsequential knob that happened to be attached to one end of it. Maybe the thing would be happier if left to roam around on its own.

On the evenings when none of his lovers had managed to lie to their husbands or equivalents well enough to spend time with him, he might go to a movie at the mall, just to convince himself he was part of a group of other people. Or he'd watch the news: more plagues, more famines, more floods, more insect or microbe or small-mammal outbreaks, more droughts, more chickenshit boy-soldier wars in distant countries. Why was everything so much like itself?

There were the usual political assassinations out there in the pleebs, the usual strange accidents, the unexplained disappearances. Or there were sex scandals: sex scandals always got the newscasters excited. For a while it was sports coaches and little boys; then there was a wave of adolescent girls found locked in garages. These girls were said – by those who had done the locking – to be working as maids, and to have been brought from their squalid countries-of-origin for their own good. Being locked in the garage was for the protection of these girls, said the men – respectable men, accountants, lawyers, merchants dealing in patio furniture – who were dragged into court to defend themselves. Frequently their wives backed them up. These girls, said the wives, had been practically adopted, and were treated almost like one of the family. Jimmy loved those two words: *practically, almost.*

The girls themselves told other stories, not all of them credible. They'd been drugged, said some. They'd been made to perform obscene contortions in unlikely venues, such as pet shops. They'd been rowed across the Pacific Ocean on rubber rafts, they'd been smuggled in container ships, hidden in mounds of soy products. They'd been made to commit sacrilegious acts involving reptiles. On the other hand, some of these girls seemed content with their situations. The garages were nice, they said, better than what they'd had at home. The meals were regular. The work wasn't too hard. It was true they weren't paid and they couldn't go out anywhere, but there was nothing different or surprising to them about that.

One of these girls – found locked in a garage in San Francisco, at the home of a prosperous pharmacist – said she used to be in movies, but was glad she'd been sold to her Mister, who had seen her on the Net and had felt sorry for her, and had come in person to fetch her and had paid a lot of cash to rescue her, and had flown with her on a plane across the ocean, and had promised to send her to school once her English was good enough. She refused to say anything negative about the man; she appeared to be simple, truthful, and sincere. When asked why the garage was locked, she said it was so nobody bad could get in. When asked what she did in there, she said she studied English and watched TV. When asked how she felt about her captor, she said she would always be grateful to him. The prosecution failed to shake her testimony, and the guy got off scot-free, although he was ordered to send her to school immediately. She said she wanted to study child psychology.

There was a close-up of her, of her beautiful cat's face, her delicate smile. Jimmy thought he recognized her. He froze her image, then unpacked his old printout, the one from when he was fourteen – he'd kept it with him through all his moves, almost like a family photo, out of sight but never discarded, tucked in among his Martha Graham Academy transcripts. He compared the faces, but a lot of time had gone by since then. That girl, the eight-year-old in the printout, must be seventeen, eighteen, nineteen by now, and the one from the news broadcast seemed a lot younger. But the look was the same: the same blend of innocence and contempt and understanding. It made him feel light-headed, precariously balanced, as if he were standing on a cliff-edge above a rock-filled gorge, and it would be dangerous for him to look down.

Gripless

The CorpSeCorps had never lost sight of Jimmy. During his time at Martha Graham they'd hauled him in regularly, four times a year, for what they called *little talks*. They'd ask him the same questions they'd already asked a dozen times, just to see if they got the same answers. *I don't know* was the safest thing Jimmy could think of to say, which most of the time was accurate enough.

After a while they'd taken to showing him pictures – stills from buttonhole snoop cameras, or black-and-whites that looked as if they'd been pulled off the security vidcocams at pleebland bank ATMs, or news-channel footage of this or that: demonstrations, riots, executions. The game was to see if he recognized any of the faces. They'd have him wired up, so even if he pretended ignorance they'd catch the spikes of neural electricity he wouldn't be able to control. He'd kept waiting for the Happicuppa caper in Maryland to turn up, the one with his mother in it – he dreaded that – but it never showed.

He hadn't received any foreign postcards for a long time.

*

After he'd gone to work at AnooYoo, the Corpsmen appeared to have forgotten about him. But no, they were just paying out the rope – seeing if he, or else the other side, meaning his mother, would use his new position, his dollop of extra freedom, to try to make contact again. After a year or so, there was the familiar knocking on the door. He always knew it was them because they never used the intercom first, they must have had some kind of bypass, not to mention the door code. *Hello, Jimmy, how ya doing, we just need to ask you a few questions, see if you can help us out a little here.*

Sure, be glad to.

Attaboy.

And so it went.

In – what? – his fifth year at AnooYoo, they finally hit pay dirt. He'd been looking at their pictures for a couple of hours by then. Shots of a boondocks war in some arid mountain range across the ocean, with close-ups of dead mercenaries, male and female; a bunch of aid workers getting mauled by the starving in one of those dusty famines far away; a row of heads on poles – that was in the ex-Argentine, said the CorpSeCorps, though they didn't say whose heads they were or how they'd got onto the poles. Several women going through a supermarket checkout, all in sunglasses. A dozen bodies sprawled on the floor after a raid on a God's Gardeners safe house – that outfit was outlawed now – and one of them sure looked a lot like his old roomie, the incendiary Bernice. He said so, being a good boy, and got a pat on the back, but obviously they'd known that already because they weren't interested. He felt bad about Bernice: she'd been a nut and a nuisance, but she hadn't deserved to die like that.

A lineup of mug shots from a Sacramento prison. The driver's licence photo from a suicide car-bomber. (But if the car had blown up, how had they come by the licence?) Three pantiless waitresses from a pleebland no-touching nookie bar – they threw that in for fun, and it did cause a waver on the neural monitor, unnatural if it hadn't, and smiles and chuckles all round. A riot scene Jimmy recognized from a movie remake of *Frankenstein*. They always put in a few tricks like that to keep him on his toes.

Then more mug shots. *Nope*, said Jimmy. *Nope, nope, nothing*.

Then came what looked like a routine execution. No horseplay, no prisoners breaking free, no foul language: by this Jimmy knew before he saw her that it was a woman they were erasing. Then came the figure in the loose grey prison clothing shuffling along, hair tied back, wrists handcuffed, the female guard to either side, the blindfold. Shooting by spraygun, it was going to be. No need for a firing squad, one spraygun would have done, but they kept the old custom, five in a row, so no single executioner need lose sleep over whose virtual bullet had killed first.

Shooting was only for treason. Otherwise it was gas, or hanging, or the big brainfrizz.

A man's voice, words coming from outside the shot: the Corpsmen had the sound turned down because they wanted Jimmy to concentrate on the visuals, but it must have been an order because now the guards were taking off the blindfold. Pan to close-up: the woman was looking right at him, right out of the frame: a blue-eyed look, direct, defiant, patient, wounded. But no tears. Then the sound came suddenly up. *Goodbye. Remember Killer. I love you. Don't let me down*.

No question, it was his mother. Jimmy was shocked by how old she'd become: her skin was lined, her mouth withered. Was it the hard living she'd been doing on the run, or was it bad treatment? How long had she been in prison, in their grip? What had they been doing to her?

Wait, he wanted to yell, but that was that, pullback shot, eyes covered again, zap zap zap. Bad aim, red spurts, they almost took her head off. Long shot of her crumpling to the ground.

"Anything there, Jimmy?"

"Nope. Sorry. Nothing." How could she have foreseen he'd be looking?

They must have picked up the heartbeat, the surge of energy. After a few neutral questions – "Want a coffee? Need a leak?" – one of them said, "So, who was this killer?"

"Killer," Jimmy said. He began to laugh. "Killer was a skunk." There, he'd done it. Another betrayal. He couldn't help himself.

"Not a nice guy, eh? Some sort of biker?"

"No," said Jimmy, laughing more. "You don't get it. A skunk. A rakunk. An animal." He put his head down on his two fists, weeping with laughter. Why did she have to drag Killer into it? So he'd know it was really her, that's why. So he'd believe her. But what did she mean about letting her down?

"Sorry about that, son," said the older of the two Corpsmen. "We just had to be sure."

It didn't occur to Jimmy to ask when the execution had taken place. Afterwards, he realized it might have been years ago. What if the whole thing was a fake? It could even have been digital, at least the shots, the spurts of blood, the falling down. Maybe his mother was still alive, maybe she was even still at large. If so, what had he given away?

★

The next few weeks were the worst he could remember. Too many things were coming back to him, too much of what he'd lost, or – sadder – had never had in the first place. All that wasted time, and he didn't even know who'd wasted it.

He was angry most days. At first he sought out his various lovers, but he was moody with them, he failed to be entertaining, and worse, he'd lost interest in the sex. He stopped answering their e-messages – *Is anything wrong, was it something I did, how can I help* – and didn't return their calls: explaining wasn't worth it. In earlier days he would have made his mother's death into a psychodrama, harvested some sympathy, but that wasn't what he wanted now.

What did he want?

He went to the Compound singles bar; no joy there, he already knew most of those women, he didn't need their neediness. He went back to Internet porn, found it had lost its bloom: it was repetitive, mechanical, devoid of its earlier allure. He searched the Web for the HottTotts site, hoping that something familiar would help him to feel less isolated, but it was defunct.

He was drinking alone now, at night, a bad sign. He shouldn't be doing that, it only depressed him, but he had to dull the pain. The pain of what? The pain of the raw torn places, the damaged membranes where he'd whanged up against the Great Indifference of the Universe. One big shark's mouth, the universe. Row after row of razor-sharp teeth.

He knew he was faltering, trying to keep his footing. Everything in his life was temporary, ungrounded. Language itself had lost its solidity; it had become thin, contingent, slippery, a viscid film on which he was sliding around like an eyeball on a plate. An eyeball that could still see, however. That was the trouble.

He remembered himself as carefree, earlier, in his youth. Carefree, thick-skinned, skipping light-footed over the surfaces, whistling in the dark, able to get through anything. Turning a blind eye. Now he found himself wincing away. The smallest setbacks were major – a lost sock, a jammed electric toothbrush. Even the sunrise was blinding. He was being rubbed all over with sandpaper. "Get a grip," he told himself. "Get a handle on it. Put it behind you. Move forward. Make a new you."

Such positive slogans. Such bland inspirational promotions vomit. What he really wanted was revenge. But against whom, and for what? Even if he had the energy for it, even if he could focus and aim, such a thing would be less than useless.

On the worst nights he'd call up Alex the parrot, long dead by then but still walking and talking on the Net, and watch him go through his paces. Handler: *What colour is the round ball, Alex? The round* ball*?* Alex, head on side, thinking: *Blue.* Handler: *Good boy!* Alex: *Cork-nut, cork-nut!* Handler: *There you are!* Then Alex would be given a cob of baby corn, which wasn't what he'd asked for, he'd asked for an almond. Seeing this would bring tears to Jimmy's eyes.

Then he'd stay up too late, and once in bed he'd stare at the ceiling, telling over his lists of obsolete words for the comfort that was in them. *Dibble. Aphasia. Breast plough. Enigma. Gat.* If Alex the parrot were his, they'd be friends, they'd be brothers. He'd teach him more words. *Knell. Kern. Alack.*

But there was no longer any comfort in the words. There was nothing in them. It no longer delighted Jimmy to possess these small collections of letters that other people had forgotten about. It was like having his own baby teeth in a box.

At the edge of sleep a procession would appear behind his eyes, moving out of the shadows to the left, crossing his field of vision. Young slender girls with small hands, ribbons in their hair, bearing garlands of many-coloured flowers. The field would be green, but it wasn't a pastoral scene: these were girls in danger, in need of rescue. There was something – a threatening presence – behind the trees.

Or perhaps the danger was in him. Perhaps he was the danger, a fanged animal gazing out from the shadowy cave of the space inside his own skull.

Or it might be the girls themselves that were dangerous. There was always that possibility. They could be a bait, a trap. He knew they were much older than they appeared to be, and much more powerful as well. Unlike himself they had a ruthless wisdom.

The girls were calm, they were grave and ceremonious. They'd look at him, they'd look into him, they would recognize and accept him, accept his darknesses. Then they would smile.

Oh honey, I know you. I see you. I know what you want.

11

Pigoons

Jimmy's in the kitchen of the house they lived in when he was five, sitting at the table. It's lunchtime. In front of him on a plate is a round of bread – a flat peanut butter head with a gleaming jelly smile, raisins for teeth. This thing fills him with dread. Any minute now his mother will come into the room. But no, she won't: her chair is empty. She must have made his lunch and left it for him. But where has she gone, where is she?

There's a scraping sound; it's coming from the wall. There's someone on the other side, digging a hole through, breaking in. He looks at that part of the wall, below the clock with the different birds marking the hours. *Hoot hoot hoot*, says the robin. He'd done that, he'd altered the clock – the owl says *caw caw*, the crow says *cheerup, cheerup*. But that clock wasn't there when he was five, they'd got it later. Something's wrong, the time's wrong, he can't tell what it is, he's paralyzed with fright. The plaster begins to crumble, and he wakes up.

He hates these dreams. The present's bad enough without the past getting mixed into it. *Live in the moment*. He'd put that on a giveaway calendar once, some fraudulent sex-enhancement product for women. Why chain your body to the clock, you can break the shackles of time, and so on and so forth. The picture was of a woman with wings, taking flight from a pile of dirty old wrinkled cloth, or possibly skin.

So here it is then, the moment, this one, the one he's supposed to be living in. His head's on a hard surface, his body's crammed into a chair, he's one big spasm. He stretches, yelps with pain.

It takes him a minute to place himself. Oh yes – the tornado, the gatehouse. All is quiet, no puffs of wind, no howling. Is it the same afternoon, or the night, or the next morning? There's light in the room, daylight; it's coming in through the window over the counter, the bulletproof window with the intercom, where once upon a time, long long ago, you'd had to state your business. The slot for your micro-coded documents, the twenty-four-hour videocam, the talking smiley-faced box that would put you through the Q&A – the whole mechanism is literally shot to hell. Grenades, possibly. There's a lot of fallen rubble.

The scraping continues: there's something in the corner of the room. He can't make it out at first: it looks like a skull. Then he sees it's a land crab, a rounded white-yellow shell as big as a shrunken head, with one giant pincer. It's enlarging a hole in the rubble. "What the shit are you doing in here?" he asks it. "You're supposed to be outside, ruining the gardens." He throws the empty bourbon bottle at it, misses; the bottle shatters. That was a stupid thing to do, now there's broken glass. The land crab whips around to face him, big pincer up, then backs into its half-dug hole, where it sits watching him. It must have come in here to escape the twister, just as he did, and now it can't find its way out.

He unwinds himself from the chair, looking first for snakes and rats and any other thing he might not wish to step on. Then he drops the candle end and the matches into his plastic bag and walks carefully over to the doorway leading into the front reception area. He pulls the door shut behind him: he doesn't want any crab attacks from the back.

At the outer doorway he pauses to reconnoitre. No animals about, apart from a trio of crows perched on the rampart. They exchange a few caws, of which he is probably the subject. The sky is the pearly grey-pink of early morning, hardly a cloud in it. The landscape has been rearranged since yesterday: more pieces of detached metal sheeting than before, more uprooted trees. Leaves and torn fronds litter the muddy ground.

If he sets out now he'll have a good chance of making it to the central mall before mid-morning. Although his stomach is growling, he'll have to wait till he gets there to have breakfast. He wishes he had some cashews left, but there's only the SoyOBoy sardines, which he's saving as a last resort.

The air is cool and fresh, the scent of crushed leaves luxurious after the dank, decaying smell of the gatehouse. He inhales with pleasure, then sets off in the direction of the mall. Three blocks along he stops: seven pigoons have materialized from nowhere. They're staring at him, ears forward. Are they the same as yesterday's? As he watches, they begin to amble in his direction.

They have something in mind, all right. He turns, heads

back towards the gatehouse, quickens his pace. They're far enough away so he can run if he has to. He looks over his shoulder: they're trotting now. He speeds up, breaks into a jog. Then he spots another group through the gateway up ahead, eight or nine of them, coming towards him across No Man's Land. They're almost at the main gate, cutting him off in that direction. It's as if they've had it planned, between the two groups; as if they've known for some time that he was in the gatehouse and have been waiting for him to come out, far enough out so they can surround him.

He reaches the gatehouse, goes through the doorway, pulls the door shut. It doesn't latch. The electronic lock is nonfunctional, of course.

"Of course!" he shouts. They'll be able to lever it open, pry with their trotters or snouts. They were always escape artists, the pigoons: if they'd had fingers they'd have ruled the world. He runs through the next doorway into the reception area, slams the door behind him. That lock's kaput as well, oh naturally. He shoves the desk he's just slept on up against the door, looks out through the bulletproof window: here they come. They've nosed the door open, they're in the first room now, twenty or thirty of them, boars and sows but the boars foremost, crowding in, grunting eagerly, snuffling at his footprints. Now one of them spots him through the window. More grunting: now they're all looking up at him. What they see is his head, attached to what they know is a delicious meat pie just waiting to be opened up. The two biggest ones, two boars, with – yes – sharp tusks, move side by side to the door, bumping it with their shoulders. Team players, the pigoons. There's a lot of muscle out there.

If they can't push through the door they'll wait him out. They'll take it in relays, some grazing outside, others watching.

They can keep it up forever, they'll starve him out. They can smell him in there, smell his flesh.

Now he remembers to check for the land crab, but it's gone. It must have backed all the way into its burrow. That's what he needs, a burrow of his own. A burrow, a shell, some pincers.

"So," he says out loud. "What next?"

Honey, you're fucked.

Radio

After an interval of blankness during which nothing at all occurs to him, Snowman gets up out of the chair. He can't remember having sat down in it but he must have done. His guts are cramping, he must be really scared, though he doesn't feel it; he's quite calm. The door is moving in time to the pushing and thumping from the other side; it won't be long before the pigoons break through. He takes the flashlight out of his plastic bag, turns it on, goes back to the inner room where the two guys in the biosuits are lying on the floor. He shines all around. There are three closed doors; he must have seen them last night, but last night he wasn't trying to get out.

Two of the doors don't move when he tries them; they must be locked somehow, or blocked on the other side. The third one opens easily. There, like sudden hope, is a flight of stairs. Steep stairs. Pigoons, it occurs to him, have short legs and fat stomachs. The opposite of himself.

He scrambles up the stairs so fast he trips on his flowered sheet. From behind him comes an excited grunting and squealing, and then a crash as the desk topples over.

He emerges into a bright oblong space. What is it? The watchtower. Of course. He ought to have known that. There's a watchtower on either side of the main gate, and other towers all the way around the rampart wall. Inside the towers are the searchlights, the monitor videocams, the loudspeakers, the controls for locking the gates, the tear-gas nozzles, the long-range sprayguns. Yes, here are the screens, here are the controls: find the target, zero in on it, push the button. You never needed to see the actual results, the splatter and fizzle, not in the flesh. During the period of chaos the guards probably fired on the crowd from up here while they still could, and while there was still a crowd.

None of this high-tech stuff is working now, of course. He looks for manually operated backups – it would be fine to be able to mow down the pigoons from above – but no, there's nothing.

Beside the wall of dead screens there's a little window: from it he has a bird's-eye view of the pigoons, the group of them that's posted outside the checkpoint cubicle door. They look at ease. If they were guys, they'd be having a smoke and shooting the shit. Alert, though; on the lookout. He pulls back: he doesn't want them to see him, see that he's up here.

Not that they don't know already. They must have figured out by now that he went up the stairs. But do they also know they've got him trapped? Because there's no way out of here that he can see.

He's in no immediate danger – they can't climb the stairs or they'd have done it by now. There's time to explore and regroup. *Regroup*, what an idea. There's only one of him.

The guards must have taken catnaps up here, turn and turn about: there's a couple of standard-issue cots in a side room. Nobody in them, no bodies. Maybe the guards tried to get out of RejoovenEsense, just like everyone else. Maybe they too had hoped they could outrun contagion.

One of the beds is made, the other not. A digital voice-operated alarm clock is still flashing beside the unmade bed. "What's the time?" he asks it, but he gets no answer. He'll have to reprogram the thing, set it to his own voice.

The guys were well equipped: twin entertainment centres, with the screens, the players, the headphones attached. Clothes hanging on hooks, the standard off-duty tropicals; a used towel on the floor, ditto a sock. A dozen downloaded printouts on one of the night tables. A skinny girl wearing nothing but high-heeled sandals and standing on her head; a blonde dangling from a hook in the ceiling in some kind of black-leather multiple-fracture truss, blindfolded but with her mouth sagging open in a hit-me-again drool; a big woman with huge breast implants and wet red lipstick, bending over and sticking out her pierced tongue. Same old stuff.

The guys must have left in a hurry. Maybe it's them downstairs, the ones in the biosuits. That would make sense. Nobody seems to have come up here though, after the two of them left; or if they did, there'd been nothing they'd wanted to take.

In one of the night-table drawers there's a pack of cigarettes, only a couple gone. Snowman taps one out – damp, but right now he'd smoke pocket fluff – and looks around for a way to light it. He has matches in his garbage bag, but where is it? He must've dropped it on the stairs in his rush to get up here. He goes back to the stairwell, looks down. There's the bag all right, four stairs from the bottom. He starts cautiously downward. As he's stretching out his hand, something lunges. He jumps up out of reach, watches while the pigoon slithers back down, then launches itself again. Its eyes gleam in the half-light; he has the impression it's grinning.

They were waiting for him, using the garbage bag as bait. They must have been able to tell there was something in it he'd want, that he'd come down to get. Cunning, so cunning. His legs are shaking by the time he reaches the top level again.

Off the nap room is a small bathroom, with a real toilet in it. Just in time: fear has homogenized his bowels. He takes a dump – there's paper, a small mercy, no need for leaves – and is about to flush when he reasons that the tank at the back must be full of water, and it's water he may need. He lifts the tank top: sure enough, it's full, a mini-oasis. The water is a reddish colour but it smells okay, so he sticks his head down and drinks like a dog. After all that adrenalin, he's parched.

Now he feels better. No need to panic, no need to panic yet. In the kitchenette he finds matches and lights the cigarette. After a couple of drags he feels dizzy, but still it's wonderful.

"If you were ninety and you had the chance for one last fuck but you knew it would kill you, would you still do it?" Crake asked him once.

"You bet," said Jimmy.

"Addict," said Crake.

Snowman finds himself humming as he goes through the kitchen cupboards. Chocolate in squares, real chocolate. A jar of instant coffee, ditto coffee whitener, ditto sugar. Shrimp paste for spreading on crackers, ersatz but edible.

Cheese food in a tube, ditto mayo. Noodle soup with vegetables, chicken flavour. Crackers in a plastic snap-top. A stash of Joltbars. What a bonanza.

He braces himself, then opens the refrigerator, betting on the fact that these guys wouldn't have kept too much real food in there, so the stench won't be too repulsive. Frozen meat gone bad in a melted freezer unit is the worst; he came across quite a lot of that in the early days of rummaging through the pleeblands.

There's nothing too smelly; just a shrivelled apple, an orange covered with grey fur. Two bottles of beer, unopened – real beer! The bottles are brown, with thin retro necks.

He opens a beer, downs half of it. Warm, but who cares? Then he sits down at the table and eats the shrimp paste, the crackers, the cheese food and the mayo, finishing off with a spoonful of coffee powder mixed with whitener and sugar. He saves the noodle soup and the chocolate and the Joltbars for later.

In one of the cupboards there's a windup radio. He can remember when those things started being doled out, in case of tornadoes or floods or anything else that might disrupt the electronics. His parents had one when they were still his parents; he used to play with it on the sly. It had a handle that turned to recharge the batteries, it would run for half an hour.

This one looks undamaged, so he cranks the thing up. He doesn't expect to hear anything, but expectation isn't the same as desire.

White noise, more white noise, more white noise. He tries the AM bands, then the FM. Nothing. Just that sound, like the sound of starlight scratching its way through outer space: *kkkkkkkk*. Then he tries the short-wave. He moves the dial slowly and carefully. Maybe there are other countries, distant countries, where the people may have escaped – New Zealand, Madagascar, Patagonia – places like that.

They wouldn't have escaped though. Or most of them wouldn't. Once it got started, the thing was airborne. Desire and fear were universal, between them they'd been the gravediggers.

Kkkkk. Kkkkk. Kkkkk.

Oh, talk to me, he prays. Say something. Say anything.

Suddenly there's an answer. It's a voice, a human voice. Unfortunately it's speaking some language that sounds like Russian.

Snowman can't believe his ears. He's not the only one then – someone else has made it through, someone of his own species. Someone who knows how to work a short-wave transmitter. And if one, then likely others. But this one isn't much use to Snowman, he's too far away.

Dickhead! He's forgotten about the CB function. That was what they'd been told to use, in emergencies. If there's anyone close by, the CB is what they'd be doing.

He turns the dial. *Receive*, is what he'll try.

Kkkkkk.

Then, faintly, a man's voice: "Is anyone reading me? Anyone out there? Do you read me? Over."

Snowman fumbles with the buttons. How to send? He's forgotten. Where is the fucker?

"I'm here! I'm here!" he shouts.

Back to *Receive*. Nothing.

Already he's having second thoughts. Was that too hasty of him? How does he know who's at the other end? Quite possibly no one he'd care to have lunch with. Still, he feels buoyant, elated almost. There are more possibilities now.

Rampart

Snowman's been so entranced – by the excitement, the food, the voices on the radio – that he's forgotten about the cut on his foot. Now it's reminding him: there's a jabbing sensation, like a thorn. He sits down at the kitchen table, pulls the foot up as high as he can to examine it. Looks like there's a sliver of bourbon-bottle glass still in there. He picks and squeezes and wishes he had some tweezers, or longer fingernails. Finally he gets a grip on the tiny shard, then pulls. There's pain but not much blood.

Once he's got the glass piece out he washes the cut with a little of the beer, then hobbles into the bathroom and rummages in the medicine cabinet. Nothing of use, apart from a tube of sunblock – no good for cuts – some out-of-date antibiotic ointment, which he smears on the wound, and the dregs of a bottle of shaving lotion that smells like fake lemons. He pours that on too, because there must be alcohol in it. Maybe he should hunt for some drain cleaner or something, but he doesn't want to go too far, fry the entire foot sole. He'll just have to cross his fingers, wish for luck: an infected foot would slow him right down. He shouldn't have neglected the cut for so long, the floor downstairs must be percolating with germs.

In the evening he watches the sunset, through the narrow slit of the tower window. How glorious it must have been when all ten of the videocam screens were on and you could get the full panoramic view, turn up the colour brightness, enhance the red tones. Toke up, sit back, drift on cloud nine. As it is the screens turn their blind eyes towards him, so he has to make do with the real thing, just a slice of it, tangerine, then flamingo, then watered-down blood, then strawberry ice cream, off to the side of where the sun must be.

In the fading pink light the pigoons waiting for him down below look like miniature plastic figurines, bucolic replicas from a child's playbox. They have the rosy tint of innocence, as many things do at a distance. It's hard to imagine that they wish him ill.

Night falls. He lies down on one of the cots in the bedroom, the bed that's made. Where I'm lying now, a dead man used to sleep, he thinks. He never saw it coming. He had no clue. Unlike Jimmy, who'd had clues, who ought to have seen but didn't. If I'd killed Crake earlier, thinks Snowman, would it have made any difference?

The place is too hot and stuffy, though he's managed to pry the emergency air vents open. He can't get to sleep right away, so he lights one of the candles – it's in a tin container with a lid, survival supplies, you're supposed to be able to boil soup on those things – and smokes another cigarette. This time it doesn't make him so dizzy. Every habit he's ever had is still there in his body, lying dormant like flowers in the desert. Given the right conditions, all his old addictions would burst into full and luxuriant bloom.

He thumbs through the sex-site printouts. The women aren't his type – too bulgy, too altered, too obvious. Too much leer and mascara, too much cowlike tongue. Dismay is what he feels, not lust.

Revision: dismayed lust.

"How could you," he murmurs to himself, not for the first time, as he couples in his head with a rent-a-slut decked out in a red Chinese silk halter and six-inch heels, a dragon tattooed on her bum.

Oh sweetie.

In the small hot room he dreams; again, it's his mother. No, he never dreams about his mother, only about her absence. He's in the kitchen. Whuff, goes the wind in his ear, a door closing. On a hook her dressing gown is hanging, magenta, empty, frightening.

He wakes with his heart pounding. He remembers now that after she'd left he'd put it on, that dressing gown. It still smelled of her, of the jasmine-based perfume she used to wear. He'd looked at himself in the mirror, his boy's head with its cool practised fish-eye stare topping a neck that led down into that swaddling of female-coloured fabric. How much he'd hated her at that moment. He could hardly breathe, he'd been suffocating with hatred, tears of hatred had been rolling down his cheeks. But he'd hugged his arms around himself all the same.

Her arms.

★

He's set the alarm on the voice-operated digital clock for an hour before dawn, guessing when that must be. "Rise and shine," the clock says in a seductive female voice. "Rise and shine. Rise and shine."

"Stop," he says, and it stops.

"Do you want music?"

"No," he says, because although he's tempted to lie in bed and interact with the woman in the clock – it would be almost like a conversation – he has to get a move on today. How long has he been away from the shore, from the Crakers? He counts on his fingers: day one, the hike to RejoovenEsense, the twister; day two, trapped by the pigoons. This must be the third day then.

Outside the window there's a mouse-grey light. He pisses into the kitchen sink, splashes water onto his face from the toilet tank. He shouldn't have drunk that stuff yesterday without boiling it. He boils up a potful now – there's still gas for the propane burner – and washes his foot, a little red around the cut but nothing to freak about, and makes himself a cup of instant coffee with lots of sugar and whitener. He chews up a Three-Fruit Joltbar, savouring the familiar taste of banana oil and sweetened varnish, and feels the energy surge.

Somewhere in all the running around yesterday he lost his water bottle, just as well considering what was in it. Bird dung, mosquito wrigglers, nematodes. He fills up an empty beer bottle with boiled water, then snaffles a standard-issue micro-fibre laundry bag from the bedroom, into which he packs the water, all the sugar he can find, and the half-dozen Joltbars. He rubs on sunblock and bags the rest of the tube, and puts on a lightweight khaki shirt. There's a pair of sunglasses too, so he discards his old single-eyed ones. He deliberates over a pair of shorts, but they're too big around the waist and wouldn't protect the backs of his legs, so he hangs on to his flowered sheet, doubling it over, knotting it like a sarong. On second thoughts he takes it off and packs it into the laundry bag: it might snag on something while he's in transit, he can put it back on later. He replaces his lost aspirin and candles, and throws in six small boxes of matches and a paring knife, and his authentic-replica Red Sox baseball cap. He wouldn't want to have that fall off during the great escape.

There. Not too heavy. Now to break out.

He tries smashing the kitchen window – he could lower himself down onto the Compound rampart with the bedsheet he's torn into strips and twisted – but no luck: the glass is attack-proof. The narrow window overlooking the gateway is out of the question, as even if he could get through it there'd be a sheer drop into a herd of slavering pigoons. There's a small window in the bathroom, high up, but it too is on the pigoon side.

After three hours of painstaking labour and with the aid of – initially – a kitchen stepstool, a corkscrew, and a table knife, and – ultimately – a hammer and a battery-operated screwdriver he found at the back of the utility closet, he manages to disassemble the emergency air vent and dislodge the mechanism inside it. The vent leads up like a chimney, then there's a bend to the side. He thinks he's skinny enough to fit through – semi-starvation has its advantages – though if he gets stuck he'll die an agonizing and also ludicrous death. Cooked in an air vent, very funny. He ties one end of his improvised rope to a leg of the kitchen table – happily it's bolted to the floor – and winds the rest around his waist. He attaches his bag of supplies to the end of a second rope. Holding his breath, he squeezes in, torques his body, wriggles. Lucky he's not a woman, the wide butt would foil him. No room to spare, but now his head's in the outside air, then – with a twist – his shoulders. It's an eight-foot drop to the rampart. He'll have to go head first, hope the improvised rope will hold.

A last push, a wrench as he's pulled up short, and he's dangling askew. He grabs the rope, rights himself, unties the end around his waist, lowers himself hand over hand. Then he pulls the supply bag through. Nothing to it.

Damn and shit. He's forgotten to bring the windup radio. Well, no going back.

The rampart is six feet wide, with a wall on either side. Every ten feet there's a pair of slits, not opposite each other but staggered, meant for observation but useful too for the emplacement of last-ditch weaponry. The rampart is twenty feet high, twenty-seven counting the walls. It runs all the way around the Compound, punctuated at intervals by a watchtower like the one he's just left.

The Compound is shaped like an oblong, and there are five other gates. He knows the plan, having studied it thoroughly during his days at Paradice, which is where he's going now. He can see the dome, rising up through the trees, shining like half a moon. His plan is to get what he needs out of there, then circle around via the rampart – or, if conditions are right, he can cut across the Compound space on level ground – and make his way out by a side gate.

The sun is well up. He'd better hurry, or he'll fry. He'd like to show himself to the pigoons, jeer at them, but he resists this impulse: they'd follow along beside the rampart, keep him from descending. So every time he reaches an observation slit he crouches, holding himself below the sightline.

At the third watchtower along he pauses. Over the top of the rampart wall he can see something white – greyish white and cloudlike – but it's too low down to be a cloud. Also it's the wrong shape. It's thin, like a wavering pillar. It must be near the seashore, a few miles north of the Craker encampment. At first he thinks it's mist, but mist doesn't rise in an isolated stem like that, it doesn't puff. No question now, it's smoke.

The Crakers often have a fire going, but it's never a large one, it wouldn't make smoke like this. It could be a result of yesterday's storm, a lightning-strike fire that was dampened by the rain and has begun smouldering again. Or it might be that the Crakers have disobeyed orders and have come looking for him, and have built a signal fire to guide him home. That's unlikely – it isn't how they think – but if so, they're way off course.

He eats half a Joltbar, downs some water, continues along the rampart. He's limping a little now, conscious of his foot, but he can't stop and tend to it, he has to go as fast as he can. He needs that spraygun, and not just because of the wolvogs and the pigoons. From time to time he looks over his shoulder. The smoke is still there, just the one column of it. It hasn't spread. It keeps on rising.

12

Pleebcrawl

Snowman limps along the rampart, towards the glassy white swell of the bubble-dome, which is receding from him like a mirage. Because of his foot he's making poor time, and around eleven o'clock the concrete gets too hot for him to walk on. He's got the sheet over his head, draped himself as much as possible, over his baseball cap and over the tropical shirt, but he could still burn, despite the sunblock and the two layers of cloth. He's grateful for his new two-eyed sunglasses.

He hunches down in the shade of the next watchtower to wait out the noon, sucks water from a bottle. After the worst of the glare and heat is past, after the daily thunderstorm has come and gone, he'll have maybe three hours to go. All things being equal, he can get there before nightfall.

Heat pours down, bounces up off the concrete. He relaxes into it, breathes it in, feels the sweat trickling down, like millipedes walking on him. His eyes waver shut, the old films whir and crackle through his head. "What the fuck did he need me for?" he says. "Why didn't he leave me alone?"

No point thinking about it, not in this heat, with his brain turning to melted cheese. Not melted cheese: better to avoid food images. To putty, to glue, to hair product, in creme form, in a tube. He once used that. He can picture its exact position on the shelf, lined up next to his razor: he'd liked neatness, in a shelf. He has a sudden clear image of himself, freshly showered, running the creme hair product through his damp hair with his hands. In Paradice, waiting for Oryx.

He'd meant well, or at least he hadn't meant ill. He'd never wanted to hurt anyone, not seriously, not in real space-time. Fantasies didn't count.

It was a Saturday. Jimmy was lying in bed. He was finding it hard to get up these days; he'd been late for work a couple of times in the past week, and added to the times before that and the times before that, it was going to be trouble for him soon. Not that he'd been out carousing: the reverse. He'd been avoiding human contact. The AnooYoo higher-ups hadn't chewed him out yet; probably they knew about his mother and her traitor's death. Well, of course they did, though it was the kind of deep dark open secret that was never mentioned in the Compounds – bad luck, evil eye, might be catching, best to act dumb and so forth. Probably they were cutting him some slack.

There was one good thing anyway: maybe now that they'd finally scratched his mother off their list, the Corpsmen would leave him alone.

"Get it up, get it up, get it up," said his voice clock. It was pink, phallus-shaped: a Cock Clock, given to him as a joke by one of his lovers. He'd thought it was funny at the time, but this morning he found it insulting. That's all he was to her, to all of them: a mechanical joke. Nobody wanted to be sexless, but nobody wanted to be nothing but sex, Crake said once. Oh yes siree, thought Jimmy. Another human conundrum.

"What's the time?" he said to the clock. It dipped its head, sproinged upright again.

"It's noon. It's noon, it's noon, it's . . ."

"Shut up," said Jimmy. The clock wilted. It was programmed to respond to harsh tones.

Jimmy considered getting out of bed, going to the kitchenette, opening a beer. That was quite a good idea. He'd had a late night. One of his lovers, the woman who'd given him the clock in fact, had made her way through his wall of silence. She'd turned up around ten with some takeout – Nubbins and fries, she knew what he liked – and a bottle of Scotch.

"I've been concerned about you," she'd said. What she'd really wanted was a quick furtive jab, so he'd done his best and she'd had a fine time, but his heart wasn't in it and that must have been obvious. Then they'd had to go through *What's the matter, Are you bored with me, I really care about you,* and so forth and blah blah.

"Leave your husband," Jimmy had said, to cut her short. "Let's run away to the pleeblands and live in a trailer park."

"Oh, I don't think . . . You don't mean that."

"What if I did?

"You know I care about you. But I care about him too, and . . ."

"From the waist down."

"Pardon?" She was a genteel woman, she said *Pardon?* instead of *What*?

"I said, from the waist down. That's how you really care about me. Want me to spell it out for you?"

"I don't know what's got into you, you've been so mean lately."

"No fun at all."

"Well, actually, no."

"Then piss off."

After that they'd had a fight, and she'd cried, which strangely enough had made Jimmy feel better. After that they'd finished the Scotch. After that they'd had more sex, and this time Jimmy had enjoyed himself but his lover hadn't, because he'd been too rough and fast and had not said anything flattering to her the way he usually did. *Great ass*, and so on and so forth.

He shouldn't have been so crabby. She was a fine woman with real tits and problems of her own. He wondered whether he'd ever see her again. Most likely he would, because she'd had that *I can cure you* look in her eyes when she'd left.

After Jimmy had taken a leak and was getting the beer out of the fridge, his intercom buzzed. There she was, right on cue. Immediately he felt surly again. He went over to the speakerphone. "Go away," he said.

"It's Crake. I'm downstairs."

"I don't believe it," said Jimmy. He punched in the numbers for the videocam in the lobby: it was Crake, all right, giving him the finger and the grin.

"Let me in," said Crake, and Jimmy did, because right then Crake was about the only person he wanted to see.

Crake was much the same. He had the same dark clothing. He wasn't even balder.

"What the fuck are you doing here?" said Jimmy. After the initial surge of pleasure he felt embarrassed that he wasn't dressed yet, and that his apartment was knee-deep in dust bunnies and cigarette butts and dirty glassware and empty Nubbins containers, but Crake didn't seem to notice.

"Nice to feel I'm welcome," said Crake.

"Sorry. Things haven't been too good lately," said Jimmy.

"Yeah. I saw that. Your mother. I e-mailed, but you didn't answer."

"I haven't been picking up my e-mails," said Jimmy.

"Understandable. It was on brainfrizz: inciting to violence, membership in a banned organization, hampering the dissemination of commercial products, treasonable crimes against society. I guess that last was the demos she was in. Throwing bricks or something. Too bad, she was a nice lady."

Neither *nice* nor *lady* was applicable in Jimmy's view, but he wasn't up to debating this, not so early in the day. "Want a beer?" he said.

"No thanks," said Crake. "I just came to see you. See if you were all right."

"I'm all right," said Jimmy.

Crake looked at him. "Let's go to the pleeblands," he said. "Troll a few bars."

"This is a joke, right?" said Jimmy.

"No, really. I've got the passes. My regular one, and one for you."

By which Jimmy knew that Crake really must be somebody. He was impressed. But much more than that, he was touched that Crake would experience concern for him, would come all this way to seek him out. Even though they hadn't been in close touch lately – Jimmy's fault – Crake was still his friend.

★

Five hours later they were strolling through the pleeblands north of New New York. It had taken only a couple of hours to get there – bullet train to the nearest Compound, then an official Corps car with an armed driver, laid on by whoever was doing Crake's bidding. The car had taken them into the heart of what Crake called the action, and dropped them off there. They'd be shadowed though, said Crake. They'd be protected. So no harm would come to them.

Before setting out, Crake had stuck a needle in Jimmy's arm – an all-purpose, short-term vaccine he'd cooked himself. The pleeblands, he said, were a giant Petri dish: a lot of guck and contagious plasm got spread around there. If you grew up surrounded by it you were more or less immune, unless a new bioform came raging through; but if you were from the Compounds and you set foot in the pleebs, you were a feast. It was like having a big sign on your forehead that said, Eat Me.

Crake had nose cones for them too, the latest model, not just to filter microbes but also to skim out particulate. The air was worse in the pleeblands, he said. More junk blowing in the wind, fewer whirlpool purifying towers dotted around.

Jimmy had never been to the pleeblands before, he'd only looked over the wall. He was excited to finally be there, though he wasn't prepared for so many people so close to one another, walking, talking, hurrying somewhere. Spitting on the sidewalk was a feature he personally could skip. Rich pleeblanders in luxury cars, poor ones on solarbikes, hookers in fluorescent Spandex, or in short shorts, or – more athletically, showing off their firm thighs – on scooters, weaving in and out of traffic. All skin colours, all sizes. Not all prices though, said Crake: this was the low end. So

Jimmy could window-shop, but he shouldn't purchase. He should save that for later.

The pleebland inhabitants didn't look like the mental deficients the Compounders were fond of depicting, or most of them didn't. After a while Jimmy began to relax, enjoy the experience. There was so much to see – so much being hawked, so much being offered. Neon slogans, billboards, ads everywhere. And there were real tramps, real beggar women, just as in old DVD musicals: Jimmy kept expecting them to kick up their battered bootsoles, break into song. Real musicians on the street corners, real bands of street urchins. Asymmetries, deformities: the faces here were a far cry from the regularity of the Compounds. There were even bad teeth. He was gawking.

"Watch your wallet," said Crake. "Not that you'll need cash."

"Why not?"

"My treat," said Crake.

"I can't let you do that."

"Your turn next time."

"Fair enough," said Jimmy.

"Here we are – this is what they call the Street of Dreams."

The shops here were mid-to-high end, the displays elaborate. Blue Genes Day? Jimmy read. Try SnipNFix! Herediseases Removed. Why Be Short? Go Goliath! Dreamkidlets. Heal Your Helix. Cribfillers Ltd. Weenie Weenie? Longfellow's the Fellow!

"So this is where our stuff turns to gold," said Crake.

"Our stuff?"

"What we're turning out at Rejoov. Us, and the other body-oriented Compounds."

"Does all of it work?" Jimmy was impressed, not so much by the promises as by the slogans: minds like his had passed this way. His dank mood of that morning had vanished, he was feeling quite cheerful. There was so much coming at him, so much information; it took up all of his headroom.

"Quite a lot of it," said Crake. "Of course, nothing's perfect. But the competition's ferocious, especially what the Russians are doing, and the Japanese, and the Germans, of course. And the Swedes. We're holding our own though, we have a reputation for dependable product. People come here from all over the world – they shop around. Gender, sexual orientation, height, colour of skin and eyes – it's all on order, it can all be done or redone. You have no idea how much money changes hands on this one street alone."

"Let's get a drink," said Jimmy. He was thinking about his hypothetical brother, the one that wasn't born yet. Was this where his father and Ramona had gone shopping?

They had a drink, then something to eat – real oysters, said Crake, real Japanese beef, rare as diamonds. It must have cost a fortune. Then they went to a couple of other places and ended up in a bar featuring oral sex on trapezes, and Jimmy drank something orange that glowed in the dark, and then a couple more of the same. Then he was telling Crake the story of his life – no, the story of his mother's life – in one long garbled sentence, like a string of chewing gum that just kept coming out of his mouth. Then they were somewhere else, on an endless green satin bed, being worked over by two girls covered from head to toe in sequins that were glued onto their skin and shimmered like the scales of a virtual fish. Jimmy had never known a girl who could twist and twine to such advantage.

Was it there, or at one of the bars, earlier, that the subject of the job had come up? The next morning he couldn't remember. Crake had said, *Job, You, Rejoov*, and Jimmy had said, *Doing what, cleaning the toilets*, and Crake had laughed and said, *Better than that.* Jimmy couldn't remember saying yes, but he must have. He would have taken any job, no matter what it was. He wanted to move, move on. He was ready for a whole new chapter.

BlyssPluss

On the Monday morning after his weekend with Crake, Jimmy turned up at AnooYoo for another day of word-mongering. He felt pretty wasted, but hoped it didn't show. Though it encouraged all kinds of chemical experiments by its paying clientele, AnooYoo frowned upon anything similar amongst the hired help. It figured, Jimmy thought: in the olden days, bootleggers had seldom been drunks. Or so he'd read.

Before going to his desk he visited the Men's, checked himself in the mirror: he looked like a regurgitated pizza. Plus he was late, but for once nobody noticed. All of a sudden there was his boss, and some other functionaries so elevated that Jimmy had never seen them before. Jimmy's hand was being shaken, his back gently slapped, a glass of champagne look-alike pressed into his hand. *Oh good! Hair of the dog! Glug-glug-glug*, went Jimmy's voice balloon, but he took care to merely sip.

Then he was being told what a pleasure it had been to have him with AnooYoo, and what an asset he'd proved to be, and how many warm wishes would accompany him where he was going, and by the way, many, many congratulations! His severance package would be deposited immediately to his

Corpsbank account. It would be a generous one, more generous than his length of service warranted, because, let's be frank, his friends at AnooYoo wanted Jimmy to remember them in a positive manner, in his terrific new position.

Whatever that may be, thought Jimmy, as he sat in the sealed bullet train. The train had been arranged for him, and so had the move – a team would arrive, they'd pack up everything, they were professionals, never fear. He barely had time to contact his various lovers, and when he did he discovered that each one of them had already been discreetly informed by Crake personally, who – it appeared – had long tentacles. How had he known about them? Maybe he'd been hacking into Jimmy's e-mail, easy for him. But why bother?

I'll miss you Jimmy, said an e-message from one.

Oh Jimmy, you were so funny, said another.

Were was a creep-out. It wasn't as if he'd died or anything.

Jimmy spent his first night in RejoovenEsense at the VIP guest hotel. He poured himself a drink from the mini-bar, straight Scotch, as real as it came, then spent a while looking out the picture window at the view, not that he could make out very much except lights. He could see the Paradice dome, an immense half-circle in the distance, floodlit from below, but he didn't yet know what it was. He thought it was a skating rink.

Next morning Crake took him for a preliminary tour of the RejoovenEsense Compound in his souped-up electric golf cart. It was, Jimmy had to admit, spectacular in all ways. Everything was sparkling clean, landscaped, ecologically pristine, and very expensive. The air was particulate-free, due to the many solar whirlpool purifying towers, discreetly placed and disguised as modern art. Rockulators took care of the microclimate, butterflies as big as plates drifted among the vividly coloured shrubs. It made all the other Compounds Jimmy had ever been in, Watson-Crick included, look shabby and retro.

"What pays for all this?" he asked Crake, as they passed the state-of-the-art Luxuries Mall – marble everywhere, colonnades, cafés, ferns, takeout booths, roller-skating path, juice bars, a self-energizing gym where running on the treadmill kept the light bulbs going, Roman-look fountains with nymphs and sea-gods.

"Grief in the face of inevitable death," said Crake. "The wish to stop time. The human condition."

Which was not very informative, said Jimmy.

"You'll see," said Crake.

They had lunch at one of the five-star Rejoov restaurants, on an air-conditioned pseudobalcony overlooking the main Compound organic-botanics greenhouse. Crake had the kanga-lamb, a new Australian splice that combined the placid character and high-protein yield of the sheep with the kangaroo's resistance to disease and absence of methane-producing, ozone-destroying flatulence. Jimmy ordered the raisin-stuffed capon – real free-range capon, real sun-dried raisins, Crake assured him. Jimmy was so used to ChickieNobs by now, to their bland tofulike consistency and their inoffensive flavour, that the capon tasted quite wild.

"My unit's called Paradice," said Crake, over the soy-banana flambé. "What we're working on is immortality."

"So is everyone else," said Jimmy. "They've kind of done it in rats."

"*Kind of* is crucial," said Crake.

"What about the cryogenics guys?" said Jimmy. "Freeze your head, get your body reconstituted once they've figured out how? They're doing a brisk business, their stock's high."

"Sure, and a couple of years later they toss you out the back door and tell your relatives there was a power failure. Anyway, we're cutting out the deep-freeze."

"How do you mean?"

"With us," said Crake, "you wouldn't have to die first."

"You've really done it?"

"Not yet," said Crake. "But think of the R&D budget."

"Millions?"

"Mega-millions," said Crake.

"Can I have another drink?" said Jimmy. This was a lot to take in.

"No. I need you to listen."

"I can listen and drink too."

"Not very well."

"Try me," said Jimmy.

Within Paradice, said Crake – and they'd visit the facility after lunch – there were two major initiatives going forward. The first – the BlyssPluss Pill – was prophylactic in nature, and the logic behind it was simple: eliminate the external causes of death and you were halfway there.

"External causes?" said Jimmy.

"War, which is to say misplaced sexual energy, which we consider to be a larger factor than the economic, racial, and religious causes often cited. Contagious diseases, especially sexually transmitted ones. Overpopulation, leading – as we've seen in spades – to environmental degradation and poor nutrition."

Jimmy said it sounded like a tall order: so much had been tried in those areas, so much had failed. Crake smiled. "If at first you don't succeed, read the instructions," he said.

"Meaning?"

"The proper study of Mankind is Man."

"Meaning?"

"You've got to work with what's on the table."

The BlyssPluss Pill was designed to take a set of givens, namely the nature of human nature, and steer these givens in a more beneficial direction than the ones hitherto taken. It was based on studies of the now unfortunately extinct pygmy or bonobo chimpanzee, a close relative of *Homo sapiens sapiens*. Unlike the latter species, the bonobo had not been partially monogamous with polygamous and polyandrous tendencies. Instead it had been indiscriminately promiscuous, had not pair-bonded, and had spent most of its waking life, when it wasn't eating, engaged in copulation. Its intraspecific aggression factor had been very low.

Which had led to the concept of BlyssPluss. The aim was to produce a single pill, that, at one and the same time:

a) would protect the user against all known sexually transmitted diseases, fatal, inconvenient, or merely unsightly;
b) would provide an unlimited supply of libido and sexual prowess, coupled with a generalized sense of energy and well-being, thus reducing the frustration and blocked testosterone that led to jealousy and violence, and eliminating feelings of low self-worth;
c) would prolong youth.

These three capabilities would be the selling points, said Crake; but there would be a fourth, which would not be advertised. The BlyssPluss Pill would also act as a sure-fire one-time-does-it-all birth-control pill, for male and female alike, thus automatically lowering the population level. This effect could be made reversible, though not in individual subjects, by altering the components of the pill as needed, i.e., if the populations of any one area got too low.

"So basically you're going to sterilize people without them knowing it under the guise of giving them the ultra in orgies?"

"That's a crude way of putting it," said Crake.

Such a pill, he said, would confer large-scale benefits, not only on individual users – although it had to appeal to these or it would be a failure in the marketplace – but on society as a whole; and not only on society, but on the planet. The investors were very keen on it, it was going to be global. It was all upside. There was no downside at all. He, Crake, was very excited about it.

"I didn't know you were so altruistic," said Jimmy. Since when had Crake been a cheerleader for the human race?

"It's not altruism exactly," said Crake. "More like sink or swim. I've seen the latest confidential Corps demographic reports. As a species we're in deep trouble, worse than anyone's saying. They're afraid to release the stats because people might just give up, but take it from me, we're running out of space-time. Demand for resources has exceeded supply for decades in marginal geopolitical areas, hence the famines and droughts; but very soon, demand is going to exceed supply *for everyone*. With the Blyss-Pluss Pill the human race will have a better chance of swimming."

"How do you figure?" Maybe Jimmy shouldn't have had that extra drink. He was getting a bit confused.

"Fewer people, therefore more to go around."

"What if the fewer people are very greedy and wasteful?" said Jimmy. "That's not out of the question."

"They won't be," said Crake.

"You've got this thing now?" said Jimmy. He was beginning to see the possibilities. Endless high-grade sex, no consequences. Come to think of it, his own libido could use a little toning up. "Does it make your hair grow back?" He almost said *Where can I get some*, but stopped himself in time.

It was an elegant concept, said Crake, though it still needed some tweaking. They hadn't got it to work seamlessly yet, not on all fronts; it was still at the clinical trial stage. A couple of the test subjects had literally fucked themselves to death, several had assaulted old ladies and household pets, and there had been a few unfortunate cases of priapism and split dicks. Also, at first, the sexually transmitted disease protection mechanism had failed in a spectacular manner. One subject had grown a big genital wart all over her epidermis, distressing to observe, but they'd taken care of that with lasers and exfoliation, at least temporarily. In short, there had been errors, false directions taken, but they were getting very close to a solution.

Needless to say, Crake continued, the thing would become a huge money-spinner. It would be the must-have pill, in every country, in every society in the world. Of course the crank religions wouldn't like it, in view of the fact that their raison d'être was based on misery, indefinitely deferred gratification, and sexual frustration, but they wouldn't be able to hold out long. The tide of human desire, the desire for more and better, would overwhelm them. It would take control and drive events, as it had in every large change throughout history.

Jimmy said the thing sounded very interesting. Provided its shortcomings could be remedied, that is. Good name, too – BlyssPluss. A whispering, seductive sound. He liked it. He had no further wish to try it out himself, however: he had enough problems without his penis bursting.

"Where do you get the subjects?" he said. "For the clinical trials?"

Crake grinned. "From the poorer countries. Pay them a few dollars, they don't even know what they're taking. Sex clinics, of course – they're happy to help. Whorehouses. Prisons. And from the ranks of the desperate, as usual."

"Where do I fit in?"

"You'll do the ad campaign," said Crake.

MaddAddam

After lunch they went to Paradice.

The dome complex was at the far right side of the Rejoov Compound. It had its own park around it, a dense climate-controlling plantation of mixed tropical splices above which it rose like a blind eyeball. There was a security installation around the park, very tight, said Crake; even the Corpsmen were not allowed inside. Paradice had been his concept, and he'd made that a condition when he'd agreed to actualize it: he didn't want a lot of heavy-handed ignoramuses poking into things they couldn't understand.

Crake's pass was good for both of them, of course. They rolled in through the first gate and along the roadway through the trees. Then there was another checkpoint, with guards – Paradice uniforms, Crake explained, not Corps – that seemed to materialize from the bushes. Then more trees. Then the curved wall of the bubble-dome itself. It might look delicate, said Crake, but it was made of a new mussel-adhesive/silicon/dendrite-formation alloy, ultra-resistant. You'd have to have some very advanced tools to cut through it, as it would reconform itself after pressure and automatically repair any gashes. Moreover, it had the capacity to both filter and breathe, like an eggshell, though it required a solar-generated current to do so.

They turned the golf cart over to one of the guards and were coded through the outer door, which closed with a whuff behind them.

"Why did it make that sound?" said Jimmy nervously.

"It's an airlock," said Crake. "As in spaceships."

"What for?"

"In case this place ever has to be sealed off," said Crake. "Hostile bioforms, toxin attacks, fanatics. The usual."

By this time Jimmy was feeling a little strange. Crake hadn't really told him what went on in here, not in specific detail. "Wait and see," was all he'd said.

Once they were through the inner door they were in a familiar-enough complex. Halls, doors, staff with digital clipboards, others hunched in front of screens; it was like OrganInc Farms, it was like HelthWyzer, it was like Watson-Crick, only newer. But physical plants were just a shell, said Crake: what really counted in a research facility was the quality of the brains.

"These are top-of-the-line," he said, nodding left and right. In return there was a lot of deferential smiling, and – this wasn't faked – a lot of awe. Jimmy had never been clear about Crake's exact position, but whatever his nominal title – he'd been vague about that – he was obviously the biggest ant in the anthill.

Each of the staff had a name tag with block lettering – one or two words only. BLACK RHINO. WHITE SEDGE. IVORY-BILLED WOODPECKER. POLAR BEAR. INDIAN TIGER. LOTIS BLUE. SWIFT FOX.

"The names," he said to Crake. "You raided Extinctathon!"

"It's more than the names," said Crake. "These people *are* Extinctathon. They're all Grandmasters. What you're looking at is MaddAddam, the cream of the crop."

"You're joking! How come they're here?" said Jimmy.

"They're the splice geniuses," said Crake. "The ones that were pulling those capers, the asphalt-eating microbes, the outbreak of neon-coloured herpes simplex on the west coast, the ChickieNob wasps and so on."

"Neon herpes? I didn't hear about that," said Jimmy. Pretty funny. "How did you track them down?"

"I wasn't the only person after them. They were making themselves very unpopular in some quarters. I just got to them ahead of the Corps, that's all. Or I got to most of them, anyway."

Jimmy was going to ask *What happened to the others*, but he thought better of it.

"So you kidnapped them, or what?" That wouldn't have surprised Jimmy, brain-snatching being a customary practice; though usually the brains were snatched between countries, not within them.

"I merely persuaded them they'd be a lot happier and safer in here than out there."

"Safer? In Corps territory?"

"I got them secure papers. Most of them agreed with me, especially when I offered to destroy their so-called real identities and all records of their previous existences."

"I thought those guys were anti-Compound," said Jimmy. "The stuff MaddAddam was doing was pretty hostile, from what you showed me."

"They were anti-Compound. Still are, probably. But after the Second World War in the twentieth century, the Allies invited a lot of German rocket scientists to come and work with them, and I can't recall anyone saying no. When your main game's over, you can always move your chessboard elsewhere."

"What if they try sabotage, or . . ."

"Escape? Yeah," said Crake. "A couple were like that at the beginning. Not team players. Thought they'd take what they'd done here, cart it offshore. Go underground, or set up elsewhere."

"What did you do?"

"They fell off pleebland overpasses," said Crake.

"Is that a joke?"

"In a manner of speaking. You'll need another name," Crake said, "a MaddAddam name, so you'll fit in. I thought, since I'm Crake here, you could go back to being Thickney, the way you were when we were – how old?"

"Fourteen."

"Those were definitive times," said Crake.

Jimmy wanted to linger, but Crake was already hurrying him along. He'd have liked to talk with some of these people, hear their stories – had any of them known his mother, for instance? – but maybe he could do that later. On the other hand, maybe not: he'd been seen with Crake, the alpha wolf, the silverback gorilla, the head lion. Nobody would want to get too cozy with him. They'd see his as the jackal position.

Paradice

They dropped in at Crake's office, so Jimmy could get a little oriented, said Crake. It was a large space with many gizmos in it, as Jimmy would have expected. There was a painting on the wall: an eggplant on an orange plate. It was the first picture Jimmy ever remembered seeing in a place of Crake's. He thought of asking if that was Crake's girlfriend, but thought better of it.

He zeroed in on the mini-bar. "Anything in that?"

"Later," said Crake.

Crake still had a collection of fridge magnets, but they were different ones. No more science quips.

Where God is, Man is not.
There are two moons, the one you can see and
  the one you can't.
Du musz dein Leben andern.
We understand more than we know.
I think, therefore.
To stay human is to break a limitation.
Dream steals from its lair towards its prey.

"What are you really up to here?" said Jimmy.

Crake grinned. "What is *really*?"

"Bogus," said Jimmy. But he was thrown off balance.

Now, said Crake, it was time to get serious. He was going to show Jimmy the other thing they were doing – the main thing, here at Paradice. What Jimmy was about to see was . . . well, it couldn't be described. It was, quite simply, Crake's life's work.

Jimmy put on a suitably solemn face. What next? Some gruesome new food substance, no doubt. A liver tree, a sausage vine. Or some sort of zucchini that grew wool. He braced himself.

Crake led Jimmy along and around; then they were standing in front of a large picture window. No: a one-way mirror. Jimmy looked in. There was a large central space filled with trees and plants, above them a blue sky. (Not really a blue sky, only the curved ceiling of the bubble-dome, with a clever projection device that simulated dawn, sunlight, evening, night. There was a fake moon that went through its phases, he discovered later. There was fake rain.)

That was his first view of the Crakers. They were naked, but not like the Noodie News: there was no self-consciousness, none at all. At first he couldn't believe them, they were so beautiful. Black, yellow, white, brown, all available skin colours. Each individual was exquisite. "Are they robots, or what?" he said.

"You know how they've got floor models, in furniture stores?" said Crake.

"Yeah?"

"These are the floor models."

★

It was the result of a logical chain of progression, said Crake that evening, over drinks in the Paradice Lounge (fake palm trees, canned music, real Campari, real soda). Once the proteonome had been fully analyzed and interspecies gene and part-gene splicing were thoroughly underway, the Paradice Project or something like it had been only a matter of time. What Jimmy had seen was the next-to-end result of seven years of intensive trial-and-error research.

"At first," said Crake, "we had to alter ordinary human embryos, which we got from – never mind where we got them. But these people are *sui generis*. They're reproducing themselves, now."

"They look more than seven years old," said Jimmy.

Crake explained about the rapid-growth factors he'd incorporated. "Also," he said, "they're programmed to drop dead at age thirty – suddenly, without getting sick. No old age, none of those anxieties. They'll just keel over. Not that they know it; none of them has died yet."

"I thought you were working on immortality."

"Immortality," said Crake, "is a concept. If you take 'mortality' as being, not death, but the foreknowledge of it and the fear of it, then 'immortality' is the absence of such fear. Babies are immortal. Edit out the fear, and you'll be . . ."

"Sounds like Applied Rhetoric 101," said Jimmy.

"What?"

"Never mind. Martha Graham stuff."

"Oh. Right."

Other Compounds in other countries were following similar lines of reasoning, said Crake, they were developing their own prototypes, so the population in the bubble-dome was ultra-secret. Vow of silence, closed-circuit internal e-mailing only unless you had special permission, living quarters inside the security zone but outside the airlock. This would reduce the chances of infection in case any of the staff got sick; the Paradice models had enhanced immune-system functions, so the probability of contagious diseases spreading among them was low.

Nobody was allowed out of the complex. Or almost nobody. Crake could go out, of course. He was the liaison between Paradice and the Rejoov top brass, though he hadn't let them in yet, he was making them wait. They were a greedy bunch, nervous about their investment; they'd want to jump the gun, start marketing too soon. Also they'd talk too much, tip off the competition. They were all boasters, those guys.

"So, now that I'm in here I can never get out?" said Jimmy. "You didn't tell me that."

"You'll be an exception," said Crake. "Nobody's going to kidnap you for what's inside your skull. You're just doing the ads, remember?" But the rest of the team, he said – the MaddAddamite contingent – was confined to base for the duration.

"The duration?"

"Until we go public," said Crake. Very soon, RejoovenEsense hoped to hit the market with the various blends on offer. They'd be able to create totally chosen babies that would incorporate any feature, physical or mental or spiritual, that the buyer might wish to select. The present methods on offer were very hit-or-miss, said Crake: certain hereditary diseases could be screened out, true, but apart from that there was a lot of spoilage, a lot of waste. The customers never knew whether they'd get exactly what they'd paid for; in addition to which, there were too many unintended consequences.

But with the Paradice method, there would be ninety-nine per cent accuracy. Whole populations could be created that would have pre-selected characteristics. Beauty, of course; that would be in high demand. And docility: several world leaders had expressed interest in that. Paradice had already developed a UV-resistant skin, a built-in insect repellant, an unprecedented ability to digest unrefined plant material. As for immunity from microbes, what had until now been done with drugs would soon be innate.

Compared to the Paradice Project, even the BlyssPluss Pill was a crude tool, although it would be a lucrative interim solution. In the long run, however, the benefits for the future human race of the two in combination would be stupendous. They were inextricably linked – the Pill and the Project. The Pill would put a stop to haphazard reproduction, the Project would replace it with a superior method. They were two stages of a single plan, you might say.

It was amazing – said Crake – what once-unimaginable things had been accomplished by the team here. What had been altered was nothing less than the ancient primate brain. Gone were its destructive features, the features responsible for the world's current illnesses. For instance, racism – or, as they referred to it in Paradice, pseudospeciation – had been eliminated in the model group, merely by switching the bonding mechanism: the Paradice people simply did not register skin colour. Hierarchy could not exist among them, because they lacked the neural complexes that would have created it. Since they were neither hunters nor agriculturalists hungry for land, there was no territoriality: the king-of-the-castle hard-wiring that had plagued humanity had, in them, been unwired. They ate nothing but leaves and grass and roots and a berry or two; thus their foods were plentiful and always available. Their sexuality was not a constant torment to them, not a cloud of turbulent hormones: they came into heat at regular intervals, as did most mammals other than man.

In fact, as there would never be anything for these people to inherit, there would be no family trees, no marriages, and no divorces. They were perfectly adjusted to their habitat, so they would never have to create houses or tools or weapons, or, for that matter, clothing. They would have no need to invent any harmful symbolisms, such as kingdoms, icons, gods, or money. Best of all, they recycled their own excrement. By means of a brilliant splice, incorporating genetic material from . . .

"Excuse me," said Jimmy. "But a lot of this stuff isn't what the average parent is looking for in a baby. Didn't you get a bit carried away?"

"I told you," said Crake patiently. "These are the floor models. They represent the art of the possible. We can list the individual features for prospective buyers, then we can customize. Not everyone will want all the bells and whistles, we know that. Though you'd be surprised how many people would like a very beautiful, smart baby that eats nothing but grass. The vegans are highly interested in that little item. We've done our market research."

Oh good, thought Jimmy. Your baby can double as a lawn mower.

"Can they speak?" he asked.

"Of course they can speak," said Crake. "When they have something they want to say."

"Do they make jokes?"

"Not as such," said Crake. "For jokes you need a certain edge, a little malice. It took a lot of trial and error and we're still testing, but I think we've managed to do away with jokes." He raised his glass, grinned at Jimmy. "Glad you're here, cork-nut," he said. "I needed somebody I could talk to."

Jimmy was given his own suite inside the Paradice dome. His belongings were there before him, each one tidied away just where it ought to be – underwear in the underwear drawer, shirts neatly stacked, electric toothbrush plugged in and recharged – except that there were more of these belongings than he remembered possessing. More shirts, more underwear, more electric toothbrushes. The air conditioning was set at the temperature he liked it, and a tasty snack (melon, prosciutto, a French Brie with a label that appeared authentic) was set out on the dining-room table. The dining-room table! He'd never had a dining-room table before.

Crake in love

The lightning sizzles, the thunder booms, the rain's pouring down, so heavy the air is white, white all around, a solid mist; it's like glass in motion. Snowman – goon, buffoon, poltroon – crouches on the rampart, arms over his head, pelted from above like an object of general derision. He's humanoid, he's hominid, he's an aberration, he's abominable; he'd be legendary, if there were anyone left to relate legends.

If only he had an auditor besides himself, what yarns he could spin, what whines he could whine. The lover's complaint to his mistress, or something along those lines. Lots to choose from there.

Because now he's come to the crux in his head, to the place in the tragic play where it would say: *Enter Oryx*. Fatal moment. But which fatal moment? *Enter Oryx as a young girl on a kiddie-porn site, flowers in her hair, whipped cream on her chin*; or, *Enter Oryx as a teenage news item, sprung from a pervert's garage*; or, *Enter Oryx, stark naked and pedagogical in the Crakers' inner sanctum*; or, *Enter Oryx, towel around her hair, emerging from the shower*; or, *Enter Oryx, in a pewter-grey silk pantsuit and demure half-high heels, carrying a briefcase, the image of a professional Compound globewise saleswoman?* Which of these will it be, and how can he ever be sure there's a line connecting the first to the last? Was there only one Oryx, or was she legion?

But any would do, thinks Snowman as the rain runs down his face. They are all time present, because they are all here with me now.

Oh Jimmy, this is so positive. It makes me happy when you grasp this. Paradice is lost, but you have a Paradice within you, happier far. Then that silvery laugh, right in his ear.

Jimmy hadn't spotted Oryx right away, though he must have seen her that first afternoon when he was peering through the one-way mirror. Like the Crakers she had no clothes on, and like the Crakers she was beautiful, so from a distance she didn't stand out. She wore her long dark hair without ornament, her back was turned, she was surrounded by a group of other people; just part of the scene.

A few days later, when Crake was showing him how to work the monitor screens that picked up images from the hidden minicams among the trees, Jimmy saw her face. She turned into the camera and there it was again, that look, that stare, the stare that went right into him and saw him as he truly was. The only thing that was different about her was her eyes, which were the same luminescent green as the eyes of the Crakers.

Gazing into those eyes, Jimmy had a moment of pure bliss, pure terror, because now she was no longer a picture – no longer merely an image, residing in secrecy and darkness in the flat printout currently stashed between his mattress and the third cross-slat of his new Rejoov-suite bed. Suddenly she was real, three-dimensional. He felt he'd dreamed her. How could a person be caught that way, in an instant, by a glance, the lift of an eyebrow, the curve of an arm? But he was.

"Who's that?" he asked Crake. She was carrying a young rakunk, holding out the small animal to those around; the others were touching it gently. "She's not one of them. What's she doing in there?"

"She's their teacher," said Crake. "We needed a go-between, someone who could communicate on their level. Simple concepts, no metaphysics."

"What's she teaching?" Jimmy said this indifferently: bad plan for him to show too much interest in any woman, in the presence of Crake: oblique mockery would follow.

"Botany and zoology," said Crake with a grin. "In other words, what not to eat and what could bite. And what not to hurt," he added.

"For that she has to be naked?"

"They've never seen clothes. Clothes would only confuse them."

The lessons Oryx taught were short: one thing at a time was best, said Crake. The Paradice models weren't stupid, but they were starting more or less from scratch, so they liked repetition. Another staff member, some specialist in the field, would go over the day's item with Oryx – the leaf, insect, mammal, or reptile she was about to explain. Then she'd spray herself with a citrus-derived chemical compound to disguise her human pheromones – unless she did that there could be trouble, as the men would smell her and think it was time to mate. When she was ready, she'd slip through a reconforming doorway concealed behind dense foliage.

That way she could appear and disappear in the homeland of the Crakers without raising awkward questions in their minds.

"They trust her," said Crake. "She has a great manner."

Jimmy's heart sank. Crake was in love, for the first time ever. It wasn't just the praise, rare enough. It was the tone of voice.

"Where'd you find her?" he asked.

"I've known her for a while. Ever since post-grad at Watson-Crick."

"She was studying there?" If so, thought Jimmy, what?

"Not exactly," said Crake. "I encountered her through Student Services."

"You were the student, she was the service?" said Jimmy, trying to keep it light.

"Exactly. I told them what I was looking for – you could be very specific there, take them a picture or a video stimulation, stuff like that, and they'd do their best to match you up. What I wanted was something that looked like – do you remember that Web show? . . ."

"What Web show?"

"I gave you a printout. From HottTotts – you know."

"Rings no bells," said Jimmy.

"That show we used to watch. Remember?"

"I guess," said Jimmy. "Sort of."

"I used the girl for my Extinctathon gateway. That one."

"Oh, right," said Jimmy. "Each to his own. You wanted the sex-kiddie look?"

"Not that she was underage, the one they came up with."

"Of course not."

"Then I made private arrangements. You weren't supposed to, but we all bent the rules a little."

"Rules are there to be bent," said Jimmy. He was feeling worse and worse.

"Then, when I came here to head up this place, I was able to offer her a more official position. She was delighted to accept. It was triple the pay she'd been getting, with a lot of perks; but also she said the work intrigued her. I have to say she's a devoted employee." Crake gave a smug little smile, an alpha smile, and Jimmy wanted to smash him.

"Great," he said. Knives were going through him. No sooner found than lost again. Crake was his best friend. Revision: his only friend. He wouldn't be able to lay a finger on her. How could he?

They waited for Oryx to come out of the shower room, where she was removing her protective spray, and, Crake added, her luminous-green gel contact lenses: the Crakers would have found her brown eyes off-putting. She emerged finally, her hair braided now and still damp, and was introduced, and shook Jimmy's hand with her own small hand. (I touched her, thought Jimmy like a ten-year-old. I actually touched her!)

She had clothes on now, she was wearing the standard-issue lab outfit, the jacket and trousers. On her it looked like lounge pyjamas. Clipped to the pocket was her name tag: ORYX BEISA. She'd chosen it herself from the list provided by Crake. She liked the idea of being a gentle water-conserving East African herbivore, but had been less pleased when told the animal she'd picked was extinct. Crake had needed to explain that this was the way things were done in Paradice.

The three of them had coffee in the Paradice staff cafeteria. The talk was of the Crakers – this is what Oryx called them – and of how they were doing. It was the same every day, said Oryx. They were always quietly content. They knew how to make fire now. They'd liked the rakunk. She found them very relaxing to spend time with.

"Do they ever ask where they came from?" said Jimmy. "What they're doing here?" At that moment he couldn't have cared less, but he wanted to join the conversation so he could look at Oryx without being obvious.

"You don't get it," said Crake, in his you-are-a-moron voice. "That stuff's been edited out."

"Well, actually, they did ask," said Oryx. "Today they asked who made them."

"And?"

"And I told them the truth. I said it was Crake." An admiring smile at Crake: Jimmy could have done without that. "I told them he was very clever and good."

"Did they ask who this Crake was?" said Crake. "Did they want to see him?"

"They didn't seem interested."

Night and day Jimmy was in torment. He wanted to touch Oryx, worship her, open her up like a beautifully wrapped package, even though he suspected that there was something – some harmful snake or homemade bomb or lethal powder – concealed within. Not within her, of course. Within the situation. She was off limits, he told himself, again and again.

He behaved as honourably as he could: he showed no interest in her, or he tried to show none. He took to visiting the pleeblands, paying for girls in bars. Girls with frills, with spangles, with lace, whatever was on offer. He'd shoot himself up with Crake's quicktime vaccine, and he had his own Corps bodyguard now, so it was quite safe. The first couple of times it was a thrill; then it was a distraction; then it was merely a habit. None of it was an antidote to Oryx.

He fiddled around at his job: not much of a challenge there. The BlyssPluss Pill would sell itself, it didn't need help from him. But the official launch was looming closer, so he had his staff turn out some visuals, a few catchy slogans: Throw Away Your Condoms! BlyssPluss, for the Total Body Experience! Don't Live a Little, Live a Lot! Simulations of a man and a woman, ripping off their clothes, grinning like maniacs. Then a man and a man. Then a woman and a woman, though for that one they didn't use the condom line. Then a threesome. He could churn out this crap in his sleep.

Supposing, that is, he could manage to sleep. At night he'd lie awake, berating himself, bemoaning his fate. *Berating, bemoaning*, useful words. *Doldrums. Lovelorn. Leman. Forsaken. Queynt.*

But then Oryx seduced him. What else to call it? She came to his suite on purpose, she marched right in, she had him out of his shell in two minutes flat. It made him feel about twelve. She was clearly a practised hand at this, and so casual on that first occasion it took his breath away.

"I didn't want to see you so unhappy, Jimmy," was her explanation. "Not about me."

"How could you tell I was unhappy?"

"Oh, I always know."

"What about Crake?" he said, after she'd hooked him that first time, landed him, left him gasping.

"You are Crake's friend. He wouldn't want you to be unhappy."

Jimmy wasn't so sure about that, but he said, "I don't feel easy about this."

"What are you saying, Jimmy?"

"Aren't you – isn't he . . ." What a dolt!

"Crake lives in a higher world, Jimmy," she said. "He lives in a world of ideas. He is doing important things. He has no time to play. Anyway, Crake is my boss. You are for fun."

"Yes, but . . ."

"Crake won't know."

And it seemed to be true, Crake didn't know. Maybe he was too mesmerized by her to notice anything; or maybe, thought Jimmy, love really was blind. Or blinding. And Crake loved Oryx, no doubt there; he was almost abject about it. He'd touch her in public, even. Crake had never been a toucher, he'd been physically remote, but now he liked to have a hand on Oryx: on her shoulder, her arm, her small waist, her perfect butt. *Mine*, *mine*, that hand was saying.

Moreover, he appeared to trust her, more perhaps than he trusted Jimmy. She was an expert businesswoman, he said. He'd given her a slice of the BlyssPluss trials: she had useful contacts in the pleeblands, through her old pals who'd worked with her at Student Services. For that reason she had to make a lot of trips, here and there around the world. Sex clinics, said Crake. Whorehouses, said Oryx: who better to do the testing?

"Just as long as you don't do any testing on yourself," said Jimmy.

"Oh no, Jimmy. Crake said not to."

"You always do what Crake tells you?"

"He is my boss."

"He tell you to do this?"

Big eyes. "Do what, Jimmy?"

"What you're doing right now."

"Oh Jimmy. You always make jokes."

The times when she was away were hard for Jimmy. He worried about her, he longed for her, he resented her for not being there. When she'd get back from one of her trips, she'd materialize in his room in the middle of the night: she managed to do that no matter what might be on Crake's agenda. First she'd brief Crake, provide him with an account of her activities and their success – how many BlyssPluss Pills, where she'd placed them, any results so far: an exact account, because he was so obsessive. Then she'd take care of what she called the personal area.

Crake's sexual needs were direct and simple, according to Oryx; not intriguing, like sex with Jimmy. Not fun, just work – although she respected Crake, she really did, because he was a brilliant genius. But if Crake wanted her to stay longer on any given night, do it again maybe, she'd make some excuse – jet lag, a headache, something plausible. Her inventions were seamless, she was the best poker-faced liar in the world, so there would be a kiss goodbye for stupid Crake, a smile, a wave, a closed door, and the next minute there she would be, with Jimmy.

How potent was that word. *With.*

He could never get used to her, she was fresh every time, she was a casketful of secrets. Any moment now she would open herself up, reveal to him the essential thing, the hidden thing at the core of life, or of her life, or of his life – the thing he was longing to know. The thing he'd always wanted. What would it be?

"What went on in that garage, anyway?" said Jimmy. He couldn't leave her alone about her earlier life, he was driven to find out. No detail was too small for him in those days, no painful splinter of her past too tiny. Perhaps he was digging for her anger, but he never found it. Either it was buried too deeply, or it wasn't there at all. But he couldn't believe that. She wasn't a masochist, she was no saint.

They were in Jimmy's bedroom, lying on the bed together with the digital TV on, hooked into his computer, some copulation Web site with an animal component, a couple of well-trained German shepherds and a double-jointed ultra-shaved albino tattooed all over with lizards. The sound was off, it was just the pictures: erotic wallpaper.

They were eating Nubbins from one of the takeout joints in the nearest mall, with the soyafries and the salad. Some of the salad leaves were spinach, from the Rejoov greenhouses: no pesticides, or none that were admitted to. The other leaves were a cabbage splice – giant cabbage trees, continuous producers, very productive. The stuff had a whiff of sewage to it, but the special dressing drowned that out.

"What garage, Jimmy?" said Oryx. She wasn't paying attention. She liked to eat with her fingers, she hated cutlery. Why put a big chunk of sharp-edged metal into your mouth? She said it made the food taste like tin.

"You know what garage," he said. "The one in San Francisco. That creep. That geek who bought you, flew you over, got his wife to say you were the maid."

"Jimmy, why do you dream up such things? I was never

in a garage." She licked her fingers, tore a Nubbin into bite-sized bits, fed one of the bits to Jimmy. Then she let him lick her fingers for her. He ran his tongue around the small ovals of her nails. This was the closest she could get to him without becoming food: she was in him, or part of her was in part of him. Sex was the other way around: while that was going on, he was in her. *I'll make you mine*, lovers said in old books. They never said, *I'll make you me.*

"I know it was you," Jimmy said. "I saw the pictures."

"What pictures?"

"The so-called maid scandal. In San Francisco. Did that creepy old geezer make you have sex?"

"Oh Jimmy." A sigh. "So that is what you have in mind. I saw that, on TV. Why do you worry about a man like that? He was so old he was almost dead."

"No, but did he?"

"No one made me have sex in a garage. I told you."

"Okay, revision: no one made you, but did you have it anyway?"

"You don't understand me, Jimmy."

"But I want to."

"Do you?" A pause. "These are such good soyafries. Just imagine, Jimmy – millions of people in the world never ate fries like this! We are so lucky!"

"Tell me." It must have been her. "I won't get mad."

A sigh. "He was a kind man," said Oryx, in a storytelling voice. Sometimes he suspected her of improvising, just to humour him; sometimes he felt that her entire past – everything she'd told him – was his own invention. "He was rescuing young girls. He paid for my plane ticket, just like it said. If it wasn't for him, I wouldn't be here. You should like him!"

"Why should I like such a hypocritical sanctimonious bastard? You didn't answer my question."

"Yes, I did, Jimmy. Now leave it alone."

"How long did he keep you locked in the garage?"

"It was more like an apartment," said Oryx. "They didn't have room in their house. I wasn't the only girl they took in."

"They?"

"Him and his wife. They were trying to be helpful."

"And she hated sex, is that it? Is that why she put up with you? You were getting the old goat off her back?"

Oryx sighed. "You always think the worst of people, Jimmy. She was a very spiritual person."

"Like fuck she was."

"Don't swear, Jimmy. I want to enjoy being with you. I don't have very much time, I have to go soon, I need to do some business. Why do you care about things that happened so long ago?" She leaned over him, kissed him with her Nubbin-smeared mouth. *Unguent, unctuous, sumptuous, voluptuous, salacious, lubricious, delicious*, went the inside of Jimmy's head. He sank down into the words, into the feelings.

After a while he said, "Where are you going?"

"Oh, someplace. I'll call you when I get there." She never would tell him.

Takeout

Now comes the part that Snowman has replayed in his head time after time. *If only* haunts him. But *if only* what? What could he have said or done differently? What change would have altered the course of events? In the big picture, nothing. In the small picture, so much.

Don't go. Stay here. At least that way they would have been together. She might even have survived – why not? In which case she'd be right here with him, right now.

I just want some takeout. I'm just going to the mall. I need some air. I need a walk.

Let me come with you. It's not safe.

Don't be silly! There's guards everywhere. They all know who I am. Who's safer than me?

I have a gut feeling.

But Jimmy'd had no gut feeling. He'd been happy that evening, happy and lazy. She'd arrived at his door an hour earlier. She'd just come from being with the Crakers, teaching them a few more leaves and grasses, so she was damp from the shower. She was wearing some sort of kimono covered with red and orange butterflies; her dark hair was braided with pink ribbon, coiled up and pinned loosely. The first thing he'd done when she'd arrived at his door, hurrying, breathless, brimming with joyous excitement or a very good imitation of it, was to unpin her hair. The braid went three times around his hand.

"Where's Crake?" he whispered. She smelled of lemons, of crushed herbs.

"Don't worry, Jimmy."

"But where?"

"He's outside Paradice, he went out. He had a meeting. He doesn't want to see me when he comes back, he said he would be thinking tonight. He never wants sex when he's thinking."

"Do you love me?"

That laugh of hers. What had it meant? *Stupid question. Why ask? You talk too much.* Or else: *What is love?* Or possibly: *In your dreams.*

Then time passed. Then she was pinning her hair up again, then slipping on her kimono, then tying it with the sash. He stood behind her, watching in the mirror. He wanted to put his arms around her, take off the covering she'd just put back on, start all over again.

"Don't go yet," he said, but it was never any use saying *don't go yet* to her. When she'd decided a thing, she was on her way. Sometimes he felt he was merely a house call on a secret itinerary of hers – that she had a whole list of others to be dealt with before the night was over. Unworthy thoughts, but not out of the question. He never knew what she was doing when she wasn't with him.

"I'm coming back right away," she said, slipping her feet

into her little pink and red sandals. "I'll bring pizza. You want any extras, Jimmy?"

"Why don't we dump all this crap, go away somewhere?" he said on impulse.

"Away from here? From Paradice? Why?"

"We could be together."

"Jimmy, you're funny! We're together now!"

"We could get away from Crake," said Jimmy. "We wouldn't have to sneak around like this, we could . . ."

"But Jimmy." Wide eyes. "Crake needs us!"

"I think he knows," said Jimmy. "About us." He didn't believe this; or he believed it and not, both at the same time. Surely they'd been more and more reckless lately. How could Crake have missed it? Was it possible for a man that intelligent in so many ways to be acutely brain-damaged in others? Or did Crake have a deviousness that outdid Jimmy's own? If so, there were no signs.

Jimmy had taken to sweeping his room for bugs: the hidden mini-mikes, the micro-cams. He'd known what to look for, or so he thought. But there'd been nothing.

There were signs, Snowman thinks. There were signs and I missed them.

For instance, Crake said once, "Would you kill someone you loved to spare them pain?"

"You mean, commit euthanasia?" said Jimmy. "Like putting down your pet turtle?"

"Just tell me," said Crake.

"I don't know. What kind of love, what kind of pain?"

Crake changed the subject.

Then, one lunchtime, he said, "If anything happens to

me, I'm depending on you to look after the Paradice Project. Any time I'm away from here I want you to take charge. I've made it a standing order."

"What do you mean, anything?" said Jimmy. "What could happen?"

"You know."

Jimmy thought he meant kidnapping, or being whacked by the opposition: that was a constant hazard, for the Compound brainiacs. "Sure," he said, "but one, your security's the best, and two, there's people in here much better equipped than I am. I couldn't head up a thing like this, I don't have the science."

"These people are specialists," said Crake. "They wouldn't have the empathy to deal with the Paradice models, they wouldn't be any good at it, they'd get impatient. Even I couldn't do it. I couldn't begin to get onto their wavelength. But you're more of a generalist."

"Meaning?"

"You have a great ability to sit around not doing much of anything. Just like them."

"Thanks," said Jimmy.

"No, I'm serious. I want – I'd want it to be you."

"What about Oryx?" said Jimmy. "She knows the Crakers a lot better than I do." Jimmy and Oryx said *Crakers*, but Crake never did.

"If I'm not around, Oryx won't be either," said Crake.

"She'll commit suttee? No shit! Immolate herself on your funeral pyre?"

"Something like that," said Crake, grinning. Which at the time Jimmy had taken both as a joke and also as a symptom of Crake's truly colossal ego.

★

"I think Crake's been snooping on us," said Jimmy that last night. As soon as it was out he saw it could be true, though maybe he was just saying it to frighten Oryx. Stampede her, perhaps; though he had no concrete plans. Suppose they ran, where would they live, how would they keep Crake from finding them, what would they use for money? Would Jimmy have to turn pimp, live off the avails? Because he certainly had no marketable skills, nothing he could use in the pleeblands, not if they went underground. As they would have to do. "I think he's jealous."

"Oh Jimmy. Why would Crake be jealous? He doesn't approve of jealousy. He thinks it's wrong."

"He's human," said Jimmy. "What he approves of is beside the point."

"Jimmy, I think it's you that's jealous." Oryx smiled, stood on tiptoe, kissed his nose. "You're a good boy. But I would never leave Crake. I believe in Crake, I believe in his" – she groped for the word – "his vision. He wants to make the world a better place. This is what he's always telling me. I think that is so fine, don't you, Jimmy?"

"I don't believe that," said Jimmy. "I know it's what he says, but I've never bought it. He never gave a piss about anything like that. His interests were strictly . . ."

"Oh, you are wrong, Jimmy. He has found the problems, I think he is right. There are too many people and that makes the people bad. I know this from my own life, Jimmy. Crake is a very smart man!"

Jimmy should have known better than to bad-mouth Crake. Crake was her hero, in a way. An important way. As he, Jimmy, was not.

"Okay. Point taken." At least he hadn't completely blown it: she wasn't angry with him. That was the main thing.

What a mushball I was, thinks Snowman. How entranced. How possessed. Not *was*, *am*.

"Jimmy, I want you to promise me something."

"Sure, what?"

"If Crake isn't here, if he goes away somewhere, and if I'm not here either, I want you to take care of the Crakers."

"Not here? Why wouldn't you be here?" Anxiety again, suspicion: were they planning to go off together, leaving him behind? Was that it? Had he only been some sort of toy-boy for Oryx, a court jester for Crake? "You're going on a honeymoon, or what?"

"Don't be silly, Jimmy. They are like children, they need someone. You have to be kind with them."

"You're looking at the wrong man," said Jimmy. "If I had to spend more than five minutes with them they'd drive me nuts."

"I know you could do it. I'm serious, Jimmy. Say you'll do it, don't let me down. Promise?" She was stroking him, running a row of kisses up his arm.

"Okay then. Cross my heart and hope to die. Happy now?" It didn't cost him anything, it was all purely theoretical.

"Yes, now I'm happy. I'll be very quick, Jimmy, then we can eat. You want anchovies?"

What did she have in mind? Snowman wonders, for the millionth time. How much did she guess?

Airlock

He'd waited for her, at first with impatience, then with anxiety, then panic. It shouldn't take them that long to make a couple of pizzas.

The first bulletin came in at nine forty-five. Because Crake was off-site and Jimmy was second-in-command, they sent a staff member from the video monitor room to get him.

At first Jimmy thought it was routine, another minor epidemic or splotch of bioterrorism, just another news item. The boys and girls with the HotBiosuits and the flame-throwers and the isolation tents and the crates of bleach and the lime pits would take care of it as usual. Anyway, it was in Brazil. Far enough away. But Crake's standing order was to report any outbreaks, of anything, anywhere, so Jimmy went to look.

Then the next one hit, and the next, the next, the next, rapid-fire. Taiwan, Bangkok, Saudi Arabia, Bombay, Paris, Berlin. The pleeblands west of Chicago. The maps on the monitor screens lit up, speckled with red as if someone had flicked a loaded paintbrush at them. This was more than a few isolated plague spots. This was major.

Jimmy tried phoning Crake on his cell, but he got no reply. He told the monitor crew to go to the news channels. It was a rogue hemorrhagic, said the commentators. The symptoms were high fever, bleeding from the eyes and skin, convulsions, then breakdown of the inner organs, followed by death. The time from visible onset to final moment was amazingly short. The bug appeared to be airborne, but there might be a water factor as well.

Jimmy's cellphone rang. It was Oryx. "Where are you?" he shouted. "Get back here. Have you seen . . ."

Oryx was crying. This was so unusual Jimmy was rattled by it. "Oh Jimmy," she said. "I am so sorry. I did not know."

"It's all right," he said, to soothe her. Then, "What do you mean?"

"It was in the pills. It was in those pills I was giving away, the ones I was selling. It's all the same cities, I went there. Those pills were supposed to help people! Crake said . . ."

The connection was broken. He tried dialback: *ring ring ring*. Then a click. Then nothing.

What if the thing was already inside Rejoov? What if she'd been exposed? When she turned up at the door he couldn't lock her out. He couldn't bear to do that, even if she was bleeding from every pore.

By midnight the hits were coming almost simultaneously. Dallas. Seattle. New New York. The thing didn't appear to be spreading from city to city: it was breaking out in a number of them simultaneously.

There were three staff in the room now: Rhino, Beluga, White Sedge. One was humming, one whistling; the third –

White Sedge – was crying. *This is the biggie.* Two of them had already said that.

"What's our fallback?"

"What should we do?"

"Nothing," said Jimmy, trying not to panic. "We're safe enough here. We can wait it out. There's enough supplies in the storeroom." He looked around at the three nervous faces. "We have to protect the Paradice models. We don't know the incubation period, we don't know who could be a carrier. We can't let anybody in."

This reassured them a little. He went out of the monitor room, reset the codes of the inmost door, and also those on the door leading into the airlock. While he was doing this his videocell beeped. It was Crake. His face on the tiny screen looked much as usual; he appeared to be in a bar.

"Where are you?" Jimmy yelled. "Don't you know what's going on?"

"Not to worry," said Crake. "Everything's under control." He sounded drunk, a rare thing for him.

"What fucking *everything*? It's a worldwide plague! It's the Red Death! What's this about it being in the BlyssPluss Pills?"

"Who told you that?" said Crake. "A little bird?" He was drunk for sure; drunk, or on some pharmaceutical.

"Never mind. It's true, isn't it?"

"I'm in the mall, at the pizza place. I'll be there right away," said Crake. "Hold the fort."

Crake hung up. Maybe he's found Oryx, Jimmy thought. Maybe he'll get her back safely. Then he thought, You halfwit.

He went to check up on the Paradice Project. The night-sky simulation was on, the faux moon was shining, the

Crakers – as far as he could tell – were peacefully asleep. "Sweet dreams," he whispered to them through the glass. "Sleep tight. You're the only ones now who can."

What happened then was a slow-motion sequence. It was porn with the sound muted, it was brainfrizz without the ads. It was melodrama so overdone that he and Crake would have laughed their heads off at it, if they'd been fourteen and watching it on DVD.

First came the waiting. He sat in a chair in his office, told himself to calm down. The old wordlists were whipping through his head: *fungible, pullulate, pistic, cerements, trull.* After a while he stood up. *Prattlement, opsimath.* He turned on his computer, went through the news sites. There was a lot of dismay out there, and not nearly enough ambulances. The keep-calm politico speeches were already underway, the stay-in-your-house megaphone vehicles were prowling the streets. Prayer had broken out.

Concatenation. Subfusc. Grutch.

He went to the emergency storeroom, picked up a spray-gun, strapped it on, put a loose tropical jacket over the top. He went back to the monitor room and told the three staff that he'd talked with CorpSeCorps Security for the Compound – a lie – and they were in no immediate danger here; also a lie, he suspected. He added that he'd heard from Crake, whose orders were that they should all go back to their rooms and get some sleep, because they would need their energy in the days to come. They seemed relieved, and happy to comply.

Jimmy accompanied them to the airlock and coded them into the corridor that led to their sleeping quarters. He watched their backs as they walked in front of him; he saw them as already dead. He was sorry about that, but he couldn't take chances. They were three to his one: if they became hysterical, if they tried to break out of the complex or let their friends into it, he wouldn't be able to control them. Once they were out of sight he locked them out, and himself in. Nobody in the inner bubble now but himself and the Crakers.

He watched the news some more, drinking Scotch to fortify himself, but spacing his intake. *Windlestraw. Laryngeal. Banshee. Woad.* He was waiting for Oryx, but without hope. Something must have happened to her. Otherwise she'd be here.

Towards dawn the door monitor beeped. Someone was punching in the numbers for the airlock. It wouldn't work, of course, because Jimmy had changed the code.

The video intercom jangled. "What are you doing?" said Crake. He looked and sounded annoyed. "Open up."

"I'm following Plan B," said Jimmy. "In the event of a bio attack, don't let anybody in. Your orders. I've sealed the airlock."

"*Anybody* didn't mean me," said Crake. "Don't be a corknut."

"How do I know you're not a carrier?" said Jimmy.

"I'm not."

"How do I know that?"

"Let's just suppose," said Crake wearily, "that I anticipated this event and took precautions. Anyway, you're immune to this."

"Why would I be?" said Jimmy. His brain was slow on logic tonight. There was something wrong with what Crake had just said, but he couldn't pinpoint it.

"The antibody serum was in the pleeb vaccine. Remember all those times you shot up with that stuff? Every time you went to the pleebs to wallow in the mud and drown your lovesick sorrows."

"How did you know?" said Jimmy. "How did you know where I, what I wanted?" His heart was racing; he wasn't being precise.

"Don't be a moron. Let me in."

Jimmy coded open the door into the airlock. Now Crake was at the inmost door. Jimmy turned on the airlock video monitor: Crake's head floated life-sized, right in front of his eyes. He looked wrecked. There was something – blood? – on his shirt collar.

"Where were you?" said Jimmy. "Have you been in a fight?"

"You have no idea," said Crake. "Now let me in."

"Where's Oryx?"

"She's right here with me. She's had a hard time."

"What happened to her? What's going on out there? Let me talk to her!"

"She can't talk right now. I can't lift her up. I've had a few injuries. Now quit fucking the dog and let us in."

Jimmy took out his spraygun. Then he punched in the code. He stood back and to the side. All the hairs on his arms were standing up. *We understand more than we know.*

The door swung open.

Crake's beige tropicals were splattered with redbrown. In his right hand was an ordinary storeroom jackknife, the kind with the two blades and the nail file and the corkscrew and the little scissors. He had his other arm around Oryx, who seemed to be asleep; her face was against Crake's chest, her long pink-ribboned braid hung down her back.

As Jimmy watched, frozen with disbelief, Crake let Oryx fall backwards, over his left arm. He looked at Jimmy, a direct look, unsmiling.

"I'm counting on you," he said. Then he slit her throat.

Jimmy shot him.

13

Bubble

In the aftermath of the storm the air is cooler. Mist rises from the distant trees, the sun declines, the birds are beginning their evening racket. Three crows are flying overhead, their wings black flames, their words almost audible. *Crake! Crake!* they're saying. The crickets are saying *Oryx*. I'm hallucinating, thinks Snowman.

He progresses along the rampart, step by wrenching step. His foot feels like a gigantic boiled wiener stuffed with hot, masticated flesh, boneless and about to burst. Whatever bug is fermenting inside it is evidently resistant to the antibiotics in the watchtower ointment. Maybe in Paradice, in the jumble of Crake's ransacked emergency storeroom – he knows how ransacked it is, he did the ransacking himself – he'll be able to find something more effective.

Crake's emergency storeroom. Crake's wonderful plan. Crake's cutting-edge ideas. Crake, King of the Crakery, because Crake is still there, still in possession, still the ruler of his own domain, however dark that bubble of light has now become. Darker than dark, and some of that darkness is Snowman's. He helped with it.

"Let's not go there," says Snowman.

Sweetie, you're already there. You've never left.

At the eighth watchtower, the one overlooking the park surrounding Paradice, he checks to see if either of the doors leading to the upper room are unlocked – he'd prefer to descend by a stairway, if possible – but they aren't. Cautiously he surveys the ground below through one of the observation slits: no large or medium-sized life forms visible down there, though there's a scuttering in the underbrush he hopes is only a squirrel. He unpacks his twisted sheet, ties it to a ventilation pipe – flimsy, but the only possibility – and lowers the free end over the edge of the rampart. It's about seven feet short, but he can stand the drop, as long as he doesn't land on his bad foot. Over he goes, hand over hand down the ersatz rope. He hangs at the end of it like a spider, hesitates – isn't there a technique for doing this? What has he read about parachutes? Something about bending your knees. Then he lets go.

He lands two-footed. The pain is intense, but after rolling around on the muddy ground for a time and making speared-animal noises, he hauls himself whimpering to his feet. Revision: to his foot. Nothing seems to be broken. He looks around for a stick to use as a crutch, finds one. Good thing about sticks, they grow on trees.

Now he's thirsty.

Through the verdure and upspringing weeds he goes, hoppity hoppity hop, gritting his teeth. On the way he steps on a huge banana slug, almost falls. He hates that feeling: cold, viscous, like a peeled, refrigerated muscle. Creeping snot. If he were a Craker he'd have to apologize to it – *I'm sorry I stepped on you, Child of Oryx, please forgive my clumsiness.*

He tries it out: "I'm sorry."

Did he hear something? An answer?

When the slugs begin to talk there's no time to lose.

He reaches the bubble-dome, circles around the white, hot, icy swell of it to the front. The airlock door is open, as he remembers it. A deep breath, and in he goes.

Here are Crake and Oryx, what's left of them. They've been vulturized, they're scattered here and there, small and large bones mingled and in disarray, like a giant jigsaw puzzle.

Here's Snowman, thick as a brick, dunderhead, frivol, and dupe, water running down his face, giant fist clenching his heart, staring down at his one true love and his best friend in all the world. Crake's empty eye sockets look up at Snowman, as his empty eyes, once before. He's grinning with all the teeth in his head. As for Oryx, she's face down, she's turned her head away from him as if in mourning. The ribbon in her hair is as pink as ever.

Oh, how to lament? He's a failure even at that.

Snowman goes through the inner doorway, past the security area, into the staff living quarters. Warm air, humid, unfresh. The first place he needs is the storeroom; he finds it without difficulty. Dark except for a few skylights, but he's got his flashlight. There's a smell of mildew and of rats or mice, but otherwise the place is untouched since he was last here.

He locates the medical-supply shelves, roots around. Tongue depressors, gauze pads, burn dressings. A box of rectal thermometers, but he doesn't need one of them stuffed up his anus to tell him he's burning up. Three or four kinds of antibiotics, pill form and therefore slow-acting, plus one last bottle of Crake's supergermicide short-term pleebland cocktail. *Gets you there and back, but don't stay until the clock strikes midnight or you'll turn into a pumpkin*, is what Crake used to say. He reads the label, Crake's precise notations, estimates the measurement. He's so weak now he can hardly lift the bottle; it takes him a while to get the top off.

Glug glug glug, says his voice balloon. *Down the hatch.*

But no, he shouldn't drink it. He finds a box of clean syringes, shoots himself up. "Bite the dust, foot germs," he says. Then he hobbles to his own suite, what used to be his own suite, and collapses onto the damp unmade bed, and goes brownout.

Alex the parrot comes to him in a dream. It flies in through the window, lands close to him on the pillow, bright green this time with purple wings and a yellow beak, glowing like a beacon, and Snowman is suffused with happiness and love. It cocks its head, looks at him first with one eye, then the other. "The blue triangle," it says. Then it begins to flush, to turn red, beginning with the eye. This change is frightening, as if it's a parrot-shaped light bulb filling up with blood. "I'm going away now," it says.

"No, wait," Snowman calls, or wants to call. His mouth won't move. "Don't go yet! Tell me . . ."

Then there's a rush of wind, whuff, and Alex is gone, and Snowman is sitting up in his former bed, in the dark, drenched in sweat.

Scribble

The next morning his foot is somewhat better. The swelling has gone down, the pain has decreased. When evening falls he'll give himself another shot of Crake's superdrug. He knows he can't overdo it, however: the stuff is very potent. Too much of it and his cells will pop like grapes.

Daylight filters through the insulating glass bricks facing the skylight window well. He roams around the space he once inhabited, feeling like a disembodied sensor. Here is his closet, here are the clothes once his, tropical-weight shirts and shorts, ranged neatly on hangers and beginning to moulder. Footwear too, but he can no longer stand the thought of footwear. It would be like adding hooves, plus his infected foot might not fit. Underpants in stacks on the shelves. Why did he used to wear such garments? They appear to him now as some sort of weird bondage gear.

In the storeroom he finds some packets and cans. For breakfast he has cold ravioli in tomato sauce and half a Joltbar, washed down with a warm Coke. No hard liquor or beer left, he'd gone through all of that during the weeks he'd been sealed in here. Just as well. His impulse would have been to drink it up as fast as possible, turn all memory to white noise.

No hope of that now. He's stuck in time past, the wet sand is rising. He's sinking down.

After he'd shot Crake, he'd recoded the inner door, sealed it shut. Crake and Oryx lay intertwined in the airlock; he couldn't bear to touch them, so he'd left them where they were. He'd had a fleeting romantic impulse – maybe he should cut off a piece of Oryx's dark braid – but he'd resisted it.

He went back to his room and drank some Scotch and then some more, as much as it took to conk himself out. What woke him up was the buzzer from the outer door: White Sedge and Black Rhino, trying to get back in. The others too, no doubt. Jimmy ignored them.

Some time the next day he made four slices of soytoast, forced himself to eat them. Drank a bottle of water. His entire body felt like a stubbed toe: numb but also painful.

During the day his cellphone rang. A high-ranking Corpsman, looking for Crake.

"Tell that fucker to get his big fat brain the fuck over here and help figure this thing out."

"He isn't here," said Jimmy.

"Who is this?"

"I can't tell you. Security protocol."

"Listen, whoever you are, I have an idea what sort of scam that creep's up to and when I lay my hands on him I'm going to break his neck. I bet he's got the vaccine for this and he's gonna hold us up for an arm and a leg."

"Really? Is that what you think?" said Jimmy.

"I know the bastard's there. I'm coming over and blow the door in."

"I wouldn't do that," said Jimmy. "We're seeing some very strange microbe activity here. Very unusual. The place is hotter than hell. I'm toughing it out in a biosuit, but I don't really know whether I'm contaminated or not. Something's really gone off the rails."

"Oh shit. Here? In Rejoov? I thought we were sealed off."

"Yeah, it's a bad break," said Jimmy. "My advice is, look in Bermuda. I think he went there with a lot of cash."

"So he sold us out, the little shit. Hawked it deliberately to the competition. That would figure. That would absolutely figure. Listen, thanks for the tip."

"Good luck," said Jimmy.

"Yeah, sure, same to you."

Nobody else buzzed the outer door, nobody tried to break in. The Rejoov folks must have got the message. As for the staff, once they'd realized the guards were gone they must have rushed outside and made a beeline for the outer gate. For what they'd confused with freedom.

Three times a day Jimmy checked on the Crakers, peering in at them like a voyeur. Scrap the simile: he was a voyeur. They seemed happy enough, or at least contented. They grazed, they slept, they sat for long hours doing what appeared to be nothing. The mothers nursed their babies, the young ones played. The men peed in a circle. One of the women came into her blue phase and the men performed their courtship dance, singing, flowers in hand, azure penises waving in time. Then there was a quintuplet fertility fest, off among the shrubbery.

Maybe I could do some social interaction, thought Jimmy. Help them invent the wheel. Leave a legacy of knowledge. Pass on all my words.

No, he couldn't. No hope there.

Sometimes they looked uneasy – they'd gather in groups, they'd murmur. The hidden mikes picked them up.

"Where is Oryx? When is she coming back?"

"She always comes back."

"She should be here, teaching us."

"She is always teaching us. She is teaching us now."

"Is she here?"

"Here and not here is the same thing, for Oryx. She said that."

"Yes. She said it."

"What does it mean?"

It was like some demented theology debate in the windier corners of chat-room limbo. Jimmy couldn't stand listening to it for very long.

The rest of the time he himself grazed, slept, sat for long hours doing nothing. For the first two weeks he followed world events on the Net, or else on the television news: the riots in the cities as transportation broke down and supermarkets were raided; the explosions as electrical systems failed, the fires no one came to extinguish. Crowds packed the churches, mosques, synagogues, and temples to pray and repent, then poured out of them as the worshippers woke up to their increased risk of exposure. There was an exodus to small towns and rural areas, whose inhabitants fought off the refugees as long as they could, with banned firearms or clubs and pitchforks.

At first the newscasters were thoroughly into it, filming the action from traffic helicopters, exclaiming as if at a football match: *Did you see that? Unbelievable! Brad, nobody can quite believe it. What we've just seen is a crazed mob of God's Gardeners, liberating a ChickieNobs production facility. Brad, this is hilarious, those ChickieNob things can't even walk! (Laughter.) Now, back to the studio.*

It must have been during the initial mayhem, thinks Snowman, that some genius let out the pigoons and the wolvogs. *Oh, thanks a bundle.*

Street preachers took to self-flagellation and ranting about the Apocalypse, though they seemed disappointed: where were the trumpets and angels, why hadn't the moon turned to blood? Pundits in suits appeared on the screen; medical experts, graphs showing infection rates, maps tracing the extent of the epidemic. They used dark pink for that, as for the British Empire once. Jimmy would have preferred some other colour.

There was no disguising the fear of the commentators. *Who's next, Brad? When are they going to have a vaccine? Well, Simon, they're working round the clock from what I hear, but nobody's claiming to have a handle on this thing yet. It's a biggie, Brad. Simon, you said a mouthful, but we've licked some biggies before.* Encouraging grin, thumbs-up sign, unfocused eyes, facial pallor.

Documentaries were hastily thrown together, with images of the virus – at least they'd isolated it, it looked like the usual melting gumdrop with spines – and commentary on its methods. *This appears to be a supervirulent splice. Whether it's a species-jumping mutation or a deliberate fabrication is anybody's guess.* Sage nods all round. They'd given the virus a name, to make it seem more manageable. Its name was JUVE, Jetspeed Ultra Virus Extraordinary. Possibly they now knew something, such as what Crake had really been up to, hidden safely in the deepest core of the RejoovenEsense Compound. Sitting in judgment on the world, thought Jimmy; but why had that been his right?

Conspiracy theories proliferated: it was a religious thing, it was God's Gardeners, it was a plot to gain world control. Boil-water and don't-travel advisories were issued in the first week, handshaking was discouraged. In the same week there was a run on latex gloves and nose-cone filters. About as effective, thought Jimmy, as oranges stuck with cloves during the Black Death.

This just in. The JUVE killer virus has broken out in Fiji, spared until now. CorpSeCorps chief declares New New York a disaster area. Major arteries sealed off.

Brad, this item is moving very fast. Simon, it's unbelievable.

"Change can be accommodated by any system depending on its rate," Crake used to say. "Touch your head to a wall, nothing happens, but if the same head hits the same wall at ninety miles an hour, it's red paint. We're in a speed tunnel, Jimmy. When the water's moving faster than the boat, you can't control a thing."

I listened, thought Jimmy, but I didn't hear.

In the second week, there was full mobilization. The hastily assembled epidemic managers called the shots – field clinics, isolation tents; whole towns, then whole cities quarantined. But these efforts soon broke down as the doctors and nurses caught the thing themselves, or panicked and fled.

England closes ports and airports.

All communication from India has ceased.

Hospitals are off limits until further notice. If you feel ill, drink plenty of water and call the following hotline number.

Do not, repeat do not, attempt to exit cities.

It wasn't Brad talking any more, or Simon. Brad and Simon were gone. It was other people, and then others.

Jimmy called the hotline number and got a recording saying it was out of service. Then he called his father, a thing he hadn't done in years. That line was out of service too.

He searched his e-mail. No recent messages. All he found was an old birthday card he'd failed to delete: *Happy Birthday, Jimmy, May All Your Dreams Come True*. Pigs with wings.

One of the privately run Web sites showed a map, with lit-up points on it for each place that was still communicating via satellite. Jimmy watched with fascination as the points of light blinked out.

He was in shock. That must have been why he couldn't take it in. The whole thing seemed like a movie. Yet there he was, and there were Oryx and Crake, dead, in the airlock. Any time he found himself thinking it was all an illusion, a practical joke of some kind, he went and looked at them. Through the bulletproof window, of course: he knew he shouldn't open the innermost door.

He lived off Crake's emergency stores, the frozen goods first: if the bubble's solar system failed, the freezers and microwaves would no longer work, so he might as well eat his way through the ChickieNobs Gourmet Dinners while he had the chance. He smoked up Crake's stash of skunkweed in no time flat; he managed to miss about three days of horror that way. He rationed the booze at first, but soon he was getting through quite a pile of it. He needed to be fried just to face the news, he needed to be feeling not much.

"I don't believe it, I don't believe it," he'd say. He'd begun talking to himself out loud, a bad sign. "It isn't happening." How could he exist in this clean, dry, monotonous, ordinary room, gobbling caramel soycorn and zucchini cheese puffs and addling his brain on spirituous liquors and brooding on the total fiasco that was his personal life, while the entire human race was kakking out?

The worst of it was that those people out there – the fear, the suffering, the wholesale death – did not really touch him. Crake used to say that *Homo sapiens sapiens* was not hard-wired to individuate other people in numbers above two hundred, the size of the primal tribe, and Jimmy would reduce that number to two. Had Oryx loved him, had she loved him not, did Crake know about them, how much did he know, when did he know it, was he spying on them all along? Did he set up the grand finale as an assisted suicide, had he intended to have Jimmy shoot him because he knew what would happen next and he didn't deign to stick around to watch the results of what he'd done?

Or did he know he wouldn't be able to withhold the formula for the vaccine, once the CorpSeCorps got to work on him? How long had he been planning this? Could it be that Uncle Pete, and possibly even Crake's own mother, had been trial runs? With so much at stake, was he afraid of failure, of being just one more incompetent nihilist? Or was he tormented by jealousy, was he addled by love, was it revenge, did he just want Jimmy to put him out of his misery? Had he been a lunatic or an intellectually honourable man who'd thought things through to their logical conclusion? And was there any difference?

And so on and so forth, spinning the emotional wheels and sucking down the hootch until he could blank himself out.

Meanwhile, the end of a species was taking place before his very eyes. Kingdom, Phylum, Class, Order, Family, Genus, Species. How many legs does it have? *Homo sapiens sapiens*, joining the polar bear, the beluga whale, the onager, the burrowing owl, the long, long list. *Oh, big points, Grandmaster.*

Sometimes he'd turn off the sound, whisper words to himself. *Succulent. Morphology. Purblind. Quarto. Frass.* It had a calming effect.

Site after site, channel after channel went dead. A couple of the anchors, news jocks to the end, set the cameras to film their own deaths – the screams, the dissolving skins, the ruptured eyeballs and all. How theatrical, thought Jimmy. Nothing some people won't do to get on TV.

"You cynical shit," he told himself. Then he started to weep.

"Don't be so fucking sentimental," Crake used to tell him. But why not? Why shouldn't he be sentimental? It wasn't as if there was anyone around to question his taste.

Once in a while he considered killing himself – it seemed mandatory – but somehow he didn't have the required energy. Anyway, killing yourself was something you did for an audience, as on nitee-nite.com. Under the circumstances, the here and now, it was a gesture that lacked elegance. He could imagine Crake's amused contempt, and the disappointment of Oryx: *But Jimmy! Why do you give up? You have a job to do! You promised, remember?*

Perhaps he failed to take seriously his own despair.

Finally there was nothing more to watch, except old movies on DVD. He watched Humphrey Bogart and Edward G. Robinson in *Key Largo. He wants more, don't you, Rocco? Yeah, that's it, more! That's right, I want more. Will you ever get enough?* Or else he watched Alfred Hitchcock's *The Birds. Flapflapflap, eek, screech.* You could see the strings where the avian superstars were tied to the roof. Or he watched *Night of the Living Dead. Lurch, aargh, gnaw, choke, gurgle.* Such minor paranoias were soothing to him.

Then he'd turn it off, sit in front of the empty screen. All the women he'd ever known would pass in front of his eyes in the semi-darkness. His mother too, in her magenta dressing gown, young again. Oryx came last, carrying white flowers. She looked at him, then walked slowly out of his field of vision, into the shadows where Crake was waiting.

These reveries were almost pleasurable. At least while they were going on everyone was still alive.

He knew this state of affairs couldn't continue much longer. Inside Paradice proper, the Crakers were munching up the leaves and grasses faster than they could regenerate, and one of these days the solar would fail, and the backup would fail too, and Jimmy had no idea about how to fix those things. Then the air circulation would stop and the doorlock would freeze, and both he and the Crakers would be trapped inside, and they'd all suffocate. He had to get them out while there was still time, but not too soon or there would still be some desperate people out there, and desperate would mean dangerous. What he didn't want was a bunch of disintegrating maniacs falling on their knees, clawing at him: *Cure us! Cure us!* He might be immune from the virus – unless, of course, Crake had been lying to him – but not from the rage and despair of its carriers.

Anyway, how could he have the heart to stand there and say: *Nothing can save you?*

In the half-light, in the dank, Snowman wanders from space to space. Here for instance is his office. His computer sits on the desk, turning a blank face to him like a discarded girlfriend encountered by chance at a party. Beside the computer are a few sheets of paper, which must have been the last he'd ever written. The last he'd ever write. He picks them up with curiosity. What is it that the Jimmy he'd once been had seen fit to communicate, or at least to record – to set down in black and white, with smudges – for the edification of a world that no longer existed?

To whom it may concern, Jimmy had written, in ballpoint rather than printout: his computer was fried by then, but he'd persevered, laboriously, by hand. He must still have had hope, he must still have believed that the situation could be turned around, that someone would show up here in the future, someone in authority; that his words would have a meaning then, a context. As Crake had once said, Jimmy was a romantic optimist.

I don't have much time, Jimmy had written.

Not a bad beginning, thinks Snowman.

I don't have much time, but I will try to set down what I believe to be the explanation for the recent ~~extraordinary events~~ catastrophe. I have gone through the computer of the man known here as Crake. He left it turned on – deliberately, I believe – and I am able to report that the JUVE virus was made here in the Paradice dome by splicers hand-selected by Crake ~~and subsequently eliminated~~, and was then encysted in the BlyssPluss product. There was a time-lapse factor built in to allow for wide distribution: the first batch of virus did not become active until all selected territories had been seeded, and the outbreak thus took the form of a series of rapidly overlapping waves. For the success of the plan, time was of the essence. Social disruption was maximized, and development of a vaccine effectively prevented. Crake himself had developed a vaccine concurrently with the virus, but he had destroyed it prior to his ~~assisted suicide~~ death.

Although various staff members of the BlyssPluss project contributed to JUVE on a piecework basis, it is my belief that none, with the exception of Crake, was cognizant of what that effect would be. As for Crake's motives, I can only speculate. Perhaps . . .

Here the handwriting stops. Whatever Jimmy's speculations might have been on the subject of Crake's motives, they had not been recorded.

Snowman crumples the sheets up, drops them onto the floor. It's the fate of these words to be eaten by beetles. He could have mentioned the change in Crake's fridge magnets. You could tell a lot about a person from their fridge magnets, not that he'd thought much about them at the time.

Remnant

On the second Friday of March – he'd been marking off the days on a calendar, god knows why – Jimmy showed himself to the Crakers for the first time. He didn't take his clothes off, he drew the line at that. He wore a set of standard-issue Rejoov khaki tropicals, with mesh underarms and a thousand pockets, and his favourite fake-leather sandals. The Crakers gathered around him, gazing at him with quiet wonder: they'd never seen textiles before. The children whispered and pointed.

"Who are you?" said the one Crake had christened Abraham Lincoln. A tall man, brown, thinnish. It was not said impolitely. From an ordinary man Jimmy would have found it brusque, even aggressive, but these people didn't go in for fancy language: they hadn't been taught evasion, euphemism, lily-gilding. In speech they were plain and blunt.

"My name is Snowman," said Jimmy, who had thought this over. He no longer wanted to be Jimmy, or even Jim, and especially not Thickney: his incarnation as Thickney hadn't worked out well. He needed to forget the past – the distant past, the immediate past, the past in any form. He needed to exist only in the present, without guilt, without expectation. As the Crakers did. Perhaps a different name would do that for him.

"Where have you come from, oh Snowman?"

"I come from the place of Oryx and Crake," he said. "Crake sent me." True, in a way. "And Oryx." He keeps the sentence structure simple, the message clear: he knows how to do this from watching Oryx through the mirror wall. And from listening to her, of course.

"Where has Oryx gone?"

"She had some things to do," said Snowman. That was all he could come up with: simply pronouncing her name had choked him up.

"Why have Crake and Oryx sent you to us?" asked the woman called Madame Curie.

"To take you to a new place."

"But this is our place. We are content where we are."

"Oryx and Crake wish you to have a better place than this," said Snowman. "Where there will be more to eat." There were nods, smiles. Oryx and Crake wished them well, as they'd always known. It seemed to be enough for them.

"Why is your skin so loose?" said one of the children.

"I was made in a different way from you," Snowman said. He was beginning to find this conversation of interest, like a game. These people were like blank pages, he could write whatever he wanted on them. "Crake made me with two kinds of skin. One comes off." He took off his tropical vest to show them. They stared with interest at the hair on his chest.

"What is that?"

"These are feathers. Little feathers. Oryx gave them to me, as a special favour. See? More feathers are growing out of my face." He lets the children touch the stubble. He'd been lax about shaving lately, there seemed little point to it, so his beard was sprouting.

"Yes. We see. But what are feathers?"

Oh, right. They'd never seen any. "Some of the Children of Oryx have feathers on them," he said. "That kind are called birds. We'll go to where they are. Then you'll know about feathers."

Snowman marvelled at his own facility: he was dancing gracefully around the truth, light-footed, light-fingered. But it was almost too easy: they accepted, without question, everything he said. Much more of this – whole days, whole weeks of it – and he could see himself screaming with boredom. I could leave them behind, he thought. Just leave them. Let them fend for themselves. They aren't my business.

But he couldn't do that, because although the Crakers weren't his business, they were now his responsibility. Who else did they have?

Who else did he have, for that matter?

Snowman planned the route in advance: Crake's storeroom was well supplied with maps. He'd take the Children of Crake to the seashore, where he himself had never been. It was something to look forward to: at last he would see the ocean. He'd walk on a beach, as in stories told by the grown-ups when he was young. He might even go swimming. It wouldn't be too bad.

The Crakers could live in the park near the arboretum, coloured green on the map and marked with a tree symbol. They'd feel at home there, and certainly there would be lots of edible foliage. As for himself, there would surely be fish.

He gathered together some supplies – not too much, not too heavy, he'd have to carry it all – and loaded up his spraygun with the full complement of virtual bullets.

The evening before the departure, he gave a talk. On the way to their new, better place, he would walk ahead – he said – with two of the men. He picked the tallest. Behind them would come the women and children, with a file of men to either side. The rest of the men would walk behind. They needed to do this because Crake had said that this was the proper way. (It was best to avoid mentioning the possible dangers: those would require too much exposition.) If the Crakers noticed anything moving – anything at all, in whatever shape or form – they were to tell him at once. Some of the things they might see would be puzzling, but they were not to be alarmed. If they told him in time, these things would not be able to hurt them.

"Why would they hurt us?" asked Sojourner Truth.

"They might hurt you by mistake," said Snowman. "As the ground hurts you when you fall on it."

"But it is not the ground's wish to hurt us."

"Oryx has told us that the ground is our friend."

"It grows our food for us."

"Yes," said Snowman. "But Crake made the ground hard. Otherwise we would not be able to walk on it."

It took them a minute to work this one through. Then there was much nodding of heads. Snowman's brain was spinning; the illogic of what he'd just said dazzled him. But it seemed to have done the trick.

In the dawn light he punched in the door code for the last time and opened up the bubble, and led the Crakers out of

Paradice. They noticed the remains of Crake lying on the ground, but as they had never seen Crake when alive, they believed Snowman when he told them this was a thing of no importance – only a sort of husk, only a sort of pod. It would have been a shock to them to have witnessed their creator in his present state.

As for Oryx, she was face down and wrapped in silk. No one they'd recognize.

The trees surrounding the dome were lush and green, everything seemed pristine, but when they reached the RejoovenEsense Compound proper, the evidence of destruction and death lay all around. Overturned golf carts, sodden, illegible printouts, computers with their guts ripped out. Rubble, fluttering cloth, gnawed carrion. Broken toys. The vultures were still at their business.

"Please, oh Snowman, what is that?"

It's a dead body, what do you think? "It's part of the chaos," said Snowman. "Crake and Oryx are clearing away the chaos, for you – because they love you – but they haven't quite finished yet." This answer seemed to content them.

"The chaos smells very bad," said one of the older children.

"Yes," said Snowman, with something he meant for a smile. "Chaos always smells bad."

Five blocks from the main Compound gate, a man staggered out of a sidestreet towards them. He was in the penultimate stages of the disease: the sweat of blood was on his forehead. "Take me with you!" he shouted. The words were hardly audible. The sound was animal, an animal enraged.

"Stay where you are," Snowman yelled. The Crakers stood amazed, staring, but – it appeared – not frightened. The man came on, stumbled, fell. Snowman shot him. He was worried about contagion – could the Crakers get this thing, or was their genetic material too different? Surely Crake would have given them immunity. Wouldn't he?

When they reached the peripheral wall, there was another one, a woman. She lurched abruptly out of the gatehouse, weeping, and grabbed at a child.

"Help me!" she implored. "Don't leave me here!" Snowman shot her too.

During both incidents the Crakers looked on in wonder: they didn't connect the noise made by Snowman's little stick with the crumpling of these people.

"What is the thing that fell down, oh Snowman? Is it a man or a woman? It has extra skins, like you."

"It's nothing. It's a piece of a bad dream that Crake is dreaming."

They understood about dreaming, he knew that: they dreamed themselves. Crake hadn't been able to eliminate dreams. *We're hard-wired for dreams*, he'd said. He couldn't get rid of the singing either. *We're hard-wired for singing.* Singing and dreams were entwined.

"Why does Crake dream a bad dream like that?"

"He dreams it," said Snowman, "so you won't have to."

"It is sad that he suffers on our behalf."

"We are very sorry. We thank him."

"Will the bad dream be over soon?"

"Yes," said Snowman. "Very soon." The last one had been a close call, the woman was like a rabid dog. His hands were shaking now. He needed a drink.

"It will be over when Crake wakes up?"

"Yes. When he wakes up."

"We hope he will wake up very soon."

*

And so they walked together through No Man's Land, stopping here and there to graze or picking leaves and flowers as they went, the women and children hand in hand, several of them singing, in their crystal voices, their voices like fronds unrolling. Then they wound through the streets of the pleeblands, like a skewed parade or a fringe religious procession. During the afternoon storms they took shelter; easy to do, as doors and windows had ceased to have meaning. Then, in the freshened air, they continued their stroll.

Some of the buildings along the way were still smouldering. There were many questions, and much explaining to do. *What is that smoke? It is a thing of Crake's. Why is that child lying down, with no eyes? It was the will of Crake.* And so forth.

Snowman made it up as he went along. He knew what an improbable shepherd he was. To reassure them, he tried his best to appear dignified and reliable, wise and kindly. A lifetime of deviousness came to his aid.

Finally they reached the edge of the park. Snowman had to shoot only two more disintegrating people. He was doing them a favour, so he didn't feel too bad about it. He felt worse about other things.

Late in the evening, they came at last to the shore. The leaves of the trees were rustling, the water was gently waving, the setting sun was reflected on it, pink and red. The sands were white, the offshore towers overflowing with birds.

"It is so beautiful here."

"Oh look! Are those feathers?"

"What is this place called?"

"It is called *home*," said Snowman.

14

Idol

Snowman rifles the storeroom, packs what he can carry – the rest of the food, dried and in tins, flashlight and batteries, maps and matches and candles, ammunition packs, duct tape, two bottles of water, painkiller pills, antibiotic gel, a couple of sun-proof shirts, and one of those little knives with the scissors. And the spraygun, of course. He picks up his stick and heads out through the airlock doorway, avoiding Crake's gaze, Crake's grin; and Oryx, in her silk butterfly shroud.

Oh Jimmy. That's not me!

Birdsong's beginning. The predawn light is a feathery grey, the air misty; dew pearls the spiderwebs. If he were a child it would seem fresh and new, this ancient, magical effect. As it is, he knows it's an illusion: once the sun's up, all will vanish. Halfway across the grounds he stops, takes one last backward look at Paradice, swelling up out of the foliage like a lost balloon.

He has a map of the Compound, he's already studied it,

charted his route. He cuts across a main artery to the golf course and crosses it without incident. His pack and the gun are beginning to weigh on him, so he stops for a drink. The sun's up now, the vultures are rising on their updrafts; they've spotted him, they'll note his limp, they'll be watching.

He makes his way through a residential section, then across a schoolground. He has to shoot one pigoon before he reaches the peripheral wall: it was just having a good stare, but he was certain it was a scout, it would have told the others. At the side gate he pauses. There's a watchtower here, and access to the rampart; he'd like to climb up, have a look around, check out that smoke he saw. But the door to the gatehouse is locked, so he goes on out.

Nothing in the moat.

He crosses No Man's Land, a nervous passage: he keeps seeing furry movement at the sides of his eyes, and worries that the clumps of weeds are changing shape. At last he's in the pleeblands; he wends his way through the narrow streets, alert for ambushes, but nothing hunts him. Only the vultures circle above, waiting for him to be meat.

An hour before noon he climbs a tree, conceals himself in the shade of the leaves. There he eats a tin of SoyOBoy wieners and finishes the first bottle of water. Once he stops walking, his foot asserts itself: there's a regular throbbing, it feels hot and tight, as if it's crammed into a tiny shoe. He rubs some antibiotic gel into the cut, but without much faith: the microbes infecting him have doubtless already mounted their resistance and are simmering away in there, turning his flesh to porridge.

He scans the horizon from his arboreal vantage point, but he can't see anything that looks like smoke. *Arboreal*, a fine word. *Our arboreal ancestors,* Crake used to say. *Used to shit on their enemies from above while perched in trees. All planes and rockets and bombs are simply elaborations on that primate instinct.*

What if I die up here, in this tree? he thinks. Will it serve me right? Why? Who will ever find me? And so what if they do? *Oh look, another dead man. Big fucking deal. Common as dirt. Yeah, but this one's in a tree. So, who cares?*

"I'm not just any dead man," he says out loud.

Of course not! Each one of us is unique! And every single dead person is dead in his or her very own special way! Now, who wants to share about being dead, in our own special words? Jimmy, you seem eager to talk, so why don't you begin?

Oh torture. Is this purgatory, and if it is, why is it so much like the first grade?

After a couple of hours of fitful rest he moves on, holing up from the afternoon storm in the remains of a pleebland condo. Nobody in it, dead or alive. Then he continues on, limpity-limp, picking up speed now, heading south and then east, towards the shore.

It's a relief when he hits the Snowman Fish Path. Instead of turning left towards his tree, he hobbles along towards the village. He's tired, he wants to sleep, but he'll have to reassure the Crakers – demonstrate his safe return, explain why he's been away so long, deliver his message from Crake.

He'll need to invent some lies about that. *What did Crake look like? I couldn't see him, he was in a bush.* A burning bush, why not? Best to be nonspecific about the facial features. *But he gave some orders: I get two fish a week – no, make it three – and roots and berries.* Maybe he should add seaweed to that. They'll know which kinds are good. And crabs too – not the land crabs, the other kinds. He'll order them up steamed, a dozen at a time. Surely that's not too much to ask.

After he's seen the Crakers, he'll stow away his new food and eat some of it, and then have a doze in his familiar tree. After that he'll be refreshed, and his brain will be working better, and he'll be able to think about what to do next.

What to do next about what? That's too difficult. But suppose there are other people around, people like himself – smoke-making people – he'll wish to be in some kind of shape to greet them. He'll wash up – this one time he can risk the bathing pool – then put on one of the clean sun-proof shirts he's brought, maybe hack off some of his beard with the little scissors on the knife.

Damn, he forgot to bring a pocket mirror. Brainfart!

As he approaches the village, he hears an unusual sound – an odd crooning, high voices and deep ones, men's and women's both – harmonious, two-noted. It isn't singing, it's more like chanting. Then a clang, a series of pings, a boom. What are they doing? Whatever it is, they've never done anything like it before.

Here's the line of demarcation, the stinky but invisible chemical wall of piss renewed by the men each day. He steps across it, moves cautiously forward, peers from behind a shrub. There they are. He does a quick head count – most of the young, all of the adults minus five – must be a fivesome off in the woods, mating. They're sitting in a semi-circle around a grotesque-looking figure, a scarecrowlike effigy. All their attention is focused on it: they don't at first see him as he steps out from behind the shrub and limps forward.

Ohhhh, croon the women.

Mun, the men intone.

Is that *Amen*? Surely not! Not after Crake's precautions, his insistence on keeping these people pure, free of all contamination of that kind. And they certainly didn't get that word from Snowman. It can't have happened.

Clank. Ping-ping-ping-ping. Boom. *Ohhh-mun.*

Now he can see the percussion group. The instruments are a hubcap and a metal rod – those create the clanks – and a series of empty bottles dangling from a tree branch and played with a serving spoon. The boom is from an oil drum, hit with what looks like a kitchen mallet. Where did they get these things? Off the beach, no doubt. He feels as if he's watching his day-care rhythm band of long ago, but with huge green-eyed children.

What's the thing – the statue, or scarecrow, or whatever it is? It has a head, and a ragged cloth body. It has a face of sorts – one pebble eye, one black one, a jar lid it looks like. It has an old string mop stuck onto the chin.

Now they've seen him. They scramble to their feet, hurry to greet him, surround him. All are smiling happily; the children jump up and down, laughing; some of the women clap their hands with excitement. This is more energy than they usually display about anything.

"Snowman! Snowman!" They touch him gently with their fingertips. "You are back with us!"

"We knew we could call you, and you would hear us and come back."

Not *Amen*, then. *Snowman.*

"We made a picture of you, to help us send out our voices to you."

Watch out for art, Crake used to say. *As soon as they start doing art, we're in trouble.* Symbolic thinking of any kind would signal downfall, in Crake's view. Next they'd be inventing idols, and funerals, and grave goods, and the afterlife, and sin, and Linear B, and kings, and then slavery and war. Snowman longs to question them – who first had the idea of making a reasonable facsimile of him, of Snowman, out of a jar lid and a mop? But that will have to wait.

"Look! Snowman has flowers on him!" (This from the children, who've noticed his new floral sarong.)

"Can we have flowers on us too?"

"Was it difficult, your journey into the sky?"

"Flowers too, flowers too!"

"What message does Crake send us?"

"Why do you think I've been into the sky?" Snowman asks, as neutrally as possible. He's clicking through the legend files in his head. When did he ever mention the sky? Did he relate some fable about where Crake had come from? Yes, now he remembers. He'd given Crake the attributes of thunder and lightning. Naturally they assume Crake must have gone back up to cloudland.

"We know Crake lives in the sky. And we saw the whirling wind – it went the way you went."

"Crake sent it for you – to help you rise from the ground."

"Now you have been to the sky, you are almost like Crake."

Best not to contradict them, but he can't let them continue in a belief that he can fly: sooner or later they might expect him to demonstrate. "The whirling wind was so Crake could come *down* out of the sky," he says. "He made the wind to blow him down from above. He decided not to stay up there, because the sun was too hot. So that isn't where I saw him."

"Where is he?"

"He's in the bubble," Snowman says, truthfully enough. "The place we came from. He's in Paradice."

"Let us go there and see him," says one of the older children. "We know how to get there. We remember."

"You can't see him," Snowman says, a little too sharply. "You wouldn't recognize him. He's turned himself into a plant." Now where did that come from? He's very tired, he's losing it.

"Why would Crake become food?" asks Abraham Lincoln.

"It's not a plant you can eat," says Snowman. "It's more like a tree."

Some puzzled looks. "He talks to you. How does he talk, if he is a tree?"

This is going to be hard to explain. He's made a narrative mistake. He has the sensation that he's lost his balance at the top of a flight of stairs.

He flails for a grip. "It's a tree with a mouth," he says.

"Trees don't have mouths," says one of the children.

"But look," says a woman – Madame Curie, Sacajawea? "Snowman has hurt his foot." The women can always sense his discomfort, they try to ease it by changing the subject. "We must help him."

"Let us get him a fish. Would you like a fish now, Snowman? We will ask Oryx to give us a fish, to die for you."

"That would be good," he says with relief.

"Oryx wants you to be well."

Soon he's lying on the ground and they're purring over him. The pain lessens, but although they try very hard, the swelling will not go all the way down.

"It must have been a deep hurt."

"It will need more."

"We will try again later."

They bring the fish, cooked now and wrapped in leaves, and watch joyfully while he eats it. He's not that hungry – it's the fever – but he tries hard because he doesn't want to frighten them.

Already the children are destroying the image they made of him, reducing it to its component parts, which they plan to return to the beach. This is a teaching of Oryx, the women tell him: after a thing has been used, it must be given back to its place of origin. The picture of Snowman has done its work: now that the real Snowman is among them once more, there is no reason for the other, the less satisfactory one. Snowman finds it odd to see his erstwhile beard, his erstwhile head, travelling away piecemeal in the hands of the children. It's as if he himself has been torn apart and scattered.

Sermon

"Some others like you came here," says Abraham Lincoln, after Snowman has done his best with the fish. He's lying back against a tree trunk; his foot is gently tingling now, as if it's asleep; he feels drowsy.

Snowman jolts awake. "Others like me?"

"With those other skins, like you," says Napoleon. "And one of them had feathers on his face, like you."

"Another one had feathers too but not long feathers."

"We thought they were sent by Crake. Like you."

"One was a female."

"She must have been sent by Oryx."

"She smelled blue."

"We couldn't see the blue, because of her other skin."

"But she smelled very blue. The men began to sing to her."

"We offered her flowers and signalled to her with our penises, but she did not respond with joy."

"The men with the extra skins didn't look happy. They looked angry."

"We went towards them to greet them, but they ran away."

Snowman can imagine. The sight of these preternaturally calm, well-muscled men advancing *en masse*, singing their unusual music, green eyes glowing, blue penises waving in unison, both hands outstretched like extras in a zombie film, would have to have been alarming.

Snowman's heart is going very fast now, with excitement or fear, or a blend. "Were they carrying anything?"

"One of them had a noisy stick, like yours." Snowman's spraygun is out of sight: they must remember the gun from before, from when they walked out of Paradice. "But they didn't make any noise with it." The Children of Crake are very nonchalant about all this, they don't realize the implications. It's as if they're discussing rabbits.

"When did they come here?"

"Oh, the day before, maybe."

Useless to try to pin them down about any past event: they don't count the days. "Where did they go?"

"They went there, along the beach. Why did they run away from us, oh Snowman?"

"Perhaps they heard Crake," says Sacajawea. "Perhaps he was calling to them. They had shiny things on their arms, like you. Things for listening to Crake."

"I'll ask them," says Snowman. "I'll go and talk with them. I'll do it tomorrow. Now I will go to sleep." He heaves himself upright, winces with pain. He still can't put much weight on that foot.

"We will come too," say several of the men.

"No," says Snowman. "I don't think that would be a very good idea."

"But you are not well enough yet," says the Empress Josephine. "You need more purring." She looks worried: a small frown has appeared between her eyes. Unusual to see such an expression on one of their perfect wrinkle-free faces.

Snowman submits, and a new purring team – three men this time, one woman, they must think he needs strong medicine – hovers over his leg. He tries to sense a responding vibration inside himself, wondering – not for the first time – whether this method is tailored to work only on them. Those who aren't purring watch the operation closely; some converse in low voices, and after half an hour or so a fresh team takes over.

He can't relax into the sound as he knows he should, because he's rehearsing the future, he can't help it. His mind is racing; behind his half-closed eyes possibilities flash and collide. Maybe all will be well, maybe this trio of strangers is good-hearted, sane, well-intentioned; maybe he'll succeed in presenting the Crakers to them in the proper light. On the other hand, these new arrivals could easily see the Children of Crake as freakish, or savage, or non-human and a threat.

Images from old history flip through his head, sidebars from Blood and Roses: Ghenghis Khan's skull pile, the heaps of shoes and eyeglasses from Dachau, the burning corpse-filled churches in Rwanda, the sack of Jerusalem by the Crusaders. The Arawak Indians, welcoming Christopher Columbus with garlands and gifts of fruit, smiling with delight, soon to be massacred, or tied up beneath the beds upon which their women were being raped.

But why imagine the worst? Maybe these people have been frightened off, maybe they'll have moved elsewhere. Maybe they're ill and dying.

Or maybe not.

★

Before he reconnoitres, before he sets out on what – he now sees – is a mission, he should make a speech of some kind to the Crakers. A sort of sermon. Lay down a few commandments, Crake's parting words to them. Except that they don't need commandments: no *thou shalt nots* would be any good to them, or even comprehensible, because it's all built in. No point in telling them not to lie, steal, commit adultery, or covet. They wouldn't grasp the concepts.

He should say something to them, though. Leave them with a few words to remember. Better, some practical advice. He should say he might not be coming back. He should say that the others, the ones with extra skins and feathers, are not from Crake. He should say their noisy stick should be taken away from them and thrown into the sea. He should say that if these people should become violent – *Oh Snowman, please, what is violent*? – or if they attempt to rape (*What is rape?*) the women, or molest (*What?*) the children, or if they try to force others to work for them . . .

Hopeless, hopeless. *What is work?* Work is when you build things – *What is build?* – or grow things – *What is grow?* – either because people would hit and kill you if you didn't, or else because they would give you money if you did.

What is money?

No, he can't say any of that. *Crake is watching over you*, he'll say. *Oryx loves you*.

Then his eyes close and he feels himself being lifted gently, carried, lifted again, carried again, held.

15

Footprint

Snowman wakes before dawn. He lies unmoving, listening to the tide coming in, wish-wash, wish-wash, the rhythm of heartbeat. He would so like to believe he is still asleep.

On the eastern horizon there's a greyish haze, lit now with a rosy, deadly glow. Strange how that colour still seems tender. He gazes at it with rapture; there is no other word for it. *Rapture*. The heart seized, carried away, as if by some large bird of prey. After everything that's happened, how can the world still be so beautiful? Because it is. From the off-shore towers come the avian shrieks and cries that sound like nothing human.

He takes a few deep breaths, scans the ground below for wildlife, makes his way down from the tree, setting his good foot on the ground first. He checks the inside of his hat, flicks out an ant. Can a single ant be said to be alive, in any meaningful sense of the word, or does it only have relevance in terms of its anthill? An old conundrum of Crake's.

He hobbles across the beach to the water's edge, washes his foot, feels the sting of salt: there must have been a boil, the thing must have ruptured overnight, the wound feels huge now. The flies buzz around him, waiting for a chance to settle.

Then he limps back up to the treeline, takes off his flowered bedsheet, hangs it on a branch: he doesn't want to be impeded. He'll wear nothing but his baseball cap, to keep the glare out of his eyes. He'll dispense with the sunglasses: it's early enough so they won't be needed. He needs to catch every nuance of movement.

He pees on the grasshoppers, watches with nostalgia as they whir away. Already this routine of his is entering the past, like a lover seen from a train window, waving goodbye, pulled inexorably back, in space, in time, so quickly.

He goes to his cache, opens it, drinks some water. His foot hurts like shit, it's red around the wound again, his ankle's swollen: whatever's in there has overcome the cocktail from Paradice and the treatment of the Crakers as well. He rubs on some of the antibiotic gel, useless as mud. Luckily he's got aspirins; those will dull the pain. He swallows four, chews up half a Joltbar for the energy. Then he takes out his spraygun, checks the cellpack of virtual bullets.

He's not ready for this. He's not well. He's frightened.

He could choose to stay put, await developments.

Oh honey. You're my only hope.

He follows the beach northward, using his stick for balance, keeping to the shadow of the trees as much as possible. The sky's brightening, he needs to hurry. He can see the smoke now, rising in a thin column. It will take him an hour or more to get there. They don't know about him, those people; they know about the Crakers but not about him, they won't be expecting him. That's his best chance.

From tree to tree he limps, elusive, white, a rumour. In search of his own kind.

Here's a human footprint, in the sand. Then another one. They aren't sharp-edged, because the sand here is dry, but there's no mistaking them. And now here's a whole trail of them, leading down to the sea. Several different sizes. Where the sand turns damp he can see them better. What were these people doing? Swimming, fishing? Washing themselves?

They were wearing shoes, or sandals. Here's where they took them off, here's where they put them on again. He stamps his own good foot into the wet sand, beside the biggest footprint: a signature of a kind. As soon as he lifts his foot away the imprint fills with water.

He can smell the smoke, he can hear the voices now. Sneaking he goes, as if walking through an empty house in which there might yet be people. What if they should see him? A hairy naked maniac wearing nothing but a baseball cap and carrying a spraygun. What would they do? Scream and run? Attack? Open their arms to him with joy and brotherly love?

He peers out through the screen of leaves: there are only three of them, sitting around their fire. They've got a spraygun of their own, a CorpSeCorps daily special, but it's lying on the ground. They're thin, battered-looking. Two men, one brown, one white, a tea-coloured woman, the men in tropical khakis, standard issue but filthy, the woman in the remains of a uniform of some kind – nurse, guard? Must have been pretty once, before she lost all that weight; now she's stringy, her hair parched, broom-straw. All three of them look wasted.

They're roasting something – meat of some kind. A rakunk? Yes, there's the tail, over there on the ground. They must have shot it. The poor creature.

Snowman hasn't smelled roast meat for so long. Is that why his eyes are watering?

He's shivering now. He's feverish again.

What next? Advance with a strip of bedsheet tied to a stick, waving a white flag? *I come in peace.* But he doesn't have his bedsheet with him.

Or, *I can show you much treasure.* But no, he has nothing to trade with them, nor they with him. Nothing except themselves. They could listen to him, they could hear his tale, he could hear theirs. They at least would understand something of what he's been through.

Or, *Get the hell off my turf before I blow you off*, as in some old-style Western film. *Hands up. Back away. Leave that spraygun.* That wouldn't be the end of it though. There are three of them and only one of him. They'd do what he'd do in their place: they'd go away, but they'd lurk, they'd spy. They'd sneak up on him in the dark, conk him on the head with a rock. He'd never know when they might come.

He could finish it now, before they see him, while he still has the strength. While he can still stand up. His foot's like a shoeful of liquid fire. But they haven't done anything bad, not to him. Should he kill them in cold blood? Is he able to? And if he starts killing them and then stops, one of them will kill him first. Naturally.

"What do you want me to do?" he whispers to the empty air.

It's hard to know.

Oh Jimmy, you were so funny.

Don't let me down.

From habit he lifts his watch; it shows him its blank face.

Zero hour, Snowman thinks. Time to go.

Acknowledgments

My thanks to the Society of Authors (England), as the literary representative of the estate of Virginia Woolf, for permission to quote from *To the Lighthouse*; to Anne Carson for permission to quote from *The Beauty of the Husband*; and to John Calder Publications and Grove Atlantic for permission to quote eight words from Samuel Beckett's novel, *Mercier and Camier*. A full list of the other quotations used or paraphrased on the fridge magnets in this book may be found at oryxandcrake.com. "Winter Wonderland," alluded to in Part 9, is by Felix Bernard and Richard B. Smith, and is copyrighted by Warner Bros.

The name "Amanda Payne" was graciously supplied by its auction-winning owner, thereby raising much-needed funds for the Medical Foundation for the Care of Victims of Torture (U.K.). Alex the parrot is a participant in the animal-intelligence work of Dr. Irene Pepperberg, and is the protagonist of many books, documentaries, and Web sites. He has given his name to the Alex Foundation. Thank you also to Tuco the parrot, who lives with Sharon Doobenen and Brian Brett, and to Ricki the parrot, who lives with Ruth Atwood and Ralph Siferd.

Deep background was inadvertently supplied by many magazines and newspapers and non-fiction science writers encountered over the years. A full list of these is available at oryxandcrake.com. Thanks also to Dr. Dave Mossop and Grace Mossop, and to Norman and Barbara Barricello, of Whitehorse, in the Yukon, Canada; to Max Davidson and team, of Davidson's Arnheimland Safaris, Australia; to my brother, neurophysiologist Dr. Harold Atwood (thank you for the study of sex hormones in unborn mice, and other arcana); to Lic. Gilberto Silva and Lic. Orlando Garrido, dedicated biologists, of Cuba; to Matthew Swan and team, of Adventure Canada, on one of whose Arctic voyages a portion of this book was written; to the boys at the lab, 1939–45; and to Philip and Sue Gregory of Cassowary House, Queensland, Australia, from whose balcony, in March 2002, the author observed that rare bird, the Red-necked Crake.

My gratitude as well to astute early readers Sarah Cooper, Matthew Poulikakis, Jess Atwood Gibson, Ron Bernstein, Maya Mahvjee, Louise Dennys, Steve Rubin, Arnulf Conradi, and Rosalie Abella; to my agents, Phoebe Larmore, Vivienne Schuster, and Diana Mackay; to my editors, Ellen Seligman of McClelland & Stewart (Canada), Nan Talese of Doubleday (U.S.A.), and Liz Calder of Bloomsbury (U.K.); and to my dauntless copyeditor, Heather Sangster. Also to my hard-working assistant, Jennifer Osti, and to Surya Bhattacharya, the keeper of the ominous Brown Box of research clippings. Also to Arthur Gelgoot, Michael Bradley, and Pat Williams; and to Eileen Allen, Melinda Dabaay, and Rose Tornato. And finally, to Graeme Gibson, my partner of thirty years, dedicated nature-watcher, and enthusiastic participant in the Pelee Island Bird Race of Ontario, Canada, who understands the obsessiveness of the writer.